Other publications by Lou Reiter

Broken Badges: Cases from Police Internal Affairs Files
Deeds Publishing, Marietta, GA 2013

Law Enforcement Administrative Investigations, 3d Edition
Public Agency Training Council, Indianapolis, 2006

SHATTERED BADGES:

More Cases from Police Internal Affairs Files

SHATTERED BADGES:
More Cases from Police Internal Affairs Files

Lou Reiter

To Sue:
BFF... hope
a couple of these
bring back memories
of our agency audits.
Lou

Deeds Publishing | Atlanta

Published by Deeds Publishing, Athens, GA
www.deedspublishing.com

Printed in The United States of America

Library of Congress Cataloging-in-Publications Data is available upon request.

ISBN 978-1-941165-73-7

Books are available in quantity for promotional or premium use. For information, write Deeds Publishing, PO Box 682212, Athens, GA 30068 or info@deedspublishing.com.

First Edition, 2015

10 9 8 7 6 5 4 3 2 1

Dedicated to the cops who strive to do the right thing: chiefs and sheriffs who lead their officers to provide professional and compassionate service and protection to their communities; the IA/OPS workers who struggle with a difficult and often unrewarding task; and advocates and protesters who keep reminding us of reality.

Contents

Author's Introduction

In this second book of the *Badges* police procedural series, Taylor Sterling continues his work in troubled police agencies...or as he calls them, "cop shops." Outside consultants frequently are brought into police agencies to help unravel and evaluate sensitive, complex or touchy police incidents. Most of these cases involve some form of potential police officer misconduct, agency mismanagement or civil liability.

Taylor Sterling is like the author, who retired from the Los Angeles Police Department and suddenly found himself a sought after police consultant. Unlike the author, Taylor's new home is now in Santa Fe, New Mexico. Taylor finds himself drawn into the dark web of police abuse, corruption and mismanagement. Some would consider Taylor a "foodie," while others might consider him a traitor to the "thin blue line." Taylor and Sandy Banks, a prominent real estate broker he met in his new home, have an open relationship that Taylor somehow seems to fill with other exciting women during his travels.

Taylor's jobs come mostly from insurance companies who cover police losses from civil lawsuits. But occasionally, the call will come from a local politician or a chief or sheriff.

Taylor Sterling's work is similar to the author's work over

the past 54 years. The stories in this book are fictional accounts derived from real police incidents or pieces of police actions in various locals. Some readers, particularly those who are law enforcement officers, may feel they know the actual incidents or cops depicted, but these are fictional accounts and any similarity is simply coincidental. These stories involve citizens and police officers in small and large, urban and rural police and sheriff agencies throughout the country. No locale is immune to the potential of some cop going off the radar, being tempted to do the unthinkable, or being swayed into actual crime.

Shattered Badges continues the pursuit of justice and professional policing. The reader is introduced to the need for and investigative techniques of the police Internal Affairs—those who police the police. When that function in a police agency is bad or malignant, corruption and police abuse soon follow. These accounts are raw, introducing you to the dark side of law enforcement.

This second novel will take you, as the reader, to new locales (New Jersey, Ohio, Kansas, Kentucky, Oregon and Indiana), new foods, and new cases of police misconduct.

A Regrettable Shooting Indictment

Complainant: Chief Samuel Pisnero
Allegation: Administrative officer-involved shooting investigation
Agency: Riverton, New Jersey Police Department
Accused employee: Officer Ray Fay

His fingers resembled thick Cuban cigars glistening under a film of sweat. He pulled back the ejector and sent an unspent AK47 round spinning back onto the wooden porch. What the bull of a man didn't realize was earlier he had accidentally hit the wrong button and the 30-round magazine carrying his firepower had ejected and was now harmlessly positioned on the planked floor under him.

By pure chance, any immediate threat to the cops had disappeared!

Ray Fay's finger had been slowly exerting pressure on his Glock .45. He was ready to squeeze off a round aimed at the big man crouched on the porch holding the menacing, but now ineffectual, AK47. Ray was conscious of Officer Mary Worth inching her way toward the porch, her Taser ready for action. Ray had worried earlier that one of his rounds might hit her. He felt an overwhelming sense of relief as he relaxed his trigger finger, recognizing the AK47 was no longer a threat.

Barbs exploded from Mary's Taser and knifed into the naked barrel chest of the enormous hulk that had command of the porch. The man dropped to his knees, but quickly grabbed the wires extending from the Taser barbs and furiously ripped them out. Small beads of blood oozed from the sharp piercings. Fat Guy lunged off the porch and followed the wires, leading him directly to Mary Worth. Like a kid capturing a June bug, he lunged and flattened her small body with his immense size.

Ray and two fellow officers rushed to ease the altercation. Handgrips were hard to secure on the sweaty, fat, shirtless form of their nemesis. Ray circled his left arm around Fat Guy's neck and grabbed his own left wrist with his right hand. He exerted pressure on Fat Guy's carotid artery in an attempt to choke him into unconsciousness.

Fat Guy rolled off Mary and in an instant Ray found himself pinned under three hundred pounds of blubber. His arms ached as he tried to cut the flow of blood to the Bluto wannabe's head. Another officer struck Fat Guy across his thighs with an extended collapsible ASP baton.

Batons have served as sidekicks for field cops since the early days of Robert Peel's police squads in London. Most English cops still carry a baton as their exclusive peacekeeping weapon. In the early days, the English instruments were called truncheons; in America they were known as billy clubs. In Boston, the short twelve-inch billy was often packed with a lead pipe. In the 1940s, the straight stick baton was uniformly adopted. This was a twenty-six inch baton usually made of ash or other hardwood. It featured a leather strap that secured the club to a cop's wrist. Exceptionally talented officers could twirl batons in artistic dances as they made their rounds on the beat. Think Officer Crumpky in "West Side Story."

After the American urban riots in the 1960s, a new style baton surfaced. It was commonly called a Monadnock after the original inventor's New Hampshire hometown. This device was similar to the straight stick, but had a short handle extending about a third up the baton. This gave a cop more striking power. Supposedly a cop could use it as a come-along device, but most street cops couldn't use a Monadnock properly for this function. It took a lot of practice and most cops didn't want to spend time performing the mundane exercise over and over again. This side-handled baton proved to be awkward and difficult to maneuver effectively. In the late 1980s, the expandable baton became the tool of record. It was constructed of metal and could be collapsed, then expanded easily and quickly. It was less obtrusive, yet very effective. Today the baton has lost luster as an enforcement tool. Chemical sprays and Tasers are far more effective and don't cause as much damage. Inflicting damage on a subject meant a cop had to spend more time with him or her, seek medical treatment, and file additional reports.

"Turn the asshole over!" one of the officers yelled.

"Shit, he's pissed in his pants," another shouted.

"Fuck. It's gettin' on me!" Ray huffed as he continued pressuring Fat Guy's neck.

Fat Guy's arms flailed from side to side as he tried to scissor-kick his legs. Suddenly all movement stopped. It felt like an additional hundred pounds had collapsed over Ray, enveloping him like a tortoise would cover her eggs. Fat Guy finally choked out, causing his largess to turn to pure dead weight.

"Roll him off me, damn it!" Ray yelled.

Fat Guy flopped onto his stomach with a mighty heave-ho. He was so big the officers needed two sets of handcuffs to restrain him. Mary retrieved a ripcord, a glorified dog leash with Velcro connectors, circled it around the guy's ankles and cinched them up to his cuffed wrists.

Ray was on his knees positioned next to the subdued hulk he had conquered. The young officer was gasping, his lungs searching for air to fill the void the intense exertion had brought on. His shirtsleeve was soaked from the river of sweat streaming down Fat Guy's neck.

Mary looked at Fat Guy and screamed, "Hey, I don't think the guy's breathing!"

Two officers grabbed Fat Guy's arms and legs and rolled him on his back. They immediately loosened the ripcord, but kept him handcuffed. One kneeled down and began chest compressions, his hands interlaced as he pumped the barrel chest. The third forceful compression caused the subject's mouth to open and the contents of his stomach spewed like a scene from *The Exorcist*. Fat Guy wrenched his body upward and began breathing heavily.

"Let's drag him over to the car in the driveway and lean him upright against the door so he doesn't croak on us," Mary ordered. "I'll call for EMS. Sergeant says he's on his way here. Seems our good Sergeant White always rides in like the cavalry when the shit's over."

Fat Guy was the poster boy for sudden in-custody death. Overweight, sweating profusely, and dancing demons released in a frenzied fight awarded him that identity.

This unfortunate phenomenon was first recorded in law enforcement actions in the 1970s when PCP, or Angel Dust, was the prime drug of choice. Ingesting the substance caused people to behave bizarrely and believe they had super powers. Users had no feeling of pain to use as an early warning system. Subjects could be smacked repeatedly with a baton and would respond only with a vacant stare. Problem was, a few subjects suddenly died when the cops were trying to get them into custody.

There was speculation that the way subjects were placed could result in positional asphyxiation. As crack cocaine took favor, additional sudden custody deaths resulted from cocaine toxicity, and what pathologists referred to as "excited delirium." Whatever the cause, subject deaths were not good lines to fill a cop's resume. When handling a druggie, there wasn't much a street cop could do other than make sure the subject wasn't in medical distress, place him on his back or in a seated position, and call EMS.

"Looks like you got a whole lot of shit going on here, Ray," Sgt. White commented as he pulled up, clipping the curb with the right front tire of his patrol car. "Heard this all started with some sort of domestic call."

Mary and Ray shot quick glances at each other.

"Geez, forgot all about her!" Mary yelled as she and Ray rushed to the steps leading to the house. They avoided the chalk circled AK47 and the wayward magazine positioned on the porch. The officers took strategic positions on either side of the open front door.

"Ma'am, are you in there?" Ray called. "It's all over. Safe to come out now."

Dead silence. No shouts, no cries, no movement.

Mary and Ray crisscrossed positions as they entered the living room, surveying as they moved. A glass coffee table stood upended and was broken in three parts. The pair quickly crossed the room and Ray checked the kitchen.

"Shit, Mary! Better call the detectives and coroner."

A heavyset woman was splayed on the floor. Her faded flannel nightgown had been a soft shade of pink once, but now was stained with deep splotches of crimson. A bloodstained knife was balanced on the edge of the kitchen counter, blade extended in challenge. Slow droplets of blood fell and patterned the linoleum floor.

"How come you didn't just shoot the fat guy, Ray?" Sgt. White asked. "Seems like you never miss an opportunity to unload your gun."

Officer Ray Fay stood silently and glared at his sergeant. He remembered how close he had come to squeezing the trigger. It would have been a justified shooting. Hell, the guy had a gun. Shit, he had just sliced his wife like a hog. This asshole didn't deserve to live.

Ray knew Fat Guy's gun wasn't really a threat. Although he had been in five, maybe six, shootings in the six years he had been a Riverton cop, Ray didn't get a thrill from shooting anybody. Well, maybe a momentary shot of adrenalin hopped him, but it never lasted long.

* * *

Ray Fay grew up in Rocky Hill, Pennsylvania, a suburb of Scranton. Rocky Hill was an extension of the poor, rough and tumble, big city. Ray never excelled at much of anything, except maybe staying one step ahead of the law. His dad put in over thirty years as a salesclerk at the local Ace Hardware. Ray watched his father pore over the annual nuts and bolts catalogue and salivate over tools touted in Sears Roebuck advertisements. His father's dream was to be a mechanic on the railroad, but had no juice to get into the union.

Ray's mother worked in the local high school cafeteria. His friends knew she served on the food line, but Ray made her promise never to say a word to him when he shuffled through the line. She would simply blow him a kiss, which was probably worse.

Ray was an only child. He figured his parents tried sex once, didn't like it, so that was that. He never saw affection flow between his dad and mom. While he would never admit it, his parents embarrassed him.

The only things that interested Ray were physical fitness and cars. His high school had a mediocre fitness room, but it was reserved exclusively for the hockey and football players. Scranton had a YMCA and a Boys and Girls Club that offered fair workout rooms, but they were too far away to use regularly. Ray didn't have a car and Scranton's public transportation didn't stretch to Rocky Hill.

Jackson's Gym saved him. Jackson's could only be entered through a door in the alley. The front portion of the Main Street building was boarded up and the front entrance was seriously padlocked with a massive chain and lock. Ray's dad mentioned the building had once been a Woolworth's, whatever that meant.

The interior of the gym was dimly lit, always dusty, and smelled of stale sweat mixed with mildew. A ragtag boxing ring stood in one corner used by guys who fancied themselves mixed-martial arts contenders. Jackson's didn't stock the fancy machines that Ray read about in muscle mags, but the gym did have a full line of bells ranging to one hundred fifty pounds. There were bars for squats and bench presses, and enough free weights to destroy anybody's back.

Ray convinced Vinny Jackson to trade workout time for a light cleaning now and then. Ray knew most of the guys at Jackson's had time logged in the joint, mostly state pens, but one boasted he'd been behind bars in the federal max prison in Lewisburg. Ray spotted the crude blue prison tats the guys sported on their arms and back that faded in the blanket of sweat they exuded. A few liked their tats shaped like crucifixes. A couple guys proudly sported swastikas that advertised their values in prominent positions on their bodies. Ray knew some guys were associated with the Aryan Brotherhood. They were the real bad asses, and most feasted on a banquet of growth hormones and steroids daily.

"Hey, kid, come over here and spot for me," a huge bald guy ordered.

He was prone on the bench press with about two fifty looking at him. Spotting wasn't the same as lifting weights. For spotting, you stand at a guy's head and steady the bar as the lifter raises it from the stays. The spotter helps with the final few pumps as the lifter strains the last of his muscles. Bald Guy looked to be about fifty, but it was hard to tell with years of hard living taking its toll. At eighteen reps Bald Guy showed strain, but slowly pressed the two more he was counting on while uttering loud obligatory guttural grunts.

Ray kept his distance from most gym guys and the candy jars of pills they carried in their gym bags. Ray fancied himself a naturalist. He was interested in tone, not bulk. He was cut, and probably had a body fat ratio less than five percent. He worked hard and consistently to keep his body in check.

Ray loved to read the car magazines left behind in the gym. He only wished he could afford one. Owning a Shelby Mustang would be his dream. Hell, anything with four wheels would do at this point in his life. Some guys his age liked Japanese cars, but Ray liked American muscle cars. Badass, big sounding ones.

* * *

Ray Fay never considered becoming a cop. He figured he'd be a mechanic or do something with cars. He tried to get a job at the dirt track on the outskirts of Scranton, but never could get hired. After working a potshot of menial jobs, Ray finally bought his first ride, an old Chevy Caprice piece of junk. But the Caprice had a 'Vette engine and could go like a bat outta hell. Ray didn't slow down until after his third speeding ticket. That $450 fine hurt him for six months.

Ray figured that once he owned a car it would be filled with pussy begging for his attention, but every morning he came out and found zilch. Most girls in Rocky Hill didn't have time for the likes of Ray. He was from the other side of the tracks in an already pathetic town. Girls didn't want their future linked with a guy like Ray. They wanted to get outta town, too.

One day Ray found himself tooling around Riverton, New Jersey. This small city was inside the sprawling mass of real estate surrounding Newark. He'd been to Newark International to check for jobs. Any job would be good. His car insurance was cancelled and he was one ticket away from his first stop in jail.

"What the fuck you want, pussy cop?" a large man demanded of the female officer who'd pulled him over.

Ray had just exited Dunkin' Donuts and was jiggling the key to open his driver's door when he heard the angry words. His coffee cup was balanced on top of the car along with a plain old-fashioned donut. He'd noticed the black and white cop car pull into the parking lot with its blue emergency lights flashing to let everyone know it was there. The car the cop stopped for whatever reason was an older model Cadillac Coupe Deville. The landau top was ragged and the car was riding on a small temporary donut wheel.

Ray watched the cop car door open and a short, stocky gal

get out. She looked around the lot before walking to the driver's side of the Cadillac. She stopped just short of the driver's door, causing the big guy driving the heavy metal piece of shit to crane his neck to look at her.

Ray could see the Cadillac's door inch open and heard the lady cop order the driver to stay in the car. She backed up a few steps as he emerged from the Caddy anyway. The guy was overweight and wore a ratty wife beater undershirt. His hair was pulled into a ponytail and knotted with a red rubber band. Grey dress slacks completed his outfit, slacks that seemed to shimmy and change color as he moved, turning from grey to green. Ray chuckled when he saw the guy was wearing turquoise plastic flip-flops.

"Sir, you ran that red light back on Stacy Street."

"Fuck if I did!"

"Sir, can I have your license, registration, and proof of insurance?"

"You know who I am, little cop lady?"

"Yeah, some asshole who just blew a traffic light!"

He didn't wait to respond. Stepping forward he grabbed the female cop around her neck with one hand while the other worked to crumple the front of her uniform shirt. In an instant he lifted her off her feet and slammed her into the rear quarter panel of the Cadillac. She tried to wrench his hand from her neck, but had no leverage.

Ray moved to Caddy Guy's rear, grabbed his ponytail and drove his foot into the guy's leg at the knee, causing the bully to lose equilibrium before landing smack on his ass. Unfortunately Caddy Guy still clutched the female cop who was now looking like a turtle desperately trying to right itself. Ray stomped on the guy's face with his right foot. His nose separated and blood gushed like Old Faithful. The female cop was able to roll off her attacker as Ray dropped his knee directly into Cadillac Guy's groin. The freakin' asshole didn't know whether to grab his nose or his nuts.

Instantly the lady cop was on her feet and was frantically shaking a little black canister.

"Better step back," she warned Ray.

The short burst of chemical spray hit Cadillac Guy directly in the face. He began to sputter and gasp before screaming like a girl. Ray saw the cop turn her head and say something into the mic clipped to her shoulder.

"Better get on the other side of my cruiser, man. There's goin' be a whole lot of cops here fast and I don't want them to misidentify you and give you an ass kicking."

She had hardly finished speaking when Ray heard sirens screaming from all four corners of the parking lot. Within less than a minute the Dunkin' Donuts lot looked like a colony of black and white mobile penguins. Ray watched as two cops drove their sticks deep into Cadillac Guy's fat gut while another gave him a short kick between his legs, ramming his nuts where the sun don't shine.

Shit, these guys don't mess around! Ray thought.

"You messed with the wrong guy, assholes!" Cadillac guy screamed as he was cuffed and stuffed into the rear of the closest black and white.

"You know who I am? I'm made—you know that! You fucked with the wrong guy. You asshole, you better get out of town!" He threw his last words directly at Ray.

The female cop came over to Ray. "Mary Worth here. Saved my ass back there. Thanks."

"Ray, Ray Fay. You're welcome. Actually it was kind of fun, Officer Worth."

She walked over to the cop car that was the last to arrive. Ray saw the gold stripes of sergeant parading up the driver's sleeve. After a couple minutes, the sergeant came over to where Ray was standing.

Extending his hand he said, "Sergeant White. Heard you jumped in and helped Officer Worth. You probably saved her from serious injury. Say, what's your name?"

"Ray. Ray Fay, sergeant."

"What you doing in Riverton, Ray?"

"Looking for a job and a good ride. My Chevy is a piece of shit, sir."

"Got a place to stay tonight, Ray?"

"Yeah, got a couple more nights before the money runs out, sir."

"Come by the police station tomorrow about two in the afternoon. That good with you?"

"Yes, sir!"

Sgt. White turned to leave, then stopped and turned back to face Ray. "Know who you beat the shit out of there, Ray?" Ray shook his head. "That was 'No Shoes' Mannette. He's not really a made guy, but he's up there. A real shit bird. But don't worry; the mob is a joke these days. See you tomorrow."

* * *

New Jersey's criminal justice system is different from those established in larger states.

Irv Katz held the position of Auburn County Prosecutor. Part of Auburn County butted the north side of Essex County. Essex County held the larger municipalities including Newark, the Caldwells, and the Oranges. Irv's domain wasn't the largest prosecutor's office in the state, but forty lawyers and nearly twenty investigators filled the desks. In most states the position of county prosecutor is an elected one. In New Jersey the governor appoints a prosecutor to the office. Once firmly in place, a Jersey prosecutor would have to step on his dick or screw somebody big to be removed. It was definitely a tenured position.

"Mr. Katz," a young man approached tentatively. "Sorry you lost the election for AG last month."

Irv nodded and thanked the kid as he grabbed his double espresso skinny latte sitting on the counter. He walked by the condiment kiosk and headed for the door of the coffee shop. Years before Irv would have dropped three packets of sugar into his coffee, but he was watching himself these days. The past election had taken a toll on him, his body, and his family. New Jersey wasn't that big, but getting around to the necessary places to collect votes wasn't easy. In the southern part of the state, communities were spread out and less populated. It hadn't proved beneficial for the election, but his handlers told Irv he had to be seen in every part of the state, even if his presence didn't result in votes. Irv often wondered if his handlers really knew anything or if they were just talking heads using bullshit statistics to confuse him, blow smoke up his ass, or pad their already huge bill.

Irv's election campaign had cost just under three million dollars and he had lost by only four points. Talking heads reported it would take closer to five million to unseat an incumbent, even one who had gone stale long before and was about ten years out of date in the prosecution arena. What pissed off Irv most was the continuous attack on his crime fighting effort. His opposition voiced loudly and often that Irv's office hadn't brought one public official to his knees on corruption charges. Thus Irv couldn't rein in support from police chiefs, even in his own county. Getting support from the state association of pompous assholes with braids on their shoulders was virtually impossible. Of course every police and firefighter union went with the guy Irv was trying to unseat—Big Bob. Most public safety unions had pension negotiations coming up and Big Bob promised the lot of them that he would float a bond issue to cover looming deficits in public safety officer retirement funds.

Environmental groups and small businesses formed the bulk of Irv Katz's support base. He had a lock on the Yiddish community in the northern part of the state that was closest to the Big Apple. Irv made tremendous inroads into many state universities, with both students and professors. Rutgers was particularly strong in support, but weak in dollars.

Everywhere Irv went after the election he was asked the same question and given the same assurance. "You gonna run next time? I'm with you if you do!"

"Mr. Katz, Chief Pisnero says he's running a little late," Irv's secretary announced as he entered his office. "Says they had a call-out last night and he has to get briefed by his ERT people."

"Is the Riverton file on my desk, Gladys?"

She nodded as Irv headed for the closet in his office. He removed his suit coat and hung it next to his camel colored cashmere overcoat. It was getting close to the time of year when he would have to get his overcoat cleaned for the winter. Irv stood in front of the full-length mirror hanging on the rear of the closet door. He was a short man, just a few inches over five feet tall. Most of his hair was gone except for wispy puffs gathered like clouds around his ears. Irv considered shaving it all off. Hell, Booker had done it and no one seemed to mind. Irv ran his fingers up the wide red suspenders that ran from belly to shoulder, straightening the braces as he did. Irv considered his red suspenders as a personal status symbol. Silly as it might be, his trademark often broke the ice and allowed him to easily move into conversations with strangers.

Irv Katz had been in the Auburn office for nearly fifteen years. When he graduated from Brooklyn Law School, he considered joining one of the five DA offices encompassing New York City. Each was a huge operation with several hundred lawyers scurrying through catacombs of hallways. Irv decided to travel the tunnel under the Hudson River and found a job in Auburn County. It wasn't the most prestigious county in New Jersey, but it was active, and the old prosecutor quickly hired him. That's what counted for a guy fresh out of law school.

Irv started his legal career doing grunt work as back up for the seasoned attorneys in the office. By the end of his first year, Irv was handling misdemeanor cases, then regular felonies, and finally graduated to major felonies like homicides. Irv's passion was focused on the laborious white-collar crimes that flowed through the county system. This was work most attorneys in the office tried to avoid. Irv was most comfortable with spreadsheets, complex contractual documents, and the lengthy pleadings necessary for this type prosecution. He proved he was good at it, very good. The Manhattan DA's office courted him for a short time until he declined its generous offer. The old prosecutor of Auburn County was getting ready to retire and had anointed Irv as his successor. At thirty-five years of age, Irv became one of the youngest county prosecutors in Jersey.

"Irv, sorry to keep you waiting, but you know, crime fighting takes a front and center position," the blustering chief muttered as he entered Irv's office. Chief Pisnero was typical of the police chiefs in Auburn County. Most had been with the same cop shop their entire career. Most had two or three generations of relatives serving in the same department. Pisnero's connection came through his wife's family. Two brothers were lieutenants on the job and his father-in-law had been Chief of Police on the day they were married. Pisnero might have been a striking force at one time, but now he was just a fat slob. The front of his white uniform shirt was stained with dribbles of spilled coffee and heavy rings of cigar spit. Pisnero's Riverton office was always thick with clouds of smoke and it irritated Irv every time he had to battle the plumes. He tried to avoid visits to Pisnero's self-claimed world.

"Got my stuff, huh, Irv?"

Irv picked up a folder on his desk and opened it. "That I have, Chief Pisnero."

"I need your approval to get my grant request sent up to the feds. We need to expand our street crime unit. It's the best way to keep that pesky crime rate down, you know, Irv. You're on board with crime fighting, I know you are."

Pisnero wore a slight smirk on his face. They both knew this comment was a jab at the recent election loss and Big Bob's nev-er-ending attack on Irv's supposed lack of support for local cops. Irv had been made out to be a prosecutor who would rather cod-dle criminals than put them behind bars. It was bullshit, and they both knew it.

"This requires a ten percent match from my office, chief."

"Yeah, but that's a small price for getting eighty percent from the feds. You put up ten and Riverton puts up ten. We're getting close to $800 grand from D.C. That's a bunch of overtime and some fine cars. We'll get more than our share back in asset sei-zures through our drug arrests. We split that shit with your office, you remember that, don't you?"

Pisnero stood in front of Irv's desk like a battering ram. He pulled on his belt with one hand and his holstered gun with the other, alternatively pumping them like pedals on a bicycle. The visiting chief finally folded his arms across his chest and stared at Irv with attitude. "*What the fuck you gonna do about it!*"

"Chief, you know this stuff doesn't flow in one direction. What have you given me in the four years you've been Riverton's police chief?"

"You playing politics with me?"

Irv didn't respond.

"You're nothing but a pipsqueak with them big red suspenders. Think that makes you some local celebrity? Well, you're wrong. You're nothing but a short little Jew outta Queens. I got Big Bob on my side!"

"Well, get your ten from Big Bob then!" With those words, Irv slammed the folder on his desk and pointed his finger at his office door.

Pisnero didn't respond. He gave a low snicker, turned and left without closing the door behind him. Irv knew the chief would go right to Big Bob and knew he'd most likely get his signature. Irv knew the Riverton chief wouldn't be supporting him any time soon, but he really didn't care.

* * *

Ray drove to the Riverton police station not knowing what might be in store for him. The sergeant said to come by and Ray really didn't have anything else to do, so why not? The job prospect at Newark airport didn't look promising. He had filled out reams of paperwork and had his fingerprints taken by computer scan before a secretary told him they *might* be contacting him. "Might be" caught his attention. Hell, he needed a job. He was down to his last couple Benjamins.

The police station wasn't imposing or impressive. The building looked like it was built back in the '20s. The brick façade was faded grey from the pollution so common in East Coast cities. Well-worn brass handles activated the old oak doors. The lobby was small and the marble floors were stained by years of shoe leather. Ray walked to the elevated desk that extended the entire length of the lobby.

"Hey, my name is Ray Fay. A sergeant told me to come by today to see him, but I forgot his name." Ray shifted on his feet, feeling uneasy.

"Told to look out for you, kid," the desk sergeant announced as he activated the buzzer under his desk. A noticeable clicking sound made by the iron gate next to the desk echoed through the lobby.

"Come on in." The desk sergeant pointed down the hallway and told him to look for the door that had 'Chief's Office' plastered on it.

Ray knocked on the door and a slight voice from inside told him to enter. An older woman looked up as he passed through the entrance and gave Ray a nice smile.

"You the kid who helped Mary, huh?"

"You mean Officer Worth? Yes, ma'am."

The woman smiled again and praised, "Polite for a young fellow. You must be from good family stock."

"Don't know about that, ma'am. But I did have a family. Too busy working to do much with me, but I learned you treat people like you want to be treated. It's worked for me, so far. But, you know, ma'am, it's getting more difficult here in the big city."

"Chief's been expecting you, son. Go on in."

"Pleasure meeting you, ma'am."

Chief Pisnero wasn't what Ray expected him to be. He was dressed in an unbuttoned silk shirt leading eyes on a trail ride to a paunchy stomach. Three gold chains dangled around his neck like shiny serpents. One chain bore a crucifix; another boasted St. Michael's emblem, and the last one featured a strange coin. When the man got up and lumbered around the desk, Ray could see black slacks and alligator loafers minus socks completed his outfit. The chief extended his chubby hand anchored with a large gold pinky ring.

"So you're the kid who helped Mary?"

Ray nodded.

"Hear you're looking for work. Is that right?"

"Yes, sir!"

"Ever think of being a cop?"

Ray hadn't. He hesitated as he considered what the chief had just suggested. A cop? Why would he want to be that? But then again, why not?

"You can just make me a cop, just like that?"

Chief Pisnero laughed and sat on the edge of his desk.

"No, it's not that easy, son. It's a long, complicated process, but I can give you a job now and we'll get you going through the process. By the way, you got a police record or been using drugs?"

"No, sir! Close on the police record, but never got caught."

Pisnero laughed again. "Me too, kid, me too."

Ray found himself suddenly employed. He started out working in the police motor pool—moving cars around, getting them washed, helping mechanics, and making sure stuff wasn't left under the seats. Over time he found a few joints, white powder residue, a used condom, leftover food scraps, and a small .25 caliber gun. All but the gun was flushed down the can by his superior. Ray wasn't certain what happened to the gun.

Six months later he was registered at the police academy in Bergen County. Ray loved the training. The procedure was controlled, regimented, and perfect for a kid who knew how to follow orders. Physical fitness training was the best. Plenty of running. It was as though instructors were trying to see who could survive the grind. Ray excelled in defensive tactics training. This was his groove. His fitness training at Jackson's quickly pushed him to rise above the couch potatoes filling his class.

The firing range was something totally new for Ray. He'd never handled, let alone fired, a gun. Riverton cops carried Glocks so that was his assigned training weapon. One of the recruits from another cop shop was assigned a Sig Sauer. The other academy recruits came close to orgasm when they saw the Sig. Most police departments used Glocks like Riverton did. Ray really didn't see the big deal or the difference…they all shot the same bullets he figured. He remembered the words of the firearm instructor: "You guys who have been shooting all your life; forget everything you've been taught. If you've never shot a gun before, I love it. You're the ones I can easily train."

Ray excelled at shooting. He had the knack for controlling trigger pressure and slowly pulling back until the gun discharged without anticipation. It seemed the weapon was simply an extension of Ray's hand and trigger finger.

The six months of training passed quickly and Ray soon found himself as Riverton's newest cop and assigned to the FTO program.

The Field Training Officer (FTO) program consists of eight to twelve weeks of closely monitored performance of new cops under the constant watch of a seasoned officer. This is the time when academy training is converted to actual on the job experience. It's also the time when a local agency can insert its unique policies and methods of police work. A regional police academy trains new cops from a number of local police departments. The academy might even enroll novice cops from local college campuses or other obscure policing departments, like transit or toll authorities so their rules and regs would be vastly different than cop shops charged with patrolling city streets. The seasoned officer, or FTO, often has a detailed checklist to record each new cop's ability and competence to handle the job. The Royal Canadian Mounted Police created one of the earliest formalized FTO programs. However, the program most U.S. police departments adopted is one known as the San Jose Model, after the city that developed it.

Ray had three FTO officers monitoring his field training. His last ride-along was Mary Worth. He really liked Mary, even though he learned she was gay. Her partner owned a flower shop in Jersey City. Mary told Ray that the pair had waterfront seats when the Twin Towers came tumbling down. Both raced to the Jersey City harbor when they heard about the organized rescue boat flotilla, later referred to as "Boatlift." In nine hours nearly half a million frightened survivors of the tragedy were rescued by party boats, tugs, ferries, and a storm of private pleasure boats. This was more than was rescued at Dunkirk in WWII, an effort that took nine days. Mary and her partner unloaded boat after boat of grey, soot-streaked survivors at the wharfs of Jersey City, all looked like cast members in an episode of the Walking Dead. Ray had followed the Twin Towers collapse, but had never heard of this boatlift effort. Real heroes are often overlooked and then forgotten, he concluded.

All units, major fight with possible guns involved, Capri Club on Main Street!

Ray happened to be driving the cop car this night with Mary riding shotgun. He immediately reached down to activate the lights and siren upon hearing the radio call.

"Ray, not yet!" Mary warned.

He looked at her quizzically. "But it's a hot call!"

"Let's take our time on this one, Ray. We don't want to get there until the shooting is over. We can pick up the losers. Take your time. We got all night to work, Ray. Remember… never rush! When you rush, you usually end up in trouble and then got to fight your way out. There's always someone bigger than you are or maybe equipped with more firepower than you have."

Females haven't always been welcome in police work. Up until the 1970s women were relegated to working as clerical help, jail matrons, or in juvenile units. Females entered cop fieldwork slowly. Female movement into the upper ranks and as chiefs of police has been as slow as their sisters faced in the private work force. The elimination of height standards was one of the early impediments removed, followed by the fight to show females could be good field cops without the upper body strength some male cops owned. It took a courageous few to initiate a series of lawsuits under Title VII to open the ranks for females to be deployed into the field as cops. Today women cops total less than fifteen percent in the field, way under the population ratio. It took time, but female cops eventually proved their worth and attained success in the field. Most use of force studies show female cops resort to the use of force less often than male cops do, yet make a similar number of arrests. Most studies show that female cops are willing to spend more time on calls and use verbal skills more effectively than their male counterparts do. Female officers have been a valuable asset to local police departments.

When Ray and Mary finally pulled in front of the Capri Club, at least twenty people were milling and massing on the sidewalk.

Several pointed to the door of the club and screamed someone inside had a gun. Ray pressed the trunk release and it popped with an audible whoosh.

"No, not yet, Ray!"

"But we need it, Mary."

"A police rifle is only going to get in the way. Takes your hands out of action. Can't fire in a crowded place anyway. Stay by the car for a few minutes and watch what's happening. Look for a person who appears out of the ordinary or stands apart in the crowd."

Without warning the club's front door burst open and a flood of partiers rushed into the street like rats leaving a sinking ship. The uniformed security guard was knocked on his ass and trampled by the stampeding horde. Three back-up police units screeched to a halt providing a law and order presence to the increasingly chaotic scene. Ray saw two males exit the club and saunter in the opposite direction to where the others were running. He thought it strange that neither man turned to look at the piercing blue strobe lights announcing the advancing police presence. Instead the cop sirens spurred them to pick up their pace.

"Mary, those two over there!" Ray shouted as he followed the two renegades. Mary took her place next to Ray, creating a team of two. The duo allowed the men to get about forty paces from the club before announcing they had them in sight and were zeroing in on them. Ray wanted the guys away from any probable drunks for safety reasons.

"Hold up, guys! Keep your hands where I can see them!" Ray commanded as he assumed the contact officer role. He knew Mary would be attempting to triangulate the two and would remain quiet. She was taking the position of cover officer.

Contact/cover positioning was a common police field tactic developed in the early 1970s. It was done to protect officers. By having one officer play the contact role and give all commands, conflicts or distractions would be minimized. Subjects would confront and interact with only one officer, keeping things simple.

The cover officer was then free to look for movement the contact officer might not be aware of and observe what might be happening around the scene. In some cases the cover officer might pull a gun and place it along his or her thigh. Most subjects or detainees would never know a gun was a couple of hundredths of a second away from being pointed directly at them.

The two men were good-sized fellows. Both wore jeans and cowboy boots. One had a leather vest stretched over a plaid shirt. The other had a hip length leather coat hanging open to reveal a denim work shirt. Both wore black cowboy hats pulled low. Vest turned and faced Ray while Leather Coat remained searching for something in the direction he'd been moving.

"Wha's up, bud?"

"Ya been at the Capri? Heard there was some sort of fight there," Ray answered as he moved into a position of advantage.

In police tactics, the most effective position of advantage for an officer when conducting a street inquiry is the L position. The officer attempts to position his body adjacent to the subject's right side, knowing only about fifteen percent of Americans are left-handed. This position also keeps the cop's gun away from the subject. All police/subject control holds start by controlling the subject's right arm. From that point, an officer can easily perform arm bar maneuvers and slide behind the subject or use the subject's right arm to drive him to the ground.

"Nope, wasn't there, bud."

Now Ray's curiosity soared into overdrive. He had seen the two guys exit the Capri. As Vest Guy turned to join his buddy, Ray grasped his right arm, swung him around so Ray was standing behind him. Ray locked the guy's arm against his back. Leather Coat was turning toward Ray in a broad arc as his hand swept his coat open. The telltale glint of a gun hidden in his waistband gleamed against his shirt.

"Gun, partner! Get both those hands behind your head, bud, NOW!" Ray commanded to Leather Coat guy.

"Do it *now!*" Mary seconded. Her piercing shriek blasting outta nowhere caught Leather Coat by surprise.

Leather Coat hesitated a few seconds, and then slowly moved his laced hands to cup the back of his head.

"Both of you, down on your knees. Do it now!"

Ray positioned himself behind the two and pushed them to the ground with an open palm thrust to the back. He ratcheted his handcuffs on Vest Guy. Mary's hands armed with cuffs suddenly appeared next to Ray, ready to secure the second guy. After Leather Coat was cuffed, Ray rolled him over and pulled out what appeared to be a Taurus four-inch .357 Magnum. A big, effective gun, even in the days of semi-automatics.

Ray enjoyed working with Mary Worth. He learned police basics in ways far different than what the academy taught, as well as unlearning many of the techniques his male FTOs used. Mary's ways were better, and safer.

* * *

The Challenger caught Ray's eye as he passed a car dealership going home one night after his shift. The beast sat defiantly in the front row of metal soldiers as Ray was coaxing his old Chevy past the brightly lit lot that boasted a battalion of shiny new cars. The Challenger looked menacing as it waited to be released. The black Dodge wore black mag rims riding under black tinted windows. A bold red stripe running from nose to ass commanded respect.

Ray parked and walked through the lot to get a closer look. *Shit, it was a six-speed!* He knew it had to be a Hemi before noticing the decal plastered proudly on the side. The Challenger's large exhaust pipes were gloriously threatening.

"Nice, huh?" came a gruff voice behind him.

Ray looked at the salesman and nodded. Next thing he knew he was racing down Newcastle Street with the red glow of the Challenger's instrument panel bleeding over his face. Ray wasn't out of fourth gear when he glanced down and saw the digital readout hovering around 70. The tac didn't redline until 6500 rpm. The four-point seat belt pocketed him in the bucket seat that clutched him like a frightened mother. The Challenger seats were gun metal grey accented with red piping. Ray was in love! Shit, was he ever in love!

"Got a job, kid?"

"Yeah, I'm a new cop with Riverton."

"Sweet. That should keep the tickets down. Cops give that courtesy thing to other cops, more than the staties do, that is. Those state guys are just pricks. The old man who owns this dealership likes you local cops. You want it? We can work it out, kid."

Ray didn't bother to say goodbye to his old Chevy. He drove his new ride to the Northside Iron Works in the fine style he had only dreamed about when he dog-eared those car magazines in Rocky Hill. The Iron Works reminded him of the old Jackson's Gym. Same stale sweat fouled the air, same dust bunnies scurried on the floor, and the same rust pockmarked the free weights. Even the lifters here had similar prison tats. But, another element characterized Northside. Many guys were members of the Pagans, an outlaw motorcycle gang. One-percenters. Overheard casual comments told Ray this crowd was heavy into drugs, guns, and prostitution.

New car...new job...maybe he needed a new life.

Ray didn't change clothes that night at the Iron Works. He retreated to his new love, the Challenger, and roared away from his old life. He'd noticed a brightly lit LA Fitness close to his apartment. Yuppies, he thought when he first saw the speared logo, but now maybe it was time he moved away from the grime and grind of pure iron. Ray found an empty parking space two rows behind the side-by-side corral of cars parked closest to the Fitness doors. Not another car within five spaces. He parked his new ride, artfully commanding two spaces and grabbed his gym bag.

The bright LED lighting in the lobby was almost painful. Ray approached the registration counter and noticed racks of clothes hanging from stainless steel poles, creating a makeshift sports boutique. A lot of purple and pink blasted his eyes and a few tees reeked of sparkly sequined stuff. How would you wash shit like that, he wondered.

"Can I help you," a sweet voice suddenly invaded his thoughts. The voice belonged to a woman about Ray's age. Slender, but obviously well cut, probably from using low weights for frequent reps in sets or maybe she was one of those new cross fitness freaks.

"Thinking about working out here, Miss...?"

"Heather," she answered, pressing a hard look at Ray. She was assessing if he was really interested in the gym or something she might put out.

"Well, Heather, I'm new around here. Just out of the police academy and working for the Riverton PD."

This caught her interest. "Super! We offer a special deal for cops. You been working out someplace else?"

"Iron Works."

Heather made a face, showing an unattractive nostril flare. "Yuck! I heard only thugs worked out there."

"I haven't always been a cop, Heather."

She cocked her head slightly to one side and said, "Let's go to the juice bar and I'll show you the plans we offer."

Juice bar? Shit, it really *was* a fuckin' juice bar! The whole place looked like a spa, although Ray had never set foot in a spa. After drinking something that looked like it should have stayed at the bottom of the sea, Heather took Ray on a tour of the facility. Lines of aerobic machines stood at attention. Stairmasters, ellipticals, and treadmills—this place had 'em all.

Ray needed more cardio than weight training in his new job as a local cop. Stamina was a definite plus; bulk just slowed a guy down. He suddenly realized there were more titties and asses surrounding him than he had ever seen in one location, other than on a soft porn site.

Ray and his Challenger had found a new home!

* * *

Ray can u handle Days Inn for me 2nite appeared as a text on Ray's phone.

"What're you doing here tonight, Officer Fay? Thought it was Wilson on duty tonight," the motel clerk asked through the bulletproof glass shielding his Days Inn office.

"Yeah, but Wilson must have gotten something better. He

sent me a text asking me to fill in for him. So, you got me for the night. Got any fresh brewed coffee in there?"

Ray was buzzed into the office, and so his night began.

Riverton was close to Newark International Airport. A dozen or more inexpensive motels catering to travelers surrounded the airport. Airlines used them to book passengers when planes were grounded for mechanical problems or when the weather suddenly turned nasty. The transient nature of airport motels was a magnet for thefts, narcotics, and occasional prostitution. Motels often hired off-duty cops to patrol the parking lots and deal with problems that might come up. It was a well paying gig, but the hours could kill a cop who later had to work his own shift at the PD.

Most police departments allow cops to work off-duty for private security venues. Grocery stores, malls, and hotel/motels hired off-duty cops regularly. They could hire private security details, but many of those officers were not allowed to carry guns. Most private cops didn't have arrest powers either so their bite was weak. Businesses liked hiring real cops because they figured the rest of the police department would help if necessary. The cops working a business usually brought their police cars with them, which was a visible deterrent. Police departments have the right and responsibility to ensure their outside hired cops are not working too many hours. Putting in too many hours could result in a cop sleeping on the job or being too tired to complete his regular tour of duty in a competent, safe manner.

Some police departments adopted policies requiring businesses to pay the city for the hire. The city would then compensate the officers after taking a cut and making normal deductions. Other cities allowed businesses to pay officers directly. Most cops loved paid details. In some instances, they earned as much from paid detail work as they earned from being a city cop. It was a win-win for everybody.

Ray worked plenty of paid details. He banked nearly $30,000 extra each year and had a portfolio worth close to $150K. His only expenses were his Challenger and his apartment. Other than visiting the gym, Ray did little else with his time. Ray began thinking of buying a business one day, but had no idea what it might be. He figured any business would have to be something he could continue after retiring from cop work. That was fifteen years out, but Ray was that kind of guy. A planner. He'd seen what happened to his dad, and wasn't going to let life sneak up on him.

"Edgar, what kind of occupancy you got tonight?" Ray asked.

The clerk glanced at his computer screen. "Pretty good, eighty-four percent. Nearly all are bunked for just one night. Travelers, I suspect. Lot of rental cars in the lot tonight. You working tomorrow, officer?"

"Nope, but I got a subpoena for traffic court. Probably won't go though. Those trials never go. Traffic judge either kicks the case out figuring the citizen spent enough time taking off work to appear, or the judge might slash the fine so the driver thinks they got a deal. But I get my four hours OT anyway."

A muffled sound came from a far section of the motel. Ray recognized it was a gunshot.

"You hear that, Edgar?"

Edgar nodded.

"Any idea what room that might have come from?" Edgar shook his head.

"That was a gunshot, Edgar! Better put out a 911 call. Tell them an off-duty cop is on the premise in uniform."

Ray opened the motel door after the buzzer activated. He quickly positioned himself outside and pressed against the wall. Ray strained to hear something. Anything that seemed out of the ordinary. A female scream pierced the silence. It came from a line of rooms to Ray's left, but he couldn't tell if the scream came from the upper or lower row of rooms. He moved from the wall's protective cloak of darkness and slithered between two parked cars, crouching while inching his head upward to catch any flicker of movement. Six rooms down the ground level hallway, a door swung open. A series of screams rang out. Ray cautiously moved down a line of four cars to reach the open door.

A lanky naked black male was backing out of the open doorway. His left hand was extended with his palm raised, sending the message—Stay away! Ray couldn't see the man's right hand.

"Stop right there! Police officer! Show your other hand *now!*" Ray commanded.

The naked black male spun around at the sound of the shout. His right hand moved upward and his left hand moved to clasp his right hand. Ray saw a chrome object gleam as the guy's hands closed.

"Drop it! Drop the gun! Don't..."

Ray wasn't able to get another word out of his mouth. He hadn't realized he'd drawn his semi-automatic from its holster. Ray was leaning on the trunk of a parked car to steady himself. His left hand grasped the lower part of his right hand under the weapon's magazine. By now the black male was only twelve feet from physical confrontation. Ray's trigger pressure was steady as the gun recoiled with a loud discharge. Ray couldn't see if his round hit the naked male, but he heard the clang of the silver object as it bounced on the concrete walkway.

"Who the hell are you?" Then the naked man slumped to his knees, his question unanswered.

The shrill screams morphed into a systematic wail. The light shining from the open doorway shadowed as another figure filled the opening. Ray could see this male was also naked. He was holding what Ray identified as a small semi-automatic handgun.

"Drop the gun! Now!"

The second naked man immediately dropped his gun and it skidded down the walkway. This naked guy was white.

"On the ground! Do it now!"

The naked man dropped to the ground and quickly put his hands behind his head. It was obvious he had followed this drill before. Ray could hear the pulsating wail of approaching police units. He waited behind the parked car until the first unit screeched to a stop.

"Cover the two on the ground! I'm going into the room," Ray yelled as he moved cautiously around the two males prone on the ground. He saw an erratic stream of blood gushing from the black male's neck. Ray still had his gun in his hand as he entered the room. A young black female cowered on the bed. Sheets were pulled around her body like a shroud. Ray figured she was probably naked, too. The woman finally stopped screaming when she saw Ray. The sight of his uniform probably calmed her down. He holstered his gun.

"You got some clothes, lady?" Ray asked. She pointed to a chair next to the TV. It was piled with a ragtag pile of clothing.

"The purple sweater and jeans, please," the female said.

As Ray handed the pieces of clothing to her he asked, "Name?"

"Claudia. Mind turning around?"

She was obviously embarrassed and Ray turned, but didn't leave the room. She didn't know he was able to see her through the mirror hung over the dresser. She had a very dark complexion. Her breasts were small, but her nipples were large and darker brown. She was a skinny thing with her ribs well pronounced. Her hipbones jutted to meet her jeans. She slithered into her clothing as fast as she could. Ray thought it strange that she hadn't asked about the two men.

"Who are the two out there?"

"Johns. You kill the motherfuckers?"

"Maybe one. Not the other one. What happened?"

"The white guy got pissed at the black guy."

"Why?"

"He came in me first. The white guy was pissed he was gonna be left with sloppy seconds. He told the black guy he had ruined his fuck. The black guy just laughed and told the white guy to suck his dick. Next thing I know the white guy pulls this gun out of someplace. Don't know where he hid it being naked and all. And then he shoots at the wall where the black guy was standing. I think he was as surprised as I was when it happened. He points it again at the black guy. That guy just wanted to get out and leave, but you shot him. Shit, he didn't have the gun. You killed the black dude for no reason. Fuckin' cops. All alike."

The woman didn't cry, shiver, or seem concerned.

"Ray," one of the arriving cops called. "Better come outside."

They had handcuffed the white guy and he was seated in the rear of a black and white. Ray noticed a trashcan was turned upside down in the walkway.

"Protecting the gun, Ray. That's all."

"What about the other guy's gun?" Ray asked.

"What gun?"

"The black guy had a chrome gun and turned on me."

The cop shook his head. "All we found was a silver hairbrush."

Ray's felt a sharp pang eat into his stomach and his mouth was suddenly dry.

"Want me to check see if anyone got a throw down or maybe a knife?" the cop asked Ray.

"No, I know what I saw. I thought it was a gun. He was handling it like you would a gun. The guy swung around and it looked like he was going into a shooting crouch."

Ray shook his head at what had happened, but he knew this was trouble. He was in deep, deep shit.

* * *

"Mr. Katz, got a fatal officer-involved shooting at the Days Inn out here by the airport. Off-duty Riverton cop working paid detail. Shot some naked black guy who was unarmed. Well, not exactly," the Auburn County prosecutor's investigator reported over the phone.

"What the hell does that mean? 'Not exactly.'"

"Well, he apparently was armed with a hairbrush."

"But, the guy was naked?"

"Yep. All three involved at the motel were naked. Some sex party. One's a hooker, boss."

"Well, get our rollout team moving."

For years, prosecutors have encouraged local agencies to investigate officer-involved shootings independently. Prosecutors generally allow police management to handle disciplinary issues and allow police-related deaths to be tried in civil court proceedings. Rarely would a cop be prosecuted for an on-duty shooting, even if someone died. However, an off-duty shooting is another matter. Too many off-duty incidents involved drunken cops, horseplay, or domestics involving a wife or girlfriend. By the 1970s, incidents involving fatal shootings by police, subjects dying after fighting with cops, or subjects being trussed like rodeo calves were increasing in numbers. Many subject deaths were being captured on camera videos as the number of personal cell and smart phones increased, along with the explosion of surveillance systems placed in most cities. Prosecutors often sent investigators to shadow cop investigators to make sure they weren't "whitewashing" cases. Some aggressive prosecutors took over case investigations using their own team of investigators. Image is always of utmost importance for prosecutors in any jurisdiction. Prosecutors must be reelected so it's important to demonstrate they're independent entities, not puppets manipulated by the local police agency. By the late 1990s it became more common to see a cop criminally prosecuted for even an on-duty death.

"Slight problem, boss. The AG activated the State Police Major Crime Unit. Seems they might try to take over."

"Get our team out there. I'm on my way," Irv ordered.

Irv was upset. The Attorney General, Big Bob, was making a point by butting his nose in Irv's cases. Irv figured it was payback after running against him in the last election.

By the time Irv Katz reached the Days Inn, a full complement of state police investigators was on the scene. Their big, black command post vehicle was holding a key position. Of course Big Bob's name was scrawled under the New Jersey state seal. For a moment, Irv fantasized it was *his* name prominently displayed.

"Mr. Katz," a young man said as he approached. The guy had the obligatory buzz cut and was slender with a face featuring a Dick Tracy square jaw. His handshake almost dropped Irv to his knees.

"Lieutenant. Smith, SP Majors here."

"Lieutenant, what's really going on?" Irv asked

The young man gave a quizzical look.

"Why are you guys down here? You've never come to Auburn County for a chicken shit cop shooting before. It'd take a politician or entertainment big shot getting shot or busted to get you guys out. Why this, and why now?"

"Hey, Mr. Prosecutor, I just follow orders. Heard the call out came from the AG hisself. You want me to give you a quick run through?"

"Sure."

Lt. Smith guided Irv through the crime scene social filled with a gaggle of cops standing in front of the motel room. A large lump mounded under a silver shock blanket on the walkway.

"That's the black guy. One shot in the neck. Nicked the carotid artery and he bled out instantaneously. Had a silver colored hair brush…and a big dick." Smith chuckled at his characterization.

"The naked white guy has been taken to the Troop Barracks. The hooker in still in the back of a Riverton unit. She thinks this whole thing is funny and figures the notoriety will net her another $10 or $20 bonus for tricks down the road."

Smith guided Irv into the motel room, pushing their way through a crowd of crime scene techs and police photographers. Irv noticed the crumpled bed linens and the leaking tube of KY jelly on the nightstand. Lubricant was seeping over the top of the stand in an expanding puddle.

"Seems one of them squeezed off a round in the room," Smith noted, pointing to a hole in the wall above the dresser mirror. "That's what alerted Officer Fay and got him moving down this way from the motel office. Seems he did a good job and was pretty tactical savvy."

"You talk with him yet?" Irv asked.

"Nope, waiting for his union rep."

"I want one of my investigators to sit in."

"Can't do that, sir. Orders, you know." A faint smirk spoiled Smith's face.

"Fuck you. This is my county! One of my guys will be sitting in!"

"Mr. Katz, you need to get that approved by my boss, the colonel, or the AG. This is my investigation and you need to stay out of it. I'll give you a heads up after we've interviewed the officer, but you can't be part of it," he said matter of factly, but with the arrogance so common with state cops.

* * *

Taylor Sterling had just returned from a four-day weekend in Taos. Sandy Banks, his Santa Fe realtor friend, had closed a two mil sale and had the urge to spend some of her fee. This was a friendship with benefits, in more ways than one. Turned out this was a really a substantial real estate coup for Sandy. She had the home listing and roped in the buyers, a gay couple from LA, too. A double header! Sandy was also the broker for the deal so she didn't have to share a dime with anybody.

Earlier Sandy tried to get Taylor to stop by the closing party her clients were hosting at the Pink Adobe. The restaurant was preparing a traditional Nuevo New Mexican feast and it would be spectacular. Instead Taylor decided to head for home. He had already spent four days with Sandy at a spa on the outskirts of Taos where the couple played a few rounds of golf, kayaked over more than ten miles of white water, consumed an immense amount of food washed down with too much Grey Goose, and enjoyed a pleasant amount of steamy sex. Life was good, very good.

Taylor was in the garage of his condo hooking the battery charger to his old Jeep Wrangler. The heap would lie down and die if he didn't drive it every four or five days. Maybe it was time to junk the Jeep and find something new. The ringing of his house phone interrupted his thoughts, allowing him to retreat from thinking about spending unearned money.

"Mr. Sterling, got a minute?" the caller asked. The voice was definitely East Coast. Taylor figured New York or New Jersey.

"Sure, actually you saved me from pronouncing death to my Jeep."

"Samuel Pisnero here. Chief of Police in New Jersey, Riverton. Need some help, Mr. Sterling."

"Boss, why me? You got lots of people who do what I do in your neck of the woods."

"You come highly rated and recommended. Heard you're the real deal. A straight shooter. That's what I need right now. What one of my men needs, too. Got your name from a friend of a friend who knows someone who knows you."

"Exactly what you need, boss?" Taylor asked, noting the chief's response sounded like an episode of the *Sopranos*. A friend of a friend of a friend who knows a guy who has a friend! Geez, could it get any more classic?

"Need you to conduct an administrative shooting investigation. One of my men killed a guy having a three-way fuck in a motel. County prosecutor pulled a kangaroo court grand jury and got my cop indicted for second-degree murder. Bullshit charge. But my guy needs help and I need a report I can give to my community and city council. We can't wait months for the trial."

"What if it isn't favorable, boss?"

"I don't need an ass-wipe, Taylor. I hear you're not that type. I want it straight…good or bad. I can handle the truth. You'll find I'm big enough to handle whatever happens."

"I can be there in a couple of days. Fly into Newark? Fair warning, gonna cost you, boss."

"Don't care. Got a good council and got my own slush fund. I skim a little off the top of my drug seizures."

Taylor already heard more than he felt comfortable hearing. Newark Liberty International wasn't one of Taylor's favorite airports. It was always under construction and was filthy. But, a fee was a fee and the Jeep was on its last legs.

* * *

After picking up his rental car, Taylor programmed his iPhone to locate the Riverton station. He drove through Newark and dropped off the Interstate when his iPhone guide Siri politely told him to exit. Taylor wondered if Siri knew where the hell she was going. Row after row of triple-decker houses and too many boarded storefront businesses filled the streets. Taylor had been to New Jersey once before on a case. That case was in the part of the state most people don't talk or know about—the quaint, pastoral south of Jersey. Once you get away from Newark, Camden, and Trenton, beautiful, idyllic countryside can be discovered.

The Riverton Police Station was typical of older East Coast stations. The last renovation was probably done in the 1950s. Well-worn steps leading from the street level to the front doors were made of granite. They dipped and waved from years of visitor and perp footfalls. Suspects were called perps in this part of the country. Large oak doors opened to a damp and musty smelling lobby. A dull marble floor beckoned and guided anybody entering to an imposing darkened mahogany desk elevated eighteen inches above the lobby floor.

"Yeah, what ya want, buddy?" the heavyset uniformed sergeant unceremoniously asked Taylor.

"Here to see Chief Pisnero."

"You expected, buddy?"

"Yes." Taylor wanted to add something obnoxious, but resisted the urge.

The sergeant picked up a phone, mumbled into the headset, and pointed to a door at the left of the desk.

"Down the hall on the right, buddy."

The hallway walls were painted that off-shade puke green so common in old government buildings. Taylor often wondered if five-gallon buckets of the slop came from ancient WWII storerooms. The walls were shaded by years of handprints and pollution. Much of the dark staining was probably residue from the days when every cop smoked three or more packs of cigarettes a day.

Chief Pisnero's office was smaller than most of the head honcho domains Taylor had visited. But the chief had his own ego wall that most in his position maintained and cherished. Certificates earned in training programs and awards bestowed by government organizations surrounded the chief's FBI National Academy cert along with a couple university degrees. Taylor noticed a football proudly perched on a plastic stand.

"Jets?"

"One of the touchdown balls the year they beat the Pats."

Sam Pisnero was right out of a Hollywood casting call. The guy rounded at 350 pounds. He was wearing shiny grey slacks hitched with a brown alligator belt. A white silk shirt deep-veed, ending just below his nipples. Three heavy gold chains teased his ample chest hair and Taylor wondered if the links ever tangled with the mat they called home. He noted the chief wore slip-in shoes without socks. An orangey-yellow tan indicative of bad tanning applications completed the look.

Chief Pisnero was a fan of bouffant hairstyles and his helmet of hair was tacked with too much product. Pisnero's style would have been awarded Buddy Holly's stamp of approval. A too broad and too white smile greeted Taylor. He couldn't tell if the chief was addicted to whitening or if he had shiny caps all in a row.

"Taylor, right on time."

"You called. Like Paladin used to say, 'Have gun, will travel.' Except I left my gun in Santa Fe."

"Yeah, heard you were in LA. Ever meet Paladin?" the chief asked.

"Actually I did once. Richard Boone was his real name. He even handed me one of his cards like on the show. Stopped him one night after he had been drinking. I was in Traffic then. He was more tired than drunk. He seemed to be a good guy. Not as big as he looked on the screen, but uglier than sin!"

"We got our share of cop shows staged here in the Big Apple, too."

Taylor Sterling had been with the LAPD for over twenty years. He loved the job, but hated the organizational bullshit. At times he wondered why he ever tested for promotion, but he retired as a Deputy Chief of Police. Taylor was good at management, better than he was as a street cop. Not every officer is cut out to be a good street cop. It takes that sixth sense, that uncanny ability to see what others don't. Taylor was more methodical and pragmatic in his thinking process. Those qualities made him a good supervisor and manager. He kept things orderly and well run. A few subordinates called him anal, but that didn't bother him. Taylor was demanding of his people, but also understood how to motivate them and draw out their distinctive talents. Each officer was different and there was no one avenue for motivation. It was a skill Taylor knew he had, and used it effectively.

"Chief, there's TV and movies and then there's the real world you and I have to work in. So, tell me what you got, boss. Tell me why you brought me clear across country."

"Got all the players ready to meet with you, Taylor. Thought it would be best to hear from everyone involved at the same time. We're meeting over at Santini's."

Santini's was located in a part of Riverton that had probably been a nice part of town at one time, but wasn't anymore. As Pisnero pulled his unmarked Tahoe to the front of the restaurant and parked at the red-painted curb next to a fire hydrant, he strung the radio mic cord over the rearview mirror. Taylor noticed the other three cars parked in front of the restaurant had mics draped over the mirrors as well. Parking was never a problem for cops in Riverton, Taylor decided.

The restaurant was typical of neighborhood Italian eateries scattered up and down the East Coast. The front showed an uninviting, red brick façade marching to a long string of small windows under the eaves of a jutting roof. The dark wood door bore crisscrossed scratches and dusky coloring from years of human oil emitted from a thousand hands pushing the door open. Inside, Taylor noticed the man behind the bar was wearing a black vest and patterned, white silk shirt. The barkeep nodded briefly, and then went back to removing telltale signs of lipstick and fingerprints on balloon wine glasses. An old Sinatra song wafted from somewhere.

Beyond the bar was the main dining room. Three U-shaped booths lined each wall and were elevated about a foot. The cushions were covered in deep red leather, possibly Naugahyde. Six tables covered with white tablecloths and silver settings filled the center of the room and stood ready for the dinner crowd.

Taylor glanced at his watch and noted it was only four thirty. He followed the chief to the back of the dining room to a pair of swinging doors. They entered a small room with only one large circular table that could easily seat twelve. Four men were already at the table. Each had a drink in front of them.

"This is Taylor Sterling," Pisnero announced. Each man got up, extended his hand for a shake, but didn't say a word. Each gave Taylor a look rivaling that of a suspicious TSA screener. Cops size up everybody the minute they make an encounter.

"Let me do the introductions," Pisnero said. "First guy on my right is Vince Palmero. He's Riverton's FOP union president." Vince challenged Pisnero in the heavy weight division. Unfortunately, he was about a foot shorter so he looked like a basketball on steroids. Taylor saw his shirttails were pulled out of his pants and one of the shirt buttons was undone, revealing a hairy stomach.

"The guy with the $3,000 Canali suit is Raymond Cavallo, the union lawyer who's the guy representing Officer Fay. Most call him "The Suit." The lawyer was Abe Lincoln tall, pushing the height of a basketball center. His steel grey hair was perfectly coiffed. Taylor noticed a large gold pinky ring bullied the rest of his hand.

"Next to Cavallo is Calvin Parker, our city attorney." Calvin Parker didn't fit the caricatures the others carried. Taylor doubted that he was Italian. He looked like he might be of Scandinavian descent. Blond hair, blue eyes, and fair skin. Parker was wearing a plain light grey suit, blue shirt, and a hand-tied blue and white striped bow tie.

"The last guy here is Rico Salvatore. He's the eyes and ears for the Attorney General. He's the AG's man on the ground. Most call the AG by his nickname, Big Bob."

Rico nodded a greeting and took a sip of a bronze, ice-cubed drink. Taylor would later realize Rico never said one word during dinner at Santini's.

A large man suddenly loomed next to Chief Pisnero. He was balding and outweighed both the chief and the FOP president combined. He was wearing a white apron with masses of red streaking the front. Taylor wasn't certain if the streams were blood or Marinara sauce stains. The big guy leaned over and whispered something to the chief. Taylor saw Pisnero peel two hundred dollar bills from a wad he pulled from his pocket and palm them into the man's hand.

"Little Paulie says he and his dad prepared special items for us and he hopes we'll enjoy. Paulie, if nobody don't, can we cut 'em up and put them through that big sausage grinder you gots in the kitchen?" Pisnero laughed and patted Little Paulie on his vast stomach.

Taylor suddenly realized this was an experience he had never had before. Here he was in the isolated back room of an Italian restaurant with the heads of the local police department. Scenes from the *Godfather* and *Goodfellas* flashed through his memory bank as Taylor allowed a small smile to crease his face. He picked up the sound of Louie Prima. At any moment he expected a dark character would blast through the door and shotgun the entire law enforcement command of Riverton, New Jersey.

This was an Italian feast Taylor would remember fondly. A large antipasti platter was served first, flanked by two bowls of fried calamari served Rhode Island style with peppers and Marinara sauce. Next to be presented were three different pastas—linguine with homemade white clam sauce, thick sausages smothered with onions and nestled in tangles of spaghetti with meat sauce, and a Bolognese version of the same.

The main course featured veal scaloppini, chicken cacciatore, veal medallions in a Madera sauce, and huge bone-in veal chops displaying prominent grill marks. Decanters of red wine remained on the table and were not allowed to go empty. Featured desserts were cannoli and tiramisu.

Except Rico, everybody at the table had a lot to say about Officer Fay's predicament and all seemed to be on the same page.

"Just so you know, Taylor, Katz's pissed because he lost to Big Bob in the last election," Pisnero explained. "He wants a big prosecution show for Fay to show he's not in bed with the cops. Katz is gearing up to challenge Big Bob again next time around. Of course Katz is upset I didn't support him the last time he ran. Right, like I'd go against Big Bob for a squirrelly Jew from Queens. Fat chance that would happen!"

Listening to this, Vince Palmero leaned back in his chair to a point where Taylor couldn't understand why the abused chair didn't topple. Suddenly Palmero dropped his chair forward with a heavy thud. His finger wildly jabbed the air.

"Little fucker with those red suspenders couldn't wipe Big Bob's ass. He'd be a disaster as AG. My members tell me he grills them whenever they bring in a probable cause affidavit for felony warrants. One told me how Katz's investigators said their boss almost had an orgasm when he could bring domestic violence charges against that poor young cop in Temple City. So the kid slapped his main squeeze a little. You work with them. You cover it up. You give the bitch something to make her go away."

Taylor noticed The Suit glance at Vince and smiled. No sense getting personally involved when he had some moron ready to badmouth Katz for him.

"There is another possibility," City Attorney Calvin offered. "Maybe Katz feels Big Bob invaded his turf. You know, the AG usually lets the county prosecutor handle shootings like this one. Maybe he's trying to send Big Bob a message. Maybe we got to give Irv Katz an excuse to get out from under his own decision. Something that will allow him to save face." Calvin saw his suggestion wasn't going over so he slumped back in his chair and crossed his arms in a defensive pose.

Taylor soon realized he was dealing with two issues. The first was a political power play between Irv Katz and Big Bob. Taylor briefly wondered what the hell Big Bob's real name was. The second issue centered on the state police investigation. Was it a good solid investigation or a hard-core hatchet job on County Prosecutor Katz at Officer Fay's expense?

"What do you think about the state police investigation?" Taylor asked. He noticed no one jumped into the conversation. "Have you all seen the report?"

"Won't let it out," Pisnero grumbled. "Even Katz hasn't got to see it. I hear Big Bob is waiting for the right moment to send it to the press and embarrass Katz."

"I've issued two subpoena duces tecums for it. One to the colonel and the other to Katz. Both say it's an open case so they don't have to disclose anything," The Suit explained. "Once Fay is officially charged, they'll have to give it to us."

"That's why I brought you in, Taylor," Pisnero explained. "I need to preempt them and get an administrative investigation going on the shooting."

"But I need basic documentation first, boss!" Taylor exclaimed. "Do you think the state cops might be helpful?"

"I can reach out to Smith. He's the lead investigator from the State Majors. I know him personally. They're not FOP, but they're friendly," Vince offered.

Calvin added, "In the end I'm probably going to have to defend the City and Chief Pisnero. But then, there hasn't been a lawsuit filed. I expect it will be coming."

"Hopefully my investigative work will help you, Mr. Parker," Taylor said in passing.

The table exchanged business cards and Taylor told the group to reach him on his cell, g-mail address, or go through Chief Pisnero. As they were leaving, Taylor saw Pisnero approach Little Paulie, give him a pat on the cheek, and heard him say the dinner bill should be sent to the station.

* * *

After he got the heads up from Vince Palmero, Taylor made arrangements to meet Lt. Smith from the State Majors unit at the area barracks. Smith indicated he had other work to do at the Bloomfield Troop Headquarters alongside the Garden State Parkway so it would be a good place to meet. Taylor told Smith he didn't need directions as his iPhone had the uncanny ability to find strange places.

The police building was a nondescript grey concrete building right out of the 1960s. It was scheduled to be rebuilt, but after Hurricane Sandy hit the Jersey coast, funding for construction was delayed. Taylor could see several marked police units parked behind the chain-link fence. New Jersey State Patrol cars had a distinctive black stripe splashed diagonally across the front doors.

Taylor knew the Jersey State Patrol was just a few years out from under the control of the U.S. Department of Justice. Back in 1994, Congress wanted to pass a bill controlling the use of excessive force by police officers. The country was still reeling from the Rodney King incident in Los Angeles. The graphic, but amateurish, video shot by citizen Hollaway had been shown incessantly through the years of the cops' trial and acquittal in Simi

Valley, the trial and guilty verdict in Federal Court in Los Angeles, and finally at the later civil trial.

As a result, some legislators were clamoring for federal legislation to rein in the cops. That never materialized. What was included in the 1994 Crime Bill were a couple innocuous paragraphs allowing government, through the Department of Justice, to bring class action civil lawsuits against any local police agency when the government encountered cops engaged in a pattern and practice of unconstitutional policing. In 1997, Steubenville, Ohio, and Pittsburgh, Pennsylvania were the first two cities to come under DOJ control. The New Jersey State Police was hit in 1999. It was the first and only state police agency to be placed under this level of governmental control. Most of their problems stemmed from a flood of allegations of racial profiling from enforcement along the interstates that bisected New Jersey. They were known as the East Coast drug highway. The agency was required to be under the DOJ thumb for only five years, but with encouragement from the agency itself, it remained under DOJ supervision for seven years. Many in the agency thought it was a good idea since there were definite benefits. State cops received improved equipment such as in-car video camera systems and were ordered additional training that the state legislature had denied for years. But, like many reform periods in American policing history, the New Jersey State Police was slowly slipping back into old ways of doing business when left unsupervised.

Lt. Smith met Taylor at the desk and led him back into a small conference room. Smith fulfilled the description Chief Pisnero had given him. Straight as a rail and suit off the rack from the Men's Warehouse.

"Heard you're retired from LAPD."

"Guilty!"

"Always heard good things about West Coast cops. Took pride in your looks and uniform. Kind of like us. Can't say the same for most of our local cops. Ignorant, lazy, fat assholes."

A small expandable file was centered on the table. Taylor resisted the urge to reach for it and spread its contents over the table to get things started. Instead, he decided to get Smith talking. Getting someone talking, Taylor had learned, allowed them to become comfortable with future interaction. Hearing themselves giving opinions and expressing thoughts seemed to open the avenue for discussion.

"Lt. Smith…" Taylor hesitated.

"It's Rob. You Taylor?"

"Yep. Say, Rob, can you give me a thumbnail sketch of what happened at the motel?" Lt. Smith didn't miss a beat.

"Pretty simple really. Only four people involved and one of them is dead. Oh, the motel clerk was there, but he didn't have anything significant to add about the shooting. So as we pieced it together, Sweet P, the hooker, responded to a call from her Craig's List solicitation. Ernest, the dead black guy, and his buddy Rusty, the white guy, were staying at the motel since they were working on a construction job close by. Company put them up at the Days Inn. Anyway, they wanted pussy so they called Sweet P.

"Say, you want some water, Taylor?" Rob walked to the small refrigerator in the corner and pulled out two bottles without waiting for Taylor's reply.

"Anyway, they wanted a three-way. Sweet P was okay with that, but balked when they said they wanted to fuck her in the ass. She absolutely didn't do anal she told them. She said they could finger fuck her asshole and brought out a tube of KY jelly from her purse. She started the three-way by giving them both blowjobs. Then the black guy started fucking her from behind, doggy style, while she was blowing Rusty.

"Ernest got his finger going in and out of her ass and he's pile driving her with that cock of his. Jeez, you should have seen the size of that guy's cock! Sweet P said Rusty yelled to Ernest that he better not come in her snatch 'cuz he didn't want sloppy seconds and nigger cum all over his cock.

"About that time Ernest let out a guttural groan and all three knows he's just shot his wad into Sweet P's pussy. Rusty pulls his cock out of Sweet P's mouth and reached down alongside the bed and came up with his .380 auto. Shit, he fires one at Ernest, but misses. Hits the wall above the mirror on top of the dresser. By this time Ernest is off the bed and backing toward the door. Rusty tries to get another shot off but his legs are tangled in the bed sheets and he slips off the bed onto the floor. Well, Ernest had opened the door and was backing out of the room when he gets shot by Officer Fay. One shot into the neck and nicks the artery. If the fucker had lived, he'd be a quad since the bullet shattered his spine at the base of his skull.

"Later Rusty tells us he thinks some asshole was shooting at his buddy so he ran to the doorway to protect him. He's damn lucky he didn't get his ass shot, too. Sweet P said all she was worried about was if she was going to get paid."

"How did the hairbrush get into the picture?" Taylor asked.

"Haven't a clue. Don't know why Ernest would grab that. Course he's dead so he can't tell us. But I do believe he did have it. Wasn't planted. Rusty verified he saw it in Ernest's hand. Sweet P is still on all fours facing the other way and didn't see nothin'." Smith shook his head and allowed a shallow chuckle to escape.

"So what happened to Rusty?"

"Oh, he was booked for aggravated assault and possessing an unlicensed firearm. He's still in jail."

"And Sweet P?"

Smith smiled and leaned back. "She's become a valuable informant for us. We're making a whole bunch of prostitution arrests with her help. She thinks we're being good to her. She still thinks we were going to arrest her for accessory to murder. Dumb broad."

"Can I take a look at your investigative file, Rob?"

He thought for a moment before sliding it over to Taylor. "Guess with you being a former cop it'll be okay."

"You give a copy to Chief Pisnero?"

"Nah! Don't want to get between the Katz and Big Bob. The bosses, either the colonel or the AG, would have to okay that action."

"Say, what's the deal between Katz and the AG?"

"You know Katz ran against him in the last election, don't you?"

Taylor nodded.

"Well, Big Bob wants to make Katz look bad to keep it from happening again. That's why we took over the investigation and dribbled the report to Katz. When Katz convened the grand jury and subpoenaed my ass, then laid a Subpoena Duces Tecum on the colonel requesting the report, Big Bob was really pissed. When Katz indicted Officer Fay you sure didn't want to be around Colonel Standard or Big Bob. That criminal indictment came out of the blue. First time that I can ever remember any on-duty cop being indicted in this kind of incident. We figured he was on-duty since he was in uniform doing official cop stuff. Shit, Fay wasn't drunk and didn't have anything in his system. No alcohol. No drugs. No 'roids. Nothing! It surprised all of us.

That fuckin' Jew from Queens didn't have any cops on his side the first time he ran for AG, and he sure ain't goin' to have any if he runs again."

Taylor could see Smith was getting agitated, clearly signaling he didn't like what Katz was doing. He knew Smith's animosity towards Katz would help him get a copy of the report or at least what he wanted from the report.

Taylor spilled the contents of the file on top of the table. He picked up the main part of the investigation labeled "Executive Summary." Taylor scanned through the report and focused on the narrative summary of the interview conducted with Officer Ray Fay.

When to interview an officer who has shot someone in the line of duty has always been a controversial subject in police circles. For many years it was thought the officer should be kept in seclusion until investigators were ready to talk with him or her. That could run hours. The interview might occur as much as fifteen or more hours after the officer began working. Police unions stepped in and some said the officer couldn't be interviewed for 48 hours or, in one case, ten days after the shooting incident. A new trend determined the interview should allow the officer to have two sleep cycles. Of course the officer would be expected to give a brief description at the scene of why he fired, how many rounds, and where he was aiming. This was for public safety reasons. It was important to know where to look for evidence and to determine if anyone else might be injured. For example, investigators would look stupid if an 80-year-old woman sitting on the toilet had been shot dead by a stray bullet and wasn't found until the odor alerted the entire neighborhood.

Another issue was if the officer should be tape-recorded during the interview and if the interview should be transcribed verbatim. Most police agencies might tape an interview, but document only a narrative summary of what was said. The problem with that approach was the investigator must interpret what the officer said and paraphrase the interview. There was real potential that the meaning might be changed, purposefully or inadvertently.

"Rob, I see you only have a narrative summary of what Officer Fay told you."

"Yeah, that's our practice. We tape it, but don't have the interview transcribed."

"But you save the tape?"

"Of course we do. But we always do a pre-interview of the witnesses, including the involved officer."

The lieutenant must have noticed Taylor's quizzical expression at his explanation. "We do a pre-interview of all of our interviews. This way the final interview isn't as long. It saves time and cost if we need to get it transcribed."

"So, let me get this straight. You discuss the interview with the person you're going to interview and then turn on the tape?"

"Yeah. Any problem with that?"

"Where did you ever learn to do it that way?"

"Don't know. We've always done interviews that way. What's the big deal?"

Taylor wasn't sure how to respond. This was such an absurd procedure, but he didn't want to piss off the lieutenant by challenging him.

"Can you see how someone might think you were coaching the interviewee?"

"I guess, but no one ever knows about it."

Taylor scanned the narrative summary of Officer Fay's interview again.

"I see you noted Fay saw the black man turn and observed a

shiny object in his hand. Did he say anything else, like how he was holding the object?"

"Don't recall that, Taylor. You think that might be important?"

Taylor wanted to lunge at Lt. Smith's throat. This was slipshod investigative reporting by Smith at best, sloppy reporting that could get an officer into serious trouble. Saving a few bucks in transcription fees could cost the officer his job and career.

"Chief Pisnero says Katz is charging Fay with giving you a false statement. What's your take, Rob?"

Smith stopped and picked up his bottle of water. He slowly took a gulp and set it down. He picked it up again, anchored the spout on his mouth and slowly sucked in a minute amount of water. He was stalling.

Finally Smith exploded. "That's bullshit, Taylor! Fay was honest and straightforward. He could have sat back and taken the Fifth, but he didn't. I don't know where Katz is coming from on that charge. It wasn't from me!"

Police officers have the same constitutional rights as any citizen when it comes to criminal matters. If the interview could result in criminal charges being filed, the officer can elect to stay silent. The Fifth Amendment of the Constitution gives everyone the right to avoid incriminating themselves in a criminal matter. Police officers, like any public employee, can however be compelled to answer questions from their public employers about administrative charges. If they don't answer, they can be fired for insubordination. However, they can't be fired if they don't waive their Fifth Amendment right. Cops rarely exercise this Fifth Amendment right. They feel obligated to tell what happened. Most never expect a prosecutor might charge them criminally even if they've made a mistake, as tragic as the outcome might be.

It was time for Taylor to see what he could get from Smith.

"Rob, I've been hired by Riverton to complete the administrative investigation into Fay's shooting. Chief Pisnero feels it's necessary to get an official announcement to the community about it. Katz is refusing to let him see the good report you and your team created. I'm really here to try to help Officer Fay. He needs someone in his corner. He can't wait the months it's going to take the criminal case to come to court. Officer Fay's hurting now!"

Taylor stopped and stared at Smith, waiting for his response. Taylor knew Smith was torn between being a stand up guy who supported a fellow cop versus being a lock-step soldier who followed orders.

Smith's bosses told him to stonewall Prosecutor Katz and avoid being cooperative. But he knew that Fay needed somebody in his corner to look out for his interests. Smith didn't know Taylor, but felt he was probably an okay fellow cop. To gain time to think, Smith took another gulp of water.

"What do you really need, Taylor?"

"The couple pages in the summary that lay out the narrative of Fay's interview and a copy of the tape recording of his actual interview. That's all, Rob."

"Tell you what, Taylor. Why don't you go down to the Dunkin' Donuts over in the Parkway Visitors' Center and get yourself a cup of coffee. You come back here in about an hour and there'll be a brown envelope left at the desk with your name on it. I'm going to put marks on the copy I give you, so I don't want to see my name on anything coming from you or Riverton. Got that?"

"Rob, I need a cup. We'll meet up again sometime. I never forget a friend and a friend of good cops."

They shook hands and an hour later Taylor was on his way back to the Riverton station carrying a thin brown envelope.

* * *

Taylor spread the contents of the envelope on the table in the sparse interview room of the Riverton station. He knew the room was wired. Most police interview rooms were. He suspected there was a video camera behind the small smoke-tinted dome in the corner of the ceiling. Taylor didn't really care. It was their case and he had nothing to hide, at least at this stage of his investigation. He had no magic wand he could wave over the file to produce missing results, if there were any.

Actually there wasn't much contained in the file after Taylor had spread it across the small table. Twelve pages of executive summary contained the bulk of the information. Bosses always wanted a thumbnail account of what any investigation covered. Usually they never ventured further into the file, taking the summary as the conclusion. There were summarized versions of the statements taken from the hooker Sweet P, the white guy, Rusty, and the motel clerk. Smith had summarized the autopsy report and listed evidence found at the motel. He also listed the criminal histories of the trio who were engaged in sex that night. There were two pages of the narrative summary of Officer Fay's interview included. The only other item included in the file was a thumb drive.

Taylor unloaded his Mac from his backpack carrying case. He was glad Smith had given him the thumb drive. Taylor had a MacBook Air, but no internal DVD player. He inserted the thumb drive and waited for the icon to appear on the computer screen. No photos or JPG files, no doc files, only a DSS file Taylor knew was indicative of an audio file made from an Olympus digital recorder. He figured it was the complete interview of Officer Fay.

Taylor went back to the paper file. The executive summary was fairly well done and basically laid out the incident and investigation information that Taylor already knew. The narrative summary of Fay's interview was the most interesting find.

The officer stated the B/M suspect emerged from the motel room with his back toward the officer. The officer commanded the B/M suspect to halt and put his hands in the air. The B/M suspect quickly turned and faced the officer. The B/M suspect carried a shiny object in one hand. The officer believed this was a gun and commanded the B/M suspect to drop the gun immediately. When the B/M suspect did not drop the gun, the officer, fearing for his life, fired one round which struck the B/M suspect in the neck, ultimately causing his death.

This was typical terse, to the point, cop reporting. But Taylor knew this summary was not what was actually said. The narrative was sterile. It had no realism. It was a report done by someone who was not there. Someone who was not scared, who was not gripped by fear. He hoped the investigator had actually done a better and more complete job during his interview with Officer Fay. Taylor figured he needed to analyze the audio file in private. He sensed this might come to more than simply his review of case documents. He didn't care if anyone observed the written review process or if the room was wired, but the audio might play a sensitive part in his final analysis determining the investigative direction he would take.

Taylor wasn't sure what the physical boundaries of the city of Riverton were. He always liked to book a hotel or motel that wasn't inside the city limits where he was conducting an investigation. This practice kept unwanted eyes and ears from peering into what he was doing. A Comfort Inn located a few miles out was adequate. He would have preferred a Residence Inn with a larger work area, but the Comfort Inn would have to do.

Police interviews or interrogations pretty much start the same way. The date and time is given and those in the room are identified. If the recording is to be transcribed, each person gives a word of introduction. This gives the transcriber a voice to attach to statements. Taylor put on his Bose headphones, sat back, and started the tape.

"This is Investigator Howard Kohn, New Jersey State Police. Next to me on my right is my partner. Want to identify who you are, John, and then we'll go around the table for additional introductions?"

"John Strange, investigator with the State Police Majors."

"Raymond Cavallo, attorney, representing Officer Fay and the Riverton FOP. May I add for the record that my client, Officer Fay, is here to assist in your investigation, but he is not here voluntarily. He knows the Riverton Police Department requires him to cooperate with any law enforcement agency conducting an investigation into any police incident. He will answer your questions and understands that if he does not, he could be subject to termination for insubordination. The fact that there is a command officer from the PD further supports his belief that his cooperation is being compelled."

"Captain Bonanero. I'm here cuz Chief Pisnero told me to sit in. I'm just going to observe." The terse voice stammered through his introduction.

"Captain, is Officer Fay being ordered to be here?"

"I guess so. Yeah, the chief told him to be here," Captain Bonanero answered.

"Is Officer Fay compelled to answer my questions?"

"I dunno. I guess so, but you'd have to ask the chief."

Kohn continued. "Officer Fay, I'm going to read you your Miranda Rights. 'You have a right to remain silent. Anything you say may be used against you in a criminal proceeding. You have a right to have an attorney present during questioning.' I guess we can jump over that since your attorney is here with you. Do you understand those rights?"

"Yep. But like my attorney said, I'm not here voluntarily. But I do want to help you because I haven't done anything wrong,"

"I'm not sure what I should do now," Investigator Kohn indicated. "So you're not waiving your rights is that correct, Officer Fay?"

"That's correct. But I want to be helpful since I'm not looking to get fired."

"You know what, guys, I'm just going to go ahead and ask my questions," Kohn apparently decided. "I'll let the lawyers argue whether Fay's answers can be used. Let's get on with it. We all want to get out of here as soon as possible." The state police investigator chuckled with those words.

Investigator Kohn allowed Officer Fay to tell his side of the story as he remembered it. Fay was articulate and very specific. He included a summary of his tactical approach. He talked about shouting commands. He was very pointed while defining the moments before he pulled the trigger and shot the naked black man.

"He was backing out of the motel room and was silhouetted by the light coming from the room. I ordered him to stop and put up his hands. He didn't follow my order. The man quickly turned to his left and when his right hand swung out I saw something shiny in it. For a moment I wasn't sure what it was. Then his left hand came up and grabbed his right hand. At that second I was positive he was holding a gun. He was going into a two-handed combat stance. I got out of the shadows and ordered, 'Drop the gun' before I cranked off one round. He immediately went down on his knees and fell to the walkway."

Fay went on to recall encountering the second naked man who dropped the gun he was holding as ordered. Police units were on the scene by this time and Fay waved officers to the subjects to handcuff them.

Taylor stopped the audio recording and slowly slid his earphones off. He thought a clerk typist could have completed this interview. Taylor was upset the investigator never required Officer Fay to be more specific regarding the timing of the incident. It was not enough to accept words like "quickly" and "brief." The investigator should have asked follow-up questions to encourage Fay to answer with different verbiage. What upset Taylor most was the investigator didn't have Fay paint a word picture of the naked black guy's hand movements and the stance he had assumed. The investigator could have described it for the record by having Fay demonstrate the stance and then methodically note his movements. Generally, people have extreme difficulty putting physical actions into words to properly depict what actually occurred. After listening to the interview, Taylor wondered if there were places Officer Fay lied or gave evasive or false statements.

Taylor pulled out a yellow tablet from his briefcase and began jotting down his preliminary thoughts about Officer Fay's interview. He knew it would be necessary to conduct his own interview and have both his and the state police interview transcribed. This case was too important to use a narrative summary exclusively. Fay's own words needed to be evaluated carefully.

Taylor knew Officer Fay's interview statement and anything resulting from it couldn't be used against him in a criminal trial. Between The Suit's comments at the beginning of the interview and Officer Fay's assertions, statements would be logically excluded as inadmissible by any reasonable court under the longtime guiding Supreme Court case of *Garrity*. Fay and any reasonable officer would have believed he was not there voluntarily and that his statement to the state cops was compelled. That meant that his statement and any leads resulting from that statement would be considered as fruits. "Fruits of the statement" is also called "fruits of the poisonous tree." This means anything found by using information from an excluded statement cannot be used against the person making the statement. In Fay's case it really wouldn't matter. The county prosecutor was likely to develop the case against Fay by indicating the dead guy, at best, only carried a hairbrush. Certainly not a deadly tool.

* * *

"Mr. Sterling?" Officer Fay approached as he hesitated at the open interview room door at the Riverton police station. "I was told to report here for an interview." Standing behind him was Vince Palmero. This time Palmero was wearing a police sergeant's uniform. The buttons on his shirt were earning their keep trying to avoid exposing his hairy belly.

"How ya doin', Taylor?" Vince asked casually. "I'm Officer Fay's union rep. Attorney Cavallo figured he didn't have to come today as it's you doin' the interview. He likes you for some reason. Why dat' be you figure?"

Taylor let Vince's comments slide. They didn't deserve an answer. He got up and shook Fay's hand and motioned for him to take a seat.

"I've asked Sergeant Viara from your department to appear at the start of this interview. He's going to give you the Garrity warning. That way anything you say can't be used to prosecute you for a crime involving the subject of the shooting we're discussing. You understand that, don't you, Officer Fay?"

"Yes, sir!" a crisp response cracked from the young man. Officer Fay wasn't in uniform since he was on administrative leave with pay. Chief Pisnero could have relieved him without pay, but he knew this was a political power play and didn't want his man to be hurt unnecessarily by losing a paycheck.

Taylor covered the same issues that the state police investigator had. Officer Fay didn't deviate from his original statement or the written report filed by the State Major Crime Unit. When Taylor reached questions about the actual shooting incident, he instructed the young officer to recount exactly what had occurred.

"Stop right there, Officer Fay," Taylor interrupted when Fay began to simulate the naked black man's hand movements showing how he handled the hairbrush.

Taylor had his digital camera prepared. He took photographs of Fay's hands showing how he recalled the naked guy's movements. Taylor took photographs from six different angles.

"Now for the transcript. I've stopped the interview and have taken six photos depicting how Officer Fay remembered the male he shot was moving and how he was holding the object that ended up being a silver colored hairbrush. Officer Fay has stated that he believed the object was a weapon. For the record, Officer

Fay demonstrated the subject raised his right hand, which was holding the object, and then brought his left hand up to cup his right hand.

"Is that correct, Officer Fay?"

Fay nodded affirmatively.

"You can't nod, officer. The transcriber can't pick that up. You must speak your answers."

"Yes, sir. That's what I showed you."

"When you said the subject quickly turned, what did you mean?"

"Just like that," Fay snapped his fingers.

"Let the record show that Officer Fay snapped his fingers to demonstrate what he meant by the word 'quickly.' Why were his actions of concern to you?"

"When the subject brought his hands together, like the way he used his left hand to grasp his right hand that held the silver object, it was the same way I hold a gun when I'm getting into a combat shooting position. I truly thought he was holding a gun," Fay insisted.

"Officer Fay, I'm doing what most police departments would call an administrative shooting investigation. It's not a criminal investigation. It's an investigation to review many other issues involved. Things like your training, tactics, use of equipment, and often aspects of risk management. Most police shootings end with a civil lawsuit, so my job is to uncover potential liability issues," Taylor explained. Taylor shot a glance at Vince who was busy cleaning his fingernails with a pocketknife.

"Officer Fay, is this your first weapon discharge?"

Fay squirmed in his chair and admitted, "No, it's not. I've had, I think, six other discharges. Two were accidental and one was at a dog. They count, Mr. Sterling?"

Taylor didn't want Fay to see the surprise covering his face so he looked down as though forming his next question. Taylor knew six discharges in less than the six years Fay had been on the job were unusual. Most cops went their entire career without ever discharging a weapon. Taylor hadn't shot his gun once in twenty years of active duty. Of course, most of those years weren't spent in the field since Taylor had been promoted to administrative ranks.

"Can you briefly describe the six discharges for me, Officer Fay?"

"The first one was an accident. I was chasing a perp through an open field. Potholes everywhere. I slipped and popped a round off. That's when I realized how sensitive the triggers on our Glocks are. The department bought those guns with a civilian pull of only five pounds. They could have gotten the NYPD model with eleven pounds. But, Mr. Sterling, my shot didn't hit the prep. We finally got him on foot."

"And the next one?"

"Let's see, I think that was the dog. I was chasing another perp through neighborhood backyards. I was going over a fence when suddenly I was eye to eye with a pit bull. I had to unload eight rounds before the motherfucker stopped charging me. Never did get that perp, but the dog was DOA."

Taylor signaled for Fay to continue.

"Next discharge was kind of funny. I was in the station's locker room changing and took my gun out of the holster to put it in my off-duty holster. I dropped the mag to be safe. But I forgot there was a bullet in the chamber. I guess I cranked off another accidental. Blew the shit out of a couple uniforms hanging on the dry cleaning rack. Chief made me pay for new ones."

Taylor couldn't wait to hear about the next three.

"I guess I'm at number four, huh? Well, that happened at the end of a pursuit. We were chasing this douche bag in a Chevy and he plows into a power pole. I ran up to the car so he couldn't jump out and rabbit on us. I pulled the door open and the guy lunges at me with a timing belt screwdriver. You know, one of those big ass ones. I only shot once and missed him. Blew the car radio to smithereens though. Scared the douche so much he pissed in his pants.

"Number five was a fatal. A domestic call. Kind of like the one I was on a few weeks ago. The guy hacked up his wife and was waving a gun and didn't drop it when ordered. When the gun came up, I had nowhere to go. I was smack in the middle of the living room and couldn't retreat to a safe place so I had to fire. Caught him with three rounds, center mass, right in the chest. You know, Katz didn't even take that one to the grand jury."

"Can't wait for the last one, Officer Fay." The young kid didn't pick up on Taylor's sarcasm.

"Liquor store robbery. Perps still inside when we got there. They couldn't go anywhere. We had them buttoned up. I had the shotgun. It was like a standoff. The two perps were packed into a corner by the glass cases holding beer. One had a knife. The other had a gun. Turned out to be a pellet gun, but it looked just like our Glocks. Didn't have any orange or red thing on the muzzle. Guy with the gun hesitated a little too long before dropping it. I unloaded with one shot of the double-ought buck. That guy's not going to be walking too good anymore. I about cut off both legs and shattered both knees."

Officer Fay wasn't gloating, but seemed unconcerned, even blasé, about his unusual record.

"You ever get any shit from the department for any of your shootings, Fay?"

"Nope. Chief talked to me about the accidentals. Like I said, he made me pay for two uniforms. Said I needed to be more careful. He knew the department owned a few guns with hair triggers. He was pissed about the pit bull I shot though. Thought I should have hit him with my baton or maybe kicked him. But, Mr. Sterling, I never got bad write-ups from the chief. I was just doing my job."

"Anybody else on the PD got as many shootings on record as you do, Ray?"

Ray Fay stopped and put his finger to his chin and closed his eyes to think. "Nope, I don't think so. But we don't discuss those things in the department. You just hear things from the grapevine. Word of mouth, know what I mean, Mr. Sterling?"

Taylor nodded in agreement. Confidentiality regarding personnel records had gone too far in police agencies. Everyone seemed to be afraid of hurting an officer's feelings. Or maybe it had to do with the old philosophy, "If it ain't writ down it cain't hurt us!" Taylor had been on the Shooting Review Board during his time with the LAPD. In fact, as Deputy Chief he was the board chairperson. The board was required to examine all firearm discharges, even accidentals, or as trainers called them, unintentional discharges. Police trainers insist there aren't any accidents when it comes to guns; sloppiness, laziness, or unsafe handling of the gun causes them to discharge.

The Review Board was charged with determining if a gun discharge was within policy, if tactics used by the officer were proper, and if there was anything learned to change written policy, training, equipment, or supervisory control. Each firearm discharge investigation was an opportunity for the agency to learn and make corrections, if necessary. Surprisingly, not all findings were unanimous. Taylor remembered heated discussions happening between board members.

Taylor surmised Chief Pisnero didn't have anything like an LAPD Shooting Review Board going in Riverton.

* * *

Taylor was pleasantly surprised when he received a quick return call from the Auburn County Prosecutor's Office. He had placed his call just that morning asking to meet with Mr. Katz and was told a conference could be scheduled that afternoon.

Taylor was glad he had emailed both interviews of Officer Fay to NetTranscripts in Arizona. Now that digital recorders were the common tool used for interviewing, they could be sent anywhere for transcription. Taylor had often used this Arizona firm and knew he could get the finished product overnight. Times had changed and Taylor had to work at keeping up to date with the constant flux.

When Taylor arrived at the prosecutor's office, the secretary at the front desk asked him to wait until the prosecutor's chief investigator arrived. Taylor guessed the man entering the office about fifteen minutes later was the investigator. He was a rather nondescript man. He must have been close to fifty, was rather short, balding, and hadn't seen the inside of a workout room in years. His suit was obviously an off the rack from JCPenney or maybe Men's Warehouse. He was carrying the obligatory brown manila folder secured with a large rubber band. The secretary ushered Taylor and the newly arrived investigator into the office of the head prosecutor.

Irv Katz's office was not as pretentious as many Taylor had seen. It was housed in an old building and so his office appeared worn and shabby. The nearly black walls might have been mahogany at one time. Taylor was surprised to see only a law school diploma and certificates to practice before the New Jersey Supreme Court and the U.S. Supreme Court hanging behind the desk. He wondered why a certificate from the U.S. 3rd Circuit Court of Appeals didn't find a home on the wall. The desk appeared almost too large for the size of the office. In one corner a small conference table with three chairs around settled as a cramped afterthought.

Katz rose as the two entered his office and moved quickly to Taylor with his hand extended.

"Mr. Sterling," Katz welcomed as he vigorously shook hands. "Chief Pisnero told me to expect you. Said you're some kind of retired cop out of Los Angeles."

"True, Mr. Katz."

"Said you were doing something with the Riverton cop fatal shooting at the Days Inn. Strange they would pull someone in from as far off as LA. Why do you think they didn't hire a guy from the East Coast, like the NYPD?"

"Maybe they wanted someone who knew zip about Riverton and not much more about New Jersey."

"Maybe so, but I think Pisnero is shrewder than that. He probably did some checking. But then, so have I."

"And, what did you find?" Taylor asked, knowing exactly where this was going.

"Doesn't anybody dislike you, Taylor? No one can be *that* good!"

"I'm not. Guess you didn't ring up the right people. Want me to give you a few negative references? My old boss doesn't have much good to say about me."

"I trust my sources, Mr. Sterling. They say you're a straight shooter. Don't hold back anything, but you're also tactful. That's a rare commodity in police circles, at least in my experience. Most of that has been here in Jersey," Katz added.

"What can you tell me about the Days Inn shooting that I don't already know?" Katz looked at his investigator for reassurance. Taylor was surprised Katz hadn't introduced him.

"Well, I pretty much got an overview from reading the executive summary completed by the State Majors."

Katz didn't allow Taylor to finish before holding his hand in the air to indicate for him to stop. "Where did you get that report?"

"Strangest thing. I found it on a counter with my name on it," Taylor admitted. He wasn't about to say it was the counter at the State Troop Barracks or that it came from one Lt. Smith. He purposefully didn't mention the thumb drive containing the audio of Officer Fay's interview.

Katz smiled, but didn't pursue the issue.

"I've interviewed Officer Fay and I've got a copy of that transcript for your review. I also have a series of photographs I took depicting how Fay said the deceased was holding the hairbrush. I noted in the executive report that the DNA testing came back with the subject's DNA on the brush." Taylor paused and waited for Katz to respond. He didn't.

"Mr. Katz, just thought you should know what my administrative investigative report will include." Taylor was ready to discuss Officer Fay's tactics and shooting at the Days Inn. He wasn't going to bring up the other shootings Fay had been involved in.

"Why would I care, Mr. Sterling?"

"You're sitting on an important case. It could have long-lasting implications for your office as well as general policing in New Jersey. When I was a deputy chief, the last thing I wanted was to be left out of the loop. Some officers who worked for me thought they were helping when they kept negative things from me. It was important for me to know the warts along with the dimples." Taylor watched Katz and caught him nodding in agreement.

"You think Big Bob is hiding stuff from me?"

"Don't know. Say, does the AG have a real name?"

Katz laughed and shot a glance at his investigator, "Yeah, Robert Benson. He's always contended he's kin to former Senator Lloyd Benson from Texas. Remember him during the presidential debates? Remember when he admonished that lightweight senator from Indiana saying, 'I knew Jack Kennedy. He was a friend of mine. You, sir, are no Jack Kennedy!' Sure unrailed that Indiana boy politician! So, what's your final take on the shooting?"

"I'm going to say that Officer Fay's tactics and his decision to shoot were in keeping with generally accepted police practices."

"You getting into the legal end of it?"

"Not from the criminal side. That's in your purview, Mr. Katz. But, I'll be discussing the shooting decision from the civil and Constitutional perspectives. I'll be putting it into the context of the 1989 Supreme Court decision *Graham v. Conner*. Even though the civil case only needs a preponderance of evidence, I think there is much more going for Officer Fay. From my perspective, it's not a close call. Any reasonable officer under the same circumstances would have felt threatened and would have used deadly force to stop an imminent threat. It's too bad the shiny object was only a hairbrush. This was a rapidly evolving situation, Mr. Katz." Taylor used lynchpin words from the Supreme Court decision.

"And you think I'm wrong, huh?"

"Mr. Katz, I'm not an expert in prosecution practices. I'm no lawyer and don't pretend to be. That's your field. It would be presumptuous for me to tell you how to run your office. I simply think you should have all the information available. You've got a big decision to make and should have all that's known on the subject. That's all."

Katz rose and walked around the table to Taylor, extending his hand again. "Nice to meet you. Always good to talk with a professional in the field."

* * *

During each investigation he handled, Taylor hopped a ride-along in the field with either a street cop or a supervisor. He got a sense of the real workings of an agency when he placed himself close and personal with department personnel. He knew field cops felt most comfortable on patrol calls since cop cars became their personal offices. Cops didn't immediately spill their guts about agency politics, personalities, or procedures, but Taylor knew most were ready to do so when a friendly ear was offered. Most field cops never had a chance to give feedback to their bosses. Bosses were usually too busy politicking to listen to what a field cop had to say. Some bosses seemed afraid to sit one-on-one with their people. Shit, they might have to answer awkward questions face to face!

Taylor reported to the Riverton station at the prearranged time of seven p.m. He had picked this particular shift because he knew it was the shift Ray Fay normally worked. He hoped he would get hooked up with an officer who knew Fay.

"Mr. Sterling?"

Taylor turned and saw a uniformed sergeant waiting for him. The sergeant was probably in his late fifties. He stood several inches shorter than Taylor, who pushed the bar at six feet. The sergeant obviously didn't hit the gym as often as Taylor did and had a few too many inches padding his middle. A thin band of grey hair circled the bottom of his head and a pencil thin grey moustache tipped skyward at each end. Wire rim glasses made him appear older than his probable years.

"Sergeant White, here."

"Yeah, I'm Taylor." Taylor extended his hand for the customary shake.

"Paul," the sergeant offered as he shook Taylor's hand with a firm grip. "You the guy used to be with LAPD?" Taylor nodded. "Heard you left with a cloud over your head."

"If you mean the chief and I didn't see eye to eye as a dark cloud, then guilty as charged."

Paul laughed. "Know the territory, Taylor. I'm not Irish or Italian, how do you think I fit into Riverton? I might as well be black. Hell, I'm not even Catholic."

Taylor squeezed into the front seat of the police car. It was a new Impala. Gone were the days of the cavernous Ford Crown Vic. The newer downsized cars made sitting as a front seat passenger difficult as well as dangerous. A body had to shimmy under the computer gear and then try to find the seatbelt attachment. It wasn't easy, especially for a big guy. Once Taylor was packed in, they left the station and promptly pulled into a Dunkin' Donuts lot.

"I know you're here about Ray Fay, huh?" Paul asked as he bit into a Belgium crème. "Funny, I just remembered this is where I first saw the kid. Right here in this parking lot. Ray saved one of my officers from an ass kicking."

"Was he on the job?"

"No, he was just a young kid looking for work at the time. He was a lost soul and not sure what life had in store for him. But, he didn't think twice before jumping in and whaling some mob wannabe."

"What kind of officer is Ray Fay?"

Sgt. White took a sip of his coffee and another bite of the doughnut. "Complicated. Loved the job once he got the hang of it. Not much else happening in his life other than going to the gym and his hotshot car. Not even sure where the guy lives."

"Why complicated?"

"Normally Ray is almost comatose. Rarely gets riled up. But once he's on a hot call, he's almost manic. Know the type? Ready to rush in like the devil was ripping his heels. Just like a frontal attack."

Unit 27 Traffic and fight at First and Main...

"That's Officer Worth, Taylor," Paul announced. "She's the cop whose bacon Ray saved. Let's back her up. I'm not sure who else is clear."

They climbed back into the marked unit as fast as age, girth, and the small car would allow. Paul turned on the emergency lights and siren as he exited through the entrance lane of the Dunkin' Donuts and screeched into the traffic lane. It had been some time since Taylor was last on a Code 3 run in a police car.

Taylor had been accustomed to taking ride-alongs when he was on the LAPD. Right up to the month he retired as deputy chief he would ride in a car with a field officer or supervisor once a week. Sometimes he would wear his uniform after removing his rank's stars. The cops knew who he was; the citizens didn't need to know. It was the cops' show and Taylor knew how to stand back and let them handle the encounters.

When Taylor first began this oversight technique, cops were hesitant, on guard, and would engage only in small talk. After several ride-alongs they became more comfortable. Taylor never discovered major problems like corruption or mismanagement on his rides, but he did find out how the field cops felt about the department and the direction it was heading. He realized most had no idea why departmental changes were made or what the administration's current direction might be. Most cops were just trying to do a good job day to day. Some were trying to be superstars. A few were lazy assholes.

The intersection at First and Main was clogged with vehicles. Two cars were mangled together. It appeared there were three people engaged in a heated argument. A heavy older man was screaming at an older woman who was standing on the crinkled hood of one of the cars. A younger male, about twenty, was pummeling the car's trunk lid with a tire iron. The older man held a small baseball bat and was cautiously approaching the kid.

"Mabel, shut the fuck up! Can't hear myself yelling at the punk beating on our car!"

"Fuck you, old man!" The sound of grinding metal screamed as the tire iron crashed down on the car, the metallic pounding overwhelmed all voices. "You, asshole. You was screaming at your old lady when you ran the fucking signal! You fucked up my ride!"

Taylor saw a short uniformed female officer appear from behind the crashed vehicles. Sgt. White began running toward the cars, focusing on the older man brandishing the baseball bat. Taylor saw the female officer had a Taser clutched in her hand. The bright yellow Taser gun commanded a presence even in this mayhem. Without warning, the younger male armed with the tire iron disappeared behind the rear of the damaged car. Sgt. White grabbed the baseball bat from the old guy's hand, threw it about twenty feet out of range, and pinned the guy against the damaged car. The older woman in a sequined purple jumpsuit was now on the ground and was circling the front of the car, heading directly at Sgt. White and her husband. She held her purse by the strap and was swinging the oversized satchel over her head like a rodeo cowgirl.

Taylor ran at the woman and ducked low as he drove his shoulder into her side. He tried to grab her around the waist, but his arm wedged between her legs. Taylor lifted the woman and slammed her onto the hood of the damaged car, sending her purse skidding across the hood, finally disappearing over the opposite side. She suddenly stopped screaming and squirming. Taylor wasn't sure if she was stunned or had passed out. He grabbed her shoulder and slid her off the hood. She slumped to the pavement, landing firmly on her butt. She stared at Taylor with unblinking eyes and opened her mouth, but nothing came out. She was apparently in shock.

Both cops handcuffed their subjects.

"Sarge, we need to call the medics. My perp has Taser barbs stuck in him," the female officer yelled to Sgt. White.

"Got my own problem here, Mary," White countered. "I think this geezer is having a heart attack."

The EMTs arrived shortly and handled both men. They must have been stationed around the corner from this neighborly battle. Neither needed more than in-field first aid, but the medics said they would take the older man in for observation.

"What's your name, ma'am?" White asked the woman.

"Sylvia Gettman! Who was that fuck who attacked me?"

"He's being taken to jail along with your husband, Sylvia."

"Not that asshole. That one!" She jabbed a finger at Taylor.

"He's one of our officers, ma'am. He was making sure you didn't get into the tussle and get hurt."

Sylvia began to cry and started shaking. "We were just going to our son's house. It's his birthday and his wife is having a surprise party for him. I was on my iPad and next thing I knew there was a big bang. I was thrown against the door, and then I heard banging on our car."

The pathetic woman looked at Taylor with her head down. "Officer, I'm sorry. I just got so scared when my husband got out with that stupid little bat. I was worried about him. I'm sorry I put you through this."

When her son arrived on the scene a few minutes later, Sylvia reluctantly left with him. She really wanted to stay with her husband, probably to continue to berate him.

Back at the police station, Taylor followed Paul White into the officers' report writing room. The short female officer was there with a cup of coffee and several reports in front of her.

"Officer Mary Worth, meet Taylor Sterling. He's here about Ray Fay's case. Some kind of consultant."

"Ray needs help, Mr. Sterling." Mary Worth offered her hand and owned a firm handshake. "He's a great kid. A little idealistic maybe, but levelheaded. He's a good friend. He's accepted me being gay. My partner and I spent some good times with Ray. I'm not sure the department has the balls to stand up for the guy. What ya think, Sarge?"

"I'm not sure, Mary. The chief talks a good game, but when the chips are down I think he worries about his own ass exclusively. Ever see him out here on the streets unless the shit's hit the fan? Nope, never! Of course if it's a guy who should be protected from 'those we're not supposed to mention' or don't exist, the chief is right there trying to smooth ruffled feathers. Those old mob farts are just a pain in the ass, if ya want my opinion. But, I'll cut him some slack this time. He brought Taylor in! Shit, you see Taylor take care of that old woman?"

"Speaking of this incident, what are you guys going to do with the men?" Taylor asked.

"I'm going to issue tire iron kid a field release from custody for vandalism. He sure beat the hell out of that car. But the old guy says the kid never threatened him personally with the iron. You have field releases in LA, Mr. Sterling?"

Cops can do a number of things with subjects they take into custody. There are very few incidents mandating a cop must make an arrest. Domestic situations require a physical arrest when there are observable injuries. Of course if there's an outstanding warrant, subjects must be brought in front of the court. Otherwise, cops have wide discretionary powers. A cop can write a singular report and let the prosecutor decide a subject's fate. The cop can write a field release from custody, which is like a traffic citation, and order the person to appear in court at a later date. Finally a cop can arrest the subject and throw him in jail. In reality, most times it depends on what occurred. Unfortunately, how a cop feels about a subject personally can come into play. That's why a supervisor should be required to review any arrest that happens after a cop and subject get into a dispute or fight. Some cops end up arresting the subject for what is known as the "trilogy of contempt of cop charges"—resisting arrest, interference, and battery on an officer. Others have referred to this type of arrest as a POP arrest: "Pissing Off the Police." In some states a supervisor can release a subject after they've been booked if they find an improper arrest has been made, as if the arrest never occurred.

"Yep, we did have field releases. What are you going to do with the old geezer?"

"He's still in the hospital, Taylor. I'm figuring I'll do nothing. All he did was get out of the car with his funny little bat. Screaming at Mabel may get him in trouble at home, but it ain't a crime.

I called a traffic unit to file a collision report. Both cars will be towed to the impound garage."

Taylor was impressed with the attitudes of Sgt. White and Mary. He knew many cops would hit the statute books to look for something to book each subject. Many cops feel if force is used on a subject, they should be charged with assault on an officer or disorderly conduct to cover their asses. Taylor felt these two Riverton cops were levelheaded and fair.

"You like using that Taser, Mary?" Taylor asked.

"Love it! It's evened the odds for me since I'm shorter than most people. Tasers aren't as messy as OC spray and not as many injury reports are required like the old days when we used the stick. I like it, Mr. Sterling. Say, weren't you the original users of the Taser?"

"Sort of, since LA started using the older version in the late 1970s. It worked, but not as efficiently as the new ones do."

"I've got to admit, I was really scared of it when I went for training. We had to take a Taser hit as part of training. Well, sort of. They attached the probes to our backs and gave a five second blast. I don't really remember, but others in the class said I screamed and was knocked on my ass. Good thing two guys were there to ease me down. You ever get Tased?"

"Nope, that's what we had academy recruits for. They'd subject themselves to anything just to make it through the academy." Taylor laughed, remembering the anguished looks on eager young faces.

The original Taser looked like a large Black and Decker plastic flashlight. A company called Tasertron developed the gun. Its inventor called the implement a TASER and said it stood for Thomas A. Swift Electronic Rifle. The first one had only seven milliamps but it packed a punch. In the '90s Taser

International took over and developed the M26. It looked almost identical to a Glock handgun. Later they manufactured the unit in bright yellow so no one mistook it for a gun. The M26 had 26 milliamps. When an officer pulled the trigger, two barbs shot out which were attached to small wires. Later, they added a laser sight and small camera. Finally they added another cartridge so two shots could be fired at a subject. Newer Tasers can also be used in a drive stun mode, meaning when placed against a subject an electric shock is emitted, but not strong enough to alter the nervous system controlling muscles. In that instance, the shock is considered a pain compliance tool. Through the years, the use of Tasers has reduced injuries to officers and the subjects being controlled. Fewer claims by officers for worker's comp injuries followed. Unfortunately, some subjects did die after being Tased. Nearly all those deaths were attributed to pre-existing medical problems or issues, such as bad hearts, use of narcotics, or assorted diseases. Several civil rights groups continue to oppose the use of Taser guns.

"Mary, you know any reason Ray Fay would be working so many hours at paid details? Seems he was at one motel or another almost as much as he was at the PD."

Mary paused to access her memory bank. "No, not really. Ray was really intense about saving money. He often shared that his investments were doing well. He didn't seem to be spending much, other than on that car of his. Hell, you just had to look at him and know he wasn't spending it on clothes."

"Could he have problems with gambling or women?"

Mary gave a loud laugh. "Ray? No way! Gambling certainly wasn't his thing. Now and then he dated a nice looking girl he met at his gym. The guy was a nut about staying healthy and in shape, but he rarely dated any girl more than four or five times. I think he was obsessed with not being like his dad. Ray didn't want to end up in a dead-end job just to make a living."

"How about you, Paul, what's your take?"

Sgt. White shook his head. "Ray is just a solid, likable young kid. I've never had any trouble with him."

"Why do you think Katz has been building a criminal case against Ray?"

"I think he's pissed about losing the election and not having the support of his own chiefs, like Pisnero. He really got upset when Big Bob and his team took over handling the Fay shooting. Never happened before. County prosecutor always had the ball, unless he dropped it big time. Katz isn't a bad guy, he's just a prosecutor, not a cop. He's worried about his win rate so he makes cops really work to get assholes prosecuted. I've worked for three different county prosecutors and they're all the same. If you don't give them a win on a silver platter, they pass or plead it out on some bullshit lesser charge. I think this case is all about revenge and Ray is blistering on the hot seat."

* * *

It had been four days since Taylor hit the ground in New Jersey and he had already completed his investigation. His written report would be sent to the Riverton police chief after Taylor returned to Santa Fe.

Before leaving any investigative scene, Taylor always met with his clients to give them a verbal accounting of what would be stated in his final report. After the Riverton investigation, Taylor felt good about the outcome of Officer Fay's fatal shooting episode, although it involved a naked black man armed solely with a hairbrush. Taylor wasn't certain Chief Pisnero would care for his analysis of the chief's shitty supervision. He was going to report the six shootings Officer Fay had been in and the failure of the chief to do a reasonable review of each one. It was the glaring liability issue in this case that stuck out. Taylor probably wouldn't mention in his report that he thought the chief was unprofessional and a real doofuss.

As expected, Pisnero chose Santini's for the debriefing. Taylor saw he was the first to arrive since the red curb in front of the restaurant was devoid of police cars with microphones hanging from their rearview mirrors. Taylor parked legally in the lot adjacent to the restaurant.

Nothing had changed in Santini's since his first visit. Hell, the restaurant probably hadn't changed in the last thirty years, other than a roll of fresh carpeting installed every ten years or so. The bartender continued his inspection of glasses and gave a slight nod as Taylor entered. Should he head directly to the back room? Maybe a secret code or handshake was necessary to avoid swimming with the fishes. Taylor slid onto a barstool, just in case.

"Ya wan' sumptin'?"

"See you got Stella on tap. Give me one of those."

"Ya got it! Meetin' the cops again?"

Taylor nodded.

"Cops seem to like this place. Always kinda surprised me. They got to know who owns and runs Santini's. Don't cops feel weird at a joint like this?"

Taylor knew the bartender was giving him a heads up about the mob. Didn't surprise Taylor. He had made that the moment he walked in, what was it, four days ago? He smiled and swigged his beer. Taylor didn't really care for Stella Artois and would have liked a heavier dark microbrew, but he was paying homage and giving respect to the apparent owners. Taylor picked up an old Al Martino song slipping through the ceiling speakers.

"Hey, Taylor! See we're the only ones here so far." The voice belonged to Calvin Parker. "Nicki, give me one of those, too!"

The men sat next to each other, drinking beers without speaking. Taylor waited. Apparently Calvin didn't talk unless he had an audience.

"Oh, you guys are already here?" Pisnero called as he entered with The Suit bringing up the rear. "Let's go to the back where it's private."

"Okay, Taylor what did you find?" the chief asked after settling in his seat.

"Vince not coming?" Taylor asked, turning to Cavallo. He shook his head.

Little Paulie appeared in the same apron he had worn four nights before. It was like a walking menu board. He whispered into Chief Pisnero's ear and disappeared as quickly as he had appeared.

"Paulie says we got antipasti, then Veal Oscar, a special fruits de mari with white clam sauce, fig pate, and something special for dessert. Don't know what da fuck fig pate is. What ya got to give us, Taylor?"

"Some good, some bad, boss."

"Let's start with the good shit, huh? I've had a shitty day with my council. They're looking to bust my balls with new cuts to the budget. Third year in a row. My guys are getting moody with no raises coming at 'em, you know?"

Taylor didn't want to go there. "The shooting is certainly defensible, boss. But you should consider building a stronger defense to protect Officer Fay. Not sure what Katz is going to do. He was hard to figure out."

"What do you mean by 'building a defense?'" Calvin Parker asked.

"I always say you got to ask, what would Johnnie Cochran do?" Taylor answered.

"You have to expect a civil lawsuit will be filed anytime someone is killed. Of course, we also have to defend Fay in his criminal trial. Not sure what Katz is going to do on that end. You're defending him, aren't you, Raymond?" The Suit nodded.

"Whaddaya mean, 'think like Johnnie Cochran,' Taylor?" Calvin asked. "By the way, did you know him? He started off in LA, too, didn't he?"

"I did, for many years. Considered Johnnie a friend. I was his expert witness in several cases. When I say 'think like Cochran,' well, let me give you an example to explain.

"Johnnie brought me in on a fatal shooting by a Chippie. Oh, I forget, you guys are on the opposite coast, but you've seen the old tube show CHIPS, right? Anyway, a California Highway Patrol motor cop stops this huge black guy in an Opal, an economy car back when they were really small. Cop says the guy jumped out and looked like he was ready to attack so he shot the guy four times. All center mass.

"Well, Johnnie grabbed that car almost before the autopsy was finished. By the time the case came to trial, Johnnie had that Opal disassembled, brought into the courtroom, and reassembled. He was able to show there was no way a guy as big and fat as the deceased could have gotten out of that car without a crowbar. Kind of like the glove trick during the OJ trial. Today you have to put on a CSI show for a jury. They expect it. If you don't give 'em bells and whistles, they feel you don't have a case."

FOP lawyer Cavallo, tonight wearing a $4,000 Versace double-breasted suit, finally said something. "He's right, you know." Cavallo paused and added, "Damn, Cochran used to wear some fine ties!"

"That's one thing I worked hard to outdo Johnnie on. I've still got forty or fifty in my closet. Those ties were all imported, mostly Italian. Buck to buck and a half each," Taylor recalled. In the days Taylor testified in court as an expert witness, he created a uniform of his own. Black blazer, dark grey slacks, black shoes, but his ties made him, like Johnnie, stand apart.

Taylor took time to savor the Veal Oscar that Little Paulie had prepared. Hand-cut veal medallions topped with a small lobster tail and smothered with a delicate white sauce. The sauce was close to Hollandaise, but had a different texture and seemed infused with a bouquet of herbs. Taylor would remember this dish fondly.

"I always thought Cochran was showboating," Chief Pisnero said with a shrug.

"Maybe, but it was for a purpose," Taylor noted, remembering his experiences with Johnnie in the courtroom. "He owned a courtroom, any courtroom. Johnnie made a point of reaching out to everyone working the court—bailiff, court reporter, clerk, even the lawyers on the other side—by saying something personal to them. 'Gladys, your boy still in college?' 'Herb, sorry to hear about your mother's passing.' I don't know how Johnnie got his information, but he used it like an expert."

"You liked him?" Calvin asked.

"I respected him," Taylor admitted, visualizing his old friend. "He was a crusader for justice. He worked as hard for a street hooker as any millionaire or a cop who was in trouble. He went too early. He believed in being fair and was a champion of civil rights. I do miss him; I do. He was one of a kind."

Calvin finally asked, "What do you figure should happen with Officer Fay's case, Taylor?"

"Three things, Calvin. First you need to create a mockup of

the scene, like in old war movies. You can get that done cheap using architectural students from the community college. Hell, make it a class project and you might get it done for free. You want to be able to move simulated small figures around.

Second, you need to get someone to perform a visual acuity evaluation. You're going to have to search for someone to do that. Get somebody good. There are machines to calibrate the light, or lumens, at the shooting scene. What could somebody like Fay have reasonably seen under the circumstances?

Last, you should consider having a forensic animation done. It will graphically show the jury what a split second actually is. It can support and substantiate the rapidly evolving situation Fay was facing. Think Johnnie Cochran!"

"What kind of cost are we looking at, Taylor?" Cavallo asked.

"Twenty thousand, thereabouts," Taylor threw out.

The men around the table weren't fazed by the estimate.

"Remember, a problem police shooting can really cost you. Johnnie got around a $16 million settlement for that state police shooting involving a minority basketball team on the Interstate up here in New Jersey, and none of them died."

"Okay, so what's the bad?" Pisnero asked hesitantly.

"Fay's shooting record," Taylor replied.

"Whaddaya mean? He had four others, right?" Calvin argued, turning to the chief.

"I think he had another one, Calvin," Pisnero answered.

"Actually he's had six, guys," Taylor corrected. "You're going to have to keep that number out of the criminal and, if it occurs, the civil trial. That six number will really shock the jury, especially if the prosecution brings up most cops don't have one shooting on record. Calvin, you should be able to exclude it as being overly prejudicial. Between you and me, Fay's record is unusual."

"How so?" Cavallo challenged.

"Raymond, how many other Riverton cops have been in- volved in six shootings and now a fatal, hell *two* fatals, in just six years? Huh?" The Suit didn't reply. There were no others.

"So what do we do with Fay?" Pisnero asked. "You know none of them other shootings cost the city any money. Well, other than the pit bull. I was pissed Fay shot that dog. Why didn't he just kick it or hit it with his baton? I told the mayor to issue the owner a check for $1,000. I saw that guy the other day and he's got him- self a new pit, one of them brown and black striped ones."

"We have to keep Fay under wraps until the trials are over," Calvin said. "Shit, that could be close to a year. Who knows what the red suspenders guy in the prosecutor's office will do? Stat- ute for filing a notice of civil claim is ninety days in New Jersey though."

"Then what? What if Ray's not prosecuted and there's no civil lawsuit? Then what?" Taylor asked. The three stared at him as if he had asked a question that had no answer.

"All I know is that you can't put Fay out there as a city em- ployee with a gun. He's too much of a liability. Next shooting he's involved with, and count on it happening, won't be a naked black guy with a shiny hairbrush. It might be a bad or indefen- sible incident. Ray Fay and Riverton could lose big. Fay might end up in prison."

Taylor eyed the chocolate cannoli. Chief Pisnero had just grabbed the biggest one and bit into it. Confectioners' sugar clouded as it landed on his dark shirt and spread like the Milky Way. Taylor decided against dessert and wondered if the chief kept a clean shirt on call at the restaurant.

"Guess we could keep Fay in another city job," Calvin suggest- ed. "Maybe a uniformed code enforcement officer?"

"Remember though, you can't cost him any money," Taylor said glancing at the FOP lawyer who was nodding like a bobble head.

"Officer Fay worked the shit out of those hotel/motel security jobs. This last shooting occurred after he had been working for twenty-two hours straight. He'd been in court, served his regular tour of duty, and then worked the extra paid detail at the Days Inn. You got a bad policy about off-duty cops working, Chief Pisnero. Besides that, you never ruled the other shootings as out of policy, boss. You're inconsistent."

The chief was too busy brushing the sugar off his shirt to pick up on that comment. Taylor saw Cavallo and Parker had gotten it, though.

* * *

Taylor had been back in Santa Fe a couple weeks. He was still contemplating what to do about his Jeep Wrangler. The battery was dead when he got back to the airport parking lot in Albuquerque. Fortunately the hotshot charger he'd thrown in the Jeep had enough juice to get the heap started for the hour trip up the mountain.

His thoughts were interrupted by a call on his cell phone.

"Mr. Sterling, this is Ray Fay."

Strange call, Taylor thought. "Officer Fay, good to hear from you."

"Don't call me Officer Fay anymore, Mr. Sterling."

"What happened?"

"Well, a lot. Katz decided to drop the criminal charge for some reason," Ray explained. Taylor smiled into the phone. "The city said I could work in a quasi-cop role, but couldn't carry a gun. They were willing to give me a bullshit job with a huge paycheck. More than I was making as a cop. But I knew it would be a dead-end job."

"So what you end up doing, Ray?" Taylor asked, expecting the answer to be party line.

"The city also offered me a settlement. Threw some money my way and asked me to go away, forever. Seemed good to me. Three hundred thousand bucks. Figured my salary, what I would have earned working off-duty jobs, and a sliver of the pension I had to give up. Wasn't much on the pension side since I'd been there just shy of seven years."

Taylor knew it was a win-win for Ray and Riverton. "What you doin' with all that money, Ray?"

"Put that together with my savings and went back home. Well, not to Rolling Rock, but Scranton. I bought myself an Elite Fitness franchise. Now those tits and asses are mine. Even get to touch some now and then. Got Vinny Jackson from my old gym to come in as a minor partner; he knows the business. He sold his shithole gym to a biker dude covered in prison tats. Even got my dad out of Ace Hardware and he works for me doing maintenance and equipment repair. Still got my Challenger for a ride. Life is good, Mr. Sterling. I'm told that you had a lot to do with my outcome."

"I'm glad it worked out for you, Ray," Taylor said. "Miss being a cop?"

"Every day, Mr. Sterling. Every day."

"Me too, Ray. Me too!"

Wrongful Justice

Allegation: Wrongful conviction
Client: Indiana Risk Insurance Pool
Agency: Livingston Police Department

Angel Martinez had been on the streets her entire life. She wondered when it really all began. Thirteen, maybe? Angel was tired of sucking dicks attached to the many men her mother brought home after drunken nights spent pandering at local bars. Angel was closing in on thirty now, but most people thought she was closer to fifty. The streets, prostitution, and drugs had aged her harshly and quickly.

"Angel, get over here," a gruff voice commanded.

"Wha' ya want, Officer Stanley?"

"Need some numbers, sweetheart. You sure still be my sweetheart, ain't you?"

Rob Stanley worked street narcotics for the Livingston Police Department, but often he strayed into county territory. Rob preferred to work alone. He didn't like other cops looking over his shoulder or second-guessing him. Out of sight, he could do police work the way he saw fit, not necessarily how it was supposed to be done or strictly in line with the book procedures the Livingston PD tried to push. Rob knew his bosses looked the other way on many of his busts. After all, he gave them what they wanted—big impressive numbers. Arrests, drug seizures, cars, and money, a lot of money. The brass particularly loved the shitload of cash Rob seized on a regular basis. Rob skimmed a little off the top to use for flash money or to pay his snitches for info. He felt it was owed him. It was just part of his job.

Angel shuffled to the unmarked, but easily identified Ford Crown Vic cop car. Her hands were stuffed deep in the front pockets of her baggy jeans that were fighting to stay on her hips. Ragged hems dragged on the ground and puddled heavily around her Doc Martins. A puffy jacket kept the cold wind at bay. Angel had short, cropped hair. Most people would mistake her for a young boy, but that didn't bother her.

"Ya got someone in mind?" Angel asked leaning deep into the driver's side of the car. The pungent odor of Whataburger onion residue assaulted her nostrils. The front seat was littered with crinkled burger wrappers, some a month old.

"I was thinking of Roscoe. You know, that colored dude you say is a good supplier of local shit. Where he work out of?"

Angel hesitated and seemed to be considering what direction she should take. "Well, yeah, he be still good. Hear he's pushing stashes of Mexican brown dis days. He work out of Baylor Park, near the Y."

"You work with me on this, Angel?" Rob asked as he patted her arm resting on the car's windowsill.

"Ya gots that kind of scratch, Officer Stanley?" Angel watched the narc lean over and pull a wad of bills from his front pocket. "Be close to $300 here. That gives you some and a small taste for me." Rob peeled off a hundred and four fifty-dollar bills.

"Sweet!" she gushed. Angel stuffed the bills inside her jacket, securing them under her bra.

"You know what you got hangin' over your head, Angel? You remember it good, don't you? I can still make that happen. You could get hard time for what I got on your ass. You'd end up going cold turkey and be some dyke's bitch. You hear? Don't fuck with me or I'll make it happen! I expect to hear from you by tomorrow. No later."

Rob screeched from the curb and didn't look back to see if he'd clipped Angel with his car's sudden acceleration.

* * *

Earlier in Rob Stanley's tenure with the Livingston Police Department

Rob Stanley had been a cop in Livingston for nearly twenty years. It was his only police job. The PD was large as far as Indiana cop shops went with nearly seventy-five cops on the payroll. Livingston was far enough away from Indianapolis to have its own identity, but close enough to deal with the residual drug problems plaguing the south side of the capital city. Rob worked patrol his first four years before being selected for investigative work.

Rob found general investigations boring and labored through two years working the burglary/theft desk. That job was simply pushing bullshit crime reports from one basket to the next. *Two potted plants removed from the front porch, lawnmower gone from the open garage, iPad missing from the desk in the den, but no serial numbers available.* Day after day the reports followed ad nauseum.

Jude Richards knocked on Rob's cubicle one afternoon as he

was dog-earing a stack of reports for the fifth time in a feeble attempt to look occupied.

"Busy, Rob?"

"For you lieutenant, I'm never too busy. These chicken shit reports flow like they're coming from a broken spigot."

"Let's get some coffee," Jude suggested. The two went out the side door and climbed into Jude's unmarked sedan. The drive to Lucky's Diner near the Interstate off-ramp took less than ten minutes.

"You get out to the river much lately, LT?"

"Nah. Don't get fishing time anymore since I took over the narc division. Fact is, haven't even thought about the water 'til you just mentioned it. Too much fun these days, Rob."

They sipped their coffee in silence. Rob took Jude up on his offer of a piece of pie. The cherry wedge was stuffed with sweet canned cherry filing and the crust was loaded with butter. Just a few bites spiked a sugar high in Rob's system.

"You want to work narc, Rob?"

"Narc? Really haven't ever thought about it."

"It's a good job. As we often say in narcotics, 'There's no crime until its overtime.' Lots of OT. Take home car. Work up your own cases. You still divorced?"

"Yep."

"No problems on the home front then. Narc gots weird hours. Shit, weird people. You end up taking the job home with you. Straight broads don't understand. Workin' the street can complicate a guy's home life."

At the time, Livingston's narc unit consisted of Jude and three cops. Rob wanted to make it four. He took the job, happy to trade potted plants for pot. His training consisted of tagging along with the other guys to observe. The unit usually operated together, but each cop developed his own cases.

Their office was located in a small corner storefront in an almost empty eight-unit strip mall. The front door and only window in the unit were boarded with plywood. Frayed posters splashed on the boarded exits announcing the Ringling Brothers Barnum & Bailey Circus that had last visited Livingston nearly three years before. The rear door was designated the entrance to the office and the narcs' parking lot was officially defined between two large dumpsters that buttressed vacant stalls at the end of the strip mall near the entrance.

Snake Evans shared Rob's small table desk in the unit office. Snake was, well, tall, lanky, and could twist his body like a serpent ready to strike. He owned high cheekbones and a protruding hawkish nose. Snake had a habit of flicking his tongue between his lips every now and then, apparently to wet his lips. For a tall guy, he had a high-pitched, squeaky voice. Even in winter he wore a thin cotton T-shirt that touted one heavy metal concert or another.

Rob often wondered how Jim Baker ever got hired; let alone finish the basic police academy. He was short and almost as wide as he was tall. His florid complexion, square shoulders, and stubby legs made the guy look like a friggin' fireplug. Jim had grown his hair 'til it was a wild, bushy mat of brown and grey rag tags. Unfortunately, the top of his head didn't get the message and nary a wisp sprouted on his saucer-shaped bald spot. Jim usually dressed in bib overalls covering a red plaid shirt. A greasy green John Deere baseball cap topped his dome.

The last member of the narc unit was Sam "Cross-eyes" Clayton. The guy's left eye was noticeably crossed and focused squarely on his nose. Sam was a big man, weighing close to three hundred pounds. He had shaved his head, but sported a full goatee braided near the bottom and secured with a silver clasp. Cross-eyes liked to wear large fake diamond studs in both ears. Sam's mouth featured a snap-on gold cap for his front tooth that he would click into place when he came into the office. He usually wore a mottled leather vest over a dirty white T-shirt. One arm displayed a large blue iron cross tattoo. The other arm was tattooed with the blade of a knife piercing a colorful snake entwined on its handle. Cross-eyes' black jeans were stiff from lack of regular washing and stood at attention over black carriage boots.

All three narcs looked at Rob the first day he showed up at the office. He was wearing tan Dockers, boat shoes without socks, and a polo shirt with a galloping horse embroidered over his left breast.

"And what frat house are you rushing, little buddy?" Snake chuckled as his flickering tongue reached an obscene length.

"Lay off him, he's gonna be my bitch," Cross-eyes ordered as he grabbed his crotch and stroked his hand up and down.

"Settle down, assholes," Jude yelled as he came out of his small office next to the rear door. "Rob's joining our team and is taking Burle's place. Burle's wife put her foot down and said it was time for him to start acting like a father to his teenage daughter."

"But, boss, *really?*" Snake groaned as he pointed at Rob.

"Don't be assholes, we'll take him to the Salvation Army and get him some proper clothes," Jude said as he laughed with the other three.

Within a month, Rob was bringing in his own cases. Some were snatched from anonymous calls that came into the police department. Most anonymous calls came from rival drug dealers trying to carve out a bigger piece of the pie by giving up information on the competition. Some calls were from parents who found their kid's stash and pressured the kid to give up a fellow student. Occasionally the team would go dumpster diving which meant going through trash cans left out by someone the team thought might be dealing drugs.

"You gotta work up some snitches," Jim ordered as he raked through his matted hair with his fingers. "Get some of your patrol buddies to let you flip some of their arrests. Your guys make a bullshit bust for a couple oxys or joints, and then you ride in on a white horse and tell the asshole they arrested you'll make the charge disappear if he gives you good info. Scare the crap outta him. Those snitches will bring you some good shit if you scare 'em bad enough."

Within three months, Rob had a stable of snitches and was making a few arrests. Nothing big, but still making arrests. Rob soon realized the team worked the arrests and search warrants together, but never shared informants. The snitches worked for one officer exclusively. When Rob had to pay a snitch for info, he simply went into Jude's office and came out with the cash he needed. Jude seemed to have an endless bag of green in his lower drawer.

"Do I need to fill out some kind of chit?" Rob initially asked.

"Nah. We keep the paper trail invisible as much as we can. You stay under a couple hundred bucks, you don't need to write paper."

Rob learned how to fill out a probable cause form to take to the prosecutor and obtain a search warrant from the magistrate. The unit had a boilerplate template in its computer. All a narc had to do was insert the specifics of his investigation, give the informant a number he pulled out of the sky, make sure the address of the place to be searched was good, and, *presto*, a warrant magically appeared! The prosecutor never asked questions; neither did the favored magistrate the team had easy access to approach.

* * *

"Rob, you and Snake ready?"

"Yeah, got the back covered. We're squatting in the alley next to a junk car on blocks," Rob quietly radioed to Cross-eyes.

Earlier Cross-eyes had worked up a dealer after getting a call from a patrol unit asking that he come to the hospital.

"Detective Clayton," the young uniformed cop said as he emerged from the emergency room. "Got a five-year-old kid who got into some shit her mother's current fuck apparently had tucked in the drawer next to her bed. Doc figures it's meth, but isn't certain yet. Kid thought it was candy. The mom's in there with the kid. She's royally pissed and wants to turn on the guy."

Cross-eyes pulled the curtain open, allowing him access to the ER cubicle.

"Ma'am, I'm Detective Clayton. Sorry to hear about your daughter. Shame when some no-good brings that death stuff into a good home."

Cross-eyes looked hard at the obese woman spilling over a metal chair close to her daughter's bed. Her faded housedress was at best two sizes too small and he could tell she wasn't wearing a bra. Her loose large breasts were stopped from dropping to her knees by a cord cinched tight around her waist. Her ankles bulged painfully over pink tennis shoes. The woman's face was blotchy and red from crying, and probably indicated the early stages of diabetes.

"That no-good man put my little baby in the clutches of the devil, Officer Clayton! He ain't worth keeping."

Cross-eyes quickly determined the location of said "no good man" who brought the meth into the home of the unsuspecting child. Just as the woman said, the asshole was sitting on a stool in the Midtown Bar on Center Street. Cross-eyes had been there many times, both as a uniformed cop and a narc. Midtown Bar was filled with a cross section of the criminal element that called Livingston home. The place reminded him of the Mos Eisley Cantina bar scene in *Star Wars* where pirates, rejects, and scum from all over the galaxy gathered to plot their plundering.

No Good had just dropped a shot glass into his beer and was tipping the glass to his lips when Cross-eyes grabbed his arm. The full glass slipped from No Good's hands and splashed onto the bar.

"Fuck, asshole!" No Good swore as he spun to confront Cross-eyes. His eyes widened as he focused on the narc's crossed eye, shaved head, and braided goatee. "Wha'da fuck you done dat for, Mister Cop?"

Cross-eyes grabbed No Good by his bicep, yanked him off the bar stool and pushed him hard to the front door. He slammed No Good into the bar door, but then realized the door opened to the inside. A rush of the early winter wind bit into both men. Cross-eyes was wearing only his leather vest and his customary T-shirt. No Good wore a black silk shirt open over a wife beater undershirt.

"Who'd you get that shit from?"

"Wha' shit?"

"The meth you brought home and left in Shamoo's bedroom!"

"Wha...?"

"The little girl ate it. Ate that shit. She be near death and you be near the chair, asshole!"

No Good suddenly realized what had happened.

"I didn't mean for dat' to happen, Mister Cop. I don't even 'member leaving any dope there. Ya gots to believe me. I didn't know!" The guy was shaking as he backed up, propping himself against the bar's far outside wall.

It didn't take long for Cross-eyes to get what he needed for the probable cause affidavit leading to a search warrant for the alleged supplier's house. He rounded up his favorite magistrate, Lionel Washington, who would sign anything put in front of him.

Jude assembled his narc team in their storefront office, ready for action.

"Cross-eyes got this here no-knock warrant for an asshole drug dealer. Says his shit put some five-year-old girl in the hospital, possibly dying from chewing what she thought was candy. Tell 'em what we got."

Cross-eyes detailed how he obtained his information and what the elements of the warrant were. He'd run the guy's rap sheet earlier and found a long string of arrests for drugs, intent to sell, trafficking, and gun offenses. Only two minor misdemeanor convictions were listed on the sheet.

Cross-eyes had driven by the targeted dealer's house a couple hours prior and reported all appeared quiet. Of course it had been after midnight when he initially cruised the house. It was now pushing five in the morning.

Jim Baker and Cross-eyes cautiously crept along the parked cars lining the street in front of the targeted house. A dog was barking incessantly about a block away. No light emitted from the house. The streetlight two houses down was smashed and telltale shards of glass indicated somebody had taken it out.

The two officers positioned themselves on either side of the front door. Cross-eyes stepped to the rear and punched the doorknob with his heavy carriage boots. The door shattered and swung open with its frame leaning like a Lincoln Log tower. Two small panes of glass in the upper part of the door battered vertically into the living room like a sheet of hard rain.

Jim Baker shot into the living room and jagged along a diagonal path across from the kitchen. He figured the opposite hall would lead to the bedrooms. Jim was about to boot the bedroom door and scream *"Police"* when the bedroom door surged at him in a fiery flash. Splinters of shattered wood and pellets blasted from a shotgun tore into Jim's body and propelled him into the wall opposite the bedroom door.

Snake and Rob were in the backyard pressed hard up against the back wall of the house when they heard the discharge and saw the shotgun flash reflected in the panes of the bedroom window. They could see a bulky figure standing next to the bed holding a long object clutched close. Taking down the mirrored figure was the only option. The recoil of Snake's Glock propelled his gun sharply upward after the shots rang out. The window exploded into a thousand pieces and the figure suddenly slumped and disappeared.

Cross-eyes was the first to enter the bedroom. A large lump was piled on the floor. The room was so dark the narc couldn't decipher exactly what he was looking at. Movement on the bed startled him and he swung his shotgun toward the action.

"No!" a piercing shriek begged.

Rob's flashlight beam illuminated the naked body of a woman. Her hands were pointed straight up as if she was reaching for the ceiling. Rob knew she was saying something, but couldn't make out her words. Distance and the reverberating shotgun blast had rendered him deaf.

"Rob, get in here and take care of this bitch!" Cross-eyes ordered as he aimed his shotgun at the lump on the floor. He inched closer with measured shuffled steps.

That night was the first time Rob Stanley encountered Angel Martinez. Jude and the team quickly realized they were in the middle of a tragic and exceptionally fucked up operation. They should have asked SWAT to conduct the raid. They should have waited until a surveillance team identified what was really going on. They should have completed a shitload of other routine police procedures. Opting for haste and glory, they were screwed.

The team had fucked up royally and now they owned two dead bodies, one was their own.

Rob was tasked with controlling the only witness, Angel. His job was getting her out of the house and out of the investigation. Angel was glad to oblige.

Back to present day

The three hundred dollars was burning a hole in her hand. Angel figured she could score a bag of Mexican smack from Roscoe. He was always good for that shit and made an easy buy for her.

Baylor Park was located in the southern part of Indianapolis. Crime had decimated the area. The once green park was barren and littered with trash that visitors felt was too much trouble to drop in cans scattered throughout the park. The city was trying, but the place was a dump. It was dusk and darkness was slowly creeping in from the east. The few operating park overhead lights hadn't flickered on yet.

Angel didn't fear the darkness or the menacing silhouettes dancing around her as she made her way through the park. Angel considered the shadows in the park to be comforting, almost welcoming. She felt the ebony milieu understood her pitiful life and offered a solitary acceptance. In a sense, Angel felt the park was a living, breathing entity that spoke to her. Maybe it was the vulnerability of living on the edge, walking a tightrope stretched between uncaring and hopelessness that inspired this feeling.

"Ya see Roscoe?" she asked one wavering silhouette. The heavy tree limb seemed to motion to the skeletal playground housing a faded jungle gym.

"Roscoe, I need some shit and I need it bad. Hears ya gots a new shipment," Angel called when she spotted her dealer perched on a spring-loaded bouncing form. Roscoe was rocking back and forth on a once colorful seahorse, grabbing its ribbed comb with his knobby fists. The dealer was keeping beat to sounds blasting in his ears through high tech ear buds. Angel's small body vibrated to the beat of the thumping heavy bass. She tapped the man on his shoulder to get his attention.

"Shit, girl!" Roscoe exclaimed, startled by the rush back to reality. Roscoe was a slight black man with a dark complexion who appeared older than his years. His claim to fame was spending more time in the joint than on the outside. Roscoe always wore the same color. Black. And then more black. Black T-shirt or turtleneck, depending on the time of year. Black leather jacket, unless he was going formal and then strutted in a black leather coat. The gap between his front upper teeth spoke of a missing tooth. Roscoe never draped himself in gold jewelry like the other shit peddlers did. His only fashion accents were a black stingy brimmed hat and mirrored shades, day or night.

"Wha' you want, girl?"

"Heard you got some Mexican brown."

"Oh yeah, from who you get that bad info?"

"Roscoe, ah gots three Benjamins in my pocket."

"Where you get dat? From dat cop buddy of yours?"

Angel drew back and clutched her arms around her waist and asked, "Why you be saying dat, Roscoe? Ah ain't no snitch. You and me goes way back. Ah ain't done nothin' to hurt you. Ah needs some of dat good Mexican shit, Roscoe, please?"

"Fuck you, Angel. Don't need you or dat cop's money. Get the fuck out of my yard, bitch!" Roscoe stumbled off the seahorse and disappeared into the black recesses of the park.

Damn, Angel thought to herself. She needed something to show Officer Stanley. She still had his three hundred and didn't want to give it up. Besides, she needed a little taste to keep her going. Angel hitched a ride back to Livingston and tried a couple of her usual sources. Nothing. No one had anything to sell. She hesitated, wondering if she should try Otto as a last resort.

Otto Graham was one of Livingston's elevated drug pushers. He was the guy who supplied most middle dealers in town and had connections all the way to Chicago and Gary. Otto was Mister Big in Angel's view of the world. She had visited Otto's place in the past. In fact, it was Roscoe who first took her for a buy at Mister Big's a couple years before. Roscoe was trying to diversify his sources, he had explained to her.

Otto lived in a house that he claimed his folks once owned. He liked to tell anyone who would listen that when the bank stole the house from his folks, he swore he would come back to Livingston one day and own it himself.

Otto's dad was one of the founders of the local Livingston Savings and Trust that was flying high in the '60s. The S&T did pretty well for about fifteen years until business collapsed due to the rolling double-digit inflation during the Carter administration. Federal regulators swooped in, padlocked the doors, and ruined the lives of all the good people who had invested in the bank. Otto's dad was one of the first to go. It didn't help that he blew his brains out in that big Cadillac Seville sitting in his garage one sunny afternoon. After that final statement, Otto, his four brothers and their mom were forced to move in with an aunt.

"What you want, Angel?" Otto asked as he opened his front door.

"Can ah come in? Got business to talk," Angel explained as she glanced down the street.

"You all by yourself, girl?"

"Yep. Just me."

"No cops? I know you work for them sometimes. I'm never sure if you know who you work for, girl." The man laughed as he opened the door wide enough for Angel to slip inside.

Angel looked inside the grandiose foyer and walked to the circular staircase leading upstairs. She glanced into the living room, then the dining room and saw the kitchen down the hall was dark.

"You be here alone, Mr. Otto?"

"Just me, my memories, and you, girl." Otto smiled and gave the once-over to the slight framed woman standing in front of him.

"What business you got tonight, girl?"

"Got three hundred burning in my pocket. Need something make me feel good," Angel said as she shuffled from one foot to the other. "Your lady not home?"

"Gone. Bitch wasn't no lady. Just another bitch."

"Well, you want to do some business, Mr. Otto?"

"You give me a blowjob and then we'll talk business, girl."

Angel hadn't considered Otto might think of her as a sex object. Most drug dealers just considered her a user. Her small frame and boyish body were a turnoff for most guys. She considered the offer. She really needed something to give to Officer Stanley to get him off her back, and a little taste of the good stuff would sure rev her up. It had been three days since she last lit up.

"You want it right here, Mr. Otto?"

"No upstairs, like grown-ups," he said with a grin and then began walking up the circular staircase. "Come on, girl. I'll be good, no rough stuff. Just want a blowjob, girl, but I want to be relaxed on the bed."

Otto dropped his pants to his ankles and fell back on the massive king size bed. He circled his penis with his long fingers and slowly began stroking up and down. His legs were dark with matted black hair and his belly moved from side to side as he fondled himself.

Angel took over working Otto's dick as she nestled between his legs. He became engorged as she moved his penis into her mouth and began to suck vigorously. Otto suddenly sat upright and forcefully pushed her head away.

"Wha' wrong, Mr. Otto?"

"Nothing, whore. Just that Mr. Otto got a little business with us," a harsh voice bellowed from a corner in the room. "Always should be business before pleasure, you know that, whore."

Angel turned and fell against the side of the bed when she saw the two men. They were dressed in black and looked threatening. Ski masks covered their faces. Both carried guns. The one talking was armed with a large semi-automatic handgun. The other guy cradled a short sawed-off shotgun with both hands.

"Where's the damn stash, Otto?"

"Fuck you. You knows who you're dealing with, assholes? Hope your insurance policy is paid up cuz your family goin' need it."

The one with the handgun moved quickly and brought the gun down between Otto's legs. The receiver of the gun landed directly on Otto's still erect penis and pushed down hard, crushing one of his testicles. Otto let out an excruciating, piercing scream and grasped his crotch. The gun swung up and around and crashed into the side of his head, opening a gash that spread deep to his upper cheek.

"Your stash!"

"Fuck you!"

The sudden shotgun explosion was deafening and shook the bedroom. The muzzle flash lit the entire room as the smell of expended gunpowder invaded the space that minutes before had been pungent with Otto's cheap cologne. Otto's stomach was ripped open by the shotgun blast and a spatter of blood pock-marked one side of Angel's face.

"What the fuck?" Handgun Guy yelled back at his partner.

"Shit, I didn't mean for it to go off!"

"Didn't mean to? What the fuck! You pulled the trigger! Didn't mean to…"

Handgun Guy stammered a string of obscenities as he re-treated two steps back. He turned and grabbed Shotgun Guy and slammed him into the bedroom wall. Two framed pictures crashed to the floor, shafted off rusty nails by the violent thrust. Glass shards dusted the carpet.

Angel realized the momentary distraction would be her only chance to escape. She slithered to one side of the bed and disap-peared into the dark Jack and Jill bathroom where she found the door to the adjoining bedroom. She could hear the two invaders screaming at each other and figured they were too pissed to no-tice she was gone. She was out the front door in a flash but could still hear screaming as she raced down the dark street.

"Officer Stanley," Angel whispered into her cell phone. "I'm in trouble, big trouble. Ya gots to halp me!"

They arranged to meet at Jerry's Chili Shack. Rob Stanley glanced at his watch—2:15 in the morning. Livingston was a quiet town after midnight. This early morning was no exception. The only movement was an old man brandishing a parking lot vacuum truck shuffling back and forth in a haphazard pattern attempting to clean the lot.

Rob looked around as he entered one of the town's icon restaurants. The Chili Shack and the Waffle House near the highway were the only places that stayed open all night. He looked down the long row of booths opposite the counter and caught a glimpse of Angel's motley head of hair. She was slumped into a corner booth with both arms clawed tightly around her body. Her legs were tucked under her butt and she looked like a bundle of rags ready for the trash. Angel's piercing brown eyes were barely visible between her hair and the collar of her jacket pulled up high as far as it would go. She didn't move a muscle, even when Rob slid into the booth across from her. He sat waiting for her to stir, move, speak, or do anything.

"He's dead."

"Who's dead?"

"Otto."

"Otto Graham? The drug dealer?" She nodded. "When? Where?" Rob hadn't heard his police radio announcing the call. A murder in Livingston should have jolted the town to life from its deep sleep.

"His house. The big place on Grant Street."

Rob punched in the number for dispatch. "Say, Sarah, Rob here. Send a car over to Otto Graham's house on Grant Street. Don't know the number, but it should be in the 911 system. Say it's a wellness check. Tell the guys to use caution. May be a crime scene." He set the phone on the table and stared at Angel. "Want to tell me about it?"

Angel closed her eyes for a brief moment. He could see her tongue reach for her upper and lower lips. Her arms still clutched her body tightly.

"I was there getting your shit for you. Keep you off my ass. It was a robbery. They was wearing ski masks. They was goin' to rob Otto of his stash." Angel stopped her recitation abruptly and looked at Rob to see his response to the story she was weaving.

"One guy whipped Otto with a handgun. The other just up and shot him with a shotgun. Weren't no reason. Maybe was some kind of accident. Even got some of his blood on me." She stopped and watched Rob curiously. He didn't offer a word.

"I ran cuz I was scared, really scared. Don't know what happened after that, Officer Stanley. I was just trying to please you. You know I wouldn't cross you."

Angel wasn't crying. She wasn't shaking. She was simply matter of fact stating what had happened. *At least from her strange point of view*, Rob thought.

"It was Roscoe, Officer Stanley."

Angel never knew why she threw out Roscoe's name. She hadn't seen the men's faces and they never took off the masks. She didn't notice anything particular about their voices. Down deep she thought a name might please Rob Stanley. Angel figured he had a hard-on for Roscoe. Maybe that was why he wanted her to buy shit off him. But now her words were out and she had to stick with her story.

Rob bought Angel a large bowl of chili and a cherry coke. That's what she asked for and her information was certainly worth a coke. He ordered a large coffee. Rob's phone began vibrating and mimicked a circle dance on the slick tabletop.

The marked unit found the front door open at the Grant Street address and found Otto splayed on the bed upstairs. His pants were puddled around his ankles. His stomach was cratered deep to his spine by a close range shotgun blast. Sarah, the dispatcher, told the investigating cops that the crime scene guys were on the way.

Rob called back to dispatch. "Tell the dicks that I've got an eyewitness. I'll bring her to the station and we'll meet them in the squad room in about an hour." Rob set the phone down and stared into Angel's deep eyes. "We've got some serious work to do, Angel."

* * *

Eight years had passed since Roscoe Blunt had been convicted of Otto Graham's murder. He had vehemently and continuously denied any involvement in the crime. Unfortunately he didn't have much of an alibi. Being in Balboa Park alone hawking drugs wasn't going to impress anybody, let alone a jury primarily paneled with white suburbanites.

Roscoe's defense attorney whaled into Angel Martinez. She was the only witness to the murder and she defiantly pointed to Roscoe as being one of the two robbers who butchered poor Otto—her longtime, dear friend.

Angel didn't deny being a drug user or buying drugs from Roscoe. She stood firm about not seeing Roscoe earlier the night of the slaughter. She said she visited Otto, her friend, and had sex with him. She was in the bathroom cleaning up when she heard Roscoe and the other robber burst into the bedroom. The bathroom door was open, just enough for her to see poor Otto get shotgunned to death by Roscoe's partner.

She testified she couldn't identify Roscoe's partner since he was wearing a ski mask. She had no idea why Roscoe wasn't wearing a mask, too. Angel testified she was able to run away when the men were tearing up Otto's house looking for whatever, probably money and drugs. She claimed she was frightened and didn't trust most cops, except her friend, Officer Stanley. She acknowledged the officer had busted her in the past, but said he was always fair with her.

So, with no place to go that night, she called Officer Stanley for help and he brought her to the police station. Angel told the jury she recognized Roscoe's face from a bunch of photographs, and again later when he and five other dudes stood in a line-up. No, she wasn't paid money to testify and she didn't have any arrests hanging over her head at the time of the murder.

Was Angel Martinez credible? The grand jury and the jury at Roscoe's trial thought so and convicted him after enjoying a hearty lunch paid for by the county and then deliberating for about an hour.

* * *

Three different sources called 911 to alert the Indianapolis Metro Police that shots were fired in the 1400 block of Ridgecrest in the south side of the city. One of the responding police units almost hit the figure that dashed from the shadows between two houses. His partner tackled the guy as he tried to clear a six-foot wooden fence across the street. The alleged perp was dressed in black and the cops discovered a black stocking mask stuffed in his rear pocket. At the base of the wooden fence, the officers found a sawed-off shotgun pumped for action.

Several additional police cars converged on the 1400 block of Ridgecrest. Mitch Reynolds was easy to spot. He was barefoot, wearing only baggy boxer shorts. Blood oozed from several gashes on his bald head. A .357 SigSauer filled his hand. Wisely he dropped it when he saw the first cop car careen around the corner with its emergency lights piercing the neighborhood's veil of black. Its siren invaded the serenity of the sleeping street and Mitch knew he was had.

Mitch was a drug dealer well known to the IMPD. But, on this particular and unusual night, he was the victim.

"Why'd you open the door?" the arriving uniformed cops asked Mitch.

"For the cop!"

"What cop?"

"There was a cop banging like hell on my front door!"

"Wha' he look like?"

An incredulous look crept over the drug dealer's face. "Like you. Same uniform. Same marked cop car. Parked right out front."

The questioning cop answered Mitch with a bewildered stare.

"That's why I opened the door at this time of night. Next minute I know these two assholes with ski masks busted in and jammed my ass into my sofa."

"Wha' happened to the cop?"

"Don't know. I'm getting whaled on by one asshole who's bashing my head with the Sig. The other one is jabbing at me with a sawed-off shotgun. All the time yelling, 'Where's your stash, where's the stash?'

"I grabbed the handgun and me and him was going round and round. Suddenly the damn thing goes off. Think he got hit somewhere cuz he lets out an awful scream. By the time I get a good tight hold on the gun, the other asshole is turning that shotgun my way. I fired four times. Don't know if I hit him, but he turned and ran out the front door. I go to run after him, but hear your sirens coming. Don't want to get shot by mistake. I turns around and the other asshole is gone. Guess he got out the back door."

"Now, you sure it was a cop? Not some make believe?"

"He's got your uniform, your car, and he looks like a cop! Seems you can find him if youse want to, huh?"

It didn't take IMPD detectives long to unravel what had happened. They isolated Officer Brad Prince from the GPS locator in his marked unit. He wasn't on duty when the attempted robbery occurred, but he was driving his take-home department patrol car. Between Prince and the shotgun-carrying robber, the third suspect was quickly located. He was bleeding from a graze bullet wound on his left thigh.

All three suspects were trying to outdo each other by giving information against the others. Turned out the trio had been pulling robberies and drug dealer rip-offs throughout the south rim of Lake Michigan to the middle of Indiana. Most drug dealers, of course, hadn't reported the robberies. None had been killed like Otto Graham in Livingston.

One of the IMPD detectives marked with grey hair recalled a similar dealer robbery in the town of Livingston years before. He told the lead prosecutor handling the IMPD cases his recollections. It took only one phone call when they realized the duo in Indianapolis was probably responsible for Otto's death as well.

Jude Richards, the same officer responsible for recruiting Rob Stanley into the narco unit, had been Chief of Police in Livingston for the past three years. The call from the DA's office in Indie surprised him initially, and then caused a sharp pain in the pit of his stomach.

Could the department have convicted the wrong man for Otto's murder?

Snake, Cross-eyes, and Rob had all retired. Well, maybe not

exactly. Up and gone, was the more appropriate term. Snake left after he hooked up with a groupie while working security at an AC/DC concert. She turned out to be sixteen; but Snake swore she fucked like a grown woman. He took a plea deal, left the department, and agreed never to go after a cop job again.

Cross-eyes got caught skimming prescription drugs from search warrant operations of pill doctors. He got three-year probation and was allowed to resign from the Livingston force. Rob Stanley retired legitimately and was living somewhere down south.

Jude sat down with the IMPD detectives and the lead county prosecutor. One of the original homicide detectives on the Otto case, Syd Shepard, was still on the job. Jude and Syd clued the Indianapolis team about the details of the Otto Graham murder and Roscoe's ultimate conviction.

With their information, the Indy cops quickly got Handgun Guy to roll over on Shotgun Guy with the promise of second-degree murder rather than first, which carried the possibility of sitting in the state's electrically charged throne as punishment for Otto's murder.

The Livingston prosecutor did the right thing. He called Roscoe's defense attorney and within a couple of weeks an uncontested Habeas was filed in court.

Roscoe walked out of the state prison after serving a full eight years.

* * *

Taylor Sterling had been working in northern Wyoming near Yellowstone National Park conducting a liability assessment for a small sheriff's office. He loved the assignment. It was late September and the tourists were long gone, but Mother Nature was putting on a spectacular show of brilliant colors accented with a cast of deer, bear, bison, caribou, and moose. A bald eagle perched on a lone pine tree was acting as sentry at the small police station each morning when Taylor showed up.

When Taylor finally emerged from the northern mountain paradise and dropped down to Laramie, his iPhone started attacking him with a vengeance. Taylor hadn't missed his electronic tether and realized how relaxing the four days he spent in rugged heaven had been. No cell service, now that was true paradise!

Forty-seven unanswered messages.

"Taylor Sterling, been trying to get you all week. Answer your phone! Ever think about getting a secretary? Austin Bean here with the Indiana Muni Insurance Pool. Need some help. Call!"

This was the first of eight calls from Austin, each becoming more intense and demanding.

Taylor called back and promised Austin he would make arrangements to fly to Indiana the following week.

* * *

The foursome found a table on the covered patio at Scalo's, taking full advantage of the beautiful Saturday night in Albuquerque. The Italian restaurant had been a mainstay in this yuppie, Nob Hill section of Central Avenue east of the University of New Mexico. UNM students congregated further west down the hill. Even further down the hill on Central, just before it dipped under I25, street people massed—the homeless, mentals, and prostitutes. A collection of misters hanging from the patio ceiling were going full blast and enveloped the four diners with welcome cooling moisture on the warm autumn evening. The wind was coming from Gallup over the high plains before reaching to the Sandia Mountains.

Taylor and Sandy, his friend with benefits, had been pried away from Santa Fe by their mutual friends, Yoshi Weinstein and his live-in friend, Armando. The four had just enjoyed a contemporary version of *West Side Story* at the UNM Fine Arts Theater. The set featured a New Mexican barrio, rather than the tenement houses of the Big Apple.

"You still avoiding New Mexico cases, Taylor?" Yoshi asked. Yoshi was a civil rights attorney in Santa Fe who was on the team taking a lot of ACLU cases. The attorneys kept plugging away at police misconduct cases and were getting beaten down by the conservative juries seated in federal court.

Yoshi was in his early forties. His mother was Cambodian and his father was an orthodox Jew living in Maryland. The Santa Fe Jewish community was sparse, so Yoshi had to settle for a Reform synagogue.

"Yep, won't touch those cases. Too many complications when you do what I do in your own backyard. I wouldn't mind doing some pro bono stuff, but the local agencies don't seem interested. I've reached out and offered training and audits, but no takers so far."

Their entrees appeared on the table as the light conversation centered on the variations of *West Side Story*.

Taylor and Sandy ordered the grilled salmon nestled on orange-infused risotto. Both found the plates beautiful and satisfying. Yoshi settled on vegetarian lasagna, while Armando polished off a huge salmon salad.

"Yoshi, I think it's finally time for me to get somebody to answer my phone when I'm out of town. Any ideas?"

Yoshi leaned back in his chair and thought a moment. "Actually I do know someone. You know Amos Munoz?" Taylor shook his head. "He's a retired state trooper. Was with some large private investigation firm, but recently headed out on his own."

"I know him," Sandy interjected. "I represented his landlord in a strip of small offices on Galisteo a couple blocks west of the capital. Small place. Just an office and a front reception area, but that's all Amos wanted."

"I've used Amos for leg work on a couple of my cases. He's good and dependable," Yoshi added. "And, the secretary who answers his phone seems like a real sweetheart. A voice from heaven. Never met her, but she's got to be a beauty with that voice. I'll call Amos to check and see if she'd be interested in helping you out, if you'd like."

"No, I'll reach out to him. What's the name his company goes by?"

"Amos Investigations. Guess he figured it'd put him near the front in the phone directory."

The next morning, after leisurely making his way through a large croissant smothered with green chili jam and enjoying a few cups of Sandy's strong coffee, Taylor returned to his condo. He couldn't find his phone book so he ended up using 411 to get Amos' number.

"Amos Investigations, Ginger here. We're having a wondrous day, hope you are, too." It *was* a voice from heaven as Yoshi had described. Soft, melodic, like the purr of a contented kitten. The voice put Taylor through to Amos Munoz.

"Amos, here," the voice commanded with a hint of a Hispanic accent.

"Taylor Sterling. I'm a friend of Yoshi Weinstein and Sandy Banks. They suggested I reach out to you."

"Need some investigation?"

"Nope, need a secretary."

"Not giving up Ginger, pal. No how, no way."

"Not asking you to. But I am interested in hiring a small share of her work."

They arranged to meet later that afternoon. Amos' office was exactly as Sandy had described. It was located in a nondescript line of eight small offices descending from street level. A sign proclaiming AMOS INVESTIGATIONS hung from the covered walkway and slowly swung in the slight breeze. Taylor opened the door to a small reception area just big enough to hold a well-used metal government desk, one chair, and a small table.

"Taylor, huh? Googled you and got reams of shit from all over the country. Popular guy, I guess," the receptionist welcomed in a husky voice.

This couldn't possibly be the woman connected to the voice he'd heard on the phone and the sweetheart described by Yoshi!

Before him sat a curvy girl, the current politically correct term for large. She pushed her chair back and stood up. She rounded the desk with agility that betrayed her size. Faded jeans were struggling with her thighs and broad butt. A sleeveless, peasant blouse hung loose at her waist. The woman's arms were muscular and a bountiful assortment of bangles hid her wrists, clinking and clattering loudly as her arms moved. Her auburn hair was bedhead tousled, but could have been styled attractively with plenty of product. The woman's broad smile was infectious as she ran her fingers through her hair and gave it a quick shake.

"You...Ginger?" Taylor stuttered.

"You...Taylor?" she mimicked and broadened her smile.

"You sound different than I pictured you."

"Shit, that's my phone persona!" The woman segued into the

purring, melodic, heavenly voice he had heard on the phone. She laughed at his reaction.

"Got myself another job at night. I'm "Allure" on 1-900-GOD-DESS. Great money, but sick bastards. Boy, they love that fuck talk! You into that sick shit, Taylor?"

Taylor noticed the flower tattoo spanning her wrist when the collection of bracelets rode down her arm. He also spied a circle of barbed wire around one of her ankles. A brilliant red stone pierced the right side of her nose. One ear was ringed with at least eight piercings. Ginger captured a ring on every finger, except her thumbs. Taylor decided not to ask this unusual creature if she had tattoos or piercings he couldn't see.

"Ginger, play nice now," a deep authoritative voice called from the other room.

Amos Munoz was a striking figure. He was close to Taylor's height, pushing near six feet. His head was shaved clean but a monstrous, bushy moustache obscured the outline of his mouth. The 'stache resembled small tumbleweeds sticking on the orifice. Starched jeans, scuffed pointed cowboy boots, and a plaid shirt mostly obscured by a black leather vest completed the look. A large silver and turquoise bolo closed the collar of the shirt.

A stainless Smith and Wesson .357 magnum on the man's belt looked to be a three-and-a-half inch on the .44 frame, finished with stag bone handles. A basket weave belt was held together with a large silver buckle proclaiming New Mexico State Police with a replica of a badge emblazoned the front and center.

Amos' small office was cramped, stuffed with a desk, two chairs, metal filing cabinet, and a trophy wall filled with New Mexico State Police mementos.

Amos noticed Taylor scanning the ego wall. "Twenty five years with the state, Taylor. Good times. Then a godawful two years in Raton. Know where that is?"

Taylor nodded. "Had four years down in Truth and Consequences, mostly up in the White Mountains. Got promoted to sergeant there and spent the remainder in Santa Fe and Albuquerque doing investigations."

"Any narc work?"

"Nope, didn't like that shit. Changes you. Hated working with those federal agencies. Checked you out with Yoshi, good attorney he is. Then I remembered Luke McKinney with State Risk had talked about you awhile back. So, Taylor, what you need from me?"

"I'm interested in renting Ginger. I'm traveling a lot more than I expected and need someone at home base to collect incoming phone calls, mail, and stuff like that. You need her fulltime?"

"Not really, but when you get good help you keep it. Not that you're good help, Ginger," he yelled, knowing the secretary was listening to every word. "I used to work with one of those national PI firms. Didn't like the work. Mostly divorce shit. Cheating spouses."

"What do you like?"

"I like working with the attorneys here in New Mexico. I'm getting a good name in civil cases. Some of my work involves cop shit. Some of it is criminal. Finding wits. Running records. Searching databases. Kind of similar to when I was a real cop."

Amos and Taylor worked out a deal they were both comfortable with. Taylor essentially bought a week's worth of Ginger's salary. He planned to put in a dedicated landline so she could stay put with no hassle. Amos offered to do computer searches for Taylor and said Ginger was pretty good at proofing written work.

"Excuse me!" Ginger's husky voice bellowed into the office. She was now filling the open doorway, hands on her hips. "I'm not a street whore and you're not my pimp, Sergeant A! I interviewed *you* before I signed onto this job. This Taylor dude ain't no john. I figure if he's gonna pick up part of my salary, I need to have some kind of relationship with him. Right now I don't know much about this stud and how he works!"

Ginger thrust her head from side to side in the bobbing way many black women master with precision. Her fists stayed on her wide hips and her lips took a defiant curl. She glared at the men. Neither could tell if she was kidding or was dead serious.

"Now, now, girl. Don't get your pussy in an uproar," Amos ordered pointing a finger in her direction and piercing the air for emphasis.

"Well, if I gots to talk with him and do his work, I think I should know him and feel comfortable with his ass. That's all I'm tellin' you dudes."

"And just what did you have in mind?" Amos asked.

"Well, let's see. It's just about lunch time and I'd like Mr. Stud here to take me to Pasqual's."

Amos looked at Taylor with a questioning tilt of his head.

"Good with me. What's with the Sergeant A?"

"That's what she calls me," Amos explained as he covered his face with his hands. "Guess it's better than anything else her mouth might come up with."

Lucky the day was a Tuesday. After a short walk, Taylor and Ginger reached Pasqual's and were surprised to find a table on the upper level close to the front door. The restaurant was a tourist destination just off the old Plaza. It featured yuppie New Mexican Nuevo food that promised to be fresh from local farms. The place was colorful with streamers and cutouts hanging from the ceiling. A circular community table in the center of the main room was loaded with rowdy conventioneers, their nametags dangling from swollen straps around their necks. The restaurant sold the T-shirts the waiters wore. Taylor actually owned a black one featuring Our Mother of Guadalupe that he bought on one of his visits to the locale.

Taylor ordered the smoked trout omelet served with thick slices of nine-grain toast. Ginger took her time pondering the menu and finally settled for the featured free-range chicken salad, after asking if it had been a happy chicken, along with a cup of cream of asparagus soup on the side.

"Well?" Taylor asked when they'd finished eating and were sipping cactus flower infused tea.

"I was just shitting you guys. Figured I could at least get a lunch out of it. Oh, I'd probably jump in the sack with you, but I figure you're not up for that, huh?" Ginger threw Taylor one of her infectious smiles. "I figure I'm not your type."

Taylor reached over, gently placing his hand on top of hers. "Actually, that's not true. I like curvy women who know who they are. And you seem to know exactly who you are. You carry yourself like a prime athlete, regardless of your size. You seem to have an intense curiosity and interest in many things. I like people who don't pigeonhole themselves."

Ginger continued smiling and reversed hands, leaving hers on top of his in a variation of the kids' old playground game.

"Thank you. I beat myself up teaching Zumba three nights a week over at a spa in the canyon. Rich bitches. Love to make them sweat and stain the $300 workout togs they wear. Gets me worked up for my night job."

"As the lovely Allure," Taylor offered without hesitation.

"Allure, at your service," Ginger replied, reverting to her heavenly voice and then let out a laugh that infected the entire restaurant.

She didn't bat an eye when tables turned to glance her way.

"You know, I've got plans, Taylor."

"And what might those plans be? Or shouldn't I be asking?"

"No, it's okay. I don't want to be a secretary, Zumba star, and phone goddess all my life," she smiled, but Taylor sensed angst overrode her assertion. "I left high school in the eleventh grade. My mom begged me to finish, but I was young and in love. Turns out my prince in shining armor was a scumbag. Left me a month later. I finally busted my ass at adult ed and got my GED."

"And?" Taylor asked, showing he was interested and wanted her to continue.

"I've been taking one night off for the past three years. Going to a vocational school. You know the type. They promise you financial aid and the guarantee of a job after you graduate. I will say they did come through with enough money to cover the cost of my education. Unfortunately, I got to pay it back some day."

"What you been studying?" Taylor asked, now genuinely interested in Ginger's story.

"You aren't going to laugh, are you?" He shook his head. "I'm going to be a paralegal."

Taylor leaned back and tried to relax in the uncomfortable ornately painted chair.

"I figure it will increase my value with Sergeant A. He gets involved in a lot of legal matters. Maybe I'll take on piecework with other local sole practitioners. Most are really stretched for office staff. I read a lot of depositions for Sergeant A and study police reports whenever I can. I'm the one in the office who knows how to search those cop databases. I can wade my way through boring legal briefs and court pleadings. I told myself, why not? What you think, Chief Taylor?"

"First of all, I left that "chief title" behind when I retired, but I think you got your act together. I'd be pleased to work with you. How could I find anyone more qualified than you?" Taylor smiled and gently stroked Ginger's hand.

"You okay now, Ginger?" Amos asked when the two returned to the PI's office.

"Yeah. We decided on a nooner rather than grab lunch, Sergeant A."

"You took over an hour!"

"The stud here just got more stamina than you, Sergeant A!"

The three shared a laugh. Taylor figured while Ginger had never been a cop, she sure had the cop humor and sarcasm down pat.

"Hey, Chief T," Ginger purred as Taylor was leaving. "Remember to call Allure when the moon rises if you want some good fuck talk."

She smiled and reverted to her heavenly voice. "It'll be a wondrous pleasure working with you, Chief Taylor Sterling."

* * *

Indianapolis International Airport was finally completed after the 9/11 tragedy. It had taken much longer than expected since civil engineers had to reroute and rebuild Interstates around the facility. Taylor liked this midwestern airport. It was huge, but convenient and easy to navigate. An expanse of windows welcomed sunshine to create a warm, friendly feeling. The city fathers of Indianapolis must have expected the entire world would be passing through so built an airport to accommodate them. The Great Recession of 2008 kept away the masses of expected travelers so the place always seemed eerily vacant.

The Indiana Insurance Pool had offices a stone's throw from the airport in a sprawling industrial park. Massive FedEx and Amazon Fulfillment centers commanded most of the buildings in the complex.

"Taylor, glad to see you!" Austin Bean greeted as Taylor was escorted to his cubicle.

Austin filled Taylor in about the series of events from Otto's murder and conviction to the recent revelations that released Roscoe from prison. A large stack of paper sat on Austin's desk that he patted protectively to accent points as he released his tale of woes.

"First got the notice to file a claim, and then got this here complaint in federal court," Austin continued. "We're worried because wrongful conviction cases have been gaining a lot of traction around the country. Think this is the first for Indiana though. Our corporate attorney isn't too anxious yet, but he keeps his emotions in check. I've arranged for the chief to be available in the morning, along with the one detective who's still on the job. Guess you can take it from there, huh, Taylor?"

It was only a thirty-minute drive to Livingston. Rush hour hadn't started yet. Taylor noticed a Hampton Inn on the first ramp signaling the city of Livingston was coming up ahead and figured it best to check-in. No matter what the date or season, highway motels filled up by seven. Taylor wondered where everybody was going in this neck of the woods on this bleak day in late September.

After settling in to his generic hotel room, Taylor decided it would be a good idea to check out the town to get his bearings. Livingston still appeared to be a farming community. Two farm equipment outlets buttressed a tractor supply store. A large banner hung over the entrance to the store announced it was Tracy Bennett Day.

The road ambled through a series of mobile home parks filled with older, scarred singlewide units. The collection appeared to be rentals judging by the lack of upkeep and the number of cars on cement blocks resembling redneck yard art.

Both sides of the road leading to downtown Livingston featured small retail shops, equipment rental locations, car repair bays, and convenience market gas stations. Abruptly the mom and pop establishments stopped, bowing to the usual faceoff between Wal-Mart and Target superstores.

Leaving the commercial district, the road pierced into what was probably the original neighborhood where the well-to-do families of Livingston resided. Large lawns circled stately brick houses that stretched almost to the edge of the property lines. Mature trees saluted the homes, proudly announcing they had stood guard over their families for thirty or forty years. What appeared to be the original high school stood like a stone statue at the entrance to the old downtown area.

The road simply ended in the center of town. Indiana towns often had a common circle like most Southern towns boasted, but rather than a courthouse anchoring the circle, a small park with an elevated, covered stage was the centerpiece. Another Tracy Bennett Day banner hung from the roof of the stage. Taylor didn't have anything particular in mind as he circled the park, but a small sign in a window caught his attention—*Livingston Courier*.

The storefront office housing the local weekly newspaper was narrow, but a twelve-foot peaked ceiling made it appear large and impressive. A long counter divided the lobby from the staff offices. Taylor heard the hum of a machine sounding from the rear of the room. A woman in her early fifties sat at one of three desks on the other side of the counter. She swiveled in her chair when he entered.

"Halp you, mister?"

"I'm in town on business for a few days and noticed Tracy Bennett Day signs all over the place. What gives?"

"Tracy's coming home next Saturday. He's been down in San Antonio at the military hospital for nearly eight months. Lost both legs and an arm over in Afghanistan. Sad, like all them young men returning with something missing. Tracy was a star athlete at the local high school. Of course he married the girl he dated through school and hadn't even seen their first child when he was shipped over to that senseless war."

The woman pulled a handkerchief from the bodice of her scoop-neck dress and dabbed her eyes.

"Never been this many saved, ma'am, even missing parts. I just hope the government keeps its word and replaces those missing parts with new prosthetics. Most cost upwards of forty thousand and they last only about five years. Sad times."

"What business you in, mister?"

"I'm a police consultant."

"Something us here at the paper might be interested in?"

"Maybe."

"Let me get John over here," she said as she yelled for John who was working at the rear of the office.

John was wearing dark dress slacks and a blue plaid long sleeve shirt. A blue Colts cap covered most of his head. The cap tucked close, allowing the grey hairs around his ears to stick straight out like a plateau skirting his skull. John wore wire-rimmed glasses on the bill of his cap that he shifted up and down to focus when needed.

"What you need, woman? You know I'm running this week's edition back there."

"Thought you might be interested in this fellow. In town on business. Says he's a police consultant." She glanced at Taylor for affirmation.

"Name's Taylor Sterling." Taylor purposefully paused since he didn't know the names of his audience.

"Mary Beth Smith," the woman replied, laughing when she realized she hadn't been polite earlier. "This here is my husband, John."

"John Smith, huh? Bet you get strange looks when you check into a motel." Straight blank faces made Taylor realize neither Smith had any idea what he was talking about.

"Well, you probably already know about the lawsuit filed by a fellow who says he was wrongfully convicted of murder and spent quite a few years in prison."

"Yeah, that was what, seven or eight years ago?" John recalled as he leaned against the counter to get closer to Taylor. "We don't get many murders in Livingston, other than domestics or migrant workers killing each other when they get to fighting. Otto's murder wasn't that newsworthy a story since everybody involved was doing drugs."

"You know them?"

"Otto? Sure I knew him. Knew both Otto and his folks. Had to pass his house on the way into town. One of them Mc-Mansions with the big front lawns. Didn't know that guy who got convicted. He was from Indy. The wit, Angel Martinez, was a regular around here. Sorry case with her nasty family, and then she just gravitated into the drug scene."

"She still around?"

Mary Beth chimed in. "Died a couple years ago. Found

dead in one of those trailers you probably passed coming into town. Medical examiner said it was respiratory complications brought on by AIDS. Another sad case. Angel looked to be about fifty, but was only a little over thirty when she passed on."

"It was pretty well known that she was an informant for the local cops," John added, puffing up a bit as he gave his inside information. "Who was that cop who seemed to be around Angel all the time, Mary Beth?"

She massaged her chin and closed her eyes to think. "Rob... Rob Stanley. Heard he's retired and living down south someplace."

Taylor told the couple he was working with the town's insurance carrier and was looking at the conviction from a police point of view.

"What's your opinion of your police department?" Taylor threw out.

"Indiana has the reputation for not having the best in law enforcement. Terrible pension system for the cops. Heard it's the worst in the country. But, Livingston is probably no better or worse than most departments around the state."

"I've heard that from a few of my friends as well, John. You're not stepping on toes with me," Taylor confirmed John's thoughts.

"I've got a pile of news accounts in our computer system, mister. Wouldn't mind sharing them with you if you promise to give me a heads up if a story breaks. What you think?"

"I'm willing to share what's not classified as confidential, John. Maybe a few details you could use as things heat up on this case," Taylor added, knowing he would have to be discreet with whatever information he could share.

"Mary Beth and I will do a search after I get this edition out.

We'll put it on a thumb drive for you. Stop by before you leave town."

Taylor glanced at his watch as he slid into his rental car. It showed 5:15. He decided to gear into food focus and pulled up the Yelp app on his iPhone. Just down the road was Grant's Country Kitchen. Taylor was surprised the restaurant had earned nearly a hundred Four-Star ratings from Yelp patrons.

Grant's parking lot was almost completely full, but Taylor wasn't in a hurry to get back to his hotel room so a wait wouldn't bother him. The restaurant was housed in a long, dark brown building stretching the entire length of the parking lot.

He was taken back somewhat as he made his way in and realized Grant's was a cafeteria. Taylor wasn't crazy about that, but relented when smells of fresh food teased his appetite. *Watch your intake, Taylor!*

The salad selection was easy pickin's—cucumber and onion. But, then the main show loomed big—Salisbury steak, chicken fried steak, baked pork chops, fried and baked chicken, fried and sautéed catfish, poached salmon, cooked (not sure how) liver, and salmon patties. *Which to pick?*

He settled on a helping of poached salmon and sautéed catfish, but passed on the starchy sides. Bright green string beans captured his attention. Taylor thought he'd finished loading at the trough until the peach cobbler begged, "Pick me, pick me!"

Taylor found a table in a far corner so he could watch the locals busily feasting on their selections. The cafeteria held a mix of working men, young families, and a fairly large gaggle of grey-haired seniors.

Rural America. This was a genuine Norman Rockwell setting.

* * *

The Livingston Police station was relatively new and was an attractive, inviting place. It was a rare cop shop that inspired comfort, but Livingston managed to create such a place. Chief Richards and the lead homicide detective, Syd Shepard, were waiting for Taylor in the chief's office.

Richards was wearing his white, long-sleeved uniform shirt, dark uniform pants, and carried a small semi-automatic resting in a minuscule holster on his belt. One gold star tipped the collars of his shirt.

Shepard was not in uniform. His pale blue button-down shirt was heavily starched and the complementary patterned tie was nondescript. Dark blue slacks completed his casual unofficial uniform. Taylor assumed they paired with a matching blue coat held hostage on a rack somewhere in the station. Shepard sported a neatly trimmed pencil thin moustache; his hair molded definitively around his head. A banker's box sat on the floor next to his chair.

Both had cups of coffee in front of them making white rings on the small conference table.

"Coffee, Mr. Sterling?" Richards asked.

"No thanks. Full tank from breakfast," Taylor answered as he took the chair that had been pulled out from the table.

"Insurance pool brought you in, huh?" Richards questioned.

"Yes. They were worried about the Roscoe Blunt lawsuit. Whadda you guys think?"

Richards and Shepard looked at each other quickly, and then sighed. Neither had a hint of a smile on their faces. On the other hand, neither showed any indication of concern either. Taylor felt he was playing a sly game of poker with these two.

"I read the full trial transcript last night," Taylor began, letting the thought settle to see the reactions he might get. Nothing!

"Seemed like a slam-dunk case for the prosecutor. Easy and quick." Still no response. Taylor figured Richards and Shepard were waiting him out to determine what approach he was going to take for what they thought would be a hostile interrogation. "Tell me about the only witness."

Shepard glanced at Chief Richards.

"They were all druggies, Mr. Sterling," Richards flatly stated.

"Wait… hold on a minute, guys. I'm Taylor. I'm not here to bust your chops. I'm here to find out what might concern the insurance pool. That group has got to make the serious decision either to fight this lawsuit or start intensive settlement discussions. They got some guy who didn't do the crime and spent eight years on death row for it. I'm here simply to offer another perspective. A different view of the incident than they've been given so far."

Richards and Shepard sat back in their chairs. Shepard crossed his arms over his chest, taking a defensive position. Richards began rubbing his chin and shot a couple quick glances at Shepard. He looked down at the banker's box on the floor. As his final act, he stretched, arched his back, and put both hands behind his raised head to intently study the ceiling for a few minutes.

"What you want to know about Angel?" Richards asked as he relaxed his hands and brought them to the table.

"Was she one of your informants? That's what Roscoe's defense lawyer was trying his damnest to prove in his cross of Angel, but struck out. He tried hard to get one of your narcs on the witness stand to testify, but was shot down by the judge. Think His Honor used the words 'fishing' and 'irrelevant' and 'not material.' What was that narc's name?"

"Rob Stanley. Used to work for me when I commanded our narc unit. Hardworking cop. Made a lot of busts. Had a long list of informants," Richards admitted.

"Was Angel one of his snitches?"

"Yeah, a very productive one."

"She working as a snitch when the murder went down?"

"Really don't know, Taylor," Richards said and once again looked at Shepard for support.

Shepard reached down and hooked his fingers into the opening at one end of the banker's box and pulled it to the tabletop like a fish on a fly.

"Why don't you take a look at the investigation reports I gave to the prosecutor, Taylor," Shepard offered without much facial expression exposing his thoughts. Taylor sensed no hostility, no sarcasm, no challenging. Just here it is, come and get it, and left it at that.

Richards stood in tandem with his cohort and announced, "I'll leave you here with the file. We'll be back in about an hour. My secretary, Judy, will get you coffee or water if you want it." They walked out of the office in single file.

Taylor opened the box and expected to find a jumbled mess of documents, photos, tapes, and marked exhibits. He was pleasantly and shockingly surprised. Two five inch three-hole binders and several manila envelopes filled the box. One envelope noted the case number and was marked "Show-up Photographs;" one was labeled "Crime Scene Photographs." A third held "DVDs of Interviews." The last envelope was identified "Handwritten Notes."

The binders had labels on the spines listing the case number, Volume I and Volume II. Inside the first was an index corresponding to numbered tabs in both binders. Taylor ran his finger down the index page and noted the appropriate documents seemed to be in the volumes. Police reports, crime scene reports and diagrams, medical examiner reports, evidence collection and analysis, criminal history sheets, communications transcriptions, court pleadings, search warrants, and arrest warrants. They were all there.

He smiled when he noticed Tab #23—"Copies of Handwritten Notes." Apparently the investigators had copied their handwritten notes, but still kept the originals preserved in one of the envelopes.

Police detectives come in all types. Homicides are one of the most critical crimes investigated by any police department. During the murder investigation, prosecution, trial, and appeal, many people review a case. It becomes even more intensive when there is the possibility of a capital crime committed or a case where the death penalty might be considered.

Homicide detectives should be the best a police department can offer. They typically are methodical, structured, and orderly. Some might consider these detectives to be anal in their methods of investigation and document preparation. It would certainly help to own a few traits of an "OCD personality." Someone characterized with an ADD personality would be a disaster as a homicide investigator. Focus and tenacity are important qualities.

The handwritten notes of any police officer, specifically a detective, have been a subject of concern in law enforcement for many years. Until recently, the detective would take notes, prepare a written report, and then destroy the original handwritten notes. Some prosecutors actually instructed detectives to do that as it precluded any challenge when handwritten notes might not be exactly as worded in the final document. Lately there have been numerous cases and policy recommendations that would require the retention of all handwritten notes by officers and detectives.

Taylor was most interested how the detectives handled interviewing Angel Martinez. He pulled out his MacBook Air, fumbled into his backpack for the external disk drive, and finally surgically inserted the drive into the computer. In the envelope holding the DVDs, he found the one with Angel Martinez's name on it.

The interview began with Syd Shepard identifying himself as the lead investigator, followed by his partner stating his name was Neil Amos. Taylor advanced the disk past the preliminaries and stopped when he reached the part where Syd began questioning Angel in specific detail.

"Did you have any money when you went to Otto's house?" Syd asked in a matter of fact manner.

"If I had money I wouldn't have been giving Otto a blow-job," Angel retorted, clearly signaling her distaste for the question.

"Why did you go to Otto's?"

"To get some shit, dummy."

"But you said earlier your regular source was Roscoe."

"Yeah, but I couldn't find him that night. I needed to score bad, man."

"Had you scored from Otto before?"

"Yeah."

"Frequently?"

"No, man. He too 'spensive."

"Now, you weren't there working for Rob at the time, were you?"

There was a hesitation and then Angel said, "No, man. I didn't see Rob for a couple of days."

"But you are one of his snitches, aren't you?"

"One of his best, he tell me that all the time."

"But not on this particular night?"

"Nope. Not on da' night Otto gets blasted."

"Why did you call Rob after you left Otto's house?"

Again there was an obvious pause before Angel admitted,

"Cuz I seen Otto get blasted by Roscoe and his buddy. Got to go to the cops. Rob good to me, but other cops sometimes are bad to me. I needed a friend. Rob is a friend to me."

"Now, you told us it was Roscoe and some other dude that shot Otto, right? You picked Roscoe's mug out of the photos we showed you. Why don't you know the other guy?"

"He face covered by the ski mask. I told you already."

"But Roscoe's wasn't?"

"It was, but after Otto got blasted he take it off. I was in bathroom and seen him. He no see me."

"The other guy had the handgun?"

"No," she sounded perturbed. "I tolds you, Roscoe had the small gun and other guy have the shotgun." She paused and then charged, "You trying to fuck me up, man? I'm the wit, shit. I ain't no perp, man. You need treat me with respect. I finger Roscoe for you. Shit, you don't need do any detecting with info I give you. Don't fuck with me! I tell Rob if'n you do."

Taylor listened to more of the interview and felt comfortable Syd was pressing Angel, but didn't believe everything she was telling him. To her credit, Angel stuck to her version of the murder without wavering. The investigative file was complete. It was very well done. But, something was still gnawing at Taylor. That feeling was tweaking his view of what seemed to be a situation that was too pat for the circumstances.

"Well?" Chief Richards asked when he and his cohort reentered the office.

"Damn fine investigation, Syd," Taylor answered. "Where did you get your homicide training?"

"OJT and watching others. Some good; most bad. I attended a couple seminars up in Indy. One was presented by a retired cop out of Miami-Dade. Nice enough fellow, but he sure told a pot full of stories."

"You never really bought the story Angel told you?"

"Nope, but she never strayed from it. Grand jury believed her. Hell, the trial jury loved her. She pushed out a version that made sense."

"But not totally to you, Syd?"

"No, but there wasn't much I could do. Hunches are good at the front of an investigation, but don't have a place at the end."

"How do you feel about Roscoe walking?"

Syd looked down and stuffed his hands into his pant pockets. He shuffled while thinking and then looked directly at Taylor and said, "Like shit. I feel like shit. No one should feel good about putting the wrong man in prison. I've been to that state facility. Even Roscoe shouldn't have to put up with that life. I know he's a drug dealer and a scumbag, but it's obvious he didn't do the crime. I'm sorry for him."

Taylor was surprised by Syd's admission. Taylor hadn't worked many wrongful conviction cases either on the job or as a consultant. Most investigators in these cases won't admit they may have made a mistake. Many shrug off any redemption by declaring the guy was scum anyway so what difference did it make? Taylor thought those reactions were face saving efforts for the detectives involved. No one wanted to believe they were responsible for taking away a person's life. Taylor respected Syd for his position. It was an unusual one given the circumstances. Taylor knew he didn't have to tell Syd how he felt about his stance.

"Chief, can we talk about your time in narcotics?" Taylor asked.

"It's Jude, Taylor," Richards said. "What about?"

"This fellow cop, Rob. Was he a pretty good narc?"

"One of the best. Made a lot of arrests and most of them stuck. D.A. loved him. Made his job easy. Rob was like a pit bull when he went after someone. Why do you ask?"

"Angel was one of his informants, I gathered."

"Yep. And a good one. Real productive for Rob."

"You got records detailing her use?"

Richards shifted in his chair, rubbed his chin, and admitted, "Not much, Taylor. We're small time here. Not like the big cities. I know what we should have been doing, but we didn't. Our snitches were pretty much the private property of each investigator. We didn't document like we should have...or like the books say we should. That's the main reason I disbanded our unit and joined the HIDTA group after I got this here Chief's job. Don't have to worry about that stuff anymore. We just supply one body to the task force and reap the rewards when they make busts and seize property."

"What about confidential monies? You know, the money your investigators use to buy info or reward their informants for help. Most places make sure their asses are covered for that."

"We had a sizable slush fund the guys used for small stuff. But, if a cop had to fork over a couple hundred or more, documentation was required. We used these little chits for records. Slips of paper. Almost like the bookies used when we focused on gambling busts," Jude said. It appeared he was researching the databank in his head to remember what they did ten years back.

"You still got those chits, Jude?"

Jude Richards leaned back in his chair, closed his eyes, and began rubbing his temples. Suddenly he jerked back and slammed his palms down on his desk, "By God, I think we might! Let's take a look."

He had to ask Judy which key on a ring loaded with at least

twenty keys was the one that opened the record storage cage in the basement. Jude and Taylor walked down metal stairs into the damp basement in the bowels of the police station. It was apparent the new station had been built right on top of the foundation of the old one. Florescent lights guiding the way flickered constantly, crying for new bulbs. The wire gate to the storage area creaked as Jude opened it and swept away the cobwebs marking an ancient spider world. Jude pushed the switch on the rubber encased flashlight he brought with him, swore mercilessly at it when nothing happened, and then tapped it into his palm until a faint beacon of light appeared. He went to a shelf near the bottom of a case and began fingering the dark brown folders at one end.

"This is where I recall we put each year's narcotic shit. There's no real rhyme or reason why or how we filed stuff, but I think the chits should be here someplace. What years we looking for, Taylor?"

"Try the year of Otto's murder and then check the year of Roscoe's trial."

Jude's fingers worked over the faded folder labels before settling on two of them. Each was about three or four inches thick. He pulled the files out and blew on each, sending a tornado of dust into the vacated hole on the shelf.

"Let's take them upstairs and I'll find something to clean them off a little. You can use my office to look at them. I got a community meeting in half an hour," Jude remembered as he glanced at his watch.

* * *

Normally police departments use informants for a variety of purposes.

Sometimes the informant is simply a concerned citizen who might have seen something or be in possession of pertinent information.

The most common informant is someone used by the police to focus on criminal activity, provide ways into the inner workings of a criminal gang, buy contraband like firearms, narcotics, or other illegal goods from criminals, or give the officer specific information needed to obtain a search warrant. These informants are called confidential reliable informants or identified as a CI.

A police officer can't identify someone as a CI simply for the sake of convenience. The informant must be vetted or shown to be reliable. Before a person can begin working with a police agency as a CI, the informant must be identified, have his or her criminal history checked, and run through a database that lists unreliable persons or informants who have turned on other cops. If a possible CI is on parole or probation, the handling officer must give approval from the CI's parole or probation officer before the CI can work with the police. A juvenile CI must have parental permission.

There are many reasons someone might become a CI. He or she may have been arrested and looking for a way to get out from under that arrest. Usually an agreement with the local prosecutor is necessary for that to happen. Others might want to get associates or criminals in trouble for their own gain. Of course, some do it for the money. Informants are paid for good information or for buying drugs from a dealer.

This active type informant should be viewed with scrutiny. They are turning on their friends and other criminals. If the person will do that, chances are they'll turn on cops just as easily. Cops use these informants, but must be leery of their ultimate motives.

A cop develops an informant's reliability by documenting performance "on the job" and by successes posted in the win column. This question must always be asked—Has the information the informant given resulted in arrests or seizures of contraband like narcotics?

It takes money to build a good informant, sometimes a lot of money.

This money must be accounted for and detailed. It's not the cop or department's money used; it's the city's cash or in some cases federal money.

Receiving cash payments, escaping an arrest charge, and focusing on personal vendettas are strong motivators and must be assessed. These motives are considered to be exculpatory, or issues that might be helpful to the criminal defendant who is arrested based on the word or actions of the informant. In 1963 and 1973 the U.S. Supreme Court heard cases referred to as "Brady" and "Giglio" and then mandated that this type evidence must be released so a jury could use it to assess an informant's credibility, especially an informant who might be the only witness accusing the person being tried.

Taylor opened the first file. The rubber band securing the folder's flap disintegrated when he pulled on it to loosen its grip on the folder. A hairy black spider escaped from the dark contents of the folder and quickly skittered across the conference table.

Getting into some dark dealings here, crossed Taylor's mind.

He stacked the contents of each folder on the table. There was no understandable file organization evident. He noticed a small sheet of paper peering from a corner of the jumbled mass of paper and pulled it out.

"Confidential Monies Expenditures" was block printed on the top of the slip. It appeared to be a quarter of one sheet of copy paper. Taylor assumed the unit clerk must have typed four chits on a page and simply cut the page into quarters.

Taylor decided to focus on these slips as he waded into the masses of paper spread before him. Ten minutes later two stacks of fifty slips each were piled in towers. Next he identified the slips with Rob Stanley's signature as the officer reporting. Rob was obviously productive and accounted for nearly half the slips in each tower.

Taylor opened his backpack and pulled out the civil complaint filed by Roscoe's attorney. Using a yellow tablet, he wrote the dates of Otto's murder, Angel's interviews conducted by Syd Shepard, the grand jury meetings, and the week the criminal trial took place. Then he went back to Rob's slips and separated them into four stacks, corresponding to the dates identified on the tablet.

Jude reappeared in his office about twenty minutes after Taylor had assembled Rob Stanley's money expenditure slips.

"What you find?" Jude asked.

"Well, let's take a look. Maybe you can tell me what these mean," Taylor suggested as he picked up one slip referencing Otto's murder date.

"The day before Otto was murdered, Rob's slip indicates he gave Angel three hundred dollars for a controlled buy. What's that mean to you? You signed as supervisory approving."

Jude picked up the slip and stared at it longer than the information warranted. "Guess he gave her money to make a narcotics buy," Jude surmised.

"Any way to know what type buy or who was the target? Whether she succeeded making the buy?"

"Not from just this one slip. Unfortunately we didn't keep good records back then. You'd have to ask Rob directly. All I know was Angel was pretty good at making buys." He shook his head at the sloppiness of the department's old record keeping system.

"But this was just a day before Otto was murdered. Shouldn't this have been part of the homicide investigation?"

"Probably, if Syd knew about it. It was Rob's responsibility to tell him about anything possibly connected to the case. Rob never indicated Otto was the focus of his investigation or that Angel was part of it. He said he was trying to get her to score a buy from Roscoe, not Otto."

Taylor picked up another slip. "Here's a slip showing Rob gave Angel five hundred the day after she was interviewed by Syd about the homicide. There's nothing saying why. Just the word "Investigation" was entered on the chit. What does that mean, Jude?"

"Don't know," Jude admitted as he realized the direction Taylor was heading. His voice became soft and hesitant.

"These last two chits are each for fifteen hundred dollars. One is dated the same day of Angel's appearance before the grand jury and the other was paid the day of her testimony at Roscoe's criminal trial. Why would you guys be paying her at that point?"

Jude dropped into the chair at the conference table after emitting a noticeable sigh.

"You know, Taylor, I just signed all these slips as they came before me. It was a perfunctory job I was assigned. I'm not sure an audit was ever done on the department's use of the confidential money fund. We always had enough to pay out and kept bringing in more to replenish the supply every time we made a dealer bust. No one cared as long as cash was available to use when a CI was needed. I assumed Rob was being honest with me about Angel. I know he picked her up and transported her to those interviews and testimonies. I figured he was doing that to make sure she showed up. Or, maybe he was trying to be nice to Angel by giving her money for her time and the shit she endured on the stand. Roscoe's attorney really tried to rip her apart."

As Jude's explanation rolled on, Taylor was becoming increasingly pissed. He kept his anger in check and didn't express his growing concern. Maybe it was time to offer the chief a little basic education in exculpatory evidence.

"Can you see how this looks?"

"What? So Rob gave his snitch a little money to help her out. What's the big deal?"

"Some might see it as payment for her testimony, a story that Rob maybe wanted told. Maybe it was the truth, but maybe not."

Jude was shaking his head, "No. That's not what happened."

"You sure?"

"Well, no, but Rob had nothing to gain."

"Do you think documentation like this might have caused someone, like the jury, to question Angel's credibility? Perhaps question her reason for giving the testimony she did?"

"Wha'd she have to gain?"

"Maybe she knew Roscoe didn't do the crime."

"Why would she do that? What's in it for her?"

"Maybe Rob forced it. Maybe her story of being with Otto wasn't the truth."

"You don't know that, Taylor!"

"I don't, but neither do you. This is something that should have been shared with the prosecutor. We're obligated by law to give over anything and everything that's potentially exculpatory or could relate to a witness's testimony. You know that, Jude, this is basic cop work."

"But we don't know that's what happened!"

"I guess we'll have to talk with Rob then. We sure can't talk to Angel."

* * *

"Rob, Jude here," Chief Richards announced when he finally got Rob Stanley on the phone. "I'm here with a retired cop from out

West who's been hired by the insurance pool on that Roscoe case. You heard he was released from prison?"

Taylor relented and allowed Chief Richards to make the call to Rob Stanley who had since retired and was living someplace in Mississippi.

"Heard that. Scumbag asshole. Got what was coming to him. Bunch of drug dealers. Who gives a shit if he wacked Otto or not. Figured he got away with a lot more during his years peddling that shit, Jude. You know his kind. We struck terror in those guys when we was rollin'. Remember those good times? Yeah, really good times. Kicking ass and making the good town of Livingston a little safer. What's the West Coast cop want with me?"

"His name is Taylor Sterling. He's here with me now. We're on speaker, Rob."

"Okay, Taylor, what ya want?"

"Where are you in Mississippi?" Taylor asked. He felt a few rounds of bantering would ease the remainder of the call.

"Bay St. Louis. Know the place?"

"Sure, just east of Slidell. I've done work in Slidell, Metairie, and a couple cases in Gulfport. You're right next to Gulfport, aren't you, Rob?"

"Yep. Got more casinos than I can spend my money at. Not that my chicken shit pension from Indiana helps that much."

"What brought you down there? Long way and culturally distant from Livingston."

"Got that right. But my wife has kinfolk down here. Lot warmer here, too. Got a job at the Hollywood Casino. Great food. Getting real good at suckin' on dem' crawfish. Ever do that, Taylor?"

"Have, and seemed to me it was too much work for a little taste. Had to buy a damn bucket of them to be satisfied."

"Okay, okay, this ain't a Chamber of Commerce call. What you got up there?"

"Want to talk about you and Angel Martinez," Taylor began.

"You know she died, Rob?" Jude piped in.

"Heard that. She lived longer than most addicts. She was a damn fine snitch, that girl."

"Want to talk about the time around the Otto murder, Rob," Taylor said.

"What about?"

"Well, Livingston may be on the tab for Roscoe's wrongful conviction."

"What's that got to do with me? I'm retired and a long way from Indiana."

"You know about punitive damages, don't you, Ray?"

In civil lawsuits there are several ways a plaintiff can be awarded money. The most common judgments and awards are for actual damages, real losses such as being unable to work or for costs associated with the case. There can be damages awarded for pain and suffering. Being locked up for years in prison can easily be shown to involve pain and suffering.

Punitive damages are rarely awarded. They are only granted when the jury and court feel punishment is appropriate regarding losses suffered by the plaintiff. If punitive damages are awarded against a cop, the department as employer isn't obligated to cover, or indemnify, the officer. The payment comes out of the cop's own pocket.

"After Otto was blasted away, Angel reached out to you."

"Yep, I was her handler and kind of a friend."

"You send her into Otto's to make a buy?"

There was a pause on Rob's end, "Nope. I gave her a few hundred to make a buy from Roscoe. Never found out why she was at Otto's that night."

"You ever ask her?" Taylor asked.

"None of my business. I was after Roscoe, not Otto."

"Whatever happened to the original three hundred you gave her?"

Another pause. "Don't know. With all she seen when Otto was gettin' his inners blown out, I figured not to press her. Then I plum forgot about it."

"How about the other thirty-five hundred you gave her?"

"Don't know what you're gettin' at Mr. West Coast fellow," Rob said, letting "West Coast fellow" drag out in his response.

"Well, here's my problem. And, I'm not accusing you of anything. Just hoping you can educate me about what was going on, Rob. Angel was a witness to a murder and she was the only one who fingered Roscoe for the crime. Now you gave her money. What for?" Taylor knew a direct approach wasn't the best one, but conducting an interview over the phone wasn't ideal.

"What's your problem, Mr. West Coast?"

"Looks bad. May not be, but sure has the appearance of evil. Kind of like you're paying her for being an eyewitness."

The long pause on the other end of the line had Taylor wondering if Rob had hung up. Jude stared at Taylor, probably questioning his blunt tactics. Taylor waited. Both heard the phone click after Rob uttered a shallow, "Fuck you, asshole!"

* * *

Taylor knew a talk with the local district attorney was next on the agenda. He also knew the county prosecutor would be reeling from Roscoe's conviction reversal. Prosecutors pride themselves on doing the right thing, but still strive for convictions. They don't like to be second-guessed. Most don't like to be shown to be wrong, even when it wasn't their fault.

"Mr. Sterling, Jude told me you wanted to talk with me about the Roscoe matter," Prudy Upton said as Taylor was ushered into his office.

"Don't like being overturned, of course, but a whole lot of stuff surfaced that proved the wrong person was convicted. Feel bad, but my office didn't know any of the new information. What can I do for you?"

"Want to know what your office thought about Angel Martinez and her eyewitness account."

The prosecutor leaned back in his chair and looked directly at Taylor. He continued to stare as Taylor realized he was probably mulling over how to answer the question. Taylor waited. He was getting used to waiting.

"Angel was a street savvy woman. She knew Roscoe from past drug dealings. She bought stuff regularly from him. She knew Otto, too. Did I like her? No. No one around here liked Angel, but the grand jury and criminal trial panelists apparently did, or maybe reluctantly accepted her version. She was pressed by me and Roscoe's attorney. I can be pretty aggressive. I tried this case myself. We don't have many, if any, murders in my county. That woman didn't budge in her testimony, ever!"

"What concerns did you have?"

"I was always concerned about Roscoe taking off his mask. I wondered about Angel's relationship with Rob, that Livingston narcotics cop. It was a gut feeling I had at the time. There was something wrong, but I couldn't put my finger on it so I couldn't bring it out in pretrial or trial."

"Did you interview the narc cop or call him as a witness?"

Taylor asked. He knew Rob Stanley wasn't on the witness roster or listed in the trial transcript, but he wanted to see what the prosecutor had to say.

Upton leaned back and folded his arms across his chest. He sat staring blankly at the wall for what seemed like five minutes. Taylor could almost hear the gears in his mind cranking. Finally, the prosecutor shook his head.

"What information did you give Roscoe's attorney about Angel, Mr. Upton?"

"He was like all defense attorneys. He asked for everything, but was weak on specifics. He did ask if she was an informant. I gave him an affidavit from Jude indicating she was."

"Did he follow up on that?"

"Sure. He asked what else we had. He asked if she was working the case when Otto was killed. We told him no. That's the information I had gotten from Jude and I had no reason to disbelieve him."

"Did you give the defense lawyer any other paper regarding her work as an informant?" Taylor inquired.

"You know, we went to the judge on that. The judge said if there was no information indicating she was actively working as an informant on that particular night, it would not be discoverable. It wasn't Brady material. That was immaterial, as I asserted."

"Were you ever told that Rob Stanley had given Angel nearly $3,800?"

"Is that a hypothetical?"

"No. It's documented in the police informant chits. Three hundred was handed over the day before Otto's murder, five big ones when she was formally interviewed, fifteen hundred the day the grand jury convened, and another fifteen hundred on the day she testified at trial," Taylor recounted. "Would you have considered that as exculpatory and an issue affecting Angel's credibility?"

Purdy Upton jerked forward and slammed both palms down hard on the desktop. "You're damn right I would have! You can't hide that kind of shit!"

"What do you think it would have done to her testimony?"

"How the hell should I know? The jury should have known about it as a point of law. Did Jude know?"

"I don't know. I haven't pressed him yet. He knows what I found in the old files though."

"This shit frightens me, Mr. Taylor. Cops keep thinking they can beat the system. I know it happens and I try to uncover it, but they band together in shades of blue. Cops are open when they need my help or help from my office, but they cluster together when they don't. It's a constant challenge," he said angrily. "I expected better of Jude, though. I hope he didn't know about it at the time. Did he?"

"I really don't know at this point," Taylor answered. He knew he was skirting the issue. Jude's signature was definitely on Rob's expense chits. There were three and only three possibilities—Jude knew about it, didn't bother to ask about the money paid, or was just lazy and didn't care.

* * *

It was a 180-mile trip to Michigan City from Livingston. Taylor had cleared the trip to the Indiana State Prison with Austin Bean at the insurance pool.

"What you figure to find up there, Taylor?"

"Don't really know, Austin. But the way this case is developing, the pool may be out major money. What's necessary might involve finding dirt on Roscoe. That might, at least, reduce your cost. Some guys take prison in stride. Others have a terrible time. Get raped or they have the shit beaten out of them. Spend time in solitary. Those things can influence a jury. The jurors start reliving the plaintiff's pain."

Taylor didn't have contacts at the prison. For that matter, he really didn't know many people involved in corrections work. In the old days he'd kept an active Rolodex with a Ferris wheel of names and numbers. These days newbie cops had no idea what the hell a Rolodex was. Taylor remembered one young officer asking if it was some kind of high-end watch. When he was on the job as deputy chief, it was easy for Taylor to reach out to just about anybody. Taylor hadn't thought about becoming a consultant after retiring or he would have developed one hellava contact file on his computer using info from that old Rolodex.

What Syd Shepard said about attending a seminar in Indiana suddenly jogged Taylor's memory. He remembered a training outfit based in Indianapolis that offered police and fire department seminars. Taylor had attended a couple when they took their show on the road to Vegas.

What was the name of that company? Ah, Public Agency Training!

"Jim Alsup," the voice said in response to Taylor's call.

"You with the Public Agency Training Council?"

"You bet. What can I do for you? Say, what's your name?"

"Taylor Sterling. I'm a consultant working for the Indiana Muni Insurance Pool. Took some of your seminars eons ago when I was on the job, Mr. Alsup."

"It's Jim. Where were you on the job?"

"LAPD."

That started a few minutes of talking shop as the two "new-found old buddies" discussed common friends they knew in cop shops around the country. Jim Alsup didn't have contacts at the state prison, but he knew someone who did. That's the way it always seemed to go, Taylor thought. When you needed to find a source, a strange but productive web was spun to get the information needed. It was the way of cops everywhere.

* * *

Indiana is a state without much interesting scenery along its highways. Flat. This time of year even the crops were down and brown. The sky was grey. It was a monotonous three hours on the road as Taylor headed to the prison.

Once there he found the place typically nondescript. Its brick façade was imposing and security fences ringed the facility with ten guard gun towers standing sentry at strategic points. Taylor didn't like prisons. They were demoralizing places. He had never worked jail assignments. Never wanted to. Maximum security prisons, like this one, were even more depressing. Inmates were incarcerated for long sentences, sometimes for life. There was little freedom of movement like you would find at the country club federal spas where white-collar criminal executives spent their time. "Extended stay in a federally gated community" some called them. The Indiana state pen certainly wasn't one of those.

"Taylor, sorry the warden is on vacation," a middle-aged guy said as Taylor was ushered through the outer security of the administrative side of the prison. "Mike Sullivan," he introduced extending his hand.

A nondescript tie hung loosely at Sullivan's neck where the

upper button of a striped shirt released a tight fit around the man's stocky neck. No starch held the shirt rigid and it matched his wrinkled pair of pants. Something hidden under a roll of fat kept his trousers in place.

Next to Sullivan stood a giant of a man. The African-American guard looked close to seven feet tall. His hands were twice the size of Taylor's and closely resembled a third baseman's mitt. The guy had broad shoulders and a massive chest, narrowing down to a sharp V at his waist. His grey uniform shirt must have been tailored to accommodate his massive biceps. Dark uniform pants strained to control defined thighs and quads. The guard's head was shaved but his face appeared soft in contrast to the rest of his lean, cut body. He had a smile that allowed glistening white teeth to contrast with his dark complexion.

"J.T. Smith, Mr. Sterling," the guard announced in a deep rumble.

"Shit, how tall are you?"

His smile spread across his face. "Six twelve, Mr. Sterling."

Taylor laughed.

"We've pulled together most of the relevant files on Roscoe Blunt's eight years here," Sullivan offered as the three sat down at the big conference table in the warden's office. "Really nothing stands out, Taylor. He was just here. No recorded incidents. No disciplinary issues. Didn't even spend time in the infirmary. Rarely had visitors. Couple of times his brother, or at least that's what he told us, came up here."

"Ah gots to echo that. Almost cain't recall the guy," J.T. added. "Ah knows he was here, but stayed out of anything that might make him different. Being on the row, he didn't have much contact with others. Tough for any of the gangs to have an impact. Kind of like that character in the movie, *Chicago*. Like that guy sang dat song Cellophane Man. Here, but not here," J.T. laughed at his recollection.

So far a real strike out...no dirt on Roscoe.

"How's it like on the row?" Taylor asked referring to the conditions on death row.

"Not like home, man," J.T. said. "Confined and little contact. Limit them guys to just two hours outside and then it's in a segregated yard."

Before he left, J.T. took Taylor on a tour of the prison. They spent more time on death row than Taylor wanted. Maybe ten minutes. Those in the cells were there for the rest of their lives. They didn't count the minutes.

* * *

The southeast corner of Balboa Park was hidden in darkness. It was a constant ongoing battle for Parks and Recreation to replace security lamps. The people who frequented this part of the park liked the anonymity the cloak of darkness provided. They weren't playing and they weren't recreating. These characters were in the drug business of one sort or another. They were criminals who needed the protection of darkness.

"Who da fuck you be, ol' man?" the young black demanded as he approached an unknown figure in his self proclaimed distribution area. The young black wore regulation 'gangsta' clothing—jeans cinched tight under buttocks that allowed a view of dirty boxer shorts that brazenly covered the guy's flat ass. His jean bottoms flopped over bright yellow Timberland boots, unlaced and flayed open. A black T-shirt proclaiming a deadhead figure draped over the loose elastic of the boxer shorts. The gangsta black had a large silver chain dangling around his neck culminating in a heavy cross glittering with stones.

"Roscoe, it is. This used to be my spot."

"Ain't no mo'. It's mine! Hear bouts you. Ancient history, though. You kilt some dealer down south, huh? How comes you ain't in Michigan City?"

"Let out," Roscoe explained as he noticed a large, imposing figure materialize from the shadows to stand behind the black kid he was talking with. He saw the metallic glint of a handgun tucked in the large figure's waistband.

"Why ya here?"

"Just visiting. Trying to see if any of my old friends are still around."

"Ah figure most are dead or in the slammer, ol' man," the young black said almost in an apologetic manner.

Roscoe had removed his hands from his pockets when he initially approached the young black. He kept them at his side with the palms facing outward. He purposefully didn't want trouble. Roscoe knew he didn't need to be dealing. His attorney told him a bundle of money was waiting for him once he sued the state. All he had to do was stay out of trouble. The attorney even loaned him money for living expenses. Not enough to live the way he wanted to live, but it was okay until the big money rolled in.

A rustling sound filled the night and Roscoe saw steady movement approaching the trio. A dark clothed figure ran at Roscoe and fired four shots directly into his chest without saying a word. The gunman turned and retreated into the darkness. The hulk standing next to the black drug dealer pulled the semi-automatic from his waistband and unloaded the entire magazine at the retreating figure. The unknown assailant stumbled and his face burrowed into the grass, still damp from the evening dew. Hulk and his boss stared at each other for a moment, then walked over and picked up the gun next to the sprawled figure on the ground. Without a word, they disappeared into the night.

* * *

"Taylor here," Taylor answered as his cell phone tweeted. He was just finishing his second cup of coffee and the remains of microwaved, water infused instant eggs served for breakfast at the Hampton Inn. Even with cheese and a liberal sprinkling of Tabasco, the eggs were barely passable.

"Morning, guy. How was prison?" Jude asked.

"Depressing. What's up?"

"IMPD found Roscoe dead."

Taylor set down his cup slowly. "Tell me the rest of the story, Jude."

"Roscoe was found in Balboa Park around three this morning. Police dispatch got a 911 call about shots fired in the park from an anonymous caller. The uniforms found Roscoe with four bullet holes in his chest. They followed the marks in the wet grass into a clump of bushes and found a second body with a bunch of bullet holes in his back. Not one gun was found. When the homicide detectives discovered the first body belonged to Roscoe Blunt, the older one remembered the Livingston murder and dropped a call to the PD.

"Guess they figured we would be happy knowing our civil suit had been settled out of court," Jude offered a laugh at his dark joke.

"Who shot him?"

"A small time drug dealer who used to work out of Livingston. We thought the guy was still in the joint or dead. Hadn't seen him in a couple of years."

"What you think happened? Was Roscoe trying to get back in the business and pissed off the new organization?"

"Could be. But that'd be pretty stupid with his payday coming soon don't you think, Taylor?"

"Pretty much. But if crims weren't stupid, we'd probably have a hard time catching them. What they find on the other one?"

"ID. Five hundred dollars. Western Union receipt. And a cell phone. Bagged his hands to see if he fired anything. But, finding no gun is strange."

"IMPD let us take a look at what they found, Jude?"

"Guess so. We're on good terms with them ever since they went back to being on their own. You know they were merged with the sheriff's department a ways back. Didn't work out. Now they're back like before. I know a couple people up there."

Two hours later Jude and Taylor were sitting at a small conference table in the Major Crimes Section of IMPD. Two detectives shared the table.

"Nope, no idea what happened out there, other than two dead. Won't know how many guns were used, but we didn't find any," one weary detective admitted.

"Any evidence of how many perps were there?" Taylor asked.

The detective laughed. "Not after the uniformed cops got there. Looked like they were having a crime scene social when we finally got to Balboa. Standing around laughing, smoking, and littering the ground with Dunkin' Donut coffee cups. Shit, they had no idea what to do inside a crime scene. Gotta do something about that."

"What about the Western Union receipt?" Jude asked.

"Apparently Justin Wakefield, the other dead guy, got the five hundred yesterday. No, wait a minute, it was the day before yesterday. Days seem to run together on these homicides. You know what I mean?"

Both Jude and Taylor nodded.

"It'll be a couple of days 'til we can get the particulars from Western Union. Told them it was a homicide. They didn't give a shit," the detective snorted.

"How about the phone?" Taylor asked.

The detective opened his notebook and flipped through a few pages. "No texts of any sort. Mostly local calls. But there were several in the last few days from a strange area code 228. Google says it's in Mississippi. Any idea what that might mean?"

Taylor and Jude casually gave each other a glance. Taylor knew the significance of the information, but waited to give Jude the lead. They both knew Rob Stanley would be found at the end of that phone line.

"I might. Let me get back to my shop and do some checking. Call you this afternoon, okay?" Jude replied.

"What you thinking, Jude?" Taylor asked as the two drove south to Livingston.

"Same as you. But I want to check a couple things first, Taylor."

Back in Jude's office Taylor was handed one of the narcotics files they had retrieved from the basement. Jude dove into the second one.

"Nothing in mine listing Justin Wakefield. How about that other one?"

Taylor shook his head. Once again the two ventured down to the basement and invaded the spiders' playground. Three files later, Jude excitedly announced, "Got it here, Taylor! Justin was one of Rob's snitches."

"How you goin' handle it, Jude?"

"Going to tell Indie what I suspect. Points to Rob, doesn't it?"

"Yep. I think for your own protection you should reach out to the local FBI. At least drop it in their lap. You got multi-state issues going on and a wire transfer that might figure into a murder. You talk with your city attorney and I'll brief Austin Bean back at the pool. Unless Roscoe had family waiting to collect, you're probably off the hook."

Jude stopped and looked pensively at Taylor. "Why do you think Rob, a cop and a good cop at that, would get involved in shit like this?"

"Only thing I can figure is he thought about punitive damages. Those would come out of his pocket."

"Could he be faced with a potential criminal charge by withholding the Angel information?"

Taylor thought long and hard about that. "I doubt it. Statute of limitations would have probably run for all possible crimes other than, maybe, official misconduct. That crime usually has a longer tail. Rob never testified, so there'd be no perjury or lying under oath. I think it was a long shot that he'd be hit with punitive damages anyway. That payment would have decimated his retirement, even living in Mississippi."

"Well, Rob might have traded his casino retirement for one at a federal gated community," Jude countered without cracking a smile.

No cop likes to envision another cop in shit like this, Taylor thought. *Even bad ones! Prison is one very inhospitable place for cops.*

Taylor suddenly remembered his promise to John and Mary Beth Smith at the paper.

"Say, Jude, can you do me a favor?" Jude looked at Taylor quizzically, but nodded.

"I promised the Smiths who publish your local weekly that

I'd keep them in the loop with any developments that weren't confidential. Could you contact them and share what you can? Apologize to them for my forgetfulness for not stopping by for the thumb drive they promised me."

"You got it. It'll give me a good excuse to keep up my contact with the Smiths. And say, Taylor, thanks for your help. You piqued some old warts, but you treated me fair. I appreciate that."

Demonstration, Rush or Lust?

Case File: Rogue Valley State College
Allegation: Unreasonable use of force
Agency: College Campus Police Department
Accused Employee: Various

He figured he was probably a junkie at best. Well, maybe a full-blown addict. He loved the rush. He found sex after a particularly intense encounter to be amazing, yet he wondered if he was getting too old for this stuff.

Oliver Pines was enjoying his usual cup of coffee, a double espresso skinny latte, at his favorite spot in Cedar City. The place was typical of most Oregon independent coffee shops. Well-worn couches and chairs scattered throughout the spacious room with the occasional green plant bringing life to small tables and corners. The aroma of roasting coffee was always in the air, even though hours may have passed since the last firing. The walls of the small bistro were covered with announcements for poetry readings, open mic sessions, and one traveling musical group or another. It was difficult for the shop staff to keep the walls current.

Oliver was fifty-eight years old. He liked being at this point in his life. Oliver worked his mountain bike on his free days, riding the numerous trails in the forest preserves lacing the low mountains circling Cedar City. He could scrape by on the salary paid by his adjunct professor's position at the local community college and his part-time job at the local Best Buy. Oliver was a computer whiz and picked up a couple hundred bucks more each month fixing seniors' machines at Mountainside, an independent living complex for oldies.

This day he brought a copy of yesterday's *New York Times* with him and was devouring an article about the numerous Occupy-inspired sit-ins around the country. The closest demonstration to Cedar City was happening in Portland. He thought about going to participate, but saw it was being held in the park smack in the center of town. Even for liberal minded Oliver, most people in downtown Portland were psycho. He doubted he could find any girl in that city who shaved her under arms and legs and didn't smell like stale body odor. Oliver was yearning for another protest of some sort; it didn't matter what the cause. He loved the rush of being with protesters and facing the local cops, wherever the cause might be. This was Oliver's narcotic of choice. It was his incessant addiction.

* * *

Oliver's passion for protesting began back in 1999. He'd been reading about the WTO Conference scheduled in Seattle. He really didn't know anything about the WTO, but began to read blogs that interested him, all on the left of the political sphere. Oliver soon adopted the mantra of radicals who contended the World Trade Organization to be akin to the coming of the anti-Christ. He accepted the premise that the WTO was comprised of only the wealthy whose efforts were designed to continue to enhance their status at the expense of laborers and the poor. Oliver didn't consider himself a member of this last group. He believed his position in life was better than that. Hell, he was an academician and an IT expert!

Oliver was concerned about the reports detailing what the "anarchists" were supposedly planning. These were the guys who dressed in black and usually wore black masks to hide their faces. He was really set off when an article he read in the *Seattle Intelligence* reported the Seattle police had been infiltrating the various groups that were organizing protests against the WTO, including the so-called anarchists. This didn't seem fair to Oliver. He believed government should be reasonable and just. To Oliver, this police action seemed sinister and enabled and validated the protesters' accusations that the police were behaving like Big Brother.

Oliver made a decision that would mark the beginning of his path to his new addiction. He went to Seattle.

He entered the basement meeting room at the Church of Life with some degree of trepidation. The Progressive Labor Party, known as the PLP, was holding an organizational meeting. Oliver didn't think the small crowd looked like a gathering of Marxists or Lenin heads. Most looked just like him. Nobody was screaming or ranting. Maps showing designated protest locations were tacked on the walls with masking tape.

"Yeah, look where they have us penned up! Six blocks from the delegate hotels and eight blocks from the Convention Center complex! Who's going to hear us from that far away?" a young woman cried in exasperation.

Oliver was immediately attracted to this woman. She looked to be the outdoorsy type. Auburn braided hair dropped to her waist. She had a darkened complexion blended from an expanse of freckles covering her face, neck, and arms. The silk tee top she wore hung loosely over jeans that hugged her butt and legs nicely. Oliver could see her breasts were small, but tight nipples piercing the silk peaks of her mountains excited the hell out of him. The woman looked wholesome and healthy and he doubted she would stoop to wearing makeup.

"We need monitors at these locations," an organizer announced pointing to several areas on the map highlighted with a bright yellow marker.

Oliver watched as the young girl raised her hand to volunteer for the monitoring position at section 11C. Oliver quickly offered to staff the same sector. When he did, the young woman glanced at him and smiled. Animated discussions followed about possible dark outcomes resulting from actions the anarchists might take; the group tried to determine how the radicals' agenda could affect their peaceful protest. Anarchists were known to be destructive, often engaging in widespread vandalism. They usually baited the cops into using excessive force.

At the conclusion of the meeting, the group organizer made sure everyone knew the next meeting was set for the following week. He emphasized it was imperative that all attend to receive their final assignments.

"You want to get some coffee?" Oliver asked the young girl who would be his section partner. "My name's Oliver."

"Greta," she said and held out her hand. "Yeah, I got some free time."

Greta recommended a nearby coffee shop. It was housed in a nondescript building, but had a rooftop patio. The breeze coming off Puget Sound was refreshing.

"You done this before, Greta?"

LOU REITER | 163

"I love these protests! For weeks I thrive on the anticipation of it all, and then during the protest I get a real rush. It's difficult to describe. How about you, Oliver?"

"First one for me, I must admit," he responded. "Aren't you worried about the cops? The reports indicate they're expecting trouble this time and are gearing up for battle."

"Cops are full of testosterone. I used to date one. Muscle-bound bonehead, that's all he was! I was at a protest where the cops lobbed in canisters of gas. God…I got so wet and almost had an orgasm."

Greta grabbed Oliver's arm and gently stroked it. "Where you staying? You said you're here from Oregon."

"Motel in Federal Way."

"Shit, that's thirty miles south of here. I live up by UW. But my two roommates are home. Can you give me a ride?"

Greta's apartment was only ten minutes away. She was impressed with Oliver's 5- Series BMW. As Oliver guided the Beemer out of the parking lot, Greta began to fondle his crotch and expertly unleashed his zipper. Her hand encircled his penis and she began to stroke it like she had sensually massaged his arm minutes earlier. Her fingers circled its bulb and then slid down to gently cup his testicles.

"Suck it," Oliver pleaded, barely able to speak.

"I don't do *that* on the first date, silly," Greta playfully announced as she continued to stroke his dick. They reached her apartment way too quickly so Oliver pulled up one building down, bouncing over the curb as he headed to a parking space.

He fumbled like a high school kid as he placed the car in park. Greta started her second act, much to Oliver's delight. Leaving the passenger's seat, she swung her body over him, pressing her back into the steering wheel. God, he hoped the horn wouldn't blare!

Oliver quickly felt bare legs straddling him, realizing the sexy protester had removed her jeans. Her fingers found his erect penis and she guided it into her wet and willing vagina. Her eyes closed as she rode him slowly and rhythmically. Oliver pushed the silk top to her shoulders and sucked her hardened nipples hungrily. Greta picked up her pace and uttered low guttural moans as she reached her *Bolero* crescendo. To Oliver's surprise and dismay, Greta dismounted as quickly as she had assumed the position.

"See you next week! Get a place closer next time," she teased as she opened the door and disappeared into the darkness. She didn't bother to tug on her jeans for the walk to her place. Instead she waved them high over her head like a conqueror's banner.

Oliver booked a room at the Residence Inn on Lake Union the following week. The WTO Conference was slated to begin the next weekend and he sure wasn't going to miss the last protest planning meeting. The PLP protest was scheduled to happen on Friday afternoon outside the designated protest areas and near the Pike's Place Market.

Their protest would be joined by a contingent of union workers from the SEIU, Service Employees International Union. Protest organizers knew their actions would result in a police confrontation since they were massing outside the designated protest zones. This was a necessary choice to generate publicity to emphasize their demands and to showcase the abuses WTO members were inflicting upon organized labor. The fact that Oliver wasn't in a union didn't matter. His aspirations resided in his crotch.

Greta was excited to hear Oliver had booked a room at the Residence Inn and that it had a lake view. She ordered him to leave the curtains and sliding door to the small porch open as the couple stripped and got it on. The thrill of an audience seemed to excite her. Greta was insatiable in her sexual demands, particularly enjoying mutual oral sex. When Oliver's condom supply was exhausted, Greta pulled a French tickler rubber from her purse, then another. This woman knew what she wanted and came prepared.

Oliver didn't want to take his sex mate home, but Greta insisted she couldn't spend the night since she had to go to work early the next morning. Oliver walked her to the front door of her four-unit apartment building. Without a word Greta dropped to her knees, unzipped his pants and performed another round of oral pleasure. Her timing was perfect. She knew exactly when to unlatch before cum filled her mouth. With a disappointed sigh, Oliver ejaculated down the leg of his pants.

* * *

Seattle's city fathers were excited when their city was selected to host the WTO Conference. This would be the first such conference held in an American city. Other world cities had been selected for similar meetings, including the G8 and G20 meetings of governments. Recent history showed that worldwide economic summits were magnets for protesters. To dissuade all but the most fervent protesters, several G8 and G20 meetings were hosted in remote locations. Unfortunately, many protest groups were becoming more violent or infiltrated by more angry groups in subtle ways to instigate aggressive tactics.

Every conceivable alphabet soup intelligence organization, government and private, were monitoring the Internet and using other sources to determine the strategies expected to be implemented by the more violent groups. Seattle would certainly become a focal point for violent protests, if newsgathering sources were to be believed.

Seattle hotels and the City Conference Center were located smack in the middle of the city in the downtown business sector. Seattle's city council and city attorney were busy trying to carve out locations where protesters and the press could have defined influence, but still remain out of range of the WTO members. Repeated calls by protest groups requesting that restrictions be removed fell on deaf ears. The courts steadfastly supported the city's efforts to control possible mayhem.

The Seattle Police Department was the lead police agency designated to handle the WTO Conference. The department was familiar with handling small protests held in the park just north of Pike's Place Market and other gathering places close to the university. Officers on bicycles were assigned to these locations usually knew the protesters by name and could work with them without confrontation. When the PD's tactical unit got involved, it was another matter entirely. The local street people referred to them as the Goon Squad.

The WTO presented the Seattle PD with new problems due to its importance and worldwide stature. The chief of police estimated that he would need 2,000 officers for 24/7 coverage of the conference. The King County Sheriff's Office would handle prisoner transportation and booking. The Seattle PD would be designated as the primary tactical response force; it was beefed up to a unit of nearly 200 strong. Regular patrol and back-up would come from a contingent of Washington State Patrol officers and groups of officers from the myriad of smaller police agencies ringing Seattle. The Emerald City received a heavy influx of federal dollars to help with expanded riot training and new equipment.

Within the police department there was constant conflict. Hardliners insisted the anarchist assembly would turn the city into a war zone and insisted the cops should be proactive and stomp them down. Another group pushed for a more conciliatory approach, similar to what the Seattle department already practiced. Between input from outside police consultants and internal hardliners, the forceful approach was eventually adopted. The state police gladly took a backseat in the operation and indicated its personnel would only become involved if a riot actually erupted, and then it would only allow troopers to be deployed as a team under its own command.

The infighting and overlapping developmental meetings foretold eventual headaches and problems. After the WTO Conference rolled up, the Seattle police chief retired almost immediately.

* * *

Oliver Pines checked into the same Residence Inn on the Thursday night before the planned weekend protest. Along with conference delegates and power hungry groupies, he had to agree to a minimum three-night stay at the hotel for $310 per night. His plastic could handle that, no problem.

After a hearty Friday morning breakfast, Oliver spent time watching several news channels covering the WTO agenda. The day before, two large protest banners had been unfolded. One was hung directly over the northbound tunnel overpass near the Convention Center and Interstate 5. The other banner was suspended from a ten-story downtown office building. The police spokesperson reported that "unknown persons" had apparently accomplished these acts without detection.

The news portrayed what Oliver believed was "all hell breaking loose" on the downtown street opposite Nordstrom's. Windows had been broken and small fires ignited in city trashcans. Media cameras were working overtime to capture images of the dark clothed, masked vandals running through the streets. Riot geared police were shown running after them. It was a circus in the making.

Oliver saw several protesters smacked over their heads with long batons wielded by stern-faced cops. He also saw several officers fire strange looking guns at the protesters. The news reporters referred to them as rubber bullet guns. A couple protesters encouraged the media to film large welts and discolored areas on their flanks and legs. One protester had apparently been hit in the eye with a rubber pellet and media coverage showed him being aided at the scene and then loaded into an ambulance. The media reported 180 people had been arrested, on Thursday alone. It was only the first day of the conference.

Oliver wasn't dissuaded from his planned assembly with the other PLP and union protesters. Of course he was looking forward to seeing Greta again. Their planned protest was scheduled to start at three in the afternoon on the cobbled street adjacent to Pike's Place Market. The street was directly in front of a long covered shopping area near the area reserved for the barrels of brightly colored cut flowers that Seattle residents and tourists rushed to buy every morning.

Oliver was walking down Pike Street and observed a parking lot overflowing with police officers dressed in black riot gear. Plastic guards protected their shins and their upper bodies were shielded by thick outer vests. Black plastic guards covered their elbows and hands, making the mass of cops look like a team of nasty hockey players. Most carried longer than usual batons. Others were holding weird guns and shotguns with large circular magazines. Oliver saw shielded helmets and clear plastic shields lying on the ground near the officers. A large black armored vehicle was parked at the rear of the lot like a sentry.

Shit, these guys were ready for battle!

His assigned group was gathering at the park just north of the string of vendor booths in Pike's Place Market. Greta's auburn hair was glistening in the afternoon sun shining brightly from the west. They smiled when their eyes met.

"Glad you showed up," she welcomed as she enveloped Oliver in a bear hug. "This being your first time, I thought you might chicken out." Greta flashed a broad and promising grin. "But then I figured you were probably more interested in what would come after the protest." She gave Oliver a sharp pat on the ass.

Within thirty minutes, close to three hundred protestors gathered in the park. Organizers began distributing protest signs attached to skinny sticks. They acknowledged these signs were difficult to hold and control, but the organizers didn't want anyone busted by the cops for carrying a "bludgeoning device." They warned the group that cops looked for anything and everything to bust protesters. Most signs screamed about the exploitation of workers, infractions by the rich, and the pitfalls of an abusive government.

"I almost have an orgasm thinking about getting arrested!" Greta exclaimed. "I've been busted at protests twice before. The cops love to do that pat-down. They usually grab a little tit, not that I have much." She looked at Oliver, expecting a comment. He obliged.

"Small, but beautiful."

A few minutes later bullhorns announced the group should begin moving down the cobbled street to the entrance of the Pike's Place Market. The largess of the group immediately clogged the street and stopped all traffic. Oliver was walking next to Greta who kept punching him in the arm. She began chanting "Down with oppression!" He saw her laughing as the words became her torch song.

The group massed where workers at the Market were usually tossing fresh fish with choreographed precision. The group's chanting become louder and drowned out the directions given by the guy commanding the bullhorn. Several protestors suddenly pointed up Pine Street. Oliver turned and saw cops rolling at them like a massive tsunami. They looked like Ninja Turtles in heat, he chuckled to himself. The cops were stationed in two lines across the street and were banging on plastic shields with their batons. It was a rhythmic thumping, almost pagan in nature. On cue, the banging ceased at exactly the same time. It was an imposing show of force.

"This is Lieutenant Simone of the Seattle Police Department. I'm declaring this an unlawful assembly. You have five minutes to disperse; I repeat, five minutes. You must turn north and disperse immediately. If you fail to do so, you are subject to arrest!" It was a sharp command issued with a strong amplification device.

Oliver looked at Greta who shrugged her shoulders and flipped the lieutenant her middle finger.

The lead organizer informed the group they should follow the lieutenant's command. He shouted the TV stations and newspapers had already captured their protest so they made the impact they wanted to make.

"Leave and walk north, but take your time. Walk slowly. Make the most of our protest!" he ordered.

Out of nowhere, Oliver heard a different sound, definitely threatening. It was the deep throaty roar of a diesel engine. Behind the riot cops lumbered the beast…their armored vehicle. As the league of police began slowly moving toward the protesters, one cop lobbed a gas grenade into the group. The can began twirling madly as it emitted the compressed gas. Many in Oliver's group panicked and began running into the vendor booths or down the stairs to reach the lower level. Greta grabbed Oliver's arm and pulled him onto the cobbled street.

The advancing cops and their mighty beast followed directly behind the protesters as the group trudged up the street. The cops kept yelling "Leave! Leave! Leave!" About three miles from Pike's Place Market, the protesting group dwindled to only a hundred diehard members. Directly across from the Labors' Hall, one of the organizers told the hundred to stop and sit on the sidewalk.

"We left," he yelled to the lieutenant who was now sitting on top of the black beast. "We complied with your order. You can't do shit now, cop!"

"Now you're blocking the sidewalk and impeding pedestrian traffic!" the uniformed lieutenant shot back.

Oliver saw they were dealing with close to sixty cops who had formed a U around the group sitting on the ground. To leave, Oliver would have to walk right through the tightly woven cops who were again beating on their shields with their batons.

"You are all under arrest for rioting, unlawful assembly, and blocking the sidewalk," the lieutenant shouted.

It took another thirty minutes for the cops to cuff everybody's hands behind their backs with plastic cord cuffs. Two yellow school buses weaved down the street and stopped near the huddle of cuffed protesters. One by one they were shoved toward the open doors of the buses and told to get on. This was difficult for some who were older and unsteady on their feet, especially with hands tied behind their backs.

Oliver wasn't sure what happened to Greta as he stepped into the bus. He sat down, and then noticed she was following right behind him. She plopped down on top of his legs, striking a playful pose. As the bus began moving, Oliver felt her hands fondling his cock and balls. This was some trick with her wrists bound in cuffs! He guessed his little fuck would get off on S&M. By the time the bus pulled into the parking lot of a large nondescript warehouse, Oliver had come in his pants.

"Get your asses out of those buses," a fat cop ordered. The Ninja cops were gone. The guys now in charge wore brown uniform shirts.

"These are deputy dogs…sheriffs," Greta explained. "They're a bunch of stupid idiots."

The protesters sat on the cold concrete floor of the warehouse for close to six hours.

"Sir," one middle aged woman said. "I've got to go to the bathroom."

"Piss in your panties, girlie! Aren't you the tough union workers?" The fat deputy laughed. "This country is for real Americans, not you commies!"

Oliver saw Greta was chatting with a woman a few years older than she was. The woman had a thick, long head of hair tightly curled. She was wearing black leggings topped with a pastel tunic covering her breasts and falling to a lace overskirt teasing her thighs. She stared at Oliver as Greta was talking with her.

"Cindy is coming with us when we get out of here," Greta informed Oliver.

"But, who knows how long that'll be?"

"They hassle you for a few hours and then issue you a ticket and tell you to find your own way home. That's what happened last time."

Greta, the professional protester, was right. Within an hour the trio found themselves on the street somewhere down by the Seahawks' stadium. They each had been issued a citation for disorderly conduct. Oliver was surprised when a cab stopped for his hail. Another thirty minutes later they were pulling into the parking lot at the Residence Inn. Oliver bought two bottles of wine at the front desk and took them upstairs to his room.

"Look at this view, Cindy!" Greta exclaimed as she opened the drapes and slid open the glass doors. The two went out onto the small porch overlooking Lake Union. Oliver saw Greta put her hand under the lace fringe of Cindy's tunic and fondle her ass. He poured three glasses of wine and joined them.

"I love protests like this one," Greta said wistfully.

"Me, too," Cindy added. "I get turned on by the rhythm of cop batons beating those shields."

"Oliver just gets turned on, period, Cindy," Greta teased. "He's got a big cock and likes to use it." She reached down and stroked Oliver's penis through his already stained pants.

Oliver and Greta were the first to drop their clothes. Oliver fell onto the bed waiting for the women to devour him. Greta began circling his dick with her eager and practiced tongue. Oliver searched for Cindy and found her studying Greta's expertise with a smile. He watched Cindy reach under her tunic and hook her thumbs under the elastic top of her leggings and sensuously glide them to her ankles. She steadied herself on a chair as she pulled each stocking off. With a startling swoop, Cindy pulled her tunic over her head exposing her naked body, excepting her full breasts that were captured in a black lace bra. She had a much fuller figure than Greta, who bordered on being anemic. Oliver's eyes were drawn to the large triangle of dark matted pubic hair nestled invitingly between Cindy's legs. With a wink, she unhooked her bra and allowed her breasts to escape. Greta raised her mouth from Oliver's erection, gave a nod of her head as Cindy opened her mouth for action. The two took turns sucking the proud, thick seven-inch cock as Oliver closed his eyes and rocked to meet the warmth of their tongues.

Something caused Oliver to stir. Maybe it was the urge to pee. Getting up, he realized only one lump shared the bed with him. He went into the bathroom and noticed the towels were still in place. Returning to the bedroom, he saw the wave of hair spilling over the pillow and realized Cindy was his bedmate. Oliver pulled the covers off, exposing her naked body. He kissed her jutting hip and ran his tongue down her thigh. Cindy rolled onto her back and slightly spread her legs in invitation.

Oliver's lips and tongue responded by licking her swollen lips, searching the moist opening of her vagina with a deep circular movement. Cindy's guttural groans accented their sensual conversation without a word being spoken. Suddenly her body became rigid…then three delicate shudders rippled through her torso as she finally relaxed. Oliver kissed his way up to her mouth and deeply penetrated her lips. Her tongue savored the collected moisture on his lips as Oliver's penis invaded her pussy. Oliver began slow rhythmic thrusting but resisted the urge to moan when he finally came inside her. He rested on top of his conquest until he was no longer hard, then rolled onto his back.

Oliver felt the bed move as Cindy left to shower. He got up and refilled his glass with wine and stood on the balcony, naked. A seaplane silently dropped over the roof of the hotel with a rush of air and glided to a landing on the lake. He heard the engine rev to turn and taxi to its mooring berth. He felt a tap on his ass and turned to see Cindy fully dressed and walking toward the door.

"I'll get dressed and drive you home," Oliver offered.

"I'd rather you didn't. Not sure I want you to know where I live."

She opened and door and left without saying another word.

* * *

Remembering his first protest gave Oliver a hard-on until he realized he was in the Cedar City coffee shop. The *Times* was still open to the article about the Occupy movements. His coffee was cold so he got a refill and picked up a local newspaper left behind on a chair.

Oliver's mind wandered as he travelled back to recall his past protest experiences. They were certainly not what he first expected they would be, but he sure wasn't complaining. He thought there had been three or four anti-war protests at the start of Desert Storm, probably in 2003 and '04. The largest demonstration took place on the docks in Oakland. He'd found a young Asian girl to seduce there. He laughed when he thought about the immigration protest at the May Day event in MacArthur Park in LA back in '07. That time he fucked a graduate student from Honduras. She was short and pleasingly plump and sex with her was satisfying. Oliver downright giggled when he thought about the two protest events he attended during the first Obama election. Both were protests at speeches made by Sarah Palin. That was the time he had his first and only sex with a black woman.

Oliver often wondered if he would enjoy similar sexual successes with Tea Party protesters. Nah, never happen. That idea was stamped with a big REJECT.

Yep, Oliver was a junkie and sure loved those civil protests! The women were all sex crazed and responded like nymphos to the taunts and actions of cops. Shit, let the cops handle the fore-play, Oliver would handle the climax.

Oliver began skimming over the local newspaper when a headline caught his attention: LOCAL PROTESTS PLANNED ON COLLEGE TUITION INCREASES. Next week. The protest would be at the Rogue Valley State College campus and was scheduled to occur every week until a tuition resolution was reached. Hmm, this could be interesting. Oliver hadn't participated in protests in Oregon before.

* * *

Rogue Valley State College was a satellite campus for the University of Oregon. It was considered a small college campus with less than 20,000 students, but most students were residential and student-housing facilities were spread throughout the campus. The campus was located in a heavily wooded area in southern Oregon, east of Medford but not quite as far as Upper Klamath Lake and Grants Pass. The campus police force was small with thirty sworn members and twelve additional staff, primarily parking control ticket writers and radio dispatchers.

Law enforcement efforts on school campuses have morphed from simple door shakers and traffic control enforcement to full service policing operations. Academic institutions and their administrations never wanted an armed police presence on campuses, but they couldn't keep crime, violence, and guns off school grounds. Slowly uniformed security guards gave way to unarmed police officers and eventually fully-certified, armed police officers with arrest powers became the peacekeepers. On college campuses, administrators tend to focus on service, rather than enforcement, the exception being parking enforcement that generates tremendous revenue.

Campus police often are pressured not to report crimes such as domestic violence and sexual assault. Administrators don't want to address these concerns with the parents of their young students. Most campus police chiefs insist they run their own departments, but in reality their direction is usually the result of consultation with the college president, dean of students, or provost. On most campuses there usually seems to be a conflict of philosophies between academicians and the campus cops.

Luther Grimes was the police chief for Rogue Valley State College. He had been on the job for nearly five years after retiring as a major with the Medford PD. His uniformed staff was similar to most campus police agencies. About half his officers were young and new to policing; the other half was made up of retired cops or ex-military.

"Luther, what do you have planned for the protest?" Susan Ames, Rogue Valley College president, asked. Susan was an attractive middle-aged woman who was famous for her tailored, no-nonsense suits usually bought at the Fashion Outlet Mall along I-5.

"We're going to take a low profile approach, Sue," Luther responded.

"What does that mean?"

"I'll have Jon meet with the primary protest organizer the day before and develop the liaison necessary. I told my people everybody had to be on duty each day of protest. I've got commitments from the sheriff's office and the Medford PD that they'll respond under Mutual Aid should we need them. I don't expect we'll have any problems. Our students and the local crowd are pretty much laid back."

"But what if there is a problem, chief?" Brett Chambers asked. He held the position of provost and handled legal and disciplinary issues for the college. Brett was the type who found a problem with just about everything. Luther generally found him to be a royal pain in the ass.

"I doubt we'll have any, Brett, but I sent Jon over to the sheriff's office to get their most up-to-date info on demonstration control. He says we're okay."

"You have to double check your people, Luther. You know that!" Brett implored with a silly ass smirk on his face. Luther didn't bother to respond to Brett's last comment.

"Well, I hope things work out as you think they will, Luther. You know I have confidence in you," Sue said. "Jon is another matter, but he's your pick."

A half hour later Luther found Jon Schilling, his second in command, in the small building that housed the police station, parking permit office, and radio dispatch. Along with police business, dispatch handled the college's radio-equipped units including building maintenance and public works.

Jon came to the college from Medford PD like Luther had, but at the time he joined the campus cop force, Jon had a cloud hanging over him. He had been in a "shoving match" with his live-in girlfriend; at least that's what Jon called it. When she didn't prosecute him for whatever reason, the DA dropped the domestic violence case. Medford might have opened an internal investigation over the incident, but Jon left the department for a job working for a logging company. Internal disciplinary action then became a moot point.

Luther knew Jon from his time on the Medford force and brought him to the college originally as an officer. Within a couple years, Jon showed he could accept additional responsibilities so Luther promoted him to lieutenant. Jon was a big guy. A little over six feet tall, but his 280 pounds was increasing every year as his belly expanded to accommodate the extra weight. He was a little slow, but Luther found him to be dependable.

"Not much of a meeting, boss," Jon said as Luther walked into the office shared by the policing supervisors.

"What you learn from the sheriff?"

"They say we need riot batons. You know, those long ass ones. Need riot gear, and shields, too, and the sheriff offered the use of their Bearcat. That big armored black thing. That'd be pretty neat, huh, boss?"

"Fat chance, Jon. Remember, we're campus service aides, not cops! You heard that prissy ass, Brett. No, get serious, what you got going on the protest?"

"I met with some hippy looking dude, let me see here," Jon said as he opened a small book he took from his uniform shirt pocket. "Cecil Parks, that's the hippy's name. He says the protest will start at noon in the quad by the founder's statue. He's looking at maybe a hundred or so to show up. Says he got good coverage in the school rag and the *Central Oregon Crier*, as well as the Medford papers."

"They gonna have monitors to control the crowd?"

"Yeah, and he got the campus Audio/Visual department to set up a speaker mic."

"They gonna have signs?"

"What you mean?"

"You know, protest signs. The kind they tack on sticks."

"Didn't say anything about that, boss."

"What's your plan, Jon?"

The lieutenant fumbled through his little book and reported, "I figure I'll be out there with three other cops. We'll be a show of force, but stay out of it unless something happens. I'll have the rest of our crew, about twenty, stand behind the police station ready for action if needed."

"What if the shit hits the fan, Jon?"

"I don't know, but I don't think that's gonna happen. If it does I'll have the troops form in a skirmish line and advance on the group as a show of force. I think that should scare the shit out of the types they're expecting at this protest. This ain't no WTO, and they're not anarchists!"

Luther thought this plan was good enough for his laid back state college campus. He figured Jon was right in his assessment of what kind of crowd would probably show up to protest.

* * *

Shelly Grant had never been to a protest demonstration before. The last time she set foot on a college campus was when she attended Oregon State. She was a Tri Delt and met her husband at a frat party. She got pregnant in her senior year and never finished her degree. Her husband graduated, however, and now they lived in the Medford 'burbs where her husband was a partner in a four-guy accounting firm. The couple had two kids; Trudy was thirteen and Bud was fourteen. Shelly was an officer in the local Red Cross auxiliary, a fairly loyal member of the Junior League, treasurer of the high school P.T.A., and was the ultimate soccer mom for her daughter's team. Even with all Shelly had going, she felt her life was boring and routine, but was trying to make the most of it. Same friends, same parties, same stories, same everything. The Peggy Lee song "Is That All There Is?" burrowed like an earworm and restlessness and discontent became her constant companions.

Her kids would be going to Rogue Valley State in a couple

years and she suddenly felt the urge to get involved when she heard about the protest. This was something that might really affect her family. It was certainly something that sounded more exciting than her garden club meeting scheduled for the day of the protest. *Garden club, whoopee!* Shelley decided to be there and make her voice heard.

She wondered what one was supposed to wear to a protest. She decided on a pair of pleated plaid blue shorts and a purple cashmere V-neck sweater. Nice match, she thought. Somehow sandals didn't seem right for a protest. Shelly searched in the corner of her closet and found shoes she hadn't worn in years—black cowboy boots imprinted with red roses. She studied herself in the mirror and liked what she saw.

The protest at the campus was to start at noon. Shelly figured the protestors expected to reach the lunch crowd. There were more protesters than she expected would be there. The crowd gathered around the speakers next to a statue of somebody she should have recognized, but didn't. She was getting excited as the crowd surged forward and people began to chant.

No more hikes! No more hikes! More teaching, less managing! More teaching, less managing!

Shelly saw the line of twenty police officers marching in one flank. They were moving kind of funny. One foot moved forward, and then the guys slid their rear foot forward to connect. As they took the sliding step, they banged their long clubs on the ground. Shelly found the choreography almost hypnotic. She was staring at the advancing army so didn't realize canisters were rolling on the ground in front of her. The gas contained in them exploded quickly and enveloped the crowd in a light grey cloud. The fog left her disoriented and confused. *What was going on!* Her eyes burned and her throat constricted. She felt an arm encircle her waist and was rushed in a direction away from the gas and screaming protesters.

"Time to leave. Let's get out of here," a calm voice suggested.

They ran until they were away from the crowd and the pervasive gas. Shelly noticed the arm belonged to a man probably twenty years older than she was. He was nice looking and trim and wore worn jeans, a mountain bike logo T-shirt, and hiking boots. He was carrying a canvas backpack.

Oliver had turned up at the protest early that day and was sitting under a tree watching people arrive and get in position. He ate a granola bar and drank the bottle of Fiji water he'd carried in his backpack. The young woman in the cowboy boots attracted his attention as he scanned the crowd. She was short, trim and fit, owned nicely toned legs, and sported short bobbed blonde hair. She appeared nervous and he surmised this might be her first protest. She seemed transfixed when the campus cops began lobbing the gas canisters. This might bode well for him.

"Slow down and breathe," he told her. "Let the wind work out the gas. Lean over and let me wash your eyes out with water."

Shelly bent at her waist and Oliver poured water into his palm and splashed it over her face. He repeated the sousing three times. As the woman leaned over, Oliver peeked down the front of her V-neck top and was rewarded with a glimpse of a small lace bra spotted with tiny pink bows.

The two retreated three blocks away from the ruckus and entered a small coffee shop featuring an outside garden area. Oliver ordered coffees.

"Would you rather have a latte or something else?"

She said coffee was good and thanked him.

"First time protesting?"

Shelly looked at Oliver and surveyed his face. It was rather attractive and tanned. She guessed he was an outdoorsy guy. This was certainly different than her accountant husband's appearance.

"Yes. I guess I got worried about the college raising tuition. I got two kids who'll be going here soon. It'll cost me, you know."

"How old are your kids?"

Shelly went on to talk about her kids, her community activities, and her life. As she talked, she shared the ennui and discontent she had been feeling. It suddenly occurred to her that she never really encountered anyone she didn't know, or who didn't know her or her husband. It felt good to unleash her pet peeves to a total stranger who actually seemed to listen to her and care.

"I love protests. I get aroused when I get in the thick of them. There's something hypnotic and sensual about the energy of the crowd," Oliver admitted.

He went on to talk about the protests he had participated in over the years. Shelly caught the excitement on his face and the interest in his voice as he related his experiences. She was surprised, but not offended, when he talked about the women he had met during demonstrations. He casually talked about the sex he had enjoyed with them. This man was talking about a life she didn't have…one that seemed exciting…and vastly different.

Shelly had never considered having an affair. Well, not seriously. But she was intrigued by Oliver's accounts. She recognized that she had also become aroused by the excitement and movement of the protest, particularly the cops banging phallic batons, and the sense of doom that fell over her when enveloped by the gas. She didn't know why she followed this stranger to the Rustic Inn on the outskirts of Medford. It seemed like the best, and only, thing to do at the time.

Shelly lay under the sheets and heard Oliver's shallow breathing next to her. The sheets were moist. She reached between her legs and felt silky moisture on her inner thighs. Her hand slid to her breast and she realized her nipples were taunt and firm. A red glow caught her attention. She turned her head and realized the digital clock was calling her. It read 5:15!

"Shit, shit!" Shelly cried as she jumped out of bed. Her foot landed on one of the used condoms Oliver had dropped over the side of the bed. "Shit, shit!"

Oliver shot up. "What the fuck's the matter?"

"My kids! I was supposed to pick them up at 4:30!" Shelly wailed as she heard the muffled sound of the cell phone ringing in her purse.

She reached down and grabbed her shorts. She stopped and dropped to her knees.

"Where are my damn panties?"

Shelly rose and stepped into her shorts and zipped them up. She tried to untangle her crumpled bra, but finally stuffed it into her purse and slipped her sweater over her head. She jammed her feet into her boots and turned, heading for the door of the motel room.

"See you at the protest next week?"

She stopped as she grabbed the doorknob. Shelly thought about the day's events and the excitement she discovered that erased her boredom. She had new mystery in her life and she welcomed it. How alive she felt! How her body tingled with new-found secrets!

"Yes, of course!" she said affirmatively as she opened the door and ran to her car.

Oliver lay on the bed and relived each moment of his sexual encounter with this new woman. His erection returned simply thinking about being with her the next week. He left the bed and jerked the covers up. Shelly's panties fell from the tangled covers. Oliver picked them up and brought them to his face. He could still smell Shelly's essence infused in the lacy garment.

* * *

"Luther, you told me you had this demonstration under control!" Susan Ames admonished her police chief. Luther knew the college president was very upset. Luther had seen the tic that danced on her right cheek before. It appeared whenever she was really pissed.

"I didn't even know we had that gas," Susan cried. "What kind was it?"

"OC, pepper gas. Makes the eyes feel like they're burning. Uncomfortable, but not long lasting and there aren't any long-term problems with it."

Luther didn't want to admit he didn't know his police agency had a stockpile of gas. He certainly hadn't authorized its use. He had taken Jon to the woodshed as Luther's dad had called his many ass-chewings as a kid.

"You may not think it's a problem, but we do! We've got at least ten complaints already," added Brett Chambers. "The phone in the provost's office had been ringing off the hook."

"We've got another protest scheduled next week," Sue continued. "What do you have planned this time? Is this debacle going to bring in a whole new crowd? I expect a detailed plan from you the day after tomorrow. You can get that to me, can't you?"

"Yes, ma'am!" Luther used "ma'am" only when he was riled up and felt out of control. Jon had fucked him this time. It wouldn't happen again!

"Who was in charge?"

"Lieutenant Schilling. I was in a training session. Remember you sent me to that program on cultural diversity, ma'am?"

"Yes, but you know how I feel about that buddy of yours. He's a misogynist."

"Sue, don't go on that trip again. You don't know him like I do. He's okay."

"Well, it seems strange that in the past two years, three female officers left your department apparently without warning. Were you the catalyst?"

"No, ma'am."

"What did the young ladies give as their reason for leaving?"

"They said they got better jobs."

"Did you ask them if your buddy was part of the problem?"

"I couldn't ask them that! You're not allowed to ask that kind of question, I don't think. I'm not just going to come out and ask anybody if Jon was a problem. If he was, they should have said something."

"They're not going to say anything with your attitude. Jon is your man. You will rise or fall on his acts. You willing to accept that condition, Luther?"

"Yes, ma'am" Luther got up to leave. He knew Sue was really agitated and he didn't want this discussion to go any further.

* * *

"Jon, get your ass in here! I don't give a shit that you're on your day off. Get your ass in as soon as you can. We have a shit storm brewing here!"

Luther saw the dispatcher crane her neck to look at him when she heard his uncharacteristic outburst.

When Jon finally made it into the station, it was obvious he had been busy working at home. He was wearing a well-worn pair of oversized grey sweat pants that appeared damp in the crotch area. His state college jersey had rings of sweat around the collar front and back, under the arms, and on the expansive stretch covering a bulging belly.

"Yard work, boss! I should have listened to you. I figured my woman had a house and the kids were about ready to leave, but she's just a bitch like all the others. You know what I mean?"

"Ever think you're the problem, Jon? Every woman I've known you to be with causes you trouble. Maybe you're the problem in the equation. Now, where the fuck did you get that gas?"

"From Simon! That sergeant from the sheriff's office. He gave it to me. It wasn't expired shit, I checked the dates on the canisters."

"Canisters? Hell, how many did you get?"

"A box. I don't know, maybe eight or ten?"

"Thankfully you didn't use them all! That sergeant know a damn thing about demonstration control?"

"Yeah, I think he even went to Seattle for the final debriefing of that WTO operation."

"Well, get him in here first thing tomorrow morning. We got to put together a written plan for next week's protest and Sue wants it pronto."

Demonstrations come in all forms. The United States Constitution and case law protects the public's right to demonstrate and express their grievances with government. However, demonstrations cannot be at the expense of public safety and the rights of others. Many demonstrations do create inconvenience and disruption in a community. The police and government officers have a responsibility to protect the rights of both parties—those who want to demonstrate and the rest of the public.

Demonstrations come in all sizes and shapes. There are public gatherings, political rallies, festivals, rock concerts, and public protests. Most are manageable and are not touched with violence. Then there are the few that progress to the point of rioting. The police must be prepared to handle every type of demonstration or public gathering. Planning for such events is methodical. There are essentially four elements to planning—intelligence, operations, logistics, and personnel

Police look to the intelligence sources to give an indication of what might be encountered during the demonstration. Reviewing past event involvement by an organization can be helpful. Intelligence gathered from the Internet, blogs, tweets, and other social media avenues are valuable sources of information that can foretell what might happen. Also important are reports from undercover operatives and informants. It has always been a slippery slope when police agencies infiltrate groups organizing a protest.

The personnel aspect of demonstration planning involves how many officers might be needed for control purposes. Where can more officers be recruited if needed? Is Mutual Aid something to implement? Mutual Aid is a term for prearranged agreements between law enforcement agencies to help each other when called upon. Which agency or organization will pay for this commitment of officers, many of whom will be on overtime, is also of prime importance.

Logistics refers to equipment. When a police agency brings in support from other agencies, will the Command Center be able to communicate with them? Are their radios compatible? Where do you obtain additional police cars? If mass arrests are necessary, how will the arrests be structured and how will the arrestees be processed and where do you put them? The logistics function must anticipate toilet needs, food and water for the people arrested. What riot tools or weapons will be needed and are the officers trained to use them?

Lastly, operational plans to manage the demonstration must be developed. This is like a football coach's game plan. This department must anticipate the unthinkable. Contingency plans from A to Z should be developed, studied, and filed. This amounts to second-guessing the mob.

Simon Loren was the stereotypical training officer. Tactical boots and starched khakis were topped by a SO logo shirt. Simon wore his Glock in a shoulder holster tight against his body. It was obvious Simon was into pumping iron as his meaty biceps stressed the seams of his short-sleeve shirt. He sported the obligatory buzz cut hair helmet, but wore it with style. Luther knew police training officers tended to be quite impressed with themselves. He allowed Simon to expound on the heavy-duty training programs he had attended and his plethora of analysis reports from the WTO episode a few years back.

Luther, Jon, and Simon worked through the morning and ended with a decent demonstration operations plan. Intelligence checks with local agencies and the restricted police intelligence network didn't show unusual interest by protest groups outside the area. They didn't pick up chatter on blogs or on the websites of anarchist groups. The three figured the college campus police could handle the protest, but this time a squad of sheriff's tactical officers would be deployed on campus. The officers from the SO would be outfitted in full riot gear.

Luther made a point to tell Simon that the Bearcat wasn't to make an appearance on campus grounds. If gas was absolutely needed for crowd control, the SO would deploy it. The SO would station a fully manned prisoner transport bus nearby and that office would handle the processing of arrests. Luther asked Jon to make contact with the protest organizer one last time.

"Boss, got a slight problem," Jon said after he hung up the phone. "Cecil, the guy organizing the protest, says they plan to call for a sit-in this time. Says a bunch of the protestors actually want to be arrested. Want to be arrested? I'll be damned!"

Simon chimed in. "I doubt they'll be using any of them bear claws. You know, those things the tree huggers used in the forest demonstration years ago. 'Member the protest up at Headwaters? Asshole tree huggers put their arms in these contraptions and you had to cut them off. The contraptions, not the arms."

Luther sought confirmation regarding this new twist and then called the college president to cover his ass.

"Sue, I think we're going to be forced to make a few arrests this time. A sit-in is in the works," Luther announced loudly into his cell phone.

"Okay, okay. Got it!"

Luther turned to Simon and Jon. "President says we can make arrests, but we got to do it peacefully. She doesn't want any bad PR coming outta this. Says there will probably be a hundred cameras shooting our mugs. Nowadays everybody has a phone that takes pictures, and video too. We got to be on our best behavior. Got that, Jon? Best behavior."

"Well, you're going to be there this time, aren't you, boss?"

"Suspect I will. The prez would be pissed if I bugged out for another training session again."

* * *

Oliver Pines checked into the Rustic Inn once again on Monday night. The protest wasn't scheduled to start until Tuesday at noon. It was easy for him to get someone to take over his classes at the community college since he was only an adjunct professor. Most of the kids in his IT classes knew more than he did anyway.

Oliver considered gift-wrapping Shelly's panties, but ended

up stuffing them into his backpack instead. His mind and body whirled with excitement and arousal when flashes of sex with Shelly teased his memory. Oliver wondered if this was something a junkie experienced knowing his next high was coming soon.

Shelly Grant spent a miserable week facing conflicting thoughts about her afternoon with Oliver. The conflict was intensified when she attended Sunday services at the Methodist Church with her family. Friday brought Shelly's Junior League meeting and the women were still planning their annual garage sale extravaganza. Looking around the storage room as she packed boxes, Shelly recounted rumors about Leaguers having affairs. The guilty—Sue Anne, Carol, and Terri—seemed to be going on with their lives without complications. About a month before, Terri had confided in Shelly about her on-going affair with the high school assistant principal.

Shelly knew she would be drawn to the next college protest. She couldn't stay away. She carefully planned what she would wear for her next encounter with Oliver. She decided on the cowboy boots she wore last time, jeans, a tank top, and a bulky green state college sweatshirt. She stuffed a fresh tube of KY jelly in an old leather purse she dug out of her closet. She was plenty sore after last week's sexual encounter with Oliver and didn't want that to happen again.

Oliver arrived early Tuesday morning. He found a tree opposite the statue in the college quad and staked it out as his leaning post. He watched as the crowd assembled, noting the same faces gathering in assigned groups. He felt a tug on his backpack and turned to find Shelly who greeted him with a shy smile and a simple, "Hello, there."

"I'm glad you came today," Oliver said. He wanted to give her a hug and reach under her sweatshirt to fondle her breasts, but he knew that was something an adolescent kid would try and it might embarrass her. Instead Oliver reached into his backpack and pulled out the panties she left as a souvenir last week.

"I thought about keeping these, but thought you might need them."

Shelly noticeably blushed as she grabbed the panties and quickly stuffed them into her purse and allowed a nervous giggle. She put her arms around Oliver and pressed against him.

The protest organizers began shouting through the mic provided by the college AV department signaling the crowd to start chanting. Shelly felt a sense of sexual excitement empower her. She noticed a mass of people move to the front of the group and organize into two lines. As if by command, they dropped to the ground across the wide pathway leading to the founder's statue. The protesters locked arms and began chanting, *"Teach, not tax…teach, not tax…"*

Most sitting on the ground appeared to be college students. Three of them, however, were much older. Two men looked to be in their sixties. One woman was well into her seventies and was helped to sit down by a younger man next to her.

"Let's go and sit with them!" Shelly whispered to Oliver.

"No, Shelly. Look!" He pointed to the approaching line of cops. He held her back a few feet behind the seated protesters.

This time the lead officer was easy to spot. He wore silver bars on the collar of his uniform shirt. He stopped two paces from the edge of the seated group.

"My name is Lieutenant Jon Schilling. You are in violation of assembly, I mean unlawful assembly. You are impeding traffic since people can't walk on the sidewalk. You gots to leave immediately or you'll be arrested. You gots five minutes to stand up and walk outta here!"

Jon obviously butchered the normal unlawful assembly pro-
vision to control unruly demonstrations. The protesters looked
at each other. Several of the younger members started to laugh.

"He didn't do that correctly," Oliver told Shelly. "I've been in
enough protests to know how police orders should be given."

Jon stepped forward and yelled, "I warned you!" He suddenly
produced a large bright red canister that he had concealed behind
his thigh. It looked like a small fire extinguisher. Jon marched
down the row of seated protesters and began spraying a thick
chemical agent on each one. Their faces were dripping with the
pepper gas mixture. Some began to cough; some were choking in
distress. A few broke the locked arm resistance stance to wipe at
their faces. Three protesters tried to stand, but could only make
it to their knees.

A young uniformed officer suddenly appeared behind the sil-
ver-barred officer who had just assaulted the seated group. He
carried a strange looking gun in his hand. It looked like something out of a sci-fi movie. The gun had a circular drum hooked
under its center. The officer was standing only ten feet from Oliver and Shelly.

Oliver saw the gun was pointed in Shelly's direction. As the
officer raised it to his shoulder, Oliver knew Shelly was directly in
the line of fire. He dove in front of her, turning his body to shield
her as best he could. Neither heard the sounds of discharge, but
Oliver was struck in the neck by a projectile. The impact was
strong enough to collapse his esophagus and crush his larynx. He
would have gasped, but then a second projectile struck him in
the eye. His eyeball exploded and the projectile continued into
its orbital cavity and shattered the small bones forming his eye
socket.

The facial explosion caused Oliver to recoil and twist away, splaying blood on everybody around him. Shelly was standing directly behind Oliver and the red spatter bled profusely onto her sweatshirt. Two projectiles struck Shelly in her left shoulder in quick succession, breaking apart as they were intended to do. She had been standing a few more feet away from the shooter, but Oliver was right on top of the cop attacker. The forceful impact caused Shelly to spin and crumple to the ground.

Simon saw a commotion brewing and realized gas had been deployed. When he heard the screaming protesters and saw the crowd run in every conceivable direction, he ordered his officers to deploy directly to the quad.

Several pepper-sprayed protesters were stumbling and bumping into each other. They were hesitant to open their burning eyes for fear of introducing more noxious fumes. Some had mucus running from their noses. Each arriving deputy took charge of a protester who'd been affected. They calmed them, localized them, and instructed them to allow the air to clear their eyes.

Luther found himself in the middle of the coughing, choking demonstrators, his cops, and the assisting deputies. He was searching the crowd for Jon. He finally saw him on his knees next to a male whose face was covered in blood.

"What the fuck happened, Jon?"

Jon looked up at Luther with a dazed stare. He was mumbling something that didn't make any sense. Luther saw tears streak down Jon's cheeks. The wail of an ambulance siren broke the tense scene. Luther ordered his officers to clear the area around the fallen bloodied man.

The ambulance crew called the fire department for back up. The fire fighters were certified in Basic Life Support, a fancy term for emergency first aid.

"The ones who were sprayed will be okay and don't need to

be taken in," the ambulance attendant told Luther. "We've got to transport the female who was shot in the shoulder though. She's suffering heavy trauma. She'll probably need an x-ray to make sure nothing's broken. Probably just some internal hemorrhaging going on."

"What about the guy?" Luther asked.

"Need to call the coroner on that one, chief."

* * *

Taylor Sterling was riding a stool at the counter at Tia Sophia's. The small restaurant was just off the square in Old Santa Fe and was only open for breakfast and lunch. It was a favorite meeting place for locals, but tourists kept finding it and spoiling it for long time regulars. Taylor was diving into his platter of huevos rancheros after anointing them with green chili sauce. The green sauce at Tia's was made with local Hatch green chilies roasted south of town. Taylor had watched the roasting process many times since he relocated to Santa Fe after retiring and leaving Los Angeles. The roasters usually were made from old fifty-five gallon drums. The operator would turn the handle of the drum over a propane flame and you could hear the chilies pop as they blackened. If you stood too close, your eyes would burn and tear.

"Taylor, how about moving to one of the booths?" a voice said behind him. The voice belonged to Luke McKinney.

Luke was the guy who introduced Taylor to the career he now called his own—police consulting. Luke worked for the New Mexico State Risk Division and was responsible for getting Taylor his first job in his new field. When Taylor retired from the LAPD, he didn't really know what he would do next. He knew he could never work for a boss and be part of a structured organization again. After a couple months of being lazy, Taylor knew he needed to get off his ass and do something interesting. Luke gave him the opportunity.

"What's up, Luke?" Taylor asked as he settled into a booth, balancing his breakfast platter and a cup of coffee.

Luke opened his companion leather folder embossed with the Seal of New Mexico. "Got a problem I'm not familiar with. Maybe you know something about it. You used to be on the Shoot Review Board in LA, right?"

"I was. So, what's your problem?"

"Got a worker's comp claim from a cop in the Chama area. Says his off-duty gun went off accidentally when he pulled it out of his jeans. Had it stuffed in his waistband, he claims. Swears he didn't have his finger on the trigger. Could that have happened that way?"

"What kind of gun was he carrying, Luke?"

"It was one of those old ones. Most cops carry semi-automatics today. I think he said it was a detective special. That mean anything to you, Taylor?"

"Yeah, had one of those babies myself when I first joined. Smith and Wesson. They were 5-shot .38s. You know if this was an air weight model? That came in aluminum alloy and was real light, but you couldn't hit the side of a barn with the damn thing. It fought you like a sonofabitch every time you fired it. The regular model was a little better. But I still had a bitch of a time qualifying with mine. Some of the guys in my recruit class bought the ones that were hammerless. Didn't hang up on clothing and you couldn't cock the hammer back and fire it in single action mode."

"What do you think about this cop's injury claim?"

"Not much, Luke. First, he's carrying it in an unauthorized and unsafe manner. No holster. Second, it couldn't have discharged the way he said unless it was already cocked. Double action took at least twelve pounds of trigger pull or more. If it was already cocked, a dumb ass way to carry any gun, it would have been about three pounds. You could almost breathe on it and it would go off. Anyway, he tells the story like he's got a lot of explaining to do. Where'd he get shot?"

"Top of his foot. Broke a bunch of bones and will be off for nearly a year until it heals."

"I'd say he was fucking around with it and cranked off a round accidentally. Maybe he was playing quick draw. He a young cop?"

"Yep. Fresh out of the state academy."

"I think you should challenge him on the duty-related status on this one, Luke. Now that I think about it, we fixed that trigger problem at LAPD a couple of years after I joined. Had so many ADs with the old revolvers, we called them 'wheel guns,' that the department modified every one of them. Couldn't cock the hammer back and fire it single action. We had some tragic incidents and killed more than a few by making that dumb mistake. Most of the time it happened when a cop ran up to a car he had been chasing and stuck his head and gun inside. Either the guy hit the gun or the car jerked and the cop cranked off a round he hadn't intended to shoot."

Taylor felt the booth bench jiggle and felt a leg brush against his. Sandy Banks slid into the booth and snuggled close to him. Sandy was Taylor's lady friend, a friendship that came with intimate benefits. She leaned into him and sniffed his neck.

"You're using the Hermes I gave you."

"I feel like a kept man. Does that make me a whore?"

She punched him in the side in response. Sandy was a large-framed woman. She was a successful real estate broker dealing in high-end properties. This day Sandy was wearing jeans, cowboy boots, a purple silk blouse and a leather jacket with bone ornaments on the front and fringe decorating the sleeves. Sandy and Taylor found each other one lucky day and were good friends as well as sexual partners when so stirred. They liked to try new restaurants together, made most local art show openings, and once in a while traveled up the highway to the Santa Fe Opera. Sandy had been a sponsoring donor since her second divorce so getting a prime seat was never a problem. Taylor wasn't into opera and would rather attend a blues festival, but Sandy liked the arias so they traded interests most of the time. Taylor had become a regular visitor at the Annual Santa Fe Folk Art Market. He also had started a modest collection of Western art. There really wasn't much room to exhibit in his small condo, but his art purchases added a splash of color to basic beige walls.

"Not working today?"

"Always working. How else could I afford to keep you, Taylor?"

Luke laughed at that crack.

"Well, you usually don't dress like this for the office, Sandy."

"Going up to just south of Las Vegas today. Looking at a ranch for some California guy. Thought you might like to come along to keep me company. I'll spring for a room at the Plaza Hotel and dinner at the Landmark Grill. You game?"

"As tempting as that is, I got to pass this time, Sandy. Got a conference call coming in from a small college in Oregon. Sorry."

She leaned over, kissed him on the cheek, and grabbed him between his legs. "Your loss, cowboy."

She left as quickly as she had arrived.

* * *

Taylor soon realized there was no easy way to get from Santa Fe to Medford, Oregon. Most flights from Albuquerque required two stops and would take up to fourteen hours total travel time. It was better to fly to Portland, rent a car and make the four-hour drive down I-5 to Medford. He would need a rental car anyway. Taylor loved living in Santa Fe, but it wasn't the most convenient place for a traveling consultant.

He knew it would be too late to arrange a meeting with the college administrators the day he arrived in the Medford area. He decided to check into a hotel in Medford rather than one closer to the college, although the college had recommended a place to stay nearby. It turned out to be a good choice since the Medford PD would become an integral part of his work on this case.

The next morning the college president, Susan Ames, greeted Taylor as he entered her spacious office in the college administration building. Already seated at the long conference table was Brett Chambers, the college provost. The third person introduced was Carlson Smithson, an adjuster from the excess insurance carrier, United Casualty.

Susan Ames was a professional looking woman wearing a rather traditional business suit. She appeared to be trim, fit, and carried herself well. Taylor liked that in a woman. Brett Chambers wore an old cashmere blend sports coat, blue button-down Oxford shirt, and an imported hand-tied red bowtie. Taylor couldn't remember the last time he had seen someone wearing a bowtie. Maybe that old senator from Illinois? Carlson Smithson had on a suede sports coat, grey turtleneck sweater, and faded jeans.

"Mr. Sterling, thanks for coming. I know we're in a place that's hard to reach. You come with glowing recommendations, by the way."

"Thanks to whomever they might have come from."

"Someone at a law firm in Eugene. Apparently you worked with the firm in a matter in their Albuquerque office."

This comment didn't need a response; besides, Taylor had no idea who she was talking about.

"Tell me what occurred and why you need my services."

Susan and Brett gave a detailed account of what had occurred, starting with the genesis of the controversy around the increased tuition, which led to the first protest, and finally covering the last demonstration resulting in the death of Oliver Pines.

"Lieutenant Schilling has been placed on administrative leave with pay. I never liked that man," Brett said with disgust. "He was Chief Grimes' pick. We tried to tell him hiring Schilling was a big mistake."

"Enough, Brett," Susan ordered. "Luther and I have been through all this. The chief acknowledged hiring Jon was a mistake, but felt some responsibility for what happened years ago at Medford PD. Luther, you know, was the supervisor who recommended that Jon be terminated for a fight he had with his girlfriend. It was that or the DA was going to prosecute Jon for domestic violence."

"Madame President, let's get back to the protest case," Taylor urged.

"Susan, please. Our concern is two-fold. First is the reputation of the college, particularly with students, their parents, and our neighbors. The second concerns the degree of liability we might be facing." She turned to the third member at the table.

"We have a lot of potential liability. Fifteen persons made complaints about being sprayed with the OC chemical. Then we have Mrs. Grant who was hit with that damn gun and, of course, we have Mr. Pines," Carlson Smithson reiterated. "My company, you know, carries the college's excess insurance. We're on tap for anything over three million dollars. Now that's total, not for each claim."

"My directions about handling the protests were very specific, Mr. Sterling," Susan offered. "This was supposed to be an extremely low profile police operation. That was the written plan Chief Grimes gave to me before the second protest was scheduled. Things weren't supposed to happen the way they did. I'm not sure where Jon Schilling got that damn gun. The newspaper photos of Mr. Pines were devastating and I've received dozens of calls and e-mails from our supporters and alumni, not to mention those from the Board of Governors."

"Now, who did the investigation of the death?" Taylor asked.

"Medford PD," Brett chimed in. "Luther doesn't like the state police."

"Is it a good department?" Taylor inquired.

"Don't know. We haven't seen the report yet," Susan answered. "The PD says it's not been completed yet. It's only been a week, you know."

"What are you looking for me to provide? You looking for something that would support firing people?"

Brett and Carlson glanced at Susan.

"Mr. Sterling, I want your professional opinion about what occurred. Who's responsible? What do we need to do in the future? And, I guess, where you think the college might be liable? I don't need or want a sugarcoated report. That's part of my concern with the PD doing the investigation. It's Luther's former department and his buddies may whitewash the events. We want you to give us a verbal report before we decide if we need it in writing."

Taylor nodded. "Let me talk with your chief. Is he available?"

"Yes, he's on desk duty at this point. I wanted him to stay out of contact with our campus people. Here are some materials to get you started, Mr. Sterling."

Susan Ames handed him a folder. She had included the written operational plan and several newspaper clippings about the unfortunate event.

* * *

Taylor found the campus police station to be similar to most others he had visited in his career. It was housed in a small building that hadn't changed in decades. The double glass doors opened to a small lobby with a counter commanding most of the room. Behind the counter was the dispatch center. The operator served as both dispatcher and receptionist.

"Can I help you?" the middle-aged woman asked Taylor as he approached the counter.

"Here to see Chief Grimes."

"Send him in, Carol," a voice called from somewhere beyond the dual-purpose desk.

Luther Grimes was a man probably ten years younger than Taylor. He was rather trim and had a full goatee. Unlike Taylor, the chief owned a full head of thick black hair. Four stars blinked on the collar of his uniform shirt. Taylor always found it strange that small department chiefs wore the same number of stars that a chief in a big city would carry.

"Mr. Sterling. The president said to expect you. She bring you in to support firing me?" Luther stuck out his hand and gave Taylor a firm aggressive handshake.

"Really don't know. I gather she's a little concerned that your old department might try to cover your ass. I understand they're doing the investigation."

"Yep, but they'll do a credible job. Better than the state cops would do. Those state guys all have some ulterior motive. Always looking for a job after OSP. Hear you're retired from somewhere in California?"

"LAPD, did twenty."

"Work detectives?"

"Nope, but supervised them now and then."

"What rank you leave with?"

"Deputy Chief."

Luther whistled and gave a serious thumbs up.

"What ya need from me?"

"Kind of a rundown of what occurred, boss."

Luther leaned back in his chair, stroked the growth on his face, and studied the ceiling before replying.

"Trusted the wrong guy, Sterling. Unfortunately he was a friend and he fucked me! Took an easy operation and turned it into my glorious campus cop swan song."

"Who are we talking about?"

"Jon Schilling. Worked with him on the PD years ago. Gave him another chance at playing cop. You probably did that sometime in your twenty, huh?"

Taylor nodded, understanding exactly what Luther meant. More than once early in his time as a supervisor Taylor allowed his emotions to make a personnel decision. More often than not, it was a bad call. He learned his lesson years ago after a warrant service went south. He expected his close friend to do the operation right. Plan it out. Have a written ops plan. Consider contingencies. Follow the book. But Taylor's friend cut corners. Totally slipshod. Three cops were caught in the crossfire and the suspect, a seventy-year-old man pushing a little weed, got his leg torn off with a shotgun blast. Luckily no one was killed. Taylor learned that you give subordinates enough room to work, but you second-guess and make sure you approve every critical op.

"Fuckin' Jon. Turned out he was a moron."

"He around so I can talk with him later?"

"Not sure, Sterling. Say, what's your first name?

"Taylor."

"Not sure, Taylor. Jon took the guy's death bad. Hell, he was even crying at the scene. A cop crying! Really took it hard. I told him to go home and the detectives would talk to him after a couple days. Strange thing, I haven't seen or heard from him since that day. Even his wife don't know where he is. Strange, and not like Jon. Jon's almost like one of them stuffed college mascots you see on the field during a football game. Everybody loves them and wants to give them a hug. Jon's kind of like that."

"Tell me about this 'damn gun' that the president referred to."

"FN 303. I'd never seen one before this incident. It wasn't one of ours."

"I never used one either," Taylor admitted, "but I'm familiar with them. You know it was the one that killed that female student in Boston. Victoria Snelgrove, if I remember correctly. When was that? Oh yeah, it was the year the Red Sox won the World Series. Think it was 2004. That cost Boston around five million bucks. Shot her in the eye. Wasn't authorized by the PD and the guy using it didn't have certification training. Boston ended up shitcanning the rest of the FN 303s in storage saying they were more powerful than the manufacturer had represented. I don't know that for a fact, though."

"Shit! Sounds exactly like what happened here! Sort of déjà vu. God, it's so similar that it's freaky."

An FN 303 is a semi-automatic weapon produced by the Belgium firm, Fabrique Nationale de Herstal. Most have a fifteen-round drum magazine that fires spheres with small fin stabilizers. The original design was developed from paint ball guns. Compressed CO2 gas projects the rounds. The specs order that the operator be trained and certified, and should use extreme caution not to hit the subject in the head or face. The weapon has a futuristic design.

"Tell me what happened, boss."

Luther related the sequence of events, beginning with the first protest. He let on that he got his ass chewed by Susan after the first event; she was pissed he wasn't on the scene. The second protest was adequately planned, he thought. He and Jon had worked up plans with a sergeant from the sheriff's office who seemed to be up on demonstration control tactics.

"Somehow Jon obtained a large canister of pepper gas and sprayed the kids and a couple older people holding a sit-in. Somebody gave one of my younger officers the FN 303. Haven't found out how he got it yet. He's a wreck, too. Between Pines's death and the injury to that woman, it was a rough day. But, you know Taylor, it was just an accident. A tragic one, but an accident."

"Can I talk with this young cop?"

"Sure, but I'll have to call him in. Probably not until tomorrow, Taylor. That okay?"

"Sure. I'm here for a few days. How about that SO guy you mentioned?"

"I'll get that arranged for tomorrow, too."

"Can you call your buds at the Medford PD and get me access to the lead investigator?"

Luther nodded and picked up the phone. The investigator would meet with Taylor at the Medford Police Department in one hour.

* * *

"You Sterling?" the young man asked, coming out of the detectives' section at the Medford station. He fit the image of most young cops. Short-cropped hair, shaved close on the sides. The detective wore a black leather jacket over a black turtleneck sweater. Surprisingly, he was wearing jeans and black cowboy boots. The jacket bulged at the hip to accommodate his firearm.

"Yes, I am," Taylor said.

"Luther says I should show you professional courtesy. Some kind of retired cop from LAPD, huh?" Taylor nodded. "You interested in the college protest investigation? What's your interest? By the way, my name's Dean Justice."

"Appropriate name for a cop, Dean. Taylor, here. College hired me to look at the matter. I do a lot of consulting for insurance companies. Liability, you know. About anything a cop does today ends up with potential liability."

"Seems that way, huh? What you want to see?"

"I'd like to see how your investigation is going up to this point. Maybe ask you a few questions after I take a look at your report."

"Tell you what. Why don't you wait in that open interview room? I'll get the file for you, but it's not finished, you know." Dean left and returned in less than five minutes carrying a dark brown folder, the flap secured with a thick rubber band. "Give me a holler when you want to talk."

Taylor settled into an uncomfortable folding chair and opened the folder. He made notes when he ran into something that aroused his curiosity. He was intrigued with the hospital intake records for Shelly Grant and he copied the unusual things he noted. After his initial review, Taylor found the detective bay, an open area holding ten desks. Dean was seated at one of them.

"Got some questions, Dean. But where's the head first."

When Taylor came back, Dean asked if he wanted coffee. The department's black brew was strong and hot.

"Noticed you didn't talk with Lieutenant Schilling, Dean."

"Haven't been able to find him. Real strange. You know he used to work here. It was before my time though. Heard he got jammed up with his taste in women."

"What do you know about Pines?"

"He was a community college instructor in Cedar City. That's near Bend on the other side of the mountain range."

"That's too far to drive down here just for the day, isn't it?"

"Well, you could, but along with his car keys, we found a motel key in his backpack."

"Find the car?"

"Nope. Figure it's parked on campus. It'll surface when it has about twenty parking tickets littering the windshield. The college makes a pot of money from parking enforcement. I did send a uniformed cop over to the motel. The Rustic Inn."

"What'd he find?"

Dean began to laugh. "Kid comes back and says Pines must have been expecting somebody. Had a bottle of Moet chilling in an ice bucket. Bed covers pulled back real nice, he said. A single long-stemmed rose was on the pillow. I've had mints on some of my hotel pillows, but never a rose. Clerk told my cop that Pines had checked in the night before. Seems he had checked in the previous week, too. Guess he was a regular on the protest scene."

"Find anything else?"

"Pines had a laptop and bottle of water in his backpack. Coroner has those."

"You know anything else about him?"

"We got ahold of his sister. Lives up near Salem. Says she and her brother were the only ones left in their family. Pines never married. She thinks he's been going to protests and demonstrations pretty regularly over the last few years. She says he was getting too liberal minded for her and her husband. Hubby is a major in the National Guard. Been deployed three times to the land of sand and mountains."

"What about this Shelly Grant? The female that was hit with the FN rounds."

"Soccer mom from an upscale golf development on the outskirts of Medford. You know, I actually know her husband. Or at least the CPA firm he's a partner in. They do my taxes."

"Any connection between her and Pines?"

"Nope, don't think so. She says she didn't know him. Just happened to be standing next to him when the young cop blasted away with the FN. She was a little embarrassed when I talked with her at her home, but her teenage kids were beaming. They thought their mom was some kind of hero. Every now and then one of them would yell, 'You go, mom!'"

"By the way, who owns the FN?"

"Sheriff's Department. Seems their tactical unit brought it and a beanbag shotgun with them. Talked with Simon who's their training sergeant and tac leader. He says he doesn't know how the campus cop got hold of it. Same with the large canister of OC. Swears he didn't give it to Jon, that's Lieutenant Schilling."

"Where was Luther when the shit hit the fan?"

"He was back at the command post where the SO unit was assembled. Jon was assigned to be the field commander, the guy in charge of the front line."

"Say, Dean, can you open the door to the coroner's office for me? I'd like to take a look at Pines's property."

* * *

The office of the County Coroner was actually part of the local hospital. It made sense, even if it was unusual.

"Sergeant Justice says you're doing an investigation for the college. Guess it's okay for you to look at this stuff. We've notified Mr. Pines's next of kin, his sister, but she hasn't arrived yet. I'm sorry, but you'll have to examine his belongings here. I need to be with you, you know. Security and all that."

She pointed to a small table about six feet from her desk. Taylor sat down and took out his yellow tablet and a pen as the lady returned with a cardboard banker's box. At one end of the box the name OLIVER PINES and a control number were written in black marker. Taylor opened the top and saw the backpack filled most of the space. A clear plastic bag containing loose change, paper money, a wallet, and car keys with membership tags from Dick's Sporting Goods, CVS, and assorted grocery stores was tucked next to the backpack.

Taylor reached for the backpack and opened it. He removed the laptop and set it aside. A black and grey composition book was also in the pack. It was the type usually seen at colleges or used to record information and journal entries. Taylor opened the book and leafed through it. Oliver Pines was obviously a doodler and strange drawings were penned throughout the book. He took a closer look and saw that the book was divided into sections with bold block capital letters identifying pages. OAKLAND PORT DEMONSTRATION; WTO SEATTLE; MACARTHUR PARK RALLY, all marked with corresponding dates. Under the headings, names of motels or hotels were listed. Taylor wasn't sure what it meant, at least not at the time.

Next he opened the Apple laptop. He liked that since it was the type he used. Taylor saw a file on the desktop labeled DEMON-STRATIONS. He double clicked the icon. It opened a series of folders, all labeled with similar demonstration or protest identifiers. He spotted Rogue Valley and clicked on it. Oliver apparently still used Microsoft Office XP and hadn't upgraded. Taylor also noticed a video file and clicked on it. It loaded quickly and the screen filed with a grainy video. He advanced to the middle of the recorded documentary.

The video showed what appeared to be a room with a bed. Probably a motel room, Taylor surmised. Two naked bodies were positioned on the bed, a man and a woman. The woman was fairly small and thin and the man appeared to be older. Taylor watched enough to see the woman's short bobbed blonde head working the man's erect penis like dunkin' dippy bird on steroids. Obviously the woman was unaware she was starring in an amateur porn flick. *So this was Pines's angle,* Taylor surmised.

Taylor glanced at the woman seated at a computer on the desk in the coroner's office. She was completely absorbed in her work. Taylor rummaged around in one of the pockets of his computer case and found a thumb drive. He inserted it into the laptop's USB port and waited for the icon to appear. Next he backed the computer to the original screen until he found the file folder marked DEMONSTRATIONS. Taylor dragged the folder to his thumb drive's icon and watched the transfer. He saw the download time was estimated to be around five minutes. That wasn't too bad since the file looked like it was close to a gig of data. He'd found video takes up a lot of space. Taylor busied himself flipping pages in the composition book until the download was complete.

"Ma'am, thank you very much," Taylor said as he finished

putting the materials back into the banker's box and closed the lid. "I'll let Sergeant Justice know how helpful you've been."

* * *

The Rustic Inn was, well, rustic. It was a vintage 1950 motel built in a large U-shape. The office was at the front near the street. A kids' play area filled the center with swings and a colorful jungle gym. Off to the side a mock-up of a covered wagon and a teepee large enough for half a dozen kids stood proud. Twenty units made the motel.

Taylor pulled up to the office and got out. Dozens of garishly painted clay figurines flanked the office door. Little men with sombreros sitting on donkeys. Leprechauns. Rabbits. Bizarre coyotes. Oxen pulling a wagon. It was a frigging menagerie! All had faded price tags attached to them.

"Yeah?" the young man behind the desk muttered as Taylor entered. He was maybe twenty years old at most. Short and stocky. No, Taylor reconsidered, he was just fat. His face was splotchy red from scratching pimples. The clerk was wearing a red shirt with the Rustic Inn logo embroidered on a sleeve.

Taylor flipped open his case hiding his retired LAPD badge, and then closed it quickly. He knew the kid would figure he was a cop authorized to be there for policing purposes.

"I'm doing a follow up investigation on the guy who was killed over at the campus the other day. Oliver Pines was his name. Heard he stayed here." Taylor used his best detective voice to establish credibility.

"I already talked to the cop who came over the day it happened. He even took Mr. Pines's toilet kit and a small gym bag filled with clothes, I think."

"Heard his room was made up like a sex den."

"Huh?"

"You know, like he was expecting a woman. Iced champagne and all. Wasn't he with some woman the week before?" Taylor threw out a probing, suggestive question.

"I didn't see no woman with Mr. Pines. I was on duty that first time. Nope, didn't see no woman."

"Did he use the same room both times?"

"Yeah."

"I need to take another look into that room, Jess," Taylor announced officially reading the nameplate on the kid's shirt.

"How'd ya know my name?"

"I'm a cop, remember?" Taylor figured the kid wasn't smart enough to realize he had his nametag on his shirt. It looked like he'd worn the same shirt the last ten days of work.

"Cops already did that."

"Yeah, but I'm from the insurance company. Doing the follow up, like I said. You want me to tell the owner you were helpful to the investigation, don't you?"

"Well, yeah, I guess. You know several people have booked that room since Mr. Pines was in there. You know that, don't you?"

"I do. Let's go take a look anyway. Anybody in there now?"

"Nope. We've only got two units rented right now."

They walked into the open courtyard and down to the corner room on the left. Unit 4. The kid in the Rustic Inn shirt opened the door with a passkey and went inside. Taylor followed him. It was definitely the same room Taylor had seen on Pines's laptop. Taylor recalled the angle of the video shot and looked around the room. Across from the foot of the bed a chest of drawers and an attached large mirror filled the wall. Taylor headed directly to the mirror. He needed additional height to reach it.

"Hey, Jess. Can you slide that ottoman over here?"

Taylor removed his shoes and used the ottoman as a stepstool and hopped onto the dresser top. He now was able to see the top ledge of the mirror.

"Hey, Jess. You guys filming your guests?"

"What you mean, mister?"

"There's a micro video camera up here," Taylor casually announced as he pulled a small pinhole camera from behind the mirror. "You do know this is against the law. Kind of kinky, if you ask me. You doing this, Jess?"

Jess began to stammer and instinctively backed up.

"Not me, officer! I've never seen that before…I," his voice trailed off.

"I believe you, Jess. Tell you what I'm going to do. I'll give you this spy shit camera and I'll forget I ever saw it. Okay?"

"Damn. Thanks, officer. I'm going to throw it away. I don't want to get in trouble. The owners are Christian people. It doesn't belong to them, I'm sure of it. You think it was Mr. Pines's camera?"

"Don't know, Jess. But I think you're doing the right thing. I wouldn't even tell the owners. That way they can deny any knowledge of it if something comes out later. But this should show you that your cleaning crew isn't doing a good job."

"Thank you, officer. I'll do what you said. Thank you so much."

Taylor was pleased how this encounter had gone. He'd confirmed what he saw on the laptop was shot in this particular room and it was the work of Oliver Pines. He had caused the camera to be destroyed and didn't leave his fingerprints on the destruction. He had a pretty good idea about what Oliver Pines was up to. Taylor wasn't surprised the detectives hadn't found the camera. They considered Oliver Pines to be a victim. Taylor had more information and was familiar with guys like Oliver. *God you're a sick puppy, Taylor.* Sometimes he felt jaded, almost stuck in the muck of police misconduct.

It was now time to talk with Mrs. Shelly Grant.

* * *

"Mrs. Grant, this is Taylor Sterling calling. I'm working for the college and its insurance company regarding the protest incident the other day when you were injured. I'd like to set up an appointment to talk with you." There was a noticeable pause on the other side of the line.

"I've already talked with the police," the female voice stammered.

"Yes, I've talked with Sergeant Justice and he told me how helpful you were to his investigation, but I'm working with the college directly and we need to ask you additional questions for our insurance carrier. I know you want to continue to be helpful. I've discovered some things about Oliver Pines that you should know." He threw that statement out there to heighten her interest and concern.

"I've already told the police that I didn't know…what was his name again?"

"Pines…Oliver Pines, Mrs. Grant. There are some things you need to know. There is new evidence I really need to share with you. My investigation concerns Mr. Pines, not you. It's important you stay informed, Mrs. Grant. You really should know what I've found."

Taylor knew this approach would force her to come to the table. It was calculated to cause her concern.

"Okay, but only if I can have a friend with me."

"That's fine, thank you. Can you pick a place to meet? I'm from out of town and don't know my way around."

"Two o'clock tomorrow afternoon at the Denny's off I-5 north of Medford. That okay? I only have an hour, though."

"See you then," Taylor agreed.

Taylor was concerned that he shouldn't sound too intimidating, but he wanted to convey the necessity for Shelly to be responsive and forthcoming. He was saving most of his found information to use during his face-to-face meeting with her. Taylor's interest in Shelly's account was simply to corroborate his suspicions about Oliver Pines. It was not intended to decimate her character.

* * *

Taylor was staying at the Rogue Valley Inn near I-5 and the Medford airport. He skipped his usual stay at a Marriott property and tried the Inn. The college had recommended it. The place was old and frayed around the edges, but adequate.

He was hoping to treat himself to a good dinner before tomorrow's meetings. Most recommendations sent him south a few miles to artsy Ashland. Taylor settled for Porter's. The restaurant was located in a restored train depot, expertly redone. He tried a local Porter beer and studied the menu, settling on the Rogue Valley salad of Oregon pears and bleu cheese, topped with lemon vinaigrette for his starter. An entrée of Sesame and Black Pepper Seared Ahi Tuna followed.

About the time he was tackling his first slice of tuna, he was interrupted.

"Mr. Sterling? I thought that was you. Susan Ames." The college president promptly staked out a place in front of him. He was locked into the booth and couldn't slide out and he doubted she wanted to slip in next to him.

"Good to see you. You're with…?"

"Some visiting college administrators." She glanced at a table of four on the other side of the room. "Boring."

"Too bad," Taylor said, and then wished he hadn't.

She smiled. "You have any preliminary thoughts about the investigation?"

"Too early, ma'am. I've got three very important interviews scheduled for tomorrow."

She bristled with the 'ma'am' and insisted, "Please, call me Susan. Luther, my police chief, calls me ma'am when he's pissed at me."

"Well, Susan, a couple more days and I'll be in to give you my preliminary thoughts."

She smiled, turned and walked to her table. She was wearing a black sheath hitting just above her knees. Sheer black stockings ended in respectable high heels. Taylor watched her behind sway as she crossed the room. She had the posture of an assured woman. Taylor admired women, well, anyone for that matter, who carried themselves well. Susan Ames was a very attractive woman closing in on fifty.

Taylor scanned the dessert menu. Nothing looked particularly interesting. He decided to settle for a Courvoisier. It was presented in an overly large sniffer with two small chocolate wafers added as chasers. Taylor peered over the sniffer and saw Susan looking at him. He tipped his glass as Susan smiled and canted her head in a quizzical way.

* * *

Taylor found Simon Loren at the sheriff's firing range. The meeting was scheduled for eight a.m. Mist hung over the range as folks told Taylor it did all the time in this part of Oregon. No one was standing at the firing line. Simon walked Taylor back to a small office with a sign over the door reading "Range Master and Tac Leader."

Simon's office was similar to most cops who held this assignment. Tactical equipment like riot shields, helmets, 36-inch batons, armor barricade shields featuring small operator's windows, shotguns, and boxes of ammunition were displayed front and center. On the walls hung advertising posters distributed by cop equipment vendors. Many posters prominently featured a thong-wearing, buxom, strikingly attractive maiden holding an assault rifle or sitting on a police motorcycle.

"Mr. Taylor Sterling. Did some checking on you, guy," Simon pronounced. A toothpick resided in his mouth and moved from side to side like a tennis ball in slow motion.

"Depends who you talk to."

"You got a pretty good rep. Say you're your own man and don't take shit from nobody. That's good enough for me, Taylor." Simon smiled as he gave his analysis and offered a strong handshake.

"Apparently you got some of my friends. But you should know, got my naysayers as well, Simon."

"We all do. Yep, we all do. What you want from me?"

"I gather the large canister of OC and the FN 303 came from your stockpile?"

"Sort of, I guess. We had them piled in our deployment area, just in case things got out of hand. Never know. Have to prepare for the worst. I was talking with Luther and we were listening to the reports from the undercovers in the crowd. Nothing really going on. Bunch of them tree huggers were sitting down across the walkway by the founder's statue. One of my men said Jon came by and grabbed the canister and FN gun, saying something about fucking with those liberal bitches."

"Know what he meant?"

"Nah. But Jon has always had a hard-on for women. I've known him for close to twenty years and he keeps getting jammed up by a woman one way or another. But, something must have really pissed him off that day."

"The young cop who used the FN, did he know what the shit he was doing with it?"

"Doubt it. I checked my records and nobody from the campus cops was trained or certified on it. We do all their firearm training, qualification, and certification. I'm the guy who actually does it. Only our Tac Team is trained to use the FN, even in our own department. The FN is a touchy piece of equipment. You got to worry about spatial distance. You know, can't be too close when you fire. Then you got to stay away from somebody's head. If you don't, it takes the shot from less lethal to a lethal use of force."

"Simon, did you talk with either Jon or the young cop?"

"I was pretty busy right after the shooting. I was having my guys round up the protesters who were sprayed and they were trying to irrigate their eyes to stop the pain. We had enough bottled water on hand to do that. They got them over to the buses and took them to the detention center. We field-released the bunch of them with just a citation. The college provost called the sheriff, the main man with the eagles on his collar, and told him to expedite their release. By the time I reached the guy who died and the woman who got hit with the FN, the medics were all over them. I saw Jon standing about fifteen feet away. He was with Luther who had his arms around him. I think Jon was crying. Don't know for sure, but it seemed like that."

"How about the young cop?"

"Stan. I think that's his first name. Don't know his last name. He was sitting on the grass with the FN placed across his legs. I went over and took control of the gun and gave it to one of my guys to make it safe. Stan had a blank stare on his face and kept saying, 'Lieutenant gave me that gun and ordered me to shoot that bitch. I never shot a gun like that.' He kept saying that things weren't meant to be like this. I had a campus sergeant take him back to their station. Last I saw of him. I feel for the kid. Think they might try to make him the scapegoat. You know how it is when the shit hits the fan. Somebody got to pay!"

* * *

Luther was still riding the desk, but Taylor noticed he wasn't wearing his uniform this morning. He was in jeans and a Rogue Valley college sweatshirt. At least he was still waving the college flag.

"Hey, Taylor, just brewed a pot. Here, use this cup. Got it back at the FBI National Academy."

"See you're still at the desk, but no uniform."

"Didn't see the need. Can't go out and meet anyone. Madame President has spoken, you know. Here I am, a retired major, graduate from the FBI NA, and chief of police, and riding the fucking desk!"

"Would have been the same even if you were back at the PD, boss. You know that."

A young man entered Luther's office. He couldn't have been

more than twenty-two or three. He should have shaved his head for all the hair he had left. He was a tall and lanky kid.

"Chief? This the guy the college brought in to bust our chops?"

"Stan, meet Taylor Sterling. He's retired from LAPD."

"THE LAPD?" the young man stammered. He waited for Taylor to approach him before he stuck out his hand. "Glad to meet you, sir. I was just kidding!"

"Don't apologize, Stan. It's a tough time for everyone."

Luther got up and said, "I'll be out in dispatch. Need to make a little small talk with Sally. You guys can use my office." He turned and left the room.

"Sir, really from LAPD? When you leave?"

"Been about six years now, Stan."

"You must have seen a lot in your years there."

"I did. You get that in any big city. The good and the bad. Both on the street and in the hallways of the department. So, Stan, tell me about yourself."

"Grew up in Medford. Needed a job and next thing I know Chief Luther hired me as a parking control guy. Got me through the police academy at the local community college. Just exchanged one uniform for another. I like being a cop. I'm not sure if I could handle the big city though, even one the size of Medford. I like the calm of the campus. People are good here."

"Stan, tell me what happened the other day."

"Well, Mr. Sterling, I was scheduled to be part of the arrest team. The plan was, if protesters were arrested, two of us would go in and take control. Cord cuff them and take them back to processing area set up near the SO bus. I saw a couple dozen people sit down across the pathway in the middle of the park. A couple of the older ones needed help getting down. Anyway, the group locked their arms together and began chanting. Lieutenant Schilling suddenly appeared next to me. He said something about liberal tree huggers and said he was going to teach them a lesson. He ordered me to put my baton away and handed me this damn Star Wars gun. Never seen anything like it before."

"Never even at training exercises?"

"No. Damn space age looking contraption if you ask me. Got this magazine barrel loader under the receiver. Well, maybe I seen something like it in a movie before, like those movies starring G-men from the Prohibition era. Kind of looked like something I've used playing a shoot 'em up video game. Jon was the boss so I followed orders."

"How'd you know how to take the safety off?"

"The lieutenant said it was already off. Then he told me I should shoot this lady standing on the other side of the sit-ins. Said she was a bitch and flipped him the finger earlier. I didn't see it myself, but he's the boss. So, I stepped around the sit-ins. Oh, I forgot to tell you I had my gas mask on. We were all told to put them on. It's hard to see with the masks on so I wasn't crazy about that idea. I imagine you've worn one in the past, huh? You know what I mean?"

Taylor nodded.

"Well, I stepped around a few protesters and advanced on the lady. By now the lieutenant was spraying the shit out of the sit-ins. I was startled when this dude suddenly jumped in front of me. Damn gun went off! God, it's got a light trigger pull that I didn't expect. Two shots fired before I realized it. The spray of blood from the dude's eye threw me again and apparently I cranked off another two rounds. Those rounds must have been the ones that hit the lady."

Stan looked at his hands resting in his lap. He started churning them as if he was washing them and suddenly placed them over his face. Taylor knew he was trying to hide tears. Taylor moved behind him and placed his hands on Stan's shoulders, gently squeezing them in support.

"Stan, it was an accident."

"No, no, it wasn't! I pulled the trigger on that damn thing! I killed that dude for no reason. I should have told Schilling to go to hell. But you don't do that under command! Worse even when you're in battle. Some battle, huh? Mr. Sterling, what you figure is gonna happen to me? I can't sleep. I can't eat. I'm turning into a wreck."

"Luther!" Taylor yelled as he opened the office door.

"What?" Luther asked as he entered. When he saw Stan he knew the kid was having a full-blown anxiety attack. Luther and Taylor held Stan under his arms and walked him outside. They relaxed their grips when Stan could walk on this own.

"Stan, take deep breaths," Luther ordered.

"It's all going to come out okay, Stan," Taylor encouraged. "We're going to be with you one hundred percent. Luther's your buddy, Stan. He's going to stay with you. It was an accident, Stan. Police work is full of accidents. We work them out and we can work this out, too."

Stan's breathing was beginning to approach normal. He asked to sit on the bench along the pathway. Luther and Taylor sat down on either side of him. Both made sure some part of their body was physically connecting with Stan. Taylor's knee was placed next to Stan's knee.

"Stan, we're going to get you to see someone. You need time to talk to someone who'll be looking out just for you," Taylor said.

"We'll set you up to see Doc Phillips, Stan," Luther advised. "I'm going to go into the station now and call for an appointment for you. Stay here with Taylor. I'll be right back."

Luther was able to get an emergency appointment with the police psychologist and left with Stan in tow.

Taylor went back into Luther's office and closed the door. He put his head in his hands and began massaging his temples with his fingers. It had been years since he was with an officer who went into crisis. It reminded him of the myriad of skills and techniques police supervisors had to develop to be effective. You never knew what might happen at any given time with your cops, most of them were friends or young officers who depended on you. But suddenly Taylor remembered the internal stress that descended on him during these encounters with a troubled officer. The job broke some; strengthened others; but changed everyone. Taylor had been changed…but, he dealt with it.

* * *

The Denny's restaurant Mrs. Grant suggested was just off I-5 and was one of the newer ones made to look like old 1950's diners found in New England or the Midwest. The sides were crafted of bright shiny aluminum and neon signs blinked red messages. At two o'clock the place was deserted. Taylor found a booth away from the counter and in the farthest corner of the diner. He ordered a coffee and glass of water.

He saw the two women as they entered and mumbled a few words to the waitress. She pointed back to Taylor's booth. One he recognized from the grainy video. Shelly Grant had short bobbed blonde hair. She appeared tan, but Taylor realized her coloring was from the expanse of freckles dotting her face. Shelly was a small woman, just a couple inches over five feet tall. She was trim, almost to the point of being scrawny. She was in jeans, yellow and white tennis shoes, and a floppy purple sweater of a thick weave, maybe alpaca.

Her friend was quite different. She was a head taller with dark hair cropped almost to a man's cut. Her figure was much fuller. She was wearing black tights that disappeared in calf length tan suede boots accented with dangling fringe on the sides. She was wearing a loosely crocheted tunic that hung down to mid-thigh and covered her black turtleneck sleeveless blouse. She spent too much time puttying her face together and used entirely too much eye makeup for Taylor's taste. He noted a sparkle of shiny flecks spattering her eyelids that was distracting. The woman was wearing heavy bright red lipstick that seemed to be so popular these days. She reminded Taylor of the women in World War II movies.

Shelly slipped into the booth first and was joined on her side by her friend. Taylor noticed Shelly circled her arms tightly around her body as if hugging herself. He detected that body language as a sign of self-preservation. This woman clearly did not want to be here.

"Thanks for coming, Mrs. Grant," Taylor greeted. "Can I get you both something?"

Shelly shook her head, but her friend said, "Cherry diet coke, no cherry in it."

"And you are?" he asked looking at Cherry Coke lady.

"She's my friend. You said I could bring a friend," Shelly said defiantly. "Her name is Terri."

"Glad to meet you, Terri. Mrs. Grant, would you rather I refer to you that way or as Shelly?"

"Shelly is fine."

"Thanks, Shelly. You know I'm here doing an investigation for the college about the protest demonstrations. I'm very sorry that you were injured, Shelly. How are you feeling now?

"I'm fine. I just had some bruising that lasted about a week."

"Why don't you tell me what happened?" Taylor began.

Taylor had vast experience interviewing people of every type. He had attended countless training programs detailing police interview and interrogation skills. Some sessions delved into the psychological and emotional reactions people had when engaged in interviews. Some training taught how to watch for telltale signs of deception by body or eye movements, particularly the significance of the direction eyes moved.

Taylor had been most impressed by the work of social science researchers at John Jay College in New York. They dismissed most premises presented in earlier investigative training as voodoo and junk science. They weren't kind showing their distaste for the initial programs developed. The John Jay premise was simply to get a subject talking. The more a subject talked, the more the information given would eventually be helpful to an investigation. Researchers discovered a good interviewer should spend no more than twenty percent of the interview time talking and the person being interviewed should use the remaining eighty percent.

Taylor adopted that approach and found it to be successful. People who are interviewed by the police, including officers under investigation, expect to be given an opportunity to tell their side of the story. They will rehearse their version in their minds over and over again. They want to give rationalization or mitigation regarding what might have occurred. This is particularly true with citizens who might be witnesses. However, as expected, interview techniques take a different slant when dealing with a hard-assed criminal.

Shelly looked at Taylor and then at her friend Terri. She began her story without unlocking her arms protecting her torso. Taylor liked that she looked directly at him when she talked.

"I'd never been to anything close to something like the protest at State College. I can't really say why I decided to go. Heck, I've got more things on my plate at home with my kids, husband, and the stuff I get involved with around Medford. But, I read the article in the *Crier* and something in it struck a chord. Maybe it was the huge tuition hike being proposed. You know, before long my kids will be going there. It'll cost us! The protest was at a good time for me—noon. My kids' stuff doesn't start until later in the day. I went to the campus, not really knowing what to expect. Certainly I wasn't thinking about getting gassed and most certainly wasn't expecting to get shot!

"When I arrived, a bunch of people were milling around close to the founder's statue. Something's always happening to that statue. It's either splashed with paint by an opposing sports team or TP'd by a frat house. I remember when I went to Oregon State I heard the tales about Rogue Valley. Oregon State is where I met Nathan, my husband. Anyway, several speakers were using the mic to berate the college administration.

"I saw a few cops standing away from the crowd. As if it was a choreographed dance, a bunch of people sat down in unison. Just plopped down on the pathway. Locked arms and began chanting something I couldn't understand. Kind of like the tree huggers did several years ago in Eureka. I remember they got maced in the eyes by a cop using a damn Q-tip. Screaming like they were being tortured!

"At first I didn't see the cop who sprayed the people who had opted for the sit-in. I heard screaming and then saw a big officer spray the seated protesters with something that had an orange hue to it. I was just off to the side looking at them and began to think I should probably run away. Just as I was about to turn to leave, this man, the one who got killed, ran in front of me.

I didn't hear anything unusual, but suddenly a spray of blood splattered over my sweatshirt. I caught a glimpse of a cop raising a space-age looking gun and then it felt like I was stabbed in the shoulder with a hot poker. You know, like something you'd use to move logs around in a fireplace. Next thing I know I'm getting loaded into an ambulance and ended up in the hospital. You know, that's about it, Mr. Sterling."

She sat back in the booth. While she had been talking, Taylor noticed Shelly had loosened her arms and occasionally used her hands to emphasize a point she was making. There wasn't much emotion shown on her face as she related the details of her harrowing experience, other than when she described being splattered with blood. At that point she winced slightly. Terri grabbed her friend's arm and squeezed it in a show of support.

"Some ordeal, Shelly. And happening your first time, too!"

"And my last time too, I might add!"

"How old are your children, Shelly?"

"Daughter is thirteen and my son is fourteen. It's funny, they now think I'm some kind of Superhero. When they heard what happened to me they kept shouting, 'Way to go, Mom!' It's been good on that front, but, of course, my husband thought I was just stupid. He's worried what people might say. We're supposed to be Republicans."

"He can be such a prick sometimes, Shelly," Terri chimed in and gave an echoing laugh.

"You're lucky you didn't have any lasting injuries."

Shelly nodded and instinctively rubbed her shoulder where she had been shot.

"I looked at your hospital records. It was good of you to give the investigator a medical release so he could share them with me. I was intrigued by one thing though," Taylor added. He stopped talking momentarily and watched Shelly carefully, figuring she was trying to think what might be concerning him.

"The hospital took an inventory of your property when you were admitted. It seemed strange that in your purse you carried a loose pair of panties and a tube of KY jelly."

Terri grabbed Shelly's arm again, but this time squeezed it vigorously.

"You know I go to the gym a lot and sometimes get chaffed from the spin bike. I always carry an extra pair of panties," she blushed. "I have bladder problems now and then. I guess it comes with having children."

Taylor was surprised she had crafted such a good story.

"Ah, yes! Certainly sounds reasonable," he admitted, looking directly at her. She dropped her eyes from his stare.

"Did you know the man who jumped in front of you? Seems he was trying to protect you."

Shelly shook her head.

"Kind of died protecting you, Shelly, as least that's what it looked like."

She shook her head again and said, "No, I don't think I've ever seen him before. I realize now he probably did save me from greater injury. Poor man."

Taylor recognized Shelly had prepared herself for his interview and he could understand why. She must have considerable conflict going on with her roles as dutiful house mom, faithful wife, and upstanding member of the community.

"Shelly, and you too, Terri, I've been in police work for many years. I started back in the early '70s. There were a lot of problems in the '60s with civil rights conflicts and war protests, followed by a mass of urban riots. Just about every big city had violent riots at some time during that era. A lot of people were killed. Police really didn't do a good job and everybody knew it. So, training programs were developed and cops had to go back to school to learn the basics. LAPD had its 1965 Watts riot and then a couple smaller ones over the next few years. I guess I was lucky coming in after those happened.

"I did work the Unusual Occurrence Command Post for nearly my entire career. That was the unit that planned and executed police enforcement during demonstrations. We went to a lot of schooling for training. I read a lot of stuff about riots and mobs. Some information dates as far back as the mid 1800s."

Taylor watched both women as he talked. Both were attentive and seemed interested.

"A lot of things happen to people when they find themselves in a mob setting. I don't use the term 'mob' in a bad sense. Mob psychology can quickly take over a person's normal senses and change their normal behavior patterns. Some peaceful people can be goaded and channeled to do violent things. Suddenly bizarre actions seem perfectly okay when they are done in the anonymity of a large crowd," Taylor continued.

"There is a little studied phenomenon that also occurs. I've talked with dozens of average people who had their normal behavior drastically changed when they were influenced by a crowd, protest, or mob setting. Quite a few told me about the thrill or rush they got during a protest. It's almost addictive they've suggested. Sometimes the rhythmic sound of chanting or cops beating their batons sexually excites them. Some expressed they found the whole experience very sensual and provocative. Some folks confided that the pulse of a protest increases their immediate desire for sex. Now I don't know that for a fact, and it hasn't done anything like that for me when I've been in riot enforcement, but, then again, I'm on the other side of the action."

Terri leaned and whispered to Shelly, "Maybe I need to try some of that protest shit!" Shelly became very still and stared at Taylor.

"You're not suggesting anything, are you, Mr. Sterling?"

"Of course not, Shelly. But there are some things that I can't figure out. Maybe you can help me."

She nodded and said she'd try.

"Did you read about the first protest? The one held the week before you were injured?" Shelly shook her head.

"See, I find that somewhat strange. The announcement of the protest and the schedules were in the first report the *Crier* published. The newspaper had extensive reporting about what happened at the first protest and how people were gassed. You'd have to be pretty dedicated to the cause if you were gassed and then went back for more abuse the following week, unless it wasn't as bad as the paper reported."

"It wasn't," Shelly insisted, and then reneged. "At least that's what the paper said."

Taylor knew Shelly realized she'd made a serious slip. He also knew staying for the rest of the interview was a good sign.

"You know, I've found out a lot about Oliver Pines."

"He's the man who was killed?" Shelly inquired innocently.

"Yes." Taylor's interest was roused that she pretended to recall his name from just his earlier mention. "You say you never met Mr. Pines?"

"No, I don't think so."

"Well, I've found that Oliver was a protest groupie. He fed on women who attended protests. He had a kinky side, too."

Terri glanced at Shelly suspiciously.

"Oliver kept pretty detailed records in a notebook. Maybe it came from him being a teacher or maybe being a full-fledged sex pervert. Perverts commonly keep records of their conquests, you know."

Shelly wrapped her arms protectively around her body again. She began biting her lower lip.

"The clerk at the Rustic Inn remembers seeing a young woman with Oliver after the first protest," Taylor said. He knew that wasn't true, but it was time to press Shelly.

"Oliver was kinkier than most guys I've investigated for this type crime. He was a criminal. He used his knowledge of mob psychology to get women to do things they wouldn't normally do. He was scum, if you ask me."

Shelly kept nibbling her lower lip and Taylor saw her body slowly begin to shake.

"He had one of those spy tiny video cameras set up at the motel. It was so well hidden that even the cleaning crew didn't notice it, but I found it the other day. It was installed just over the top of the dresser mirror. It's the type of camera you can download into a laptop. He had a laptop in his backpack that I reviewed at the coroner's office."

Shelly's hands unlocked from around her middle and moved to her face as she began to cry. Terri circled her arms around Shelly's shoulders and hugged her.

"It's okay, baby. It'll be okay," Terri crooned.

"No it won't, Terri! Just 'cuz you're fucking that guy at the high school doesn't mean it's okay. It's not!" Terri didn't respond, but teased Taylor with a smirk.

"Mr. Sterling, I'm not on that laptop, am I? Please tell me I'm not!"

"Shelly, I'm only interested in Oliver Pines. He was a scummy stalker. He took advantage of many women. I'm not here to do you any harm. You're a hero to your kids. I want you to stay their hero. It's Oliver Pines's reputation that I want to document and discount."

Shelly opened up like a proverbial faucet. "He was so interesting. He told me about all the protests he had been to, but now I find I'm just like those women you told us about. I admit I was aroused by the excitement and the threatening and menacing presence of the cops. Somehow it was infectious. I did things with that man I've never thought of doing with my husband! Well, I may have thought about them, but would never bring them up. I didn't have to hide anything with Oliver. It was wonderful, but at the same time repugnant. Please tell me I'm not on his laptop, Mr. Sterling!"

Taylor lied. "I don't know, Shelly. But it won't get out if you are. I've made certain the video won't get out. Your kids will always think you're their hero. I've just got to make sure that Oliver's estate isn't awarded money from the college because he was killed being a sexual predator. That's what he was, you know. He was a criminal. You were his victim, Shelly, that's all."

"It's the last thing I'd want, too. I just want to put this entire mess behind me. I don't want any part of it anymore. My life and my family are fine for me now. Damn, I sure don't want this kind of excitement in my life."

Taylor left Shelly and Terri sitting in the booth. He was sure Terri wanted to hear every salacious detail from Shelly. Taylor smiled and wondered whether that sexual stimulation theory was real or just some urban myth. It really didn't matter. It gave Shelly a face-saving hook to grab onto if she needed something to blame for her indiscretion.

* * *

"Sergeant Justice, thought I'd drop by and let you know what I've found so far," Taylor said as the Medford investigator came out to the station lobby to greet him.

"Anything I should know about?"

Taylor figured the sergeant's investigation was focused exclusively on the police use of force and not what Pines might have been doing. From the police investigator's point of view, Pines and Shelly Grant were the victims in this case. Taylor assumed that was why Justice hadn't gone to review Pines's property at the coroner's office. Taylor was the only one who had signed the review sheet inside the box.

"Things are pretty much as you already found out," Taylor said, consciously avoiding information about Pines and Mrs. Grant, or what he had discovered at the coroner's office and Rustic Inn.

"Nobody at the campus station was trained on the FN by the sheriff's office. That young officer who used the FN, Stan was his first name, never got his last name. Anyway, he's not in good shape. Luther got him in to see the department psychologist on an emergency basis. By the way, what do you think the prosecutor might be considering?"

"You know prosecutors. Keep things pretty much close to the vest. He hasn't said much to us other than he's interested in finding out more about Lieutenant Schilling and that Stan guy. He still remembers Jon and his domestic issues when he was on the Medford PD. Thinks he should have been prosecuted back then. You might be interested to know that Pines's sister is arriving at the coroner's about six tonight. Had to wait until her husband got off work to get a ride. Need to talk with them?"

"I do. Thanks for the heads up. Six o'clock at the coroner's office, huh?"

The couple walked into the coroner's office fifteen minutes late. Pines's sister was about fifty and overweight. Her husband was in much better shape. Taylor figured he had to be as he was still a member of the National Guard and held the position of major.

"Excuse me, Sergeant Justice told me to expect you. I'm Taylor Sterling. I'm working for the college and am looking into the incident that resulted in your brother's death. Can I have ten minutes of your time?"

"Of course. I'm Carla Smith and this is my husband, Joe. What can we do for you?"

"Joe, I'm envious of your service with the Guard. Major, huh? That's pretty good." Taylor knew noting this would keep the door open for discussions with Carla. Joe smiled broadly and shook Taylor's hand.

"You close to your brother, Mrs. Smith?"

"Please, call me Carla. Not at all. Joe didn't like him. Thought there was something weird about him. Never told me what exactly, just weird. Maybe 'cuz he was such a geek working on computers all the time. Besides, we lived on the opposite side of the mountain. Oliver lived over in Cedar City around Bend. Hot up there, you know."

"Well, I've got some bad news for you," Taylor said. He related what Oliver had been up to over the past several years and the real attraction that drew him to protests.

"That doesn't excuse what happened to him at the college here though," Taylor continued. "I wanted you to know that there's some nasty stuff on his laptop. Apparently he filmed women in sexual positions without their knowledge. Stuff that would devastate any person."

"Oh, God, heaven help us!" Carla exclaimed, putting her

hands to her mouth. "We're good Christians, Mr. Sterling. We don't have no place for porn in our lives. Maybe you could just take Oliver's laptop and dispose of it?"

"I really can't do that in my position. Were you able to retrieve his computer and software from his home in Cedar City?" She nodded.

"My suggestion is you take that equipment, along with any external drives, you know what they are, don't you?" Joe nodded. "Take that stuff and the laptop that's in his backpack and have them all wiped clean. Probably will cost you around a hundred bucks."

Carla and Joe thanked Taylor for his honesty, even though the packaged information disgusted both of them.

"You planning on suing the college, by the way?" Taylor let the question slide as he shook their hands.

"Had some attorney call us about that," Joe replied. "Told him to pound sand. Me and Carla never had need for Oliver, and sure don't now!"

* * *

Taylor felt it had been a good day. Tomorrow would be his last in Oregon. It would take him another day to get back home to Santa Fe. Tomorrow he would talk with Luther and schedule his exit briefing with the college administrators.

Luther was in his office early the next morning. He looked like he hadn't slept the night before. A stubble growth of beard shadowed his jowls and he reeked of stale body odor and beer.

"They found Jon, Taylor," Luther announced as Taylor entered his office carrying a fresh cup of coffee from the dispatch communal pot. Taylor gave Luther a questioning turn of the head.

"Jon's wife called me about seven last night. She said she still hadn't heard a word from Jon, but figured he was someplace in their new Chevy Tahoe since it was gone from the garage.

"It dawned on me that the truck was still under warranty and probably still had the OnStar activated. We called the On-Star communication center and they located the Chevy in the national forest. I didn't know that thing worked when the car wasn't running. Rangers found the car in about thirty minutes and within an hour they found Jon. He was propped against a big pine overlooking Eagle Lake. An empty bottle of Jack Daniels sat between his legs along with his Glock. Apparently Jon ate his gun. Top of his head was gone."

"I'm really sorry for your loss, Luther. I know Jon was your friend."

"Thanks, bud. You know, I'm at fault. Should have known Jon had his demons. I just gave him the rope. Hell, it appears he took young Stan down with him. Stan's a basket case. We got him committed to a rehab place across the line in California."

Luther got up and walked out to dispatch. Taylor followed him and watched him fill two coffee cups.

"Take a walk with me, Taylor?"

They left the building and ended up sitting on the same bench they had shared with Stan the day before. Luther was silent for several minutes.

"I think I'm getting too old for this shit, Taylor. Years ago I wouldn't have let this happen." Luther wasn't asking for conversation so Taylor didn't respond.

"I haven't had my heart in this job for a couple years now. I kept it because I thought I needed the extra money, but I really don't. Wife and I got this trailer, an old restored Airstream. Sweet to pull. She says we need to use it before we get too old. She was right and I told her to start packing."

They shook hands. Luther told Taylor he would take his coffee cup back to dispatch so he could be on his way. Luther had a smile on his face and his eyes told Taylor he was looking to the future.

* * *

Taylor parked in front of the small bar across from the Rustic Inn. He couldn't schedule a meeting with Susan and the others at the college until four that afternoon. The motel clerk saw him and waved as he got out of his rental car.

"Say Jess, how's it going?" Taylor called, crossing the street to say hello. The young clerk was straightening the clay figurines surrounding the office door. "Cleaning up your version of 'It's a Small World?'"

The kid laughed. "Just like Disneyland, huh? Funny, Officer Taylor, very funny." Taylor didn't correct him. "Got some good local brews across the street. Try the Bear Paw Stout, if you like a heavy beer."

"Thanks for the tip. See you around, Jess."

Taylor ordered the Bear Paw and found it pretty good. He tried two other beers and an order of stuffed jalapeño peppers before it was time to head to the college.

The same cast of characters was present and seated in the same places they'd parked the first day Taylor arrived. Susan Ames, college president; Brett Chambers, college provost; and Carlson Smithson, United Casualty insurance adjuster. Taylor took a seat directly across from Susan.

"Tragic what happened to Lieutenant Schilling," Susan commented.

"Yes, all deaths are tragic in some way. They all drag a tail that seems to touch many people if they care or not," Taylor mused. He had been in the death and dying wars for a long time.

"What else you know that we don't, Mr. Sterling?" Brett shot out. Taylor decided he definitely did not like this man.

"You do know the young officer who shot Pines is in a rehab hospital? He won't be coming back. That just might get the prosecutor off the hot seat," Taylor surmised as the three nodded their heads.

Susan had something to say. "Luther came in early this afternoon and told me he was quitting. You know anything about that, Taylor?"

"I had coffee with him this morning, so yes I do. We all come to a crossroads in our careers at some time. Smart folks know when to recognize it and make the right move. Others don't see a choice or wait too long and eventually become bitter and jaded. I think Luther made the right choice."

"That from personal experience, Mr. Sterling?" Carlson asked. Taylor nodded. "What about the potential for lawsuits?"

"Well, that's really your field, Carlson, but I have some pretty good ideas for you to mull around." Carlson leaned forward and picked up his pen.

"Pines was your potential biggest liability. College professor with no criminal record. No record of drug use. But, he was one sick puppy. He was a protest demonstration groupie. In the past eight or ten years he participated in more than fifteen of them. All kinds, and for all causes."

"What has that got to do with his death?" Brett asked.

"Oliver Pines was a serial stalker. After each demonstration he ended up in bed with one or two women protesters. He capitalized on their fascination with the rush and sexual thrill that some find when they are involved in demonstrations. Added to that, Oliver was kinky and a real weirdo. He filmed these women with a video camera and transferred the sexual escapades to his computer." Taylor produced his thumb drive and slid it across the table to Susan. "I got this off his laptop. It would destroy any credibility Oliver would have in any court. Everyone would hate this creep."

"And where did you get this data? How did you find out about the video camera?" Brett quizzed.

"I didn't steal it, if that's what you're insinuating. On top of that, old Oliver had never been married and his only next of kin, his sister, had pretty much pushed him out of her family's life. She said she wasn't interested in pursuing a lawsuit and I believe her. She and her husband, who's a major in the National Guard, were sickened by the thought that he made and enjoyed sex tapes. The major is going to have them erased professionally."

"Did you determine if there was a connection between Mrs. Grant and Oliver?" Susan asked.

"Not that I'm aware of. I spoke with her yesterday," Taylor answered.

"She on that thumb drive?"

"No!" Taylor wasn't lying. He had deleted the file that contained any reference to the Rogue Valley State College protest, including the sexual encounter with Shelly.

"Was she?" Susan asked again.

"What, you're saying I purposefully deleted something from the file? Susan, that wouldn't be ethical. And you know I'm an ethical consultant."

"Of course some might say deleting a particular event was an ethical act, either as a consultant or a decent human being," she said with a smile.

"Mrs. Grant has become a hero to her teenage kids. They consider her Supermom. Soccer mom morphs into Supermom, now that's a headline for you! It's kind of sweet, actually. Mrs. Grant told me she just wanted to put everything connected with this incident behind her."

"So, where does that leave the college and my firm, Mr. Sterling?" Carlson asked.

"You've got maybe fifteen people who were sprayed and suffered some discomfort. A few of those will wear the action as a badge of honor. Others might want something more tangible. I imagine if you offered each a few thousand they would take it as a good faith gesture. If you do it soon, most won't have hired a lawyer they'd have to share it with."

"Taylor, I'm going to need a new police chief. You interested?" Susan asked.

"No ma'am." He knew that would tweak her. "And, you couldn't afford me."

After a few more minutes of casual small talk the group of four stood. Susan approached Taylor and said she would walk him out.

"Nice thing you've done for that soccer mom."

Susan smiled broadly and Taylor mimicked tipping his hat and grinned.

* * *

"Taylor?" the female voice said when he picked up his cell phone.

"Yes?" he said hesitantly.

"Do you get so many calls at this hour from strange women that you don't recognize me? It's Susan. I know you're leaving in the morning. I was wondering if you'd like some company on your last night in town."

"Actually, I was getting ready for bed."

"That's even better. You won't have to change."

Taylor always enjoyed watching women dress. He enjoyed watching them undress even more. Susan put on her clothes in a way he specifically enjoyed. Very methodical, almost ritualistic as she draped her clothing in the proper places. She turned and looked at Taylor as she settled into her heels.

"Make sure to send me your bill, Taylor."

"That sounds so cheap, Susan!"

"Taylor, one thing I know, you're not cheap."

She blew him a kiss, turned with her head held high and he watched the door of his room close softly behind her.

Speed is fun, but kills and costs

Complainant: Kansas Municipal Insurance Pool
Allegation: Pursuit fatalities
Agency: Barrington, Kansas Police Department
Accused employees: Chief Reginald Batts and Officer Jason Day

The tires on the small vehicle smoked as it escaped the parking lot of the nearly defunct strip mall on Center Street. There weren't many businesses still up and running in the shabby string of buildings that had seen far better days. Many had plywood panels covering broken windows. Those still operating were closed at this late hour—eleven o'clock. Sal's Liquors was one store still open, the place for booze buyers never closed for long. The raging car missed the lot entrance and careened over the curb, its undercarriage banging on the pavement sending a cascade of sparks to illuminate the night sky.

Officer Jason Day was evaluating the developing situation he'd just come upon, but wasn't sure what was going on. He had been assigned to highway interdiction duty for over six months and was making his way to Highway 54 to begin his shift when he caught the unexpected action. Jason thought maybe there'd been a robbery at the liquor store. That thought would enter the minds of most cops considering the convergence of events.

Jason was well known to the guys manning Sal's. He'd often drop in and shoot the shit with whatever clerk was on duty. Jason knew friendly visits made the clerks feel a little safer. He thought it must be unnerving to be working alone in a liquor store late at night, never knowing who or what might walk through the door. Jason had noticed the sawed-off shotgun under the counter, but knew most of the twenty-somethings working the late shift would never use it or didn't have a clue how to handle it.

Jason moved into high gear when the exiting car picked up speed. The disappearing taillights offered a good plausible stop opportunity for him. Maybe nothing had happened at Sal's, but then again, maybe the clerk had been robbed or was lying in a pool of blood behind the counter, dead.

"Unit 21 to dispatch."

"Go 21."

"Got a suspicious car leaving Sal's Liquor at a high rate of speed. Gonna try to catch up. Send a unit to check the store."

"Roger that, 21. Unit 24, Unit 24 check on Sal's Liquor for 21. Suspicious circumstances."

"24, Roger that. ETA five or six minutes."

Jason Day had been off plebe police probation and FTO, field training officer, status for nearly six months. New cops would graduate from the regional basic police training academy and then go back to the police department that originally hired them. Before new cops could work alone, they would have to spend eight or ten weeks riding with a seasoned officer. The older officer, sometimes with only a few more months on the job, would teach the new guy how to do police work on the street and would evaluate how they handled whatever calls came their way. Jason liked driving alone. During training, Jason didn't like justifying every stop or turn he made to the FTO riding with him. Constantly being evaluated and second-guessed was trying, to say the least. But Jason was smart enough to realize he didn't know enough about policing just yet. His radio conversations were awkward and talking with the subjects he stopped made him uncomfortable. Actually, talking to *any* person was a lot different than texting and conversing on Facebook. Jason had liked the anonymity of texting. But as a cop, you had to be on your toes to watch and read how people reacted to what you said. This was something new for the self-proclaimed techie.

Jason mashed his foot on the accelerator of the year-old Dodge Charger. He loved the throaty sound the Hemi made when it dropped into low gear, but he really got off on the powerful thrust that pinned him against the seat. Jason knew he commandeered a fast interceptor; his cop shop chief bought the car for that very reason. He decided not to flip on the emergency lights just yet. The pulsating accusation might spook the driver ahead who was still racing down the road like a bat outta hell. As he gave chase, Jason reviewed what he learned at the academy. He could still hear his instructor ordering, "Wait until you're almost on top of the violator before you flick the lights. Otherwise, you might tweak a pursuit and give the suspect the feeling he can out run you."

60…70…80…almost 90 miles per hour! Jason saw his speedometer climb like a monkey on a ladder.

The side streets were flying past as he gained on the small car. Its taillights were becoming more visible now. The car must have slowed, he figured. When Jason was three car lengths back, he matched the pace.

"21…Vehicle KUM 325 Kansas. Looks like two inside."

"Roger, 21. Registered to a Cynthia Snyder in Roscoe, no wants or warrants."

Jason couldn't determine the sex of the two in the car. He looked around to get his bearings since he was still trying to learn the streets in Barrington.

Barrington, Kansas was a sleepy suburb west of Wichita along Highway 54. There wasn't much west of Wichita other than farmland and a few small towns like Barrington. Known as the Sunflower State, Kansas was flat as a pancake and it was joked cows outnumbered the people and trees, and cornfields outnumbered the cows.

Jason had graduated from Kansas State in Manhattan with a degree in Criminal Justice. He planned to join the KCPD Kansas or KCPD Missouri police departments one day. They were the big boys in law enforcement, places where the real stuff happened. Living vicariously, Jason was a news junkie for the two big city agencies he lusted after. Some days he thought he was watching the Murder Channel with the excessive number of shootings, stabbings, and killings the crime reporters covered. Barrington wasn't like that. At best, the town was slow and predictable. Only thirty cops on the job to keep peace and order.

"Dispatch to 21."

"Go, dispatch."

"24 reports everything's okay at Sal's."

Jason still sensed the occupants of the small car had been up to something. He could now determine he was chasing an older Maxima. He figured he would make the stop and see what the two runners were up to.

Jason spent a few seconds rationalizing why a stop was necessary. He'd come upon a scene in a high crime area late at night where the subjects peeled out recklessly, thus his decision to make the stop under "reasonable suspicion" was justified. Settled, at least in his mind.

Police officers make "suspicious persons stops" as a regular part of protecting the community. Back in 1968, the U.S. Supreme Court gave street cops that authority in Terry v. Ohio, a case involving a Cleveland officer. The court ruled a street cop could stop, inquire, and frisk a subject when the officer had a "reasonable belief that the person had committed, was committing, or was about to commit a crime."

As a result, a cop is now allowed to conduct a cursory frisk if he or she has a reasonable belief the suspect "may be armed and presenting dangerous conditions" for the officer and community. This is less than the "probable cause" that is required to arrest a subject. The real coup is how the officer reports his reasonable suspicion to be of "specific and articulable facts."

Verbiage created problems for the NYPD when the courts tested the NYPD 'Stop, Question, and Frisk' program in 2013. It wasn't that cops were doing something illegal, the issue was street cops didn't write enough to support and substantiate their stops and frisks, especially since a higher percentage of blacks and Hispanics were being stopped and searched. Commonly, street cops will note a suspect was observed in a high crime area, appeared to be a lookout for a crime being committed, or was ducking into the shadows as police made their rounds. Giving a cop the "street fisheye" can also be described as suspicious. It doesn't take much to document reasoning, but some cops aren't very articulate; some are just lazy. Others simply don't think about why they're stopping and frisking somebody on the street; they may make up reasons after the stop.

Jason looked at the street sign the speeding car had just passed and noted it was Dexter Way. This was only a few streets from where the town of Barrington ended and the county took jurisdiction.

This was the time to pull out the stops. Jason activated his emergency overhead lights with the toggle switch on the dash. The blue strobes circled above him and bounced off the rear window of the Maxima. Jason saw both heads whip around to look out the back as the rear of the Maxima dipped when the car once again accelerated. Jason flipped the siren toggle and the searing wail shrieked as he punched his accelerator. The Charger lurched, growled, and leapt forward like a tiger.

"Unit 21 in pursuit of vehicle westbound on 54 from Dexter Way."

"All units, 21 in pursuit westbound on 54 from Dexter. All units clear the frequency."

Jason's decision and actions immediately instigated a well-rehearsed chain of procedures.

"Clearing the frequency" is commonly done when police enter an emergency situation and it is necessary to restrict other units from broadcasting. If more than one unit broadcasts, it could negatively impact an emergency help call from the primary involved officer. Keeping the frequency open also allows the dispatcher to stay focused on the emergency and not become distracted by mundane or routine calls.

Jason was able to stay a couple hundred yards behind the Maxima. This gave him enough time and space to maneuver if the Maxima crashed or suddenly stopped. The city limits were long behind him, but Jason figured he was involved in a fresh pursuit so it was okay to continue the chase. He knew the state police and sheriff's units were not close by and wouldn't be patrolling this lonely stretch of highway in rural Kansas.

Jason glanced at the speedometer and the digital printout read 102. The Maxima was going even faster and was slowly pulling away. Jason contemplated ending the pursuit, but decided to give it a few more miles.

It was pitch dark on this stretch of highway and with the speed both cars were traveling, the sudden emergence of a dark pickup from a dirt road was almost impossible to see. Jason saw sparks fly as the Maxima hit the left front wheel of the truck. The Maxima careened to the left on two wheels before becoming airborne. The car rolled three times before flopping onto its roof, spinning like a top in a whirlwind of fiery frenzy. The motion sent the car over the side into a deep drainage ditch. The front end of the pickup was torn from the firewall and what was left of the big truck spun in a clockwise circle, settling in the middle of the highway.

Jason stomped his foot on the brakes but was having trouble handling the Charger while executing moves to avoid the truck. The Charger slid into a four-wheel skid with its anti-lock brakes powerless to respond. Jason squeezed by on the right of the truck, close enough to skim the paint. He felt the Charger hit something and then bump over something else. He was too busy trying to guide his police car to a stop to wonder what, if anything, he had struck.

* * *

Billy Snyder had earned his permanent driver's license only the week before. In fact, he was carrying a paper temporary license; the plastic official issuance would be mailed to him within the month. Billy had been waiting a long six months in trainee status, driving his mom to errands all over town. Even though Mrs. Snyder rode shotgun wearing white knuckles on the edge of the passenger seat, she usually gave in to her son's incessant pestering to let him take the wheel. She hoped the extra driving would give him good experience.

A milestone had been reached. Billy was in the driver's seat on his first night out alone, in his own car! He picked up his good friend Tommy Olsen and the two headed to a party at a nearby lake house. He had collected Tommy at the corner down the street from where he lived. Tommy set the location because he didn't want his mom to know where he was going and certainly didn't want her to notice Billy was driving. He knew that would freak her out.

They were headed to one of those "Internet invite parties" when one friend tells a friend about a party, and they tell another and on and on. Billy suspected there might be a couple hundred kids showing up at the house.

"I hear that fine babe, Sue Beth, is going to be there, Tommy. Last time I hooked up with her at a party, she let me wet my finger in her pussy. She rubbed my cock so good I almost came in my pants!" Billy grinned, remembering the experience and fantasizing about what was to come.

"My mom's psycho about me riding with my friends. Thinks none of us know shit and don't know how to drive worth a damn." Tommy laughed as he climbed into Billy's Maxima. "Sue Beth is sure fine, but Bev is the one I'm out for. She sucked my cock last time at Brett's party. Tonight I'm going all the way, count on it!" Tommy proudly displayed a three-pack of condoms.

"Where'd you get those?"

"Dad's nightstand. Shit, he has a full box there. Hasn't used one in the last six months. He's not gonna miss three."

"We need to get some beer?"

"Yeah, good idea. Swing by Sal's. We can always get a few

brews there. They never check IDs. Probably glad to get the sale with all the other stores closed."

Billy glided the Maxima into the parking lot of Sal's Liquor Store. Only two other cars filled the lot. As Billy geared his car into Park, he noticed a cop slowly drive by and saw his brake lights blink. As the cop car turned around to enter the lot, Billy dropped the gearshift into Drive, gunned the Maxima and peeled out like his ass was on fire. He bounced over the curb before turning onto the highway heading out of town.

"Billy, what the fuck you doing, man? We ain't done nuttin'!"

"Shit, we were there to buy booze!"

"Cop don't know that, asshole!"

"Too late now. Hang on, Tommy, I'll outrun him."

"What the fuck...Billy, stop!"

Billy looked back and saw the cop turning his car around. Maybe he wouldn't be following them after all. No such luck. The cop car's headlights soon showed it was gaining on them fast.

Billy stomped on the gas pedal. He'd never gone faster than 50, and that was with his mom issuing non-stop orders and warnings. He remembered her screaming at him to slow down. He took a quick glance at the dash and the glowing red numbers indicated he was topping 110. One thing Billy was happy about—the highway was flat and straight. He took another look in the rearview mirror before setting his eyes on the road ahead. This race was going to take his full concentration.

Out of fucking nowhere, a dark object loomed directly in front of the Maxima. Billy tried to wrench the wheel to the left, but his car was going so fast it only seemed to drift idly. Billy had the sensation his life was traveling in slow motion and he was simply watching it unfold like a curious bystander.

The Maxima hit the front of whatever it was that blocked the highway and suddenly it rode like a carnival ride from hell. The Maxima rolled several times, gave a groan, and shed parts until it landed topside and began a slow, easy spin. The roof collapsed over Billy and Tommy, compressing their spines and fracturing both backs.

Suddenly everything stopped. A hissing sound snaked from the engine. Black muck oozed into the passenger compartment through the shattered windows. The drainage ditch that had become their landing field was only three feet deep, but deep enough to smother Billy and Tommy, sucking whatever life essence each had left.

* * *

Edgar and Hazel Bennett had farmed their green 180 acres all their lives. They were the third generation Bennetts to till this soil, and were proud to say it was still fertile and promising. This year Edgar split the fields into crops of corn and soybeans. It had been a better year than the previous two when Kansas farmers were beaten down by dry summer days. The drought had won the war those years, but God was good now.

"Let's go into town tonight," Hazel casually mentioned as she watched Edgar get up from his chair. Scott Pendley and the nightly news had signed off.

"Good idea. The Cafe okay with you, Hazel?"

"Edgar, I know you like that place so you can catch up with your old friends, but Sylvia stopped serving dinner a few months ago."

"Well, how about the Granary then?" Hazel nodded her approval.

The Bennett's farm bordered on Highway 54. The house sat

300 yards from the highway at the end of a dirt road. Their brand new Ford F250 Crew Cab was parked under the aluminum carport. Edgar carefully maneuvered the Ford down the bumpy dirt drive at a top speed of 20 miles per hour. It seemed to shake and shimmy less at the lower speed. He crossed over the metal cattle guard and stopped at the entrance to the highway. As he always did, Edgar looked both ways and then crept onto the highway to make his left turn.

The speed of the approaching cars combined with the slight rise in the highway obscured Edgar's ability to see the approaching cars, even with the emergency lights twirling on the cop car. At the speed the Charger was going, it was outrunning its siren.

Edgar finally saw the headlights but had only a fraction of a second to turn the steering wheel to the right with his left hand while throwing his right arm across Hazel to offer protection. She hadn't taken the time to latch her seatbelt.

The collision was immediate and intense. The Ford F250's front end was nearly torn off with a deep jagged laceration marking its right fender. Both front tires were blown out, causing the truck to spin twice before coming to rest in the center of the highway. The passenger door enclosing Hazel whipped open from the force of the collision and propelled the old farmer's wife onto the highway. Shep, the Bennett's mixed-breed border collie, leapt over the front seat and jumped from the truck cab to run to where his mistress lay in a crumpled mass of blood and bones. The police car veered to the right of the F250 and the Charger's left front bumper struck Shep as the dog howled over Hazel. The Charger's right tires bounced over the sprawled body of Hazel Bennett and its undercarriage dragged her nearly 100 yards down the highway like a lassoed calf at a two-bit rodeo.

* * *

Adrenaline shot through Jason's system as the high from the active pursuit gave him a rush like he'd never experienced before. He was relieved he had controlled his Charger so well and hadn't crashed into either vehicle. His heart was pumping and his mind was screaming, "Yes, yes, yes!" But his hands were shaking as he clutched the steering wheel in a death grip.

"Unit 21...multiple collisions...somewhere on Highway 54 past the county line. Need back up, sergeant, and ambulance immediately. Probable injuries. Maybe fatals!"

Jason really didn't have a sense of what had happened. His recollections stopped at seeing the Maxima disappear and the dark F250 explode in a shower of sparks, finally shooting a litter of debris along the shoulder of Highway 54. Jason got out of his car and was about to start running to the F250 when he saw a mangled and bloody body wedged under his car. Remnants of a floral patterned cloth covered the corpse like a shroud. He looked closer and saw the mass had once been a woman. Jason puked on the pavement and tried to control sobs.

Edgar Bennett ran to the police car, but stopped when he saw the body crushed under the carriage. The old man dropped to his knees and began to wail, an eerie heart-wrenching sound Jason would remember for the rest of his life. The man's cry pierced his soul and found burial deep in his memory.

Jason rushed to the drainage ditch and saw the Maxima. It was submerged upside down with filthy water lapping at the lower window level. He jumped into the muddy ditch and trudged to the car as fast as the muck would allow. Jason was able to force his arm into the open driver's side window. His search stopped abruptly when it hit the mass that once was Billy Snyder.

A blast of sirens announced back-up had arrived. A loud gun-shot intensified the night's confusion; a thunder that Jason later learned was a deputy putting down the wounded Shep. Jason pulled himself out of the ditch and realized a half dozen police units were surrounding his Charger. The EMT unit from the county fire department arrived shortly after the cops closed the area. Clyde Bartlett, another Barrington officer on duty, arrived and rushed to Jason.

"Jason, you okay?"

"Yeah, I guess. I thought they were robbing Sal's! I thought they were robbing Sal's!" Jason knew then that his life as he knew it was over.

Many years before in Ohio and Wisconsin

To Reginald Watts, Barrington, Kansas was a long ass way from Milwaukee. Reggie, as most called him, was originally from a small town in central Ohio near Columbus. This was one kid who knew he wanted to be a cop while coming of age in Mansfield, a forlorn, rusty industrial town far past its glory days.

Reggie dreamed of being a cop in a big city like Columbus. After working the system and trying hard, he got his wish and entered the Columbus Police Academy. The academy was considered to offer state-of-the-art law enforcement training. Of particular note was an indoor room that could simulate rainy conditions so all-weather training could be well controlled and monitored. The academy also boasted a complete forensic training lab where hands-on experience was top notch.

The Columbus PD was accredited by a national group called the Commission on Accreditation for Law Enforcement Agencies, and was at the top of the law enforcement game, by cop standards. As with any department, even the best ones, there were problems. The Civil Rights Division of the Department of Justice spent an inordinate amount of time scrutinizing Columbus police policies. Federal attorneys considered the PD to be racist and brutal.

As a recruit at the academy, Reggie was molded into what the Columbus police department thought street cops should be. Reggie loved the drills, regimentation, and orderliness of life at the academy, but he was itching to be out on the streets in uniform so he could start catching the bad guys and keep that scum away from the good citizens of Columbus. Without warning, his dreams and hopes were shattered when the budget crunch hit and his entire recruit class was laid off with no plan in place for rehiring.

Reggie didn't want to go back to Mansfield so he worked odd jobs in the Columbus and Cleveland areas. He heard a few cop shops in Wisconsin were hiring and decided to go for it; Reggie knew he had no future in Ohio. The application and vetting process took nearly six months until finally the Brookside PD offered him a spot and shipped him to the Milwaukee Police Academy.

Brookside was a pleasant suburb outside Milwaukee and had close to 100 officers assigned to the police department. Reggie was back on the job he thought he would love. It didn't take long for him to realize the Milwaukee academy was not of the same caliber he had experienced in Columbus.

Reggie's first fifteen years as a Brookside cop were a blend of daily routines, mundane street police work, short stints in vice and liquor enforcement, and four years in detectives working property crimes. Reggie had not done well on his first and second tries at the sergeant's exam, but lucked out on the third. He wasn't high on the list for promotion, but eventually the department shuffled him into place and he was back on the streets with gold sergeant stripes marching up his sleeves.

When Reggie joined the suburban department, the Milwaukee force, the big neighboring police agency next door was under scrutiny. The turmoil began back in 2004 when Frank Jude, a male stripper, was caught in an unfortunate incident when he and his friends ended up at a party with off-duty Milwaukee cops. Frank was almost beaten to death by these officers for unknown reasons. However, there certainly were hints of racial animus. On-duty officers were involved in the abortive attempt to cover up the beating and place blame on Frank and his friends. Years of trials wore on before the local DA ended up losing the only felony trial in his 38 years in office when the officers weren't convicted. Later, several of the same officers were indicted, pled guilty, or were found guilty in federal trials. Lingering community unrest persisted and ended with an out-of-area police chief being selected to run the Milwaukee police department. The stigma of "police brutality" and the "Code of Silence" clouded the reputations of all neighboring departments, much like happened after the Rodney King incident with the LAPD in 1991. Brookside got caught up in the cloud of police misconduct.

"Mr. Sergeant," the old black woman began. She was old in appearance, but probably not in chronological age. The woman was overweight and had an enormous bosom that spilled out of her frayed dress. The pungent fragrance of a heavy application of perfume filled the air around her. She wore a small hat pinned to her hair and her hands were hidden in soiled brown gloves. This woman was a throwback to the memory of her mother who lived at a time when women wouldn't venture in public without a hat, gloves, and clutching a purse.

"My son Clarence done been abused by your men, Mr. Sergeant. He only a chile, but he look like a man. He not too bright, but he be kind-hearted."

"Ma'am, what's your name, ma'am?"

"Beatrice. Beatrice Manson." The woman looked directly at Reggie and he could see moisture filling her eyes. She tried to draw attention from her tears by fumbling with her gloves and placing them in her purse.

"Here, take this, Mrs. Manson," Reggie said as he handed her a tissue from the box on his desk. "Tell me what happened to your son Clarence."

"My son comes running up onto the porch and running right behind him is these two officers, Mr. Sergeant. Clarence, he be huffing and puffing and saying he do nuttin'. Dem officers come running right up onto my porch and one of dem hit my Clarence top of his head with a flashlight. Big black thing. Blood gusted out and filled my Clarence's face. The other cop bounced up and kicked Clarence in, well, you know wheres." Mrs. Manson raised her hand to cover her mouth.

"Weren't right, Mr. Sergeant. Clarence jus' hanging onto me when dat happened. I tried to ast the officers what my Clarence done and dey told me to shut my mouth or I'd get some of dat too. Ain't right what dey do to my Clarence. Don't matter what Clarence done, it just ain't right, Mr. Sergeant."

Reggie had owned the rank of sergeant for only a month. He didn't know what the routine was for handling a citizen's complaint like this. He knew what the manual said should be done, but he also knew sergeants didn't always follow the written word. Besides, he didn't know anything more than what this woman was telling him. He knew there were usually three sides to every story—the complainant's version, the officer's side, and finally, what really happened.

"Mrs. Manson, I'll try to help you," Reggie encouraged as he placed his hand over the plump fingers resting on his desk. A thin wedding band on Beatrice's left hand was buttressed by rolls of fat and Reggie thought the only way it could ever be removed from her third finger would be to cut it off with a jeweler's saw.

"I'm going to look into this for you, don't you worry." Reggie watched as the old woman struggled to wiggle out of her chair and gain solid footing before adjusting her hat and taking her gloves from her pocketbook. Once accomplished, she slowly walked out the lobby doors.

Reggie rotated his chair that groaned at the maneuver and looked at his computer screen. His fingers moved the mouse as he searched for dispatch information. He first logged Mrs. Manson's address with no results, and then typed "Clarence Manson." The screen popped with the arrest report.

"*Officers on routine patrol obs. 3 m/b congregated outside ABC Market. This has been known to officers to be a hangout for the local street gang, "21 boys." When officers alighted from their marked squad, suspect Clarence Manson ran. Believing susp. was hiding evidence, officers gave chase. As susp. began to run up the stairs to a house, he slipped and struck his head on the concrete stairs. Susp. taken into custody for obstruction, hindrance, and disorderly conduct. Susp. treated at Fire Station 1 by EMTs. Susp. found to be juvenile, so released to his mother with citation.*"

Reggie saw the arresting officers were Smith and Bronson. Bronson was working and he responded almost immediately to Reggie's text to come into the station.

"Sarge, you want see me?" Bronson asked as he entered the watch commander's small office.

"Yeah, I do. Had a visit from Clarence Manson's mom. She's

making a complaint that you whopped on him. Different story than what you wrote in your report, though. What's your side?"

"This something gonna end up with discipline, Sarge? If it is, then I get to have my union rep present."

Reggie knew Bronson was right. The bargaining agreement with the local Fraternal Order of Police unit gave all officers that right.

"This is just a preliminary inquiry, Bronson. Don't make it a federal case."

"Well, it's my right, you know. You're new here. None of us know much about how you're gonna supervise, Sarge."

"Bronson, sit your ass down!"

Bronson stuck to his version of what had happened to Clarence. Gave exactly the same story he filed in his report.

After Bronson left, Reggie turned back to his computer. He plugged in "Early Warning System" and checked the complaint histories for both Bronson and Smith. Each had discourtesy complaints, but no use of force complaints. Time to call Clarence's mother.

"Mrs. Manson?" Reggie inquired when a female voice answered his phone call. "I checked with the officers who visited your home and there's not much I can do now. But I did call the Juvenile Court and the clerk said she would pull the citation the officers gave to Clarence. You and Clarence won't have to appear down at the juvenile center."

"Thank you, Mr. Sergeant, it still ain't right, but my Clarence is okay now."

Reggie knew he should have opened an Internal Affairs complaint investigation, but he didn't want to start his career as supervising sergeant on a negative note with only four weeks under his belt. He was more concerned with showing his men he would cover their backs than open an investigation that probably wouldn't result in specific findings. Mrs. Manson seemed to be placated by the work he had done on her behalf. No sense making a big deal of this, Reggie thought. He knew the Brookside PD didn't initiate many citizen complaint investigations. Reggie never had one in his fifteen years and he'd certainly used his stick and flashlight a few times when he shouldn't have.

* * *

Brookside Lanes was a regular Saturday night hangout for the wealthy kids living in Brookside. This particular night was bitterly cold and a flurry of snowflakes swirled in the night sky in the parking lot. A young female bowler had come out to her car to get a sweater and quickly returned to the front desk. She told the attendant she had seen a large man lurking in the parking lot near the tree line. The attendant spit his wad of gum on a plastic cup lid for safekeeping and put in a call to the Brookside Police.

Officers Scott Matthews and Chris Shaw were sent to the bowling alley, each in a cop car. It was 24 degrees with the wind blowing from the northwest, making the wind chill close to zero. The officers approached the parking lot from opposite ends. They intended to make a couple passes, stop and talk with the attendant, and then clear the call. Last thing they wanted to do was leave the warmth of their patrol cars.

"Chris, you see there in the shadows by that Suburban?" Scott Matthews squawked on the tactical channel.

"Sort of. Big guy, huh? Looks like he's smoking. I can see a faint glow," Chris Shaw reported.

"Let's light him up, Chris!"

The officers directed their cars toward the Suburban and simultaneously turned on high-intensity takedown lights. A large man was silhouetted leaning against the big SUV. He immediately turned his head away from the piercing lights aimed in his direction. Both officers reluctantly exited their cars and approached the large form from opposite sides.

"28 to dispatch. We have a male in the Brookside Lanes parking lot. 27 and we are approaching to investigate."

"Hey, buddy, what you doing here?" Scott called to the hulky figure. The guy didn't answer. "Police here, we just want to talk, buddy."

"I ain't your buddy!"

"What's your name, man?" Scott changed his approach and lowered the pitch of his voice.

"Clarence."

"Say Clarence, can you come over here. Let's talk," Scott continued.

"Nope! I ain't doing nuttin'."

"Got some folks scared here in the bowling alley, Clarence. Why you think that be, huh?"

"Dunno know why. I'm minding myself having a smoke. My momma don't like me smoking so I light up where she can't see me. Don't want no trouble. Never do, but people just gets scared when I'm around. Dunno know why."

Chris was now positioned behind the giant.

"Throw the cigarette down, Clarence," Chris ordered from his obscured position in the dark in a sharp authoritative command voice.

"What the fuck?" Clarence whirled around swinging his arms toward the voice behind him.

One of the massive arms caught Chris on the side of his head and set him on his ass. Scott jumped on Clarence's back in an attempt to throw him off balance and drive him to the pavement. Clarence moved back and forced Scott into the side of Suburban, nearly knocking the wind out of him.

"27…need help NOW!"

Within two minutes, three sheriff's cars and the only other Brookside unit were racing into the parking lot. The collective emergency strobes made the lot look like the honky-tonk carnival at the County Fair. Clarence was now standing in the lane between parked cars and was growling unintelligible sounds at the six officers circling him. One deputy pulled out his Taser, fixed a dot on the hulk and shot Clarence without warning.

The barbs fired and impacted, piercing into Clarence's back. One barb sunk into his left shoulder blade and the other pierced his lower right side near the spine. The electrical current worked exactly as it was supposed to do, causing interference to Clarence's muscular nervous system. He dropped to his knees, and then hit the pavement, landing on his stomach with a thud. Four officers pounced on Clarence to control him and fought to bring his arms behind his back for handcuffing. Eventually two sets of cuffs were hooked together to restrain the big black man's flailing arms. One officer straddled Clarence's legs to control his extremities. The intense struggle exhausted the four cops as their captive fought with all he had. Finally, the sound of Clarence's last breath on earth was thundering as a strange silence filled the parking lot. What the hell had happened?

Eventually the medical examiner stated the cause of death was a combination of compression asphyxia caused by multiple officers on his back and a congenital heart defect. The toxicology report indicated there were no drugs or alcohol in Clarence's system.

The investigation of Clarence's death by the District Attorney's office uncovered the inquiry report completed by Sgt. Reginald Watts one month prior which detailed his encounter with Clarence's mother. The DA accepted Reggie's explanation of his course of action and the absence of need to initiate a complaint investigation. In the end, the DA and the coroner found Clarence Manson's medical condition was the primary cause of his unfortunate demise.

Reggie considered paying a visit to Mrs. Manson. In the back of his mind, he worried his lack of follow up on her complaint might have been an error in judgment. He struggled with the thought that he might have been able to help Mrs. Manson by referring her son to one of the area's mental health facilities for treatment. Reggie questioned his choice not to make that simple referral, but what did it matter now?

Internal Affairs investigations don't only clear officers. They search for the truth of what might have occurred in questionable situations. These investigations can assist citizens caught in the criminal justice system's morass and the closed rank silence of police agencies.

* * *

Twenty years passed quicker than Reggie expected. Before he knew it, he was vested with a pension from Brookside and could retire and receive a nice monthly check. It was something to consider.

Reggie was married to Patsy McClendon. It was his third try at marriage. Patsy was an RN at the local trauma hospital. She was ten years Reggie's junior and the third time the groom felt he had collected a fine trophy wife who could also cover her own keep.

Patsy longed to return to where her family lived near Wichita, Kansas. The McClendon family settled in this part of Kansas four generations before and was considered to be a clan of political movers and shakers. Patsy's dad was the president of the local Farmers and Merchants' National Bank in Barrington, about fifty miles from Wichita. Reggie's retirement gave the couple the opportunity to move to another state without much financial worry, and so they settled in Kansas. Patsy was quickly snapped up by a local physician-run hospital where her family's position assured her a job. Reggie wasn't anxious to jump back into any employment, but was open should something interesting come up.

One afternoon Barrington's chief of police called a press conference and announced he had accepted the position of police chief at a larger department in Colorado. One of Patsy's uncles happened to be on the Barrington City Council and it wasn't long before one retired Reginald Watts was sworn in as the town's seventh police chief.

Reggie soon found policing Barrington was vastly different than policing around Milwaukee. For one thing, the biggest city, Wichita, was far to the east and had little impact how cops in Barrington would be handling matters.

But the biggest difference Reggie found was there wasn't much crime in Barrington. The community was most interested in seeing marked police cars drive up and down the town's manicured residential streets. Residents wanted their cops to raise a hand in a friendly wave and help them drag garbage cans to the curb on trash day.

Local businesses wanted Barrington cops to stop by, shoot the breeze, and maybe spin crazy cop stories that everybody knew would never happen in a place like Barrington. Reggie felt he was living and working in a real life Mayberry.

What the hell, Reggie often thought. I got a pension check coming in every month from Wisconsin, got a small salary from the good people in Barrington, and I even got a car to use whenever I want. Life is good. I can play this silly game if that's all the town people want of me.

The Barrington PD didn't have to worry about dispatching or jailing subjects; the county sheriff handled those mundane tasks. All Reggie had to do was control his small band of thirty cops. Barrington's department was like so many throughout the country—a stepping-stone for young officers who wanted to move on to a city where real crime happened. Full-blown testosterone ran in the veins of those young studs. Of course, there were always a handful of cops who were lazy and welcomed the laid back routine typifying the cop business in Barrington.

"Boss, welcome to the job," a heavy-set cop greeted as he entered the chief's small office carrying a cup of coffee. "I hear you've been getting around town and visiting with cops on the job. I had to take family medical leave that put me out for the past couple weeks. Sorry I wasn't here for your swearing in ceremony."

Roscoe Stedman was one of the older cops Reggie inherited. He was short and fat and Reggie doubted he could pass a physical in most police departments. He found it interesting that they actually made gun belts big enough to accommodate Roscoe's girth. The front of his belt wasn't visible since a roll of fat hung over it like a protective shield. His upper pant legs were strained to the max trying to contain enormous thighs. A bushy moustache obscured Roscoe's upper lip. The old-timer was Barrington's senior officer with nearly fifteen years on the job.

"Yeah, Roscoe. Have a seat and let's talk." Roscoe had great difficulty squeezing his butt into the wooden chair with the confining arms defining its perimeter. Rolls of fat rippled over the arms, chair back, and molded seat. Visions of Tweedle Dum and Tweedle Dee floated in Reggie's head.

"Hear you're the senior man around here."

"Yes, sir, that I am. Kind of like the department historian." The fat man laughed as coffee spilled over the lip of his cup marking his uniform shirt with Rorschach blots. "Know the good, the bad, and the ugly, boss. Mostly good, though."

"What'd you think we need to do most on the job, Roscoe? I want to hear your ideas since you're the most experienced cop on the squad."

Roscoe relaxed and put his free hand to his chin. "Don't know, I reckon. Things seem to be going okay. Those young bucks, though, they can be tough to rein in. They want to fight crime and there just ain't any here in Barrington. We need to give them something to do, boss."

"That's what I was thinking, Roscoe. Glad you brought it up. What you think we should give them to do?"

Roscoe shook his head. He'd probably never considered this before.

"I notice nobody seems to be writing traffic tickets."

"Yep, that's right. The council doesn't want the town folk getting riled up and the cops giving tickets would sure do that!"

"Well, we got that main highway running right through Barrington. What if we put the cops on that stretch? We might even pull in a few bucks of seizure money to boost ticket revenue. What you think, Roscoe?"

Reggie knew the big, older cop wouldn't go for the idea. It meant he might have to work for a change.

"Well, maybe, but these young cops don't really know how to do that shit. Whadda they call it? Highway interdiction or something like that. I took a training class that troopers from Nebraska gave and they taught us what to look for and how to stay out of trouble with the feds." Roscoe brought his finger back to his chin like the great thinker he was. "I think it was just a bunch of bullshit, if you want my humble opinion."

Drug trafficking in the U.S. still depends largely on transportation on public highways once narcotics or illegal drugs reach the country. Drugs go in one direction and money flows in the other direction. Aggressive cops began patrolling major highways in the late 1970s and early 1980s looking for shipments of narcotics and/or money.

When a federal program allowed police to seize the illegal assets of drug traffickers, stopping shipments quickly became a lucrative activity. Some early highway cops were sloppy with their arrests and often cut corners and stepped on the Constitutional rights of the criminals they stopped.

Well-intentioned officers documented the methods used to confiscate drugs and money without violating the Constitution. Their methods were organized into training programs presented to police departments around the country.

In the late 1980s, the advent of video filming and audio recording of drug stops produced valuable evidence to support highway cops' methods which added much to the training programs. Criminal defense attorneys often challenged indices commonly thought to give an officer additional justification for a stop.

Actually, many alleged items that might justify a stop were rather mundane like trash, fast food wrappers, maps, and other things most every driver would carry in a car. Advanced training gave cops information detailing secret hiding places where drugs and money might be discovered in stopped vehicles.

Training also offered a scripted scenario a highway cop could follow when talking to a suspected driver. Stopping vehicles became a choreographed stage play captured on video and audiotape demonstrating that searches were, in fact, consensual. This training is commonly referred to as "highway interdiction tactics." Conversely, those on the receiving end of the stops frequently referred to the practice as "highway robbery."

Reggie convinced Barrington's city council and city manager to pop for funds to buy two new vehicles and the in-car video and audio equipment necessary to begin a highway interdiction program on Highway 54.

The new cop cars shining in the department lot were black Dodge Chargers with Hemi engines, equipped with heavy-duty suspension and brakes, massive front push bars, and reflective grey decals signifying Barrington Police. Reggie handpicked his youngest and most aggressive cops to initiate the program that targeted travelers passing through Barrington on the main highway. The council and manager were very explicit that the enforcement effort only be directed at passing drivers, not the good residents of Barrington.

* * *

Jason Day was one of the young aggressive cops handpicked by Chief Watts. Jason loved the mandatory two-day training program given by a quartet of troopers from Oklahoma. He was impressed with the troopers' professionalism, skill, and the successes they shared with the class. He salivated when he saw the trophy photos the troopers proudly flashed up on the screen. Automatic weapons and piles and piles of bundles of cash. One showed bricks of cocaine that could have filled a dumpster. Jason was even more excited that Chief Watts picked him over the more seasoned officers. He figured this highway interdiction stuff was a skill he could capitalize on when he made the move to a bigger city police force.

Dusk was falling and Jason was sitting in his usual spot on the median separating the east and west lanes of Highway 54. He was watching westbound traffic that particular day. He saw a small dark vehicle moving in the fast lane and radar-pegged it traveling at 72. When the chief instituted his new highway interdiction program, he and the City convinced the State to lower the speed limit from 65 to 55.

Jason saw the vehicle quickly veer to the right and settle behind an 18-wheeler chugging along in the slow lane. Jason watched as the driver stared directly ahead into the rear of the truck rather than glance sideways at him in his marked police car. The driver appeared to be dark in complexion and Jason thought he might be Hispanic. This could definitely be a catch.

Jason punched his accelerator, spraying dirt as his car bounced onto the pavement and turned left. He was behind the suspect Ford Escort, possibly a rental car commonly used by drug mules moving contraband into the country and money out of it. The Escort maintained a constant 55 mph speed and stayed behind the truck as other westbound cars sped by the three vehicles ambling in the slow lane. Jason called in the license plate number and dispatch returned that it was a Budget rental out of Chicago.

Jason waited until his parade of three passed the next off-ramp before turning on the overhead emergency light full force. He watched the Escort driver glance into the rearview mirror and signal his intent to pull onto the shoulder. Jason planned to use the right side approach he'd recently learned for stopping a subject, and gradually pulled his car onto the shoulder to investigate. He executed the maneuver turning the wheel aggressively to the left, positioning his cruiser at a sharp angle directly behind the

Escort. This tactic gave Jason protection when he exited his car and created a barrier between the stopped suspect and himself. This right side approach also gave Jason distance when he walked to conduct his investigation.

Just as Jason exited his squad car, the Escort shot out and deposited lines of rubber disfiguring the highway. The Escort quickly caught up to the 18-wheeler and passed it. Jason raced back and jumped into his car, shooting a dump load of gravel into the drainage ditch as he accelerated to catch the speed freak.

The Escort suddenly veered in front of the big truck as Jason was starting to pass it on the left. The suspect was heading to the approaching off-ramp and careened in front of the truck before bouncing wildly onto the ramp. By the time Jason passed the truck, the Escort was long gone.

21 to Dispatch. That suspect in the dark Escort got off at Exit 3. I'm turning around. Alert the SO to BOLO that car.

It took Jason three minutes to turn around in the median before he could take the off-ramp. At the bottom of the ramp he looked both ways for a sighting. Nothing to see. He figured the Escort wouldn't travel eastbound since that would take him back to Barrington. The young cop approached the next intersection leading to the frontage road. He didn't see any vehicle traveling north and slowly turned to head into a new subdivision on the outskirts of town. The new homes were built with short driveways ending at metal carports. The third house down had a dark Escort parked in the carport. Jason slowed and stopped, blocking the entrance to the driveway.

The car looked empty. Suddenly a head popped up and the Escort shot back directly into the left side of Jason's cop car, caving in the passenger door. The Escort turned left and drove across the newly seeded lawn, bouncing over the swale for drainage and onto the residential street.

21...found the car. In pursuit northbound on, I think, Daisy Lane. We're approaching 60 and climbing.

The subdivision was a jumble of streets that wound and snaked like a vipers' pit. The streets were meant to be aesthetic, but they were a pain in the ass for fire trucks and speeding police cars to navigate. Jason followed the Escort, maneuvering around cars parked on the street edges. Startled residents were standing on their lawns watching as both cars screamed past. Two teenagers on bikes dropped their bikes and dove into a thicket of bushes as the cars raced by. Jason knew there was only one exit street in the neighborhood that could be used. The rear of the subdivision bordered on a farm and went nowhere.

Jason watched in amazement as the Escort shot between two houses and plowed directly through a chain-link fence, blasting through the barbed wire fence isolating the farm. The Escort disappeared into rows of shoulder high corn.

Shit, Jason thought. Here I am in a fuckin' cornfield! Hell, the guy could be anywhere and I could be his target!

Jason heard sirens approaching and elected to stay at the fence line watching the now empty Escort. Roscoe Stedman was in the first car to arrive, followed quickly by a sheriff's car. There weren't enough cops to establish a perimeter. That was big city stuff. Jason rushed to search the abandoned car. Other than the rental agreement, trash, empty beer and soda cans, and an assortment of McDonald's wrappers, there wasn't anything else to find. No drugs. No money.

"Looking to make another big one, huh?" Roscoe threw out when he approached Jason and the Escort. He was wearing a shit-eating grin. "You get a cut of what you find on these stops,

Jason? Chief's not going to be happy about you damaging his chariot, particularly when you got nothing to show for it!"

Jason thought about giving a flip response, and then realized his words wouldn't be productive.

Two hours later a deputy called the Barrington PD and reported he had picked up a Mexican guy with papers from Chicago. The Mexican insisted he was just a day laborer and some guy had picked him up for work. Nothing on him except a little corn stalk residue.

* * *

The call from Rachel Mendez was a delightful distraction. Taylor had been lamenting, once again, about what to do with his aging Jeep Wrangler. He and the Jeep had weathered many years of good times, trials, and tribulations together, but lately he was getting tired of going out to the carport to rev up the old Jeep, only to have the starter click in response, not answering with the anticipated roar.

Rachel was calling to suggest a weekend rendezvous at Taylor's place. She was an attractive attorney in the DA's office in Gunnison. Taylor met her during his Colorado adventure while driving back from Grand Junction to Santa Fe in Sandy Banks' new bright yellow Porsche 911. The Porsche had been targeted by a cop from a little burg called Juanita Springs. Profiled would probably be a better description of what had happened that go around. The Juanita Springs cops were trying to perform a highway interdiction, but in this case, they aced a highway robbery game. The cops figured the Porsche would be a good addition to the drug task force's fleet of seized cars and would produce a couple months' salary for the task force guys.

Rachel, assisted by the local chief of police, got the Porsche back in Taylor's hands so he could return it to his steady friend, Sandy. In the process, Taylor was able to help the chief avoid a civil lawsuit and started in motion an investigation that rid the world of several dirty cops from Utah.

Rachel and Taylor hit it off right from the start and enjoyed each other's company. They kept in touch and the young attorney was willing to travel to keep the relationship alive.

This was Rachel's third visit to Santa Fe to see Taylor. Recently she had been captivated by an episode of "Diners, Drive-ins, and Dives" on the Food Network which highlighted restaurants in the Santa Fe area; she wanted to try each establishment featured during her weekend stay.

Dinner at the Tune-Up Café was good and diverse. The café had been a house, or maybe a garage, and was located on a small residential street. The inside looked to be decorated by a commune hippy who had taken a wrong turn in Alice's Wonderland. A kaleidoscope of colorful zigzags on the walls mimicked a LSD experience from the '60s. The menu was Mexican, with South American hints thrown in for flavor.

Rachel chose Mole Colorado Enchiladas for her entrée and pronounced them to be very good. Taylor tried the El Salvadoran Combo and found the banana leaf wrapped tamale to be excellent. It was good to find tamales with the perfect amount of masa rather than be served in a cannoli of dough accented with only hints of carnitas.

Rachel meandered into Taylor's kitchen the morning after their dinner experience, wakened by the aroma of fresh coffee and the loud clanking of pots. She was wearing one of Taylor's oversized LAPD tee shirts and he doubted much else. She took a seat at the table and watched him work on breakfast.

Taylor was busy whisking eggs, stirring in measures of cumin, dried cilantro, diced green chilies, a hearty dose of pepper, and a splash of cream. He poured the thick mixture into a hot frying pan, threw in a couple pinches of salt, and finally topped the concoction with shredded sharp cheddar cheese before sliding the pan into the heated oven. They would enjoy their breakfast in about forty-five minutes, Taylor estimated.

"Got some good news, Taylor," Rachel announced as she mulled over her coffee. He looked at her, expecting her to tell him what it was. "Got a new job."

"That's great! But, why leave DA Sanders? You said you liked working for him."

"I did. But the work got boring. Same old, same old. DVs, DWIs, assaults, juvie problems. I was getting stale."

"So what's the new job?"

"Department of Justice."

"What, up in Denver?"

"No D.C."

"You ever been to D.C., Rachel?"

"Once," she said, and paused for effect. "Eighth grade field trip." They both laughed at the thought.

"So what division of DOJ?"

"Civil Rights, Special Litigation Section. You've done some work for them, haven't you?"

Taylor had worked with that section of DOJ a few years back. In 1994, Congress passed a law allowing the DOJ to conduct investigations of local police agencies when it was suspected the agency was involved in widespread Constitutional violations. They were called "pattern and practice investigations." Close to twenty agencies were initially investigated, including municipal offices, sheriff departments, and one state police agency. The

DOJ continued to be active and conducted similar investigations throughout the country. Taylor had been a consultant for DOJ on several of them.

"I was. Also worked on the city side of a couple investigations. Why did you pick that section?"

"I've taken a liking to cop work for some reason." She smiled at Taylor. "You do get to the East Coast, don't you?"

"Occasionally."

After breakfast Rachel nosed around Taylor's small condo.

"You've done a lot to your place lately. I like that piece," she said pointing to a carved wooden statute.

"That one was crafted by a Polish carver. I bought two pieces from him at the Folk Art Festival a few months ago. He specializes in religious pieces. Tudeusz Kacalak was brought over by one of the owners of a shop just off the old square. I had him make this piece for me. It's Saint Michael, the patron saint of law enforcement."

"I didn't know you were so religious, Taylor!"

"I'm not. I just like St. Michael and folk art."

For lunch, the couple tried another of Guy Fieri's Santa Fe picks. Rachel was eager to try the green chile cheeseburger at Bert's Burger Bowl. Sloppy and flavorful, just the way she liked it.

"Doesn't your friend with benefits get upset when I come down and stay with you?"

"You mean Sandy? No, not at all. We both have other friends. We simply enjoy each other's company when we can. We don't have any preconceived ideas or commitments. No, it's not a problem."

Taylor suggested they attend a gallery opening that night at one of the many art shops lining Canyon Road. The winding narrow street was dotted with art galleries showcasing every imaginable medium. Art ranged from inexpensive tourist souvenirs to fine art, or at least promising fine art.

Taylor's special gallery opening invitation was one of many he received since his move to Santa Fe after retiring from the LAPD. He liked art, was willing to pay for it, and so his name was quickly added to the golden list.

Gallery parking, as always, was a bitch. Rachel drove her car since Taylor hadn't gotten around to struggling with the canvas top on his Wrangler. It was already November and the chill in the air at this altitude was constant. Taylor reminded himself he had to get that top in place before the weather turned really bad.

"Taylor," a voice called as he guided Rachel into the crowded gallery. The voice belonged to Sandy Banks. She elbowed through the crowd like a linebacker, grabbed Taylor, planted a wet kiss on his lips, and flicked a sensuous smack on his ass. Sandy was the type woman who filled any room she entered. She pulled away as quickly as she'd grabbed and glanced at Rachel.

"I hope you're going to introduce me to this lovely Latina, Taylor."

Taylor saw both women scanning each other with an intensity that would put a TSA agent to shame. Sandy was wearing a bright floral peasant dress, dropping to just below her knees. Her long suede coat touched her ankles provocatively. A large amber piece suspended on a long chain nestled between her heavy breasts. Sandy was a foot taller than Rachel, and only a couple inches shorter than Taylor. She was a large-boned woman with about fifty pounds over Rachel's trim figure.

Polar opposite, Rachel had chosen a short black leather skirt, black turtleneck sweater topped with a black leather vest for her night on the town. She gained height from four-inch platform heels. Thick shiny black hair framed her dark face that was adorned only by small diamond earrings.

"Sandy Banks, this is Rachel Mendez. She's visiting from Gunnison."

"Rachel, you must be the wonderful lawyer who saved my Porsche that Taylor allowed to get away!" Sandy laughed and placed her arm in Rachel's.

"Come with me and meet Calvin. He owns this overpriced gallery."

Later that night Taylor had a question to ask Rachel. "Well, did you girls talk about me?"

"Of course we did, silly." Rachel would only say how different she found Sandy from Taylor's description. Taylor knew Sandy would throw something in the next time they were together. He couldn't wait.

A teary goodbye wasn't on the agenda when Rachel packed to leave. Taylor promised he would contact her if he was ever anywhere near D.C. He actually was looking forward to making a trip east. It would give him a reason to prowl around the District again. He hadn't visited the new Native American Indian Museum since it opened in the ring of Smithsonian buildings on the mall, and that was definitely on his bucket list.

Taylor walked Rachel to her car, gave her a hug and kiss, and waved her on her way.

Once back in his condo he saw the message light on his phone was blinking for attention.

"Taylor, Bob Turner. Kansas Muni Insurance Pool. Got a job for you. How fast can you get to Wichita?"

* * *

"Don't think we've ever met, Taylor," Bob Turner said as they found each other at the baggage carousel in the Wichita Airport. It seemed like a good place to meet a stranger. After Taylor grabbed his bag, the men made their way to a Starbucks outside the TSA checkpoint.

"Taylor, here's the story. I got a nasty claim from Barrington, a small town a few miles down the road from here," Bob began as they sat down and opened their coffee lids to let the dark brew cool.

"Barrington hasn't had much activity in the claims department, other than the usual car crashes and officer slip and fall workers' comp claims. This claim, however, involves three deaths. All locals. Happened when a cop was chasing a couple kids. Sixteen years old...both of them. They were just dumb kids. Then a 72-year-old woman who was riding with her husband was run over by the cop's car. Killed their dog, too."

Bob dropped his head, shaking it in disbelief. "Community is up in arms about it and not happy with the local cops. Particularly the chief!"

"Not much in the way of a federal claim, Bob, but maybe you got liability on the state claim. You guys have a cap on claims here in Kansas?"

"Sort of," Bob admitted. "It's not quite that easy in Kansas. Laws limit liability to five hundred thousand per incident, but then there are other laws on the books that say it's the limit of insurance, which in this case is five million."

For many years, police pursuit deaths and injuries were litigated in local courts under state laws. Usually they were classified as wrongful deaths. A case in 1978 opened the floodgates for litigation in federal courts. That case allowed citizens to sue cities and counties, and allowed citizens to collect additional funds for attorney fees, if they won their case. Citizens were required to show that a city or county actually created the problem or situation and didn't do anything in an attempt to resolve it. Of course, a Constitutional violation had to be proved; usually a 4th Amendment use of force/seizure or a 14th Amendment due process claim. Allowing officers to engage in uncontrolled high-speed pursuits which resulted in death or injury could lead to litigation. In other situations, it might be proved a police agency wasn't overseeing or monitoring this dangerous police tactic adequately.

The trend ended with a case out of Sacramento filed as Lewis v. Sacramento. Like many police pursuit cases, the ending was tragic. In this case the officer was chasing two young boys on a motorcycle. The officer either lost sight of the cycle or he stopped the chase. He did not know that a short distance down the road, the boy driving the motorcycle stopped. When the officer approached the standstill cycle, his cruiser still traveling at a high speed, he couldn't stop and hit the pair, killing the passenger. The court concluded that the officer didn't intentionally strike the motorcycle. Slowly, pursuit cases lost steam at the federal level.

Around 2010, the U.S. Supreme Court heard the case of a Georgia sheriff's deputy chasing, and eventually ramming, a young man running from a traffic ticket stop. The Supreme Court viewed the deputy's in-car dash camera as evidence. The pursuit never exceeded 70 miles per hour, but the justices found the deputy's actions were "objectively reasonable" under the conditions. That ended federal litigation affecting police pursuits.

In state courts, statutes may limit how much money can be awarded in lawsuits against public officials. For example, the collection limit in New Mexico is $400,000. In Florida the limit is $200,000. In some Florida cases when the jury verdict awards more, the case can be taken to Tallahassee, where the Florida state capitol is located, for a special legislation award.

"Problem is, Taylor, I'm not sure what's been going on in Barrington. Hadn't heard from them in years. Then over the last two years, there were ten filed claims for dings and dents on cop cars. Nothing really major, except one brand new vehicle that was totaled when it ran off the road and hit a tree. Got a couple workers' comp claims out of those accidents. I need someone to take a look and give the insurance pool concrete info so we can evaluate claims more effectively."

People working for insurance companies that cover police agencies usually have a good idea of the inner workings of police operations. Many have been officers in the past or just being around the police departments give them a heads up on how the agency should be operating. Taylor had discovered that he was often called in to give a little weight to the insurance company's final decision. The company could point the finger at Taylor and say it was his opinion and the company agreed with it. There were times, Taylor had discovered, when the insurance people were at a loss or didn't know how to access the right information or ask the right questions. Taylor's experience frequently allowed him to get into the nitty gritty of the operation, open a few doors, find some contacts, and occasionally poke a hornets' nest.

Taylor drove the short distance from the airport to Barrington. Highway 54 bypassed the center of town, as so many new highways did. Three off-ramps from the limited access highway identified where the town could be found. Wasn't like Interstates that had zero cross traffic. Between the off-ramps, intersecting roads crossed the highway. Taylor took the ramp noting "City Center." As he exited, he spotted a Hampton Inn and figured it would have to do for his Barrington base. Taylor usually picked motels some distance away from the ears and eyes of locals, but here he would probably end up in another county.

Taylor traveled less than a mile before reaching the acclaimed "City Center." Barrington's center consisted of a roundabout of two intersecting business streets leading to a couple blocks of one-story retail shops and professional offices. Barrington wasn't home to a big box shopping center as many towns boasted these days.

It was close to 1:30 when Taylor rounded the circle and found the Barrington Inn Café. Most restaurants in smaller towns were open for breakfast and lunch, but closed by two in the afternoon. Some might reopen for dinner at five if there was enough traffic. Barrington's streets offered angle parking and Taylor pulled his rental car into a spot directly in front of the café.

This hometown eatery was similar to the many others Taylor had visited during his years on the road as a consultant. Gone was the counter, replaced by tables lined in long rows. At the back of the café, there was usually one large round table that could easily seat ten and was identified as the old-timers or regulars' table. How someone was privileged to be invited to sit at these designated tables was always a mystery to Taylor. He found a small Formica table next to the honored rounder that was vacant this time of day.

"Coffee?" a voice asked from behind a curtain of beads.

"Sure, black," Taylor answered the unseen voice.

A large beige mug with wisps of steam circling the top was set before him by a pudgy hand attached to a long-sleeved faded green dress. A woman in her sixties, at best, was apparently going to be Taylor's first conduit to the workings of the little town. She wore an apron with splashes of the breakfast meals she had served earlier that day. Her hair was bound in a net that health departments often require food service employees wear. After depositing the cup on the table she stepped back and placed her thick hands on her large hips.

"You not from around here?"

"Nope."

"Lost?"

"Nope."

"Sightseeing?"

"Nope."

"Well, you win. I'm plum out of reasons why anybody would come by here this time of day."

"My name's Taylor Sterling. I've come to work with your police department."

"Not thinking of taking a job with them, are you?" she laughed.

Taylor complimented her by chuckling with her. "No, used to do policing, but don't anymore."

"You been a cop?"

"Yep. LAPD. Seems like eons ago."

"Sylvia Peters, Mr. Sterling. I own this place, or at least own it along with the bank and my husband. He doesn't come around much, which is better for business."

Taylor looked around and noted the café was empty. "Not busy, huh?"

"Gettin' ready to close. Just do breakfast and lunch. You interested in lunch?"

"Got any soup?"

"Split pea with ham."

"My favorite," which it really was. When Sylvia returned with the soup, she pulled out the chair across from Taylor and took a seat.

"What the cops do to bring in a fellow from the LAPD?"

"I'm working with the Kansas insurance pool."

"Hazel Bennett and those two young kids, huh? Real shame. Hit our town pretty hard. Edgar, Hazel's husband, hasn't been the same since she was killed. Before the accident, Edgar would make the regulars' table a couple times a week when he could get away from the farm. Haven't seen him in here since that awful day. Hear he's thinking of selling and moving to KC to live with one of his boys. Nice people. Yep, it was a real shame." Sylvia looked at the ceiling as if searching for heaven and Taylor saw tears begin to form.

"Good soup, Sylvia," Taylor said, trying to avert her attention from memories of death. "Cops ever come in here?"

"Old ones do, not that there are that many. That big guy Roscoe is always in here for feed. Difficult to fill that guy up! Young ones rarely come in here. Guess they like the Hardee's and Waffle House better."

"How about the chief?"

Sylvia leaned back in her chair and explored her chin with nail bitten fingers. "Couple of times he's been here, I guess. He's not from around Barrington, you know. He comes from someplace up in Wisconsin. Retired cop, and I don't think he was a chief before taking the job here. His wife has kinfolk in Barrington. All of us figure that's how he got the job. He's not like our last chief who really worked the community. The old chief would come in at least once a week and sit at the regulars' table and bullshit with the old farts. The old chief was active in the local Rotary Club, too. I think he even was president one year. Sorry to see the guy leave, but he got a bigger and better job in Colorado."

"What do the old farts think about this new guy?"

She hesitated. Taylor figured she was wondering if it was appropriate for her to say anything. "Most don't know him. Some say he's playing hard ass cop on the highway. But he don't stop locals, so doesn't bother them so much. He's nice enough, though. Always pleasant, just sort of standoffish."

Taylor finished his soup and dropped a ten on the table. "You got good hash browns, Sylvia? I consider myself a real expert on hash browns."

She granted him a toothy smile. "You come by for breakfast and rate me, Mr. Sterling. I might even get you a seat at the old farts' table."

* * *

The Barrington police station was just off the roundabout. Taylor noticed the fire department had been connected to it at one time by the large bay doors off to one side. The station was housed in a single story brick building with two glass doors commanding the front. Several marked police cars were visible in the lot behind a high chain link fence. The glass doors opened to a small lobby. A cubicle with small sliding opaque window panels, like you'd find in a doctor's office, was centered in the lobby. Taylor was sure a buzzer sounded when a warm body entered the building, but he jabbed the brass bell sitting on the counter for extra attention. A panel slowly slid open in acknowledgement and an elderly, frail woman asked, "Can I help you?" He gave his name and almost immediately the door to one side of the counter opened and a uniformed officer appeared

"You Taylor Sterling?"

"Guilty, boss." Taylor knew this had to be Chief Watts by the proud flock of eagles on the collar of his uniform shirt. County sheriffs or heads of state police departments would scoff if they saw a chief of a meager 30-person department wearing eagles as a rank designation. Stars would be okay, but eagles were definitely another matter.

Reggie Watts was a big man, but well trimmed. He was wearing a dark blue uniform bisected with a polished leather equipment belt. Many cops these days wore nylon combat-style equipment belts. Watts obviously was a man who followed tradition.

Reggie led Taylor to a small room in the far corner of the police station. There was just enough room for a desk and chair, two arm chairs, a bookcase, and a coat rack. Very little decorated the walls of the chief's office. The only souvenir Taylor noticed from Watts' former job was a sergeant's badge encased in a shadowbox resting on top of the bookcase.

"The insurance pool must be nervous, huh?"

Taylor was surprised the chief didn't open with the usual bantering to qualify Taylor's credentials, followed by laying out his own personal experience.

"That they are! Think it's warranted, boss?"

Reggie slumped into his desk chair and leaned back. In a blink he shot forward and placed his large hands on the desk with a bang.

"Nope! Tragic accident, that's all. My guy Jason Day was doing honest police work. He thought he'd come upon robbers and needed to take action. That's what good cops do, Taylor. You were one once, huh?"

"Was he in pursuit, boss?"

"Yep. Called it out and all that. Got the dispatch tape to prove it. It's a shame that old Mrs. Bennett wasn't wearing her seatbelt. Would have saved her life, most likely. A real shame."

Reggie could tell Taylor wasn't exactly pleased with his explanation so he continued. "You know I did suspend Officer Day for one of his other pursuits."

"What was different about that one?"

"He was chasing a dope smuggler in a rental car. He momentarily lost the guy, but found him hiding in a driveway in a residential neighborhood. Day parked his Charger across the entrance to the driveway figuring it would block the dirtbag. But the doper jammed his rental car in reverse and rammed our cruiser. Crushed the right side bad. Then the guy took off in a flash. Oh, we caught him eventually, but he stashed the shit he was transporting."

"What'd you suspend Day for?"

"Wrecking my car! Shit, it was out of service for nearly two weeks. He shouldn't have parked it like that. He made a tactical error. I told Day and the other guys on highway duty that they got to protect our cars. Can't make busts and seizures if we got no cars." Reggie sat back satisfied with his response this time.

"What I'd like to do, chief, is get a copy of your procedural manual. Take it back to my motel room and give it a look. Then I'd like to ride with one of your officers tonight and another one tomorrow morning. I'd prefer a seasoned officer. I'll get back with you later tomorrow afternoon. How's that sound? That way we don't pussy foot around today since I don't have any understanding of what I'm looking at. Is this good with you, boss?"

Taylor already sensed he didn't like Chief Watts and this would give Taylor a chance to take a fresh look, maybe…at least come to the table without his initial hostility.

Chief Watts nodded, got up, and ambled to the bookcase and pulled out a three-inch thick binder. He handed it to Taylor who saw Barrington SOP Manual was embossed in dark blue on the cover.

"Come back about seven tonight, Taylor. Officer Jason Day is on. He's the one who ran over Mrs. Bennett. You can ride with him. That okay?"

Taylor nodded and took the binder. He checked into the

Hampton Inn and settled into his room. After grabbing a bottle of water from the vending machine down the hallway, he opened the manual and found the index. "Emergency Vehicle Operations and Pursuits" was listed as General Order 2/100.00. It appeared to be a well-organized and complete written order. It was similar to the ones Taylor provided to several insurance pools he had worked with.

* * *

Jason Day was waiting in front of the police station when Taylor drove up at precisely seven o'clock. Jason was driving one of the town's new Dodge Chargers. Taylor heard the door locks open signaling him to squeeze into the passenger seat.

"Sorry I can't move all that computer gear, Mr. Sterling."

"No problem, Officer Day. I understand why you can't. It's Taylor since we're going to spend a couple of hours together."

"Okay. It's Jason on this end. What you want to see or do?"

"Just spend some time with you. Normal patrol. Just do what you normally do, Jason."

"I usually work the highway. Interdiction. We got another unit doing routine work inside the city limits to handle regular calls. Frees us highway cops to do our thing."

"Which is what, Jason?"

The young cop turned to Taylor. "You know anything about highway interdiction?"

"I do."

"Well, that's what I do, day in and day out. Tickets. Stops. Searches. Seizures. Been good at it, too. You have that stuff when you were with LAPD?"

Someone did a good job prepping him, Taylor thought. "Actually it's a procedure that's become more common since I left the job, Jason, but I know about it."

"You got a problem with it?"

"Nope, do you?"

Jason started the Charger and they pulled onto the road, circling the roundabout in the center of town. Jason drove east until he reached the sign indicating the city limits and then pulled onto a dirt cutout and stopped, facing north in the center median of Highway 54.

"I wait here and use radar on the westbound traffic. Speed limit drops back a few hundred yards from 65 to 55. I don't bother anybody unless they're doing over 80. Figure they know at that high speed, they're doing something wrong."

Traffic was light and only two or three cars came by every ten minutes or so.

"Jason, I was told you were the pursuing officer in the incident that ended with the fatalities."

Jason gave a serious nod.

"You okay?"

The young cop nodded again.

"Get any discipline for that?"

Jason turned, stared at Taylor and shook his head.

"Tell me what happens when an officer gets involved in a pursuit here in Barrington, Jason."

A quizzical expression covered Jason's face. "Like what, Taylor?"

"Do you have to file a pursuit report?"

Jason shook his head.

"Does the supervisor complete one?"

Shook his head again.

"You got a review board that looks at it?"

"Don't think so. Never heard of anything like that. I do reports if I arrest someone or seize contraband like drugs, guns, or money."

"You been trained in pursuit driving?"

"At the academy we had a few classes in defensive driving. They filled a section of the local airport parking lot with water and had us race around and slam on the brakes. Said it was designed as a skidpan and would give us training on what to do if we skidded out. Actually, those sessions were a lot of fun, Taylor."

Unfortunately, actual pursuit driving training, not simply driving around cones and sliding around a manufactured skidpan, hasn't been available to most law enforcement agencies. High-speed emergency driving training began in the late 1960s. Departments used any space they could find in the community, such as an old airfield, for training.

The Los Angeles County Sheriff's department created a training track on the Fairgrounds in Pomona. Eventually the LAPD developed another in the harbor area. Some states created high-speed tracks in expanded and new police academies, like the one at the Georgia Public Safety Training Academy in Forsyth.

Some programs overinflated the tires of the vehicles used on the high-speed track to simulate greater speeds while maintaining a lower speed.

Unfortunately real hands-on training is very expensive, time-consuming, and labor intensive. Safety considerations required many eyes and strong control. Budgets were always a problem and many high-speed, hands-on training programs have been severely limited or eliminated entirely.

Taylor Sterling fondly remembered his emergency driving training. It started with a day of classroom instruction to discuss LAPD policies, the dynamics of vehicles traveling at high speeds, and the safety procedures used on the track. Defensive driving included simulated last minute decision-making using flashing lights to direct choice of lane. Instruction was also given in backing and turning in tight spaces as well as parking techniques.

One exercise Taylor remembered was designed to demonstrate the limited effect of the cop car siren. He and three cops were loaded into a police car and told to drive at 60 miles per hour. Another police car raced up behind them with its siren blaring. Taylor and the other three were told to raise their hands when they first heard the siren. It amazed Taylor that when he raised his hand and looked back, the pursuing car was less than one car length behind his.

The skidpan simulated handling out-of-control cars and taught proper control methods that were often contrary to how a driver would normally be expected to respond.

But the real thrill for Taylor happened on the high-speed track. He learned how to cut the curve, accelerate entering the curve, and ways to handle the steering wheel with both hands using the shuffle method. The instructor in the car would scream orders to punch the accelerator when Taylor instinctively wanted to slam on the brakes.

Taylor knew he was fortunate to have this extensive training. As a consultant, he realized most new cops didn't receive much driving training or experience as part of their curriculum.

Jason raised his laser radar gun with a flourish and focused it on an approaching car. With a disappointed sigh, he lowered it. "Just 73."

He raised it again, aiming at another car. He studied the readout, dropped the radar gun into the center console, and jammed the gearshift down. "86, we got an 86!"

The Charger kicked up dirt as Jason accelerated and swung onto the highway. Taylor saw the speedometer digital begin to climb...*45...60...80...95...100.*

When Jason was about fifty yards behind the racing car, determined to be a newer model Mustang, he activated the overhead blue strobe lights and siren. Taylor noticed the small video camera near the rearview mirror was activated showing a red light.

"21 stopping Kansas 345KTA."

"Roger 21, new registration not on file."

They saw the driver of the Mustang glance into the rearview mirror, and then sharply focus forward. The Mustang's rear dipped as it accelerated with a jolt. It quickly caught up to the three westbound cars. The Mustang snaked between the cars. Brake lights glared bright red on the three cars as the drivers realized they might be part of something big. As usual, the cars slowed down. The drivers appeared confused. Should they pull over or continue straight down the road?

Jason swung to the left of the car in the fast lane and onto the sloping shoulder. The rear end of the Charger began to break away, but Jason punched the gas and straightened it out, coming back onto the highway. The Mustang gained distance during this movement.

Taylor noticed the digital readout peaking at 120.

"21…Looks like he's running."

Jason's Charger was closing the distance between them. The Mustang was approaching an 18-wheeler lumbering in the slow lane and a car barreling down in the fast lane. The Mustang swung onto the right shoulder and kicked up a cloud of gravel and dust as it wildly circled the truck. The car traveling in the fast left lane suddenly braked and swung into the right lane as the truck passed. The left lane was now open for Jason and he punched the Charger full throttle. The engine screamed as they left the two vehicles behind. Within a mile, the Mustang began to slow and eventually pulled onto the right shoulder. Jason followed and pulled sharply left behind the Mustang. The two racers were but a car length apart.

"21...*Stopping car just west of mileage marker 184.*"

Jason reached up and canted the video camera slightly to the right to compensate for the angle of his car. He opened his door and crouched behind the V it created. Jason had his gun in one hand and activated the mic clipped on his shoulder with the other.

"Driver!" The sound of Jason's voice echoed through the siren's PA system. "Put your hands on top of your head. Do it now!" The commands were slow and sharp.

"With your left hand, reach over and turn off your car and then drop the keys out your window. Do it now!" A hand emerged and a shiny object dropped to the ground. "Now slowly open your door and get out with your hands on top of your head. Do it now!"

A young woman emerged and did as Jason directed.

"Now slowly turn around 360 degrees. Do it now, please!" She again did as ordered. She was a large woman wearing jeans and a sweater that clung to her frame. "Now get on the ground and put your arms out from your side. Do it now, please!"

The woman hesitated and then slowly dropped to her knees, finally finding her position flat on the ground.

Jason slowly approached her. He wasn't aware Taylor had exited the car and was now crouched near the right front fender of the Charger. Jason holstered his gun and moved to the woman's right side, bringing one arm then the other around her back and ratcheting a pair of handcuffs.

"I'm sorry, officer," the woman stammered. "I don't know why I just didn't stop."

Jason steadied her as she got up and turned her to face the

trunk of her Mustang. Taylor noticed Jason used his flashlight to glide it around her waist and down each leg instead of using his hands in his cursory search for weapons.

"Lady, you could have killed us and yourself. What the fuck were you thinking?"

"I didn't know you were behind me until I heard the siren and then you scared the shit out of me! I was thinking about stopping, but then I didn't really know if you were the real cops or a guy who was going to rape me. I was just scared and acted like a stupid ass. I'm going to Colorado to meet friends. It's the first time I've had my Mustang on the open road and I guess I was pushing her to the limit."

"Well, you and your Mustang are going to be corralled for awhile, lady!"

Jason stuffed the young woman, Julie she called herself, into the caged rear of his police car and called for a tow service to haul the Mustang to the station's car corral.

Taylor had a flashback to his early days at the LAPD as he waited with Jason. Police pursuits were common in the years before Taylor became a cop. In fact, written policies were just becoming the standard of operation about the time Taylor first started patrolling the streets of LA. During the mid 1970s there were serious questions about the necessity for high-speed police pursuits. Studies showed it was rare for a pursuit to capture a subject who had committed a serious crime. Most pursuits collected drunks, young kids, or drivers who had outstanding traffic warrants. Studies also showed an increased frequency of deaths and injuries of those being pursued, as well as harming innocent third party individuals who happened to be on the road.

One tragic incident involved an Oklahoma police chief who responded to a multiple fatal police pursuit crash. He found the innocent third party victims to be his entire family. Policies since have fluctuated from a position of "no chase" to a restrictive policy of chasing only known violent felons. Close monitoring, limiting the number of police cars involved, and restricting the speed of the chase were also instituted.

Another common concern were the unnecessary beatings at the conclusion of the pursuit when the involved officers' adrenalin was pumping, overriding their common sense.

Taylor had been involved in a few pursuits during his early years as an LAPD street cop. He recalled the times he was the driver of the police car and captured the subject who was challenging authority by running. Taylor knew he was in control of the car regardless of the speed. It always brought a rush he found exhilarating.

He particularly remembered a chase that happened on the graveyard shift. Taylor and his partner were parked on the Mulholland on-ramp to the 405 Freeway. The ramp was located at the top of the mountain ridge between Brentwood and the San Fernando Valley. Graveyard shifts can be boring and slow. Taylor remembered hearing the screaming engine coming up the hill and topping the crest. Up rushed an exotic sports car with its highly tuned engine in the red zone. Taylor punched his accelerator and started down the on-ramp, giving his napping partner a serious wake-up call. The northbound lanes descended rapidly while curving to the right. By the time Taylor approached the ramps for the Ventura Freeway, he caught a glimpse of the sports car's taillights as it slowed to take the westbound ramp that snaked under the northbound lanes. Taylor was ready to follow, but glanced at his speedometer and saw it bouncing at the 145 mark. Wisely, he chose to drive straight. He knew his cop car would flip at that speed. His heart was beating so wildly it could have flown out of his chest.

When Taylor was the passenger in an LAPD ride, it was a different matter entirely. There weren't enough "Oh shit handles" to make him feel secure. Pursuits scared the shit out of him, regardless of the speed. Looking back, Taylor realized how stupid most of the chases had been. No driver ever caught had committed a serious crime and everybody's life had been placed in jeopardy as cars raced down the roads.

Once he realized this, Taylor became committed to promoting a restrictive pursuit driving policy and a formalized scrutiny and evaluation of any pursuit, regardless of the outcome. Without strong oversight, Taylor knew there were a few officers who would act stupidly.

"So what are you going to do now, Jason?" Taylor asked when they were back at the station and the Mustang had been hauled away.

"I'm going to see if Ms. Julie, the daredevil, will give me consent to search her car. If she doesn't, I'll search it under 'incident to an arrest' or in the guise of an inventory search of an impounded vehicle."

"What if it's clean?"

Jason paused. "If I don't find any shit in her car, I'm going to cite her for reckless driving, excessive speed, evading, and whatever else I can find in the book. She'll be able to bond out in a few hours. The chief doesn't like us booking too many people into the county jail. Costs the city too much money."

"You do any kind of pursuit report?"

"Nah. Just give a ticket in a case like this. Chief doesn't like us to clutter up his in-basket with reports."

* * *

Taylor tossed and turned that night and was up and out of the Hampton at six in the morning. He'd scheduled another ride along, had an appointment with the city manager and then would meet with the chief at the end of the day.

Taylor pulled up to the Barrington Inn Café and found the

parking spaces in front full, so he swung a U-turn and parked on the opposite side of the street. The Café was almost half full. Taylor figured the townsfolk had to get an early start to face the cow pastures and cornfields of Kansas. He saw Sylvia waddle from the kitchen, her arms loaded with plates of breakfast choices.

"Taylor, over here," she ordered as she passed the regulars' table occupied by three men, all at least ten years older than Taylor. She turned and said to the trio, "Make room for my new friend Taylor, you old farts."

Taylor drew one of the seats and sat down. "Hope you guys don't mind. Not sure what the qualifications are for taking a seat at your table."

"Not much, and not sure I even know. Course, Sylvia trumps whatever we think anyway," the man next to Taylor said. "Rob Stevens is my name. Retired from Public Works about seven years ago."

"Retired, my ass," the second man countered. "Rob was retired a couple years after the city hired him." The third man began to chuckle. "Name's Seth Martin. Retired from school maintenance five years ago."

"Say, how'd you talk Sylvia into getting you a seat our table?" the third man piped in.

"Ralston, shut your mouth. Shoot, you're not even retired," Rob said and turned to Taylor. "What's your business here in Barrington?"

"Looking into the pursuit that killed those kids and the farmer's wife."

Rob leaned forward and rested his chin on his hands. "Who's doing the looking?"

"I'm working for the insurance pool that covers the city."

"You some sort of insurance agent?" Seth asked.

"Nope, retired cop."

"That's enough qualification in my book," Rob said.

Sylvia appeared and dropped a platter of food in front of Taylor. He looked at the heaping plate as heat rose to flush his face. Three eggs were presented over easy accompanied by two short, fat sausages done very well. Hash brown potatoes mounded to the perimeter of the plate.

"Well, you said you were a connoisseur of hash browns. Rate these, fellow!"

Taylor leaned over his plate and inhaled the aroma of the morning meal. The potatoes were fried to a dark crust. They were obviously not packaged or processed potatoes, as each string and cube was irregular in shape. There was enough oil or grease to give the mound a glistening sheen. Small flakes of red and green added interest to the pile. Taylor plunged his fork into the mound and shoveled a hefty bite into his mouth. Now, these were hash browns! A complexity of spices teased his taste buds.

Taylor enthusiastically smacked his lips, put down the fork, and clapped three times.

"Wonderful, Sylvia! I can see the bits of red and green bell peppers. How did you slice them so small? The onions seem almost caramelized. I can pick up the salt, pepper, and cumin, but what's the other spice?"

"Smoked paprika!" Sylvia announced with a proud smile.

"I'd rate this dish a 9 out of 10."

"What would make it a 10?"

"Maybe a dash of diced green chilies and a little shaved ham? I've developed a taste for fire in my food. But, these are great as they are, Sylvia. My compliments to you."

Taylor lifted the eggs and plopped them on top of the hash

browns. He stabbed each yoke with his fork and watched the yellow ooze bury into the crisp potatoes. All three men were watching him as he scooped a forkful and slid it into his mouth.

Sylvia laughed and returned to her kitchen.

"How come he gets to sit at our table?" Ralston challenged again.

"Ralston, I said shut your mouth. 'Cuz Sylvia said so," Rob retorted. "What you really looking for, mister?"

"Like I said, I'm interested in what caused the deaths of those people."

"Chief Watts, that's what caused it. He come to our town and makes a Gestapo gang out of his cops. Chasing people up and down Highway 54 like banshees. Never had to worry before, but nows I got to always look for them blue lights. Young cops don't seem to know them cop cars they drive can go under 70 or 80. Racing all over the damn place." Rob scowled as he leaned back in his chair.

Seth leaned forward and added, "Yep, Rob said it right. Poor Edgar ain't been the same since Hazel got run over. Hear he's gonna move in with one of his kids. Just ain't the same."

"How come no one has taken this up with the chief?" Taylor asked.

"He don't listen. We hardly ever see him, and Barrington ain't that big a place," Rob explained. "The McClendons have run this town for three generations. They must have gotten the city manager to hire Watts. Manager don't do nothin' without running it by the McClendons. Got no one to listen to us complain, so we shut up."

"Why he get to sit here?" Ralston roared indignantly.

"Ralston, for the last time, shut it!" Rob and Seth ordered simultaneously.

"I'll try to get back here tomorrow morning for breakfast, guys," Taylor announced, scooping up the last of his eggs and hash browns. "You be here?" Turning, he added, "If that's okay with you, Ralston."

"That'll be just fine, Mr. Sterling," Ralston said, beaming at the acknowledgement. Rob and Seth shook their heads and gave a feeble salute.

* * *

Taylor arranged to ride with a senior officer from the police station. Once again he rang the brass bell on the counter to get attention. An exceptionally large man opened the door to the right of the counter.

"You Taylor?"

Taylor nodded and the officer continued, "Chief says I need to let you ride along with me. Whatcha want to see?"

"Nothing special, just see the city and talk some."

"Talk, huh? Okay, whatcha really looking for, Taylor?"

"Well, the insurance pool is a little nervous. Got three dead and they're worried about their exposure. You can understand their concern, can't you?" Taylor was trying to read the nametag on the officer's uniform. "What's that? Stedman?"

"Hey, I'm sorry, man. It's Roscoe. Roscoe Stedman." The two shook hands. In the parking lot, Roscoe headed for a Ford Crown Vic marked police car.

"You get one of the new Chargers, Roscoe?"

"Nah. They're for the young guys doing highway interdiction. Besides I can't fit in those suckers. You maybe noticed I'm kinda big? Actually I'm fat as a hog ready for the kill!" The hulk squeezed into the driver's seat.

"Got to use an extension for the seatbelt. It's a bitch, but it's my own fault. I just love to eat, and love to eat wrong."

Roscoe swung the car out of the lot and drove slowly to the main business district. He waved to everybody on the sidewalk and occasionally called them by name. He pulled into the parking lot of Barrington Feed and Grain, parked, and got out. Several green John Deere tractors lined the side of the parking lot. Taylor followed Roscoe into the large building where stacks of bagged feed hugged one wall. The store boasted lines of work clothes with a large display of heavy boots towering in one corner.

"Sadie, how's it going?" Roscoe called to the woman behind the counter. "Hear your old man George is down with his old back problem."

"That's what he claims, Roscoe. I think he's just faking and wants to retire. This drought has been a bitch for business the last couple years."

Roscoe continued the conversation, hitting on some of the other problems local businesses were experiencing. He and Sadie chatted about their grandkids and the hard times facing young families today. Each worried hard times might eventually chase their families out of Barrington and force them to move to the city. Roscoe spent time talking with each customer who came into the store. Nearly an hour passed before Roscoe and Taylor drove out of the lot and slowly moved up and down the other streets in town.

"You seem to like being a cop here in Barrington."

"Nearly twenty years on the job. It's been good to me, until recently."

"What changed?"

Roscoe turned quiet and stared ahead. Taylor could almost hear his thoughts colliding. Taylor figured Roscoe was debating with himself, deciding if he should open up or hedge his comments. Taylor found most young cops didn't care what they said and would flap their traps indiscriminately if they thought they had an audience. Older experienced officers were more calculating. Taylor figured they didn't speak until they determined what was in it for them.

"New chief basically. Change is now most important. I like the people here in Barrington and they like me. I'm really not sure the chief gives a shit about the people who live here." Roscoe paused to collect his thoughts. "This highway shit bugs me."

"How's that, Roscoe?"

"When the chief first got this harebrained idea to send the young bucks out there with those souped up Chargers, he figured they'd be scooping up carloads of drugs and money. He figured it'd make him famous in these parts."

"And did it?"

"At first they produced amazing results. Figure the end result was close to netting half a million bucks. City manager and council spent weeks high fiving themselves and dancing a jig."

"And?"

"Wasn't more than six months before the drug mules figured it out. Stopped using 54 as their conduit. Now the bucks just write speeding tickets and come across an occasional stolen car. Of course a few drunk drivers are stopped and that's good. The young cops are still out there racing up and down the highway for no good reason. Gives 'em a hard on, I think."

"What about those deaths in the pursuit by Officer Day?"

"Tragic thing. Chief didn't really think much about it and that surprised me. I even wondered why the city manager and council haven't been out front of it. They're just sitting back like nothing happened. Can't figure that out. None of them came to Hazel's funeral. Townspeople all noticed that and have been talking trash ever since. Chief don't listen to me, though."

Roscoe drove to the outskirts of town by way of Highway 54. He turned onto a dirt driveway and crossed a cattle guard with the car's tires rat-a-tatting over the metal bars. They drove a few hundred yards and came to a small white frame house with a new Ford F250 parked in front.

"This here is the Bennett farm. I try to come by now and then to see how the old man is doing."

The door opened as Roscoe and Taylor reached the top step of the front porch.

"Roscoe, how you doing, my friend?" Edgar Bennett welcomed the two as he stepped aside waving them to enter the house. Edgar had a stooped, crooked carriage and his round pot-belly seemed out of place with the rest of his frail body. A band of steel grey hair circled the lower part of his head while the rest of it was bald dotted with large liver spots. Edgar wore thick black-rimmed glasses.

"Good. Doing good, Mr. Bennett," Roscoe insisted as they were ushered through the living and dining rooms to a small kitchen. The three sat at a bright blue table in one corner of the room. The kitchen chairs were made of matching blue Nauga-hyde capped with chrome slides like would be found in a retro diner.

"Coffee? It's from this morning, though."

"No, just here to see how you're doing, Mr. Bennett. This here is a guy from the insurance pool. Taylor Sterling is his name. He's looking into the crash that took Hazel," Roscoe shared as he turned to Taylor.

"So sorry for your loss, Mr. Bennett," Taylor offered, not knowing what else to say to this man he didn't know.

Edgar Bennett nodded at Taylor and then focused on Roscoe. "Can't bring my little flower back, you know." Taylor could see tears swelling in Edgar's eyes.

"I got a new truck, but I miss her so. Miss Shep, too. I'm leaving this farm soon. It hurts to see my wife's stuff in the closets. Don't have the will to clean them out. Just going to leave and let somebody else do that. Ever lose someone close to you, Mr. Sterling?"

"Not like your Hazel, Mr. Bennett. Attended several funerals of cops who used to work for me. Most died in traffic accidents like your wife. A couple took their own lives. One was shot and killed in a robbery. But, no, I haven't suffered a loss like you have," Taylor admitted. He wanted to say more, but couldn't find the right words.

"How soon before you go live with your son, Mr. Bennett?" Roscoe asked to break the silence.

"About a month."

"You excited?"

Edgar stared at Roscoe and his anger was suddenly exposed. "No I'm not! But, I know it's for the best. What else can I do?"

They sat for several minutes with Roscoe and Edgar making idle, meaningless chatter. The three shook hands and Roscoe and Taylor headed to the Crown Vic.

"Thanks. Thanks a lot, Roscoe," Taylor said as they reached the highway to head back into town.

"Thought you ought to see the residue from Day's pursuit. Spared you meeting the boys' parents. They're worse wrecks."

* * *

City Hall was a fairly new building a block from the old police station. Red brick and single story, it covered most of the block. A large black granite slab was embedded in the walkway on the right side of the entrance. Taylor noticed it was a tribute to Barrington's military who had given their lives in combat dating back into the Civil War. He was surprised by the number of fallen in World War II. Then Taylor remembered watching a program on PBS that told the story of many rural midwestern towns that had sent platoons of young men into that war; many were slaughtered in the Normandy invasion. In some cases, the war's cost had taken all the young men in a single family or town.

Taylor was ushered into a well-organized, uncluttered office. Zack Stanton was already rounding his desk to meet Taylor with his hand extended.

"Let's sit down at the conference table," Zack offered. "I've taken the liberty of asking my risk manager, Bob Clements, to join us. Can I get you anything, Mr. Sterling?" Taylor shook his head. "I was really surprised when the insurance pool told us they were sending a consultant from out west. Have you done work for them in the past?"

"Actually I haven't. This is my first time working with the Kansas pool."

"Why'd they pick you?"

"That's been something I wondered about myself, Mr. Stanton. Never really know what starts my phone ringing. Most of my assignments seem to come by word of mouth. Networking. That kind of thing."

"Zack, Taylor. Call me Zack," the city manager encouraged as he turned to the small-framed man who had entered the room.

Bob Clements fit the profile, if there was one, of what a risk manager should look like. He was barely over five feet tall, maybe weighed in at 130, was bald, wore wire rimmed glasses, and sported a bushy moustache. His buttoned-down shirt had rolled up sleeves and his tie was pulled away from his neck. A vintage pocket liner was loaded with pens and Bob Clements' reading glasses hung around his neck on a gold chain. He carried the obligatory clipboard.

"Sorry to be late, Zack," Bob apologized as he sat down opposite Taylor.

They both looked at Taylor, signaling he should start the conversation.

"What's the city's position regarding the pursuit deaths?" Taylor began; looking for an indication of the direction the Barrington city officials were taking.

"Tragic," Zack said flatly as Bob nodded. "We figure it was just a tragic accident."

"Ever have anything like that happen in the past?" Taylor was still trying to pry information from the two.

Zack and Bob shook their heads. "No, we haven't, Taylor. I guess that's what worries us somewhat," Zack admitted. "Chief Watts doesn't seem too concerned about the whole thing."

"That bother you?"

"Yes!" Bob shouted. His outburst was a surprise as the risk manager exploded from his passive posture. "That bugs the shit out of me. Those were our people and it just seemed so unnecessary."

Zack looked quickly at his manager. "Bob, that's the first time I've heard you get so riled up!"

"Well, I've been biting my tongue since Hazel and those boys were killed. Just so unnecessary, Zack. I've been hurting over it and no one in the city government seems to care. I care deeply, and I want you to know that."

"And what do you think about it, Taylor?" Zack asked.

"Bob probably knows the most about your actual insurance liability, but you seem to have issues with your police department that you need to address, Zack."

The city manager leaned back as Bob leaned forward in seesaw fashion. Taylor continued to explain his findings.

"Not everybody is pleased with what the chief has happening on the highway. I get a feeling your chief hasn't spent much time building social capital."

"What do you mean by social capital?" Zack asked.

"Police work is usually fairly routine, almost bordering on the mundane. But, it always has the potential for high risk and critical tasks, even in a place like Barrington. These tasks can go bad real quick. Accidents can happen. When that occurs, the police must go to the bank where they've deposited social capital. People remember the good things cops do to help, and if they like the cops personally, particularly the chief of police, they are forgiving. When a police department hasn't developed and grown much social capital, residents often point fingers and accuse the department of being out of control or unaccountable. It takes effort and consistency to build social capital. I've gathered your chief and the young cops haven't done a good job of that here."

Zack and Bob were both nodding in agreement. They were getting it.

Taylor continued. "Now, it seems you guys didn't build much capital either by not attending Hazel's funeral. Town folks noticed your obvious absence."

Zack replied, "The town attorney told us it would be best if we didn't attend. I felt bad, but we got to follow his advice."

"Actually you don't! Lawyers can give advice, but each individual must make their final personal decision. Right is simply right sometimes. Lawyers typically don't get involved in the emotional side of issues. You can understand why, they'd be emotional wrecks if they did."

"So you think we got some problems in our burg, huh, Mr. Sterling?" Zack asked haltingly.

"I think you got three things you should seriously consider." Taylor began his summation, knowing they probably didn't want to hear it.

"First, you got a chief who hasn't connected with the Barrington town folks. Don't know why, but he apparently hasn't even tried. Next you got an agency that allows street cops to chase people at will and they're not documenting those vehicular pursuits like most police departments do. You really don't know how many pursuits your young Turks engage in unless there's a crash, arrest and seizure, or random violation. Lastly, you got some obvious and serious financial exposure. Have you been served with any civil lawsuit notices?'

"Have we?" Zack asked, looking at Bob for the answer.

"Zack, two attorneys have filed the required notice of intent to sue. One is representing the boys' families and another represents the Bennett side. We've just received the initial notice, though."

Taylor responded, "I doubt if they're going to go the federal route. That opportunity pretty much dried up with the last Supreme Court ruling in a Georgia case. But your exposure is definitely there on the state level. If the attorneys bring in agency issues regarding lack of adequate reporting and management, it's a whole other matter entirely. You need to consult with your attorney and the Kansas insurance pool."

"What about Officer Day? Should we fire him?" Zach Stanton was beginning to realize what might be ahead.

"You itchin' for another lawsuit?" Taylor demanded. "He was doing exactly what your chief told him to do. The chief didn't find his cop did anything wrong. I sure wouldn't consider firing the young guy. That would open a whole new can of worms."

* * *

"Been looking through your manual, boss," Taylor began as he settled in the worn chair in Chief Watts' small office.

"What do you think of it? Pretty good, huh?"

"Where'd you get it?"

Reggie Watts looked at Taylor and grinned. "Some consultant made it up. Kind of like you, I guess. Paid $1,500 and got us a manual worthy of accreditation, not that I'm particularly interested in that."

"You read it, boss?"

Reggie squinted. "Yes, why do you ask?"

"Well, let's start off with your pursuit policy. It's pretty good, all seven pages of it. There are a couple things I have questions about, however."

Reggie didn't say a word as he rested back in his chair.

"Says the pursuing officer should request an air unit get involved at the earliest possible moment. You got an air unit, boss?" Reggie didn't respond.

"Also says that an officer involved in any pursuit must complete a separate pursuit report that is evaluated by the traffic safety committee. You got a committee that does that, boss?"

Reggie stretched, got up, and walked around his desk and sunk into the chair next to Taylor. His hands were on his knees as he leaned forward toward the consultant.

"So what the fuck do you want me to say? This is a small hick police department stuck in the middle of nowhere. I got thirty cops to manage and the town is on my back. It's a shame about those boys and Mrs. Bennett. Shit happens in police work, Taylor. You know that. Shit happens!"

"You're right, boss. Problem is you put those young Turks out there in Hemis without guidance or oversight. All you were looking for was to collect riches from your highway robbery program. That young cop, Day, is lucky he's not being prosecuted. This being the Midwest, Barrington might get off cheap, but my report to the insurance pool might stir up shit for your tenure here as chief of police. You dropped the ball, no doubt about it. From what I've heard, you got no public or social capital with your community. No one in Barrington really cares whether you keep your job or not. I imagine a few would like to see you go. That's going to be tough for your wife and her influential family. What will you do if that happens? What if they show you the door and slam it behind you?"

Reggie rose and returned to the chair behind his desk. "Don't rightly know, Taylor. Haven't really considered that happening. You really going to stick it up my ass?"

"Yes, sir, I am!"

The men didn't shake hands as Taylor got up and walked out of the Barrington police station, flicking the bell as he left.

* * *

The next morning, Taylor sauntered into the Barrington Inn Café at nine. Earlier he had called Bob Turner at the Kansas Muni Insurance Pool and they decided to meet in town. That was fine with Bob since he had plans to meet with the crowd at City Hall and the town attorney. Taylor figured meeting at the Café at a later hour would avoid the usual morning crowd and would give them a semblance of privacy.

"Well, Mr. Hashbrowns, hello there!" Sylvia called a greeting from the kitchen.

"Hey, Sylvia, good morning. Can I sit at this table by the front window? I'm expecting someone to join me." She nodded.

"What, too good to sit with us?" Ralston yelled from the regulars' table in the back. "It's okay with me if you sit here. Sylvia told me to be nice."

"Thanks, Ralston, but I got to meet with someone."

A few minutes later Taylor was giving Bob his observations and the information he'd gleaned from his time at the Café, on the ride a-longs, and from his meetings with Zack, Bob, and Chief Watts.

"Gonna need a written report on this one, Taylor," Bob reminded. "What kind of turnaround can you give me?"

"Week after I get back home?"

"That'll be good. You think the chief will survive?"

"Don't know, Bob. He's apparently got political pull from his wife's family, but no one else. Depends on which camp is stronger. But I don't see he's made the move from field sergeant in Wisconsin to chief. Not everybody can, you know. It takes a different kind of thinking. Don't know if he's capable of that."

* * *

It had been nearly a year since Taylor had visited Barrington. A morning e-mail from Bob Turner was a surprise.

Taylor—Update on Barrington. Settled with the families. Chief Watts apparently left town. Don't know where he went. Seems his wife didn't want to go with him and has filed for divorce. Sylvia at the Café keeps asking for you. Something about green chilies. What the heck is that about?

Taylor smiled, looked down at his omelet and reached for the bottle of Valentina Salsa Picante.

Too Many Guns, Too Little Training

Allegation: SWAT fatal shootings
Client: Kentucky League of Cities Municipal Insurance Pool
Agency: Spirit Lake Police Department
Accused employees: Numerous officers

"Put your motherfuckin' hands up! All of you! You too, lady!"
the muffled voice ordered from behind a filthy stocking mask
pulled deep over a big head. The head belonged to a large man,
well over six feet tall and probably weighing close to 300 pounds.
The large AR15 with its modified, shortened stock and extended
magazine added power to hulk's commands as he whipped the
weapon back and forth at the terrified line of shoppers standing
at the supermarket check-out.

Majors Market was akin to a Wal-Mart or Menards in this
part of the great state of Kentucky. Stacked on rows and rows
of towering shelves were cartons piled nearly to the ceiling.
Forklifts rushed up and down rows carrying fresh supplies bundled in cellophane to add to the cardboard skyscrapers. Majors
Market was open 24/7 and on this particular Monday at two in
the morning, most employees were busily restocking the shelves
for the weekly rush ahead. Only a few customers marked by

vacant expressions on drawn faces wandered the store's endless aisles.

The six armed men assaulting Majors this night were dressed in black BDUs similar to military or cop shop issues. Each carried an automatic weapon. Handguns were strapped to their legs and dozens of plastic zip cuffs hung from their belts. Large black plastic bags dangled from rear pockets like shiny tails.

"Where's the on-duty manager?" a masked man barked at the two startled cashiers. Three customers were getting a rude wake-up call as their knuckles blanched white grasping steel rails on shopping carts. One of the cashiers, a young girl in jeans and a shirt straining to confine an inner tube of belly fat, pointed to a row of opaque windows positioned above the cash registers.

"You two, secure the rear!" the apparent leader yelled at two of his cohorts. "Hey, you two, herd these people and stand guard at the entrances. Butch, you come with me!" The leader used a sharp tongue on his men as he headed for the stairs leading to the windowed room perched like a skybox above the grocery aisles.

The door at the top of the stairs was made of reinforced metal and had a numbered keypad located directly above the doorknob. Butch carried a sawed-off, pump action Ithaca 12-gauge shotgun and knew how to use it. He fired one blast of double-ought buck into the lock and quickly jacked another round into the shotgun's chamber. The expended shotgun cartridge bounced erratically down the metal staircase to the concrete floor below. At the short distance, the blast blew a massive hole in the door and the keypad imploded violently into the room.

Benny Biggs, the store manager, thought he heard muffled shouting, but wasn't able to make out what was being said, probably because he was deep in the zone. Ear buds were crammed into Benny's ears as Garth Brooks wailed on his iPod. Sensing something was happening below, Benny pulled one ear bud from its cavity and placed Sunday's tabulations he'd been studying on his desk. He started to walk to the door to investigate when the keypad shot by him and almost tore off his leg. Benny had totally forgotten to push the emergency button that would have triggered an alert to the alarm company and the town's local police department, Spirit Lake PD.

"Get over here!" Butch's partner shouted to the terrified manager. "Open the safe and do it now!"

"It's timed. Cain't til nine in the morning. Look at what is says on the front. Ah cain't!"

The burly robber approached the safe and dropped to one knee. He was carrying a small black nylon bag that he now unzipped and spread wide. He reached into the bag and pulled out a small rectangular beige object that he stuck against the safe next to the digital keypad. He pushed a small object into the pliable rectangle, moved it back, and finally nudged it to the side.

"You best be gettin' back with me, fella," the man ordered as he activated a switch causing a contained blast on the surface of the safe. Yellow smoke clouded the room and slivers of metal exploded like rockets, some embedding into the opposite office wall. The masked man went to work on the safe and pried it open with a small wrecking bar he'd taken from the black bag.

Several stacks of banded bills, three bags of coins, and a wad of checks secured with a large rubber band were the treasures hidden inside. The masked man scooped only the paper money and jammed the banded booty into a trash bag he pulled from his rear pocket.

"Tie him up!" he shouted to Butch before walking through the damaged office door and down the stairs. He saw two of his partners standing by the cash registers with their black bags bulging and was happy to see the cashiers and customers on the floor with their hands bound tightly in zip cuffs. The captives' eyes were wide, flickering back and forth watching the movements of the masked men.

The last two robbers rushed from the back of the store and the six men left the building with a casual swagger. A total of twelve minutes had passed from the bandits' entrance into the store and when the customers heard a vehicle roar in escape. It would be another twenty minutes until a clerk working in the back room could wrestle out of his restraints and place a call to the Spirit Lake PD. Within the hour at least forty police cars surrounded Majors Market, led by officers from Spirit Lake and supported by a fleet from the Laurel County Sheriff's Department and the Kentucky State Police.

"Six big men wearing stocking masks, black military clothing, and carrying cannons!" the captives cried as they offered descriptions, adding the half dozen robbers made their escape in a noisy vehicle.

Art Summers, Spirit Lake Chief of Police, caught the KSP sergeant's eye and exclaimed in frustration, "Don't know if they were black, white, or polka dotted! Only clue is one is named 'Butch' and it seems he was carrying a 12-gauge, judging from the expended shell casing my men found by the office stairway."

"Chief, sounds like the same crew that hit the Wal-Mart down in London," the KSP sergeant offered. "Looks like a military type crew. They sure know their shit! How much did they get this time?"

"Manager was pretty evasive about that, but said it was the entire weekend take," the Spirit Lake chief said with a heavy sigh. He knew there would probably be more robberies coming down the pike soon.

* * *

The investigative task force assembled to work the market crimes became known as the "Big Box Robbery Task Force." The local press loved the name, of course. People who didn't usually read the local papers now became fixated on the stories any reporter armed with a tape recorder, laptop, or tablet generated.

The Big Box force was comprised of investigators from the FBI office in Louisville, two Kentucky State Police investigators assigned from the Frankfurt headquarters, one detective from the Laurel County Sheriff's Office in London, and Captain Lewis Shakelford representing the Spirit Lake Police Department. Chief Art Summers was present nearly 24/7 during the initial days of the investigation, but then tried to take a back seat to Shakelford. That effort didn't always work well.

The task force spent its first few days together reviewing statements taken from employees and customers at both stores—the Wal-Mart in London and Majors Market in Spirit Lake. The investigators spent hours squinting at grainy surveillance tapes capturing the movements inside and outside each store. Through the FBI office, the task force was able to obtain enhanced versions of the outside surveillance tapes and found the vehicle used in each robbery was a white Ford Super Cab F250 stolen from the Kentucky Department of Transportation lot, displaying decals and all. The captured truck carried no viable trace evidence, but the task force knew the robbers had been wearing gloves.

The only tangible lead was the name "Butch" heard when the robbery was going down at Majors. Most on the force believed the bandits had military training. The FBI took over researching recently discharged military personnel or National Guard enlistees named Butch.

The money taken in the robberies wasn't marked in any way. Between the two heists, it was estimated the take was close to one million bucks.

* * *

"Chief, whaddya hear on those robberies?" a member of the Spirit Lake Rotary Club asked during dessert at the group's weekly meeting.

"Sam, I'm not privy to let you people in on the nitty-gritty of the task force investigation," Art Summers explained to the Rotary members. "Anytime the FBI gets involved, you know everything goes hush hush real fast."

In reality, Art didn't know anything more than he did the first couple days following the robbery. It was a dead-end deal as far as he was concerned. Art hoped no one in Spirit Lake was involved and wished the task force would find an out of town crew committed the crimes. Some *way* out of town crew, he thought to himself.

Spirit Lake originally was a four-way intersection with a gas station and general store standing on one corner of the old highway between Lexington and the pass going over the mountains near Jellico, Tennessee. Interstate 75 changed things drastically on many fronts for this rural eastern section of Kentucky.

Corbin, Kentucky was the home of Colonel Sanders; London boasted Daniel Boone National Park and later the Chicken Festival. Up the road the college town of Berea led to Lexington. Spirit Lake tried to capitalize on Interstate 75, but it proved to be more difficult than the early townspeople thought it would be.

One of the major problems was Spirit Lake had no lake. Most of the recreational water for boating and fishing in the area was to the west at the massive Lake Cumberland formed by the Tennessee Valley Authority.

Yet, Spirit Lake had been able to garner a slow growing population that was now hovering near 20,000. Several large distribution centers consistently caused traffic jams as 18-wheelers rushed to reach their retail destinations. The good thing was decent jobs were plentiful.

Art Summers had been a cop in Spirit Lake since he was twenty years old. Now he was one year shy of fifty and had held the title of Chief of Police for the last five years.

Art was a hometown boy. In the nearly thirty years he had been in the department, it had grown from fifteen officers to forty officers and seven dispatchers. Art was next up to be the president of the Kentucky Police Chiefs' Association. He had gone to all the right schools and taken all the right courses to make this happen. His advanced degree in criminal justice was earned from Eastern Kentucky University and he was a graduate of the Southern Police Institute Managerial program as well as the prestigious FBI National Academy.

Art had taken a liking to hostage negotiation when he found a place on the newly formed Spirit Lake SWAT team about mid-phase in his career. There wasn't much need for a SWAT team in the town, but the former chief wanted to grab the federal money available to set a team in position.

A big black panel truck with large white SWAT letters painted on the sides was parked large as life in the police department lot. Spirit Lake responded to only three or four incidents each year when SWAT operations and equipment were needed. The trappings were used more for grabbing attention at public gatherings, like the Spirit Lake County Fair and the annual police open house.

SWAT stands for Special Weapons And Tactics. Police departments with similar tasks may be called ERT—Emergency Response Team or SRT—Special Response Team. These police units were created following the Austin-based University of Texas tower shooting in 1967. Back then local police hadn't been trained or equipped for such a sniper encounter.

The LAPD and NYPD first formally developed these specialty units, but in slightly different ways. Since those early years there has been a proliferation of rapid response units in both large and small police agencies. There has been some concern about the over-militarization of the police through this style of aggressive tactical response.

These teams are the most heavily armed police units in any police agency. Many agencies have purchased armored vehicles, tanks, and bulldozer-type equipment to build their presence and effectiveness. With American wars winding down, local police departments have been snapping up an excess of military equipment under the 1033 program. One small Georgia police department without one lake or river to patrol secured boats and scuba gear from the surplus military supplies.

Tactical units tried to standardize operations by creating national and state professional associations, such as the National Tactical Officers Association. Common requirements demand that reasonable tactical units receive sixteen hours or more training each month. That's a difficult requirement for most departments, particularly the smaller ones. Many tactical units require intensive screening before a cop can become a tactical officer, including psychological assessments, physical agility tests, and extensive oral interviews.

Unfortunately, once an agency creates a tactical unit, it wants to use it. Some units are activated when concentrated levels of force, including automatic weapons and grenades creating smoke, loud distracting noises, and intense heat aren't warranted. Reasonable units use threat assessment tools to help the commander determine whether the unit should be involved. Any time a SWAT unit is used, the potential threat to citizens and members of the team increases, even when everything goes as planned.

* * *

Butch Philpot pulled into the Huddle House restaurant parking lot just off the highway leading from Perry County, with its famous county seat in Hazard, to Laurel County. Bull Higgins had called him on his cell when Butch was working at the small engine repair shop he and his brother Smiley owned on the outskirts of Spirit Lake. He asked for a meeting in a back booth of the restaurant.

"Nice ride, Butch," Bull commented as he slid into the molded plastic seat defining the booth. "New?"

"Yeah, my other truck was getting to be a piece of shit. Spent way too much time working on it. Transmission finally went out. Had to get a new one."

"Cain' understand that, but how come you had to get a brand new one?" Bull asked as he looked out the restaurant window at the Harley Davidson Limited version Ford F250 with paper tags still fluttering on the license plate holder.

"I told you guys not to start spending that money and especially not to be foolish about it either. Looks like you been foolish, Butch."

"Bull, I guess I didn't think too smart. But ah about had an orgasm when ah sees it setting in the Ford lot. Jest had to bring it home."

Bull leaned forward and softly said, "Fuck you, Butch. You put us all in a fuckin' bind." He settled back into the seat, disgust written over his face.

* * *

Lewis Shakelford was smiling as he entered the small task force office Spirit Lake had provided in an unused space in City Hall.

"What's up, captain?" one of the FBI agents asked.

"Butch Philpot is up, that's what. He bought a new Ford truck the other day and paid cold cash. He and his brother can't make that kind of money on that damn engine shop of theirs."

The FBI agent picked up the phone and dialed his Louisville office. In less than an hour the task force was pulling together a roster of likely connected suspects. Butch and his brother Smiley were connected to a loose group of survivalists calling themselves the "Kentucky White Nation." They were regulars at the shooting range outside Lexington run by a guy named Johnny Johnson. Johnson was a licensed gun dealer, primarily doing business at gun shows. Another of the survivalists was Bull Higgins, a reserve deputy sheriff for a small county, Harlan, south of Hazard. He had a brother on the job in that same county.

Before long the entire Big Box Robbery crew had been identified. The information was sufficient to obtain search warrants for each member's residence and work place. The task force mulled over how to best execute the warrants. The locations of the targeted houses and businesses spread over four counties. The investigators' concern was that once they hit one location, the word would get out quickly and anything hidden at the other locations would be lost.

They discovered the Big Box gang was planning to meet at a turkey shoot at Johnson's range, but that wasn't scheduled for another two weeks. The investigators were itching to get on with the bust. They were tired of sitting on their asses holed up in a crappy room looking at each other and drinking bad coffee.

"I'd wait for the turkey shoot, if it was up to me," Lewis

Shakelford told the assembled group. "There are a lot of people usually at them folks' houses. Breed like rabbits, they do."

"Lewis, you are my tether," Art Summers said in an exasperated voice. "I know you're just looking out for me, but I think we can do it in one concerted, well planned operation. We come in early in the morning before anybody is up so there's less chance of anybody getting hurt. We can split our SWAT team and hit both Philpot locations in Spirit Lake. You other boys can figure out who's goin' do what and where to grab the other four assholes."

By the time the task force had plotted the operation, over thirty cops were involved coming from locations around the area. Art had gotten the okay to move the growing operation-planning group to the larger City Commission meeting room. The walls of the room were lined with maps, collections of photographs of houses and businesses, Google aerials of each targeted location, and pictures of the targeted men. The actual planning by each tactical unit was left to the unit commander assigned to each target. The task force settled on a coordinated hit the next Friday at five in the morning. Each team would stay connected to the other teams by cell phone since the various departmental cops were on different radio frequencies so they couldn't talk to each other any other way. This was always a problem for large-scale police operations.

The Spirit Lake SWAT team was composed of ten officers. Sgt. Bruce Adams was the team leader and had been ordered to be at the planning meeting at City Hall.

"Now ah knows that Butch Philpot lives in that little cinder block house down by Goose Creek," Art said to his assembled group of two—Lewis Shakelford and Bruce Adams. "You know those places that Jeeter owns? Whole string of them little houses.

Lives there with his wife and ah think they have a little girl about eight."

The other men nodded. "Now Smiley, don't he live in that single wide in Lazy Acres?"

"Yes he do," Bruce Adams replied. "Ah knows the one. It's off by itself since the other two next to it burnt down last winter."

* * *

As he left work for the day, Butch chugged the beer he'd grabbed from the engine shop refrigerator. The refrigerator was covered with equipment decals and stickers featuring scantily dressed women perched provocatively on cars and motorcycles. He finished the beer by the time he swung his new Harley Davidson Limited truck into the driveway of his house.

Thursday night football was on his agenda. He wondered who was playing that night.

Butch knew something was different the second he walked through his front door. High-pitched squeals emitting from six little girls romping in the center of the living room assaulted his ears. The girls were playing a board game that featured colorfully plumed ponies.

"Selma, what's goin' on? Ain't this a school night?"

"Teacher planning day tomorrow, Butch. Ah told Gina she could have a sleep over with her friends. You can watch your ball game in the bedroom," Selma added.

Selma and Butch weren't always friends, let alone married. In high school they hated each other. Both watched the other date wildly, almost to the point of promiscuity; that was just the way things were at Spirit Lake High. It was during their senior year they found themselves thrown together at an illegal beer party at Swamp Holler. Gina was conceived in the rear seat of Butch's ratty old Buick Electra. Their families convinced them to get married for the sake of the coming child. Their years together had developed from acceptance to fondness to a genuine loving relationship.

"Daddy! Daddy! Lisa told me about a birthday party she just went to. It was a Princess Party. She got to dress up like a princess and everything! I want one of those on my birthday. Can I, daddy, can I?" Gina screamed as she danced around Butch. "I want to be Lady Gaga. She's a princess, right, daddy?"

Butch hugged her and said, "Of course ya cain. You be my princess always." He turned to Selma after Gina ran back to her friends. "What the fuck is a Princess Party, Selma?" Selma simply shrugged.

Selma and Butch fed the half dozen potential princesses a supper of hotdogs wrapped in crescent roll dough, Stouffer mac and cheese, and slices of juicy watermelon. Butch retreated to the bedroom and hunkered in for Thursday night football. He was a diehard Steelers fan but, unfortunately, they were being thrashed by the Pats. It was nearly nine when Selma staggered into the bedroom.

"Well, they're down, but I don't think they're out. Giggling and telling stories," Selma sighed. She wiggled out of her jeans, pulled off her blue UK sweatshirt and ambled into the bathroom to brush her teeth.

Butch watched her bending over the sink and enjoyed the view. Her small, firm butt jiggled as she moved the brush vigorously over her teeth.

"I guess a fuck is out of the question?" Butch asked. Selma flipped him the finger in response.

* * *

Bruce Adams gathered his SWAT team together at City Hall at three in the morning. This would give him enough time to brief the squad, split it into operational teams, and still allow time for each team to plan for the raid they would make on the Philpot houses. With only ten men on his team, Bruce would be limited to small operational units of five for each targeted location. The ten gathered around the big oak table used for city council meetings.

To get things going, Bruce turned to his brother Hal who was one of the men assigned to the Philpot raids. Bruce and Hal had served together as original members of the Spirit Lake SWAT team. "Hal, you take Zeke, Tyler, JT, and Bubba and plan the raid on Smiley's trailer. You've been over there before, ah reckon?" Hal gave his brother thumbs up.

"You other four come over here," Bruce said to the remaining guys seated at the table.

Bruce had been dispatched to Butch Philpot's house once on a domestic. The call didn't result in an arrest, but he knew where the Philpot house was located in the small subdivision. Since he had been there, he figured immediate surveillance and a drive-by to verify location wasn't necessary. He knew the area well and felt certain there was no chance his team would hit the wrong house. The Google photomap supported his recall of the target location. Bruce figured that Butch and his wife would be asleep in the master bedroom and their daughter would be safe in one of the other bedrooms. All the bedrooms were located at one end of the small tract home.

When Bruce walked to the front of the conference room to grab a pad of flipchart paper, he noticed Chief Art was surveying the operation. Standing in front of his team, Bruce tacked a sheet on the wall with a strip of masking tape.

"This here is Butch's house," he told the four he had picked for his team. "I don't think we should use the SWAT truck on this one. It's too damn big and noisy. Ah figure we'll use two of our marked units and come at the house from two directions. You three guys come in from the east and I'll come in from the west. We'll park two houses away from Butch's place. Stay on Tac1 for all communication."

Bruce looked at the four men. Gunther and Big T were also original members of the SWAT team, but he had two rookies, too. Josh had just returned from a second deployment at one of those sand places in the Middle East. Bruce could never keep the countries straight and wasn't sure he could even find them on a map. Didn't matter to him anyway since he had finished his commitment in the Guard and had been out for the last four years.

Timmy Gould was the last member of Bruce's team. Timmy was a tall, lanky kid who had joined Spirit Lake two years earlier after being an Explorer Scout in the department's post. He still had that goofy high school look and sported a perpetual cowlick on the back of his head, even with a buzz cut haircut. Timmy had been on the SWAT team only four months.

"We got a search warrant for the house," Bruce told his team. "Lookin' for guns, masks, and money from the Big Box robberies. Remember, these guys are probably armed to the teeth and aren't afraid to use whatever weapons are handy. Warrant is a no knock because we don't want anyone to have time to figure we're at the door. Don't want anybody hurt. Ya gots to remember one thing—Butch may have done the crime, but he's got a wife and kid in the house, too.

"Gunter, Big T, and Josh, you be in this car," pointing to the vehicle rounding the corner from the east. "Timmy, you'll ride with me. Gunter and Big T, take the back of the house and Josh, you cover the southeast corner. Gunter, you'll cover the north-west so we got eyes down all sides. When I give the word, Big T, you break the sliding glass door leading off the patio in back and throw in a distraction device.

"Take the smaller ram with you, Big T. When Timmy and I hear the device go off, we'll boot the front door with the big ram. The three of us will converge in the hallway leading to the bedrooms. The master is the first on the right. Timmy and I will take that one. Big T, you get the daughter's room. Any questions?"

"What guns will we have, boss?" Gunter asked.

"Gunter, you and Josh take the pistol grip Mossbergs. Big T, you'll be throwing the distraction device so you better take one of the MP5s. It's smaller and won't get in the way. I'll take a Mossberg. Timmy, you've fired the MP5 ain't you?" Timmy nod-ded although he had only shot it a few times during last month's training at the range. "You be my back-up then, Timmy."

The two police cars approached the subdivision together, and then split, waiting for Bruce to give the order to position the cars. They parked at a quarter to five under a still dark sky and slowly crept across the front lawns of the houses on either side of the targeted house. The men had to circle around a motor home set on cinder blocks in the driveway of one home.

Big T was a little off center carrying the ram and nearly tripped over four bikes piled haphazardly in one of the yards. The team was dressed in black BDUs, but they weren't carrying usual SWAT gear that would have included full ballistic vests and Kevlar helmets. It was nearly show time as the five cops quietly settled into position.

Police raids were haphazard before the advent of SWAT units during the highly volatile era of the "War on Drugs." The advent of SWAT situations developed approaches designed to protect officers as well as people in the houses they would be raiding. Professional units used various threat assessments. These assessments evaluated the raid target, considering such factors as the criminal history of the persons expected to be inside, the possibility of weapons stored in the targeted house, potential fortification, surveillance cameras or barriers, guard dogs, and the general layout of the house and property. The more threat indicators established, the bigger need for specialized units, powerful weapons, and gas or distraction devices. The same threat indicators could be used to change the function of the search warrant obtained from the court. Higher threats allowed officers to obtain a no-knock warrant. Most warrants require officers to knock and announce their presence while waiting a reasonable length of time before breaking down the door. In a North Las Vegas case, the Supreme Court ruled that twenty seconds would be a reasonable amount of time for someone inside to hear the announcement and answer the door.

In this type raid, weapons and munitions are vastly different than what street cops would use. It's common to find SWAT units using semi and fully automatic weapons such as the Heckler Koch MP5 and AR15. Pistol gripped shotguns are still used.

The most common type of gas/diversion grenades used is a flash bang. These devices spew gas while creating a loud explosion, momentary high heat, and a brilliant flash of light. They are designed to shock and stun house inhabitants and allow the officers to get inside quickly to control the situation. The intense heat generated can cause nasty burns if the device lands on an individual and frequently the explosion results in a fire.

The planning for high-risk raids is formalized. It's important that each member of the SWAT team know who they're after, who they should expect to encounter, and what evidence they're looking for. It is critical to find out as much about the location as possible. It's imperative the team leader completes a site inspection immediately before the raid. This would avoid conducting a raid when another officer was on premise answering an unrelated call and reduce the chance of hitting the wrong location.

The team leader is responsible for developing a written plan detailing all aspects of the raid. The plan defines all known information and lists the steps taken prior to the raid. The plan also details each officer, what assignment that officer has, and what equipment and armament each officer will be carrying. The plan should also contain information such as specific radio frequencies to be used, medical support stationed within a reasonable range, and anticipate other needs such as female officers required to search females or a dog handler if it's determined dogs are at the raid location. Sometimes a unit will plan for a fire department contingent to be on standby if distraction devices are used.

"Go!" Bruce ordered as his digital watch clicked exactly 5:00.

Big T swung his ram into the sliding glass door, although it apparently was unlocked. Shards and plates of jagged glass blasted into the living room. Big T pulled the pin and threw the distraction canister into the living room. The blast was deafening. A brilliant flash of light momentarily assaulted the small room as the canister twisted violently on the floor in the middle of six little girls bundled in colorful Hello Kitty, Princess Aurora, Cinderella, and Rapunzel sleeping bags.

The girls bolted from sleep as a symphony of screams filled the room. Big T dropped the ram and tried to pull the MP5 strap over his head as he turned to begin moving down the hallway to what he had been told was the daughter's bedroom. He never looked around the living room. Big T tripped over the mound on the floor and went down hard, sprawled in the middle of the terrified children.

Timmy hit the front door with the large ram the moment he heard the distraction device detonate. The door wasn't solid core and disintegrated on contact. Bruce was first through the front door and yelled, "Search warrant...Police! Police! Search warrant!" Bruce headed for the hallway with Timmy following directly behind him.

Butch and Selma were in bed. Selma was lying on top of the covers to combat the stuffiness in the bedroom. Normally the bedroom door was wide open, but Selma had closed it to muffle the non-stop giggling coming from the front room. Butch was rolled securely in the covers and snoring heavily. He had finished the six-pack of beer watching the football game, causing a deep sleep.

Selma heard the glass breaking followed by the explosion and cacophony of screams. She bolted out of bed and ran to the bedroom door. Wearing only her underwear, she flung the door open, turned left and shot into the living room. Selma ran into Bruce and he careened against one wall as Selma rushed by him.

When Timmy followed Bruce through the front door, he reached for his MP5 and braced it forward. His left hand was on the magazine extending down from the gun and his right hand was on the pistol grip. He thought he had indexed his finger along the housing of the gun directly above the trigger guard and trigger. Timmy saw the blur exit the bedroom hallway and race toward him. He wasn't sure who it was or what was happening. Suddenly Timmy heard three pops and felt the recoil of his MP5. He looked down and found his finger was inside the trigger guard and on the trigger.

Bruce stuck out his arm and clotheslined Butch as he ran to follow his wife to the front of the house, causing him to fall on his back. Bruce spun his capture on his stomach and secured his hands with flex cuffs he'd pulled from his belt.

"Easy, Butch, we're cops," Bruce yelled into Butch's ear.

"What the fuck! What the fuck!" Butch stammered. "Selma! Selma!"

The girls were now in full panic mode as they staggered to their feet. Big T was scrambling to disengage himself from the twisted mass of sleeping bags. Bruce noticed Timmy standing ramrod straight in a corner next to a hutch with colorful plates balanced on the rim. Timmy's head was bent down looking at the MP5 hanging idly from the strap around his neck. Timmy wore a distant stare and appeared frozen in place.

"Timmy, what the fuck?" Bruce exploded.

Bruce focused his eyes on a spot on the floor directly in front of Timmy. Selma was lying across a Hello Kitty sleeping bag still occupied by a young girl who had her eyes strained shut and her palms over her ears. Blood was spurting from Selma's neck and the right side of her face was gone. Hello Kitty was bathing in a widening pool of red.

Selma's body wasn't moving. Bruce knew she was dead, but still went to her to help. He grabbed an empty sleeping bag with Cinderella waiting for her prince smiling up at him and pressed it hard onto Selma's neck to try to stop the blood flow. He knew a bullet had severed her carotid artery by the large volume of blood gushing like a broken fire hydrant.

Josh and Gunter were now positioned in the living room. Josh tried to herd the screaming girls to one side as Gunter yelled into his mic, "Shots fired! Shots fired! Butch Philpot's house. Send help. Send rescue. Hurry! For God's sake, hurry!"

Gunter could only mutter, "Shit! Shit!"

One girl corralled by Josh began yelling, "Mommy! Mommy! Daddy, where are you?" Gina found her mother's body on the floor and began to shake and cry and fell to the floor clutching Josh's leg.

Bruce looked at Timmy and saw tears streaming down his cheeks. "Gunter, get Timmy out of here now!" he ordered.

* * *

Taylor Sterling ambled out to his carport. He planned to stop at his bank and then grab a bite to eat before meeting Sandy Banks for their date later in the day. Sandy wanted somebody to convince her that she needed a new dining room table. She'd already made up her mind, but was looking for confirmation and justification.

For the umpteenth time, Taylor climbed into his not-so-trusty Jeep Wrangler. The familiar dull clicking sound when he turned the key sent imaginary electrodes shooting through his body.

Shit, shit, shit! Taylor thought to himself.

He walked to the rear of the carport and grabbed the battery charger from the shelf it called home. The time had finally come, he thought. It had been a good run, but it was time to junk his old Jeep friend. Yep, it was time, past time. Taylor made a decision.

Taylor pulled into Sandy's driveway and sat behind his steering wheel for a couple minutes. From the hilltop perch defining Sandy's house he could see most of Santa Fe beneath him. It was a clear day, but soon fireplace burning would leave a band of smoke hovering over the valley like a thick grey blanket.

"Well, look at you, cowboy!" Sandy exclaimed as she opened the front door and stepped on the landing.

Taylor climbed out of his new acquisition—a beautiful new ride. The Dodge Ram 1500 extended cab truck was an off-road version 4x4 featuring large knobbed tires. The truck proudly wore gunmetal metallic grey paint with a black leather interior accented with bright yellow trim and piping on the seats.

Taylor really didn't need a pickup truck, let alone a 4x4. He wasn't into hunting or off-roading, but the vehicle just felt right and he convinced himself it would fit his new image, whatever that turned out to be. Hell, Taylor thought, every man needed a truck. A big ass one. A bad one. *Arrrr!*

"Well, howdy there, lil' miss. Figured I needed something healthy to ride when I'm not ridin' you."

Sandy smiled. "And what proper burial did you give your old steed, big fella?"

"Gave it to the Boys and Girl's Club. They even came over and towed it away. Sad day for us. Me and my Wrangler had bonded well over the years," Taylor admitted, clenching his fist to his chest.

This happened to be Sandy and Taylor's official date night. Each half of the couple was in charge of finding something interesting or new to do on date nights, maybe both. Taylor and Sandy walked hand in hand to his new steed. Even though Sandy was a tall athletic woman, she had to figure out the best way to mount the Dodge. She put her right foot on the protruding chrome step and grabbed the handle on the doorframe. Taylor nestled his hand on her rather broad ass covered in tight sequined jeans and gave a gentle shove to help her mount.

"Where to, Sandy? Will I need to use my 4x4 extra features?"

She laughed and looked at him. "You know how to use them? My plan might get this shiny truck dirty. Didn't I tell you we were going mud bogging for our date?" She laughed even harder. Taylor knew there was no friggin' way she would get anywhere near mud. She might scuff and dirty her pricey Stetson boots and that sure as hell wasn't gonna happen.

"Head north toward Taos," she ordered.

Sandy had discovered a new restaurant with an owner who was looking to expand into Santa Fe. Taylor knew Sandy had an ulterior motive for this venture, she usually did. Sandy was one of the top realtors in the area and motives of any kind were her stock in trade. He didn't mind trying a new place, as long as the food was interesting and good.

They pulled into the parking lot of a small building outside the square in Taos. It was clustered among several art galleries that Taylor was glad were closed at this hour.

"Raul, surprise us!" Sandy exclaimed to the man who was embracing her as Taylor watched the show with amusement. "This is one of my steady squeezes, Taylor Sterling. He's my favorite taste tester, amongst other attributes. He has culinary panache."

Sandy avoided looking at Taylor to see if he was reacting to her off-the-wall comments. Actually he didn't mind her words one bit. He knew Sandy had other intimate friends and that was okay with him. Their relationship was full of fun and had enough intimacy to satisfy both.

They started their meal with a heady assortment of smoked locally caught fish accented with pungent goat cheese. Taylor asked for a Grey Goose l'Orange on the rocks and passed on wine, saving it for the main course.

The poached pear salad with Gorgonzola cheese crumbles teased with light orange vinaigrette was unexpected and very tasty. The main course was a whole baked bass encased in a terracotta pot that Raul cracked open at their table. Sprigs of fresh rosemary sprinkled over the entree gave a pungent aroma. The bass was smothered in yellow and red peppers and onions. Raul expertly carved the head away, mercifully, and butterflied the bass while removing the bones. Accenting grilled vegetables were seasoned with a rich balsamic glaze. Green chili grits complemented the entrée. Taylor and Sandy ended their meal with half a ripe red papaya serving as compote bowl for fresh berries.

"Well, what do you think?"

"Food was absolutely superb and served with an informal, but attentive flair. The joint's decor, however, is a little blah," Taylor responded.

"We can improve on that in Santa Fe."

Taylor thought the meal was well worth the time to get there. "You get some sort of deal from our host Raul?"

"Of course, I do! How can I afford you and the others without making deals?" Sandy's body shook as she suppressed a chuckle.

The next morning Taylor's new truck was still standing proud in Sandy's driveway.

* * *

Spirit Lake spilled with a dichotomy of opinions about the capture of the Big Box Robbers. Most citizens were pleased that the dangerous guys had been captured. The same group thought Selma Philpot's death was a tragedy, but she shouldn't have been living with that scum Butch anyway. A smaller group was incensed about what they called a botched, military-style police raid turned execution. Most had no understanding of what had occurred or why it had happened. Facts didn't get in the way of these well-meaning people.

The Commonwealth's attorney was caught in the usual police predicament. He knew there was more to the story, but the officers involved all gave similar versions of the tragic events. The most told version was that Selma had apparently not heard Bruce's command that they were conducting a police search. Timmy was simply trying to protect his leader, Bruce, from

Selma's assault. Because it was such a confined space, there was no other option for action. The attorney knew he wasn't getting the full story, and suspected the young girls wouldn't be able to clarify much. Butch had come on the scene after the actual shooting had taken place and heard only confused noises, screaming, and yelling, followed by the rapid fire of gunshots.

Butch and Smiley Philpot's folks lived in eastern Kentucky in Perry County, just outside the city of Hazard. They lived in the hill country where most people wouldn't venture without someone vouching for them. If a stranger, or even an uninvited friend, didn't announce their name loudly, they would be met with buckshot. After the shooting, the grandparents took Gina to live with them.

Gina would never get her Princess birthday party.

It was nearly a year to the date of the Spirit Lake robbery when the entire gang was finally convicted after exhausting several appeals. They received prison sentences ranging from 15 to 30 years. Justice was dispensed swifter in this part of Kentucky than say in the state of California or without the media circus trials in Florida.

* * *

Ezra Blair was sixty-eight years old, the last thirty of which were spent in Spirit Lake with his wife of fifty years. Ten years earlier he had been diagnosed as bipolar. There had been many incidents that had given his wife, Sadie, cause for alarm. On more than one occasion she had fled to her sister's house across town during Ezra's manic periods. He had never hit her or threatened her with violence, but his size and erratic mood swings frightened her.

When his fits raged, Sadie said Ezra acted like a wild bull in a china shop.

For the past three years, a nurse from County Health had visited Ezra every week to make sure he was taking his medication. Ezra might bluster, huff, and puff about doctor's orders, but the nurse was able to control him and cajole him to comply. Ezra was a big man. He weighed over 280 pounds, most of it flab.

Because of his diagnosis, Ezra was on SSI disability. Before that kicked in, he had been working as a forklift operator at a distribution center along I-75. It was a good job and Ezra was making a decent living. Ezra and Sadie had simple tastes and rarely were extravagant, but they did like to go into Lexington when Ezra got tickets for UK basketball or football. Once they traveled to Louisville and spent the night at the famous Brown Hotel, basking in the old Southern tradition of opulence. Ezra finally enjoyed one of those Hot Brown sandwiches. He chose an open-face turkey sandwich topped with a generous supply of bacon, and then covered with a sauce called something like moor-nay. It was Ezra's idea of the perfect lunch, ever.

One summer Ezra and Sadie drove over to Branson and saw Wayne Newton and an Asian guy who played a mean fiddle. Ezra knew it was really a violin, but he figured the way the fellow played the damn thing, it was closer to a fiddle.

This particular Thursday night was like every other Thursday night in the Blair household. Ezra was slumped in his lounge chair watching a strange program on A&E. Sadie thought it had something to do with guys going around buying junk, or treasures, as they sometimes referred to their finds. Ezra would carry animated conversations with the TV, screaming at the top of his lungs, "That's just a piece of junk. You're paying how much for that piece of shit? You gotta be crazy!"

As if on cue, the ranting pushed Ezra into his nasty zone and he began yelling at Sadie about not doing the laundry to his specifications. His demands made no sense, but when in that state, nothing coming out of Ezra's mouth made sense. He bolted from his chair and charged directly at Sadie. She cringed and covered her head with shaking hands waiting for the blow, but Ezra stopped just short of where she was cowering and started to jump up and down.

"Get out! Get out! You're nothing but a lazy woman living off my money. Get out!" Ezra pointed at the door.

"Let me get some clothes together first, Ezra."

"No, get your ass outside now!"

She'd faced these episodes before. Sadie knew she had to get away from Ezra and give him time to calm down. She tried to remember the last time she saw him take his medication but her mind drew a blank. Weeks before she stopped looking into his little plastic box with compartments for each day's pills. Now she knew that was probably a mistake.

Sadie opened the front door and it nearly slammed into her as Ezra forcibly flung it closed. The impact was so great that the knocker chimes clanked with an erratic, violent pulse. Sadie knew the county nurse was due to visit the next day. Sadie went to her sister's house and planned to call the nurse in the morning to alert her about what had happened.

The next morning Sadie met the county nurse outside the Blair's home. She again explained what had happened the previous evening.

"I think it's time I spent a few days at my sister's house. Ezra is getting worse. I'm not afraid of him, but it's just so hard on me dealing with his moods. I never know when he's going to go off on a tantrum. Could you talk with Ezra while I go inside to pack a small suitcase?"

Both women walked up the short sidewalk to the front door. Ezra must have seen them or heard their cars pull up. He yanked open the front door and stood with a carving knife clutched in his hand.

"Don't come any closer or I'll use this on you! You know I will!"

"Ezra, I'm Thelma. Remember, this is Friday. I visit you every Friday. I need to talk with you. Sadie needs to get inside her house."

"Not *her* house! My house! My money; my house! You bitches get out. Don't need no bitches. I'm the man here!" Ezra screamed a string of obscenities and slammed the door shut.

"Sadie, I hate to do this, but I think we need to call the police. We must get Ezra committed for his own good. We need to get him back on his meds so he won't hurt himself or anyone else."

Sadie was silent and began to cry. "They'll only hurt him. I don't want him hurt. He doesn't know what he's doing. I don't want him hurt."

"We need to get him to the hospital. We need to get him back on his meds. You know that, Sadie."

Sadie nodded as Nurse Thelma punched 9-1-1.

* * *

Bruce and Hal Adams were pumping iron at the World Gym. Hal was spotting for Bruce, positioned prone on a bench grasping the iron bar with talcum-laced hands. He had just added two 25-pound disks to the bar, making his bench-press an even 300 pounds. Bruce readied his hands at his favored distance and took two slow breaths. With a jerk he raised the bar and steadied it high above him. Slowly he allowed the bar to fall, took a deep breath and brought the horizontal iron back up again.

Hal counted slowly, 9…10…11…12 before Bruce lowered the bar back to the uprights at the count of 15. Bruce waited a few seconds while hungrily sucking deep breaths before swinging upright off the bench.

"Hear about Timmy?" Bruce asked, still trying to catch his breath. Hal shook his head.

"Got pensioned off. Disability. Guess killing that Philpot woman was just too much for him. He was always kind of a pussy, though."

"What's happening with that lawsuit the ambulance chaser filed?"

"Don't know. Those things get lost in the hopper. Takes forever to get to court, if it ever does! What the fuck?" Bruce exclaimed as he looked at the text that just arrived over his phone.

"What's up?" Hal asked.

"Call up for SWAT."

Bruce and Hal hadn't finished their workouts so they weren't dripping wet. The duo dumped their gear in gym bags and threw on jeans, T-shirts and windbreakers emblazoned with the SLPD logo. Within fifteen minutes they were walking through the station door.

"Everybody up?" Bruce asked the sergeant on duty.

"Yup. Ya gots only nine on the team these days, right?"

"Unfortunately. Haven't had time to get someone to replace Timmy. Wasn't sure he wasn't comin' back," Bruce told the sergeant. "Okay, what we got?"

"Ol' Ezra Blair, The guy's off his meds again. Ran his wife

out of the house last night. She come back with Ezra's psych nurse from county and he won't let them in the house. All the wife wants to do is grab some clothes so she can go to her sister's house. Ezra's in one of his states. I've seen him like this before. Need to let him calm down. The nurse says he's got a knife and was flinging it around threatening her and the wife. Nurse says he should be committed. Chief says to activate you guys. Up to me, I'd let him calm down like always. But, what the fuck do I know?"

Bruce radioed Art Summers, "Boss, where you at?"

"I've got a command post over at Spring and Market. It's about two blocks away from Ezra's house. I've got his wife and the county nurse with me. Come up to the command post without the van, Bruce. We'll work it out from here."

Bruce told his men to stay with the van and made his way to the command post. Bruce made a quick change into his BDUs, but left his SWAT gear in the van. He figured it might unnerve the wife and nurse to see the arsenal.

The official Spirit Lake command post was simply a Chevy Tahoe marked unit driven by the field sergeant. Bruce saw the tailgate was lowered and a map of the area covered the shelf. Art, Sadie, and Nurse Thelma converged on Bruce as he walked to them. Thelma again described what had occurred and added she believed Ezra should be involuntarily committed. Sadie Blair nodded her head in agreement.

"Let us handle it initially," Art told the women. "Once we have him controlled, we'll call you at your sister's house. You both don't need to be here now. It's okay for us to go into your house, isn't it, Ms. Blair?"

"Of course it is, Chief Summers. But, please don't hurt my husband."

"I've visited Ezra every week for the past four years. I can help you get him under control. I know how to talk with him. He's not an easy person, particularly when he's off his meds," Thelma shared with Art.

"It doesn't work that way, missy," Art explained. "You called us. Now the situation has become a police operation. You'd only be getting in the way. I'm an expert at this type stuff. I'm a certified trained hostage negotiator. Let us handle it." Art put his arm around Thelma and moved her away from the command post.

"I don't care what you are! I know my client and I know his problems. Don't tell me to walk off!" Thelma was noticeably upset and her fist was shaking as she pointed at Art.

"Now, now. Don't go threatening me. You don't get to do that. That's interfering with our investigation. You don't want to get yourself arrested, missy!"

"Don't you go 'missy' me!" The nurse stormed off, grabbing Sadie by the arm.

"Nurses, geez," Art muttered to the officers gathered around the Tahoe. "Think they know everything. Real ego nut there." He turned to Bruce and asked, "What you want to do with your guys?"

Bruce and his team had been to Ezra's house once before. They were able to talk him down that time and got Ezra into an ambulance to take him to the hospital for a psych evaluation. Bruce figured the same would happen today.

"I think we'll first knock on the door and see if he opens it. If we don't get an answer, I'll have a couple guys look through the back windows to see if we can pinpoint his location. If worse comes to worst, we'll go through the front door. Got his wife's consent so there's no need for a warrant. Seems like a righteous welfare check to me." Art nodded in agreement.

Bruce and Big T approached the front door while Josh and Zeke covered both sides of the house. Bruce told TJ to cover the back of the house. The rest of the team stayed back at the SWAT van.

"Ezra, police here!" Bruce called as he knocked loudly on the front door. No answer. He banged on the doorframe with his metal flashlight. He tried yelling two more times with no response. The other three officers were peering into windows trying to get a fix on the situation. They radioed to base that no one was visible in the house. Bruce grabbed the front door handle, heard a click, and pushed the door open.

"Police! Ezra! We're here to check up on you. Sadie is concerned about you and wants to make sure you're okay. Where are you, guy?" No answer. It was less than a minute before the five officers had checked each room and didn't find Ezra.

"He must be in the cellar," Big T offered.

The team hadn't yet checked the house cellar. Bruce opened the door to the tunnel of old steps. The entrance was dark and malodorous. His eyes quickly adjusted and he could see the wooden staircase descending down and then turning to the left at the midway mark. Bruce found the light switch and a flick caused a single bulb to cast a faint light on the cellar steps. Bruce could feel dampness rush at him and saw the walls were made of basic foundation rocks.

"Ezra, you down here?" Bruce heard faint scuffling. "Ezra, I hear you; come show yourself. This is Sergeant Adams. Your wife is concerned about you. We're here to help you, Ezra, not hurt you. Come out and talk with me."

"Go away, you fucker! Got no right to be in my house! Get the hell out of my house! I don't need your help. I'm okay. *She's* the one off her rocker. Give her the help she needs. I don't need you or your help!"

Bruce couldn't determine exactly where Ezra was in the cellar. He slowly began to walk down the steps.

"Ezra, this is Sergeant Adams. Bruce. I'm coming down to talk."

"You better not. I've got a knife with me and I'll use it. You got no right to be in my house."

"Now calm down, Ezra. I just want to talk," Bruce said softly as he dropped down two more steps. His flashlight surveyed the cellar's four walls. It appeared to be a tactical nightmare. Small, no more than fifteen feet square. He could see the walls were a combination of rock and cinderblock. Joists holding the first floor were bare on the ceiling and the room appeared to have low clearance. There were no lights, other than the single bulb Bruce had turned on. There was little ambient light peeking through the dirty, smudged small cellar windows hugging ground level.

"Don't come any further or I'll cut you!" Ezra screamed, revealing his hiding place under the stairway in a corner of the cellar. Ezra stuck his arm through the open stairwell menacingly. He had a large kitchen butcher knife duct taped to his arm and was waving it back and forth like Blackbeard's sword.

Bruce went back upstairs and closed the door behind him.

"Big T, we're gonna have to force him out. He's barricaded under the stairwell and he's got a knife taped to his arm. It's obvious he's delusional. Let's get the team assembled. Want you to get four others. Bring the gas, and you'll need gas masks if we deploy it. It's gonna be a bitch getting him up once we get him in cuffs. He's a big fellow so it will be dead weight. Brief the chief at the van. Ask the boss if he wants to try negotiation."

Ten minutes later Big T entered the living room of Ezra's house. He had Josh, Gunter, Zeke and JT with him. Josh was carrying the Sage, Zeke had the beanbag shotgun with the yellow stock, and Gunter lumbered in with the large red gas canister dangling from his hand. It looked like a small fire extinguisher. Each officer wore a ballistic vest with POLICE lettered on the front. Gas masks were secured in pouches worn on their thighs. The men were wearing kneepads and leather gloves. Bruce figured he'd give Ezra one more chance and called Art to see about negotiating with him.

"Chief says Ezra had the chance to talk. Chief thinks negotiation won't work," Bruce relayed to his team.

"Ezra, come up now. If I don't hear or see you in a couple minutes, we'll be coming down. Believe me; you don't want that, Ezra."

"Hell with you. Come on down and see what I've got for you, assholes!"

Bruce shrugged and gave his team the signal to descend the stairs. The five officers rushed down the steps and jumped over the outstretched arm taped with the knife that was sticking out under a stair slate. The men fanned out and discovered the ceiling clearance was so low that each had to squat so their helmets wouldn't hit the exposed beams.

Ezra was butt heavy with his legs extended, and was crammed into the corner of the cellar under the mid-landing of the stairwell. He kept waving his left arm with the knife taped to his forearm. His chattering was more like a high-pitched squeal making his words unintelligible. Ezra's eyes darted from one officer to another like a snake about to strike.

"Men, put on your masks now! Give him a couple bursts of gas, Gunter," Big T ordered.

Fog emitting from the activated OC cylinder filled the area under the stairwell and enveloped Ezra in a cloud. Ezra pulled a dishtowel from behind his back and pressed it to his mouth. He was coughing harshly, but the gas wasn't having the effect expected. Ezra wasn't moving.

The officers looked through the small openings of their gas masks to check out the situation. They sounded like Darth Vader with a bad case of laryngitis when they tried to communicate with each other.

"Juice it up! Give him some more gas!" Gunter unloaded the entire canister. Ezra stayed put, coughed, but kept swinging his knifed arm.

"Less lethal, Zeke!" Big T shouted.

Zeke fired one of the winged beanbags from his shotgun. It impacted Ezra's left thigh and he flinched, but still didn't leave his position under the stairwell. Zeke pumped and fired two more rounds, hitting Ezra again in the thigh and his left bicep. Nothing happened.

"Josh!" Big T yelled.

Josh swung the Sage up and pulled it back to rest on his shoulder. The weapon had six rounds attached to the drum positioned on the stock. Josh made sure it was loaded with foam rounds. The weapon could also fire wooden dowels, but they were more devastating and injurious.

Josh fired the first round and saw it strike Ezra's left thigh. There was no response, other than Ezra swearing loudly at his antagonist. Josh quickly fired the remaining five rounds. Ezra kept yelling at the officers. Josh fumbled through the large cargo pockets of his BDUs and inserted round after round into the chamber, pulling the trigger sending the foam projectiles flying at Ezra. Several more times he retrieved rounds from his pocket when finally he was out of Sage ammo.

"I'm out!"

Big T keyed the mic on his shoulder and hollered, "More Sage rounds!"

One of the cellar windows broke open and a box of Sage rounds scattered over the cellar floor. Barney scooped them up and handed them to Josh who quickly jammed them into the cylinder and fired. It wasn't until after the incident was over that they realized the new box of Sage munitions held the wooden dowel version.

"I think he's finally out," Big T called as he looked at Ezra's slumped figure. The officers hesitated to approach the unconscious man.

"Got fire guys up there?" Big T radioed. "Have them send down one of them probe poles."

Bruce captured the pole and inserted the hook at the pole's end into the masking tape around Ezra's arm and pulled up. The masking tape split and the knife clanked to the ground. The officers grabbed Ezra and pulled him out of his sanctuary. Ezra was not moving, just moaning as they moved him onto the cellar floor. It took a while to secure him to the rigid backboard one of the firefighters had brought down, strap him on, and maneuver his dead weight out of the cellar into the waiting ambulance. The old wooden steps groaned and creaked as six large police and fire officers guided the backboard up the steps.

Ezra languished in the hospital for nearly six months. He had been struck by 124 projectiles—beanbags, foam rounds, and wooden dowels. Welts, bruises, knots, and lacerations marked his body from the top of his head to the bottom of his feet. He struggled with the trauma, mentally and physically. His bodily condition welcomed pneumonia and this affliction severely impacted his lungs and breathing. Ezra finally died from a laundry list of physical deficiencies.

* * *

Art Summers was rarely ever called to appear before Clyde Smith at the County Commonwealth Attorney's office. In Kentucky, this legal position was similar to a district attorney's job in most other states. It was unusual for Art to be summoned, but he wasn't concerned since he had known Clyde since the days Clyde was chasing ambulances to rope in clients.

"Art, come in and sit yourself down, buddy," Clyde welcomed as his secretary opened the office door for the chief.

Clyde was approaching sixty, had a full stock of grey hair, his face accented with black horn-rimmed glasses. The attorney was probably forty pounds overweight for his five foot six frame. He wore a white dress shirt without a tie and the top two buttons were open. He should have worn suspenders, as his belt was well hidden under the enormous belly that flapped over his middle. Clyde stood, but didn't come around his file filled desk to greet his old friend.

"Clyde, how you been?" Art asked.

"Good, Art. Your boys and them London and Laurel County cops been keeping our courthouse open," he chuckled at his classification of the steady increase in arrests made by local agencies.

Art settled into the chair in front of the desk and asked, "So, what's so important you got to call me down here, Clyde?"

"You know, I never really believed that bullshit story your guys came up with about the Philpot shooting. I took a beating for not prosecuting your boys or even bringing the case to a coroner's inquest." Clyde looked directly at Art as he made the comment.

"You had the facts, Clyde."

"I had the facts you guys put together, Art, that's all." The attorney continued to stare daggers at the chief.

"What you saying, Clyde? You think my men lied? Hell, it was the KSP that done the investigation. Don't shoot them evil eyes at me!"

"I couldn't disprove their stories, Art. That's all it was. Shit, there weren't any credible witnesses. You know I got to prove 'beyond a reasonable doubt.' That's a high burden of proof."

"So why the invite today?"

"Can't do the same on the Ezra incident, Art. Your boys blasted the shit out of the old guy and that's what caused the complications that ended Ezra's time with us. Got to take this one to the coroner's inquest. Thought you should know before I talk with the press. Local press is on my ass. This is the second fatal your boys have been involved in over the last year. Doesn't smell right to me. I think you got something else going on in your little police station, Art."

Art leaned back in the chair and brought his fingers to his temples and began massaging them in a circular motion. He knew he could argue with Clyde, but he sensed the decision had been made. Art's men would be blindsided by the Commonwealth Attorney's decision. Art couldn't remember the last time a county attorney had convened a coroner's inquest for something a cop had done.

"Will we be able to present a defense?" Art asked, not being familiar with the protocol for the inquest.

"Seems reasonable, Art. You know this ain't like a real court. It's a lot less formal. We'll have six people on the panel and a circuit judge will officiate."

"How much time 'til all this happens?"

"Three weeks."

* * *

"Taylor," the strange voice on the telephone began. "Heard you talk at a risk management seminar a couple of years ago. People say you're the man to call for sticky police matters. I got one. You interested?"

"Who's asking?" Taylor responded as he got off the elliptical machine at the LAFitness gym next to the mall on Cerritos. Taylor fluctuated going between this gym and the smaller one at his condo complex. Sometimes he liked the solitude of the usually empty condo gym. No one seemed to use it much anymore. Other times he liked to be around people as his workout was energized by them. Over the years Taylor had met a few interesting people at the gym. But then again, he'd met obnoxious ones as well. He usually went to the gym in the late morning after the early pre-work rush and before the social rush began in the evening.

"Oh, sorry! I'm Ben Franks from the KLC. That's the Kentucky League of Cities. I run the law enforcement risk section."

"Haven't done any work in Kentucky yet, Ben."

"Well, we got something for you if you can be here in about a week."

"Where's 'here?'"

"Laurel County. It's in the eastern part of the state. Need to fly into Lexington if you can. Closest airport without going to Louisville or over the mountains to Knoxville."

"What you got?"

"Small police department. Maybe forty strong. Two SWAT incidents within the past year; both ended up with a fatality. We just got the civil papers on the first one and expect to get hit with the second round after the coroner's inquest. That's why we need you up here next week. We'd like you to attend the inquest and give us your initial feedback. Then, depending on what you sense, maybe look into the department. You game?"

"You know my fee?"

"Sort of. Checked you out and everybody says you aren't cheap. I'm looking for quality, Taylor. But, better send me a fee and expense schedule though. I'd like to make plans for you to be here by Tuesday, next week."

"Okay, see you Tuesday in eastern Kentucky, Ben."

For the past five years this had become Taylor's life away from Santa Fe. He enjoyed consulting. It allowed him to continue to be involved with police work, but on a slower pace, at least most times. Taylor knew sometimes he accepted more work than he should, and worried about running into commitment conflicts, but so far, none had materialized.

Taylor was also aware many times he became involved in the worst arena of policing and sometimes met the most malignant cops. Taylor continually reminded himself that such incidents and cops were the exception as the vast majority of officers and cop shops never fielded negative news or the breath of a scandal. But, Taylor appreciated that bad cops did step into shit so he figured he'd never be out of work as a cop consultant. This viewpoint validated the decision he made when he retired from the LAPD that he would never again work as a chief or in a position of having an official boss. Taylor felt good about what he was doing.

* * *

Most courtrooms look pretty much the same. Some are smaller than others and a few, particularly the old renovated federal courthouses, are very ornate. But, most are functional and bland. Tax money at work.

Taylor was surprised when he entered the new courthouse in

the center of London, Kentucky, and the courtroom designated for the coroner's inquest. A large wooden structure stood opposite the jury box that was built to avoid obstructing the judge's view from his elevated position. Taylor estimated the unusual structure was about fifteen feet square with a staircase in one corner. The ceiling was lower than found in most structures, less than six feet in height. The sides were covered with clear plastic sheeting so one could see inside without obstruction. Taylor thought someone had put a lot of work into creating this display.

The courtroom was crowded with spectators. Taylor noticed a TV cameraman and photographers gathered outside the courtroom in the hallway. He had to wind his way through the unexpected throng and hoped he wouldn't be late for the show. He surmised TV crews wouldn't be allowed inside the courtroom. Taylor was lucky and found a seat on the aisle so he could grab a good view of the expansive front of the room.

The bailiff announced everyone should stand as the judge entered. The judge was young, as judges went. He was wearing a sport coat rather than a traditional judicial robe. He adjusted narrow reading glasses, glanced at papers covering his desk, and waved to the bailiff to bring in the jury. The bailiff left through a doorway next to the jury box and quickly reappeared leading the six jurors to their seats.

"You may take your seats," the judge said. "Mr. Smith, it's your show."

Clyde Smith casually strolled around his counsel's table and approached the railing separating him from the six jurors who had finally finished wiggling and sliding into their chairs. A strange mix of men and women filled the jury box. It was Clyde's time to question each juror to discover reasons they should not be seated on the panel.

One potential juror, a bearded man in his late twenties was wearing a blue UK sweatshirt and was busy picking at something lodged in his nose. He acknowledged he was out of work and couldn't find a job in the area, despite having a PhD in ancient Roman literature. He assured the questioning attorney that he didn't read the local newspapers and hadn't heard about the Blair incident.

A young woman closer to twenty was staring at Clyde intently. She was dressed in a black turtleneck sweater and a very short black leather skirt accented with a kaleidoscope of colored patterns squiggled on leggings. A black leather jacket featuring pockets outlined in bright rhinestones completed her outfit. Her blond hair was in the current style of long rolling curls highlighted with an uplifted tuff in lieu of bangs. She captured the eye of most of the men in the courtroom when she wiggled her way into the jury box. She acknowledged she was a cashier at a local bikers' bar, but hoped to land a job with the county, maybe with the sheriff's office.

A man in his forties was wearing an Amerigas logoed shirt and blue jeans. He had a toothpick sticking in the corner his mouth that he adroitly moved from left to right with a combination of movements using his lips and tongue. The round outline of a canister of smokeless tobacco in his upper pocket indicated he would be longing for a pinch or two sometime during the day.

A woman in her late sixties was dressed in a dark brown tweed suit with a cream blouse. She was clutching a small brown leather purse planted on her lap. Taylor felt confident she had a pair of brown leather gloves in her purse. She was a retired secretary from the Land Conservatory. She nervously glanced left and right at the others sharing the small jurors' box.

The fifth juror was decked in a corduroy sport coat probably saved from his high school days thirty years earlier. He wore rimless glasses and had a small moustache he surely manicured daily. He proudly announced he was the assistant principal at a local middle school where he had been teaching for the past two decades.

The last juror was a tall, overweight man wearing bib overalls over a red plaid shirt. He identified himself as a local farmer raising mostly hogs. He beamed when he told the court that one of his hogs had placed first in the county fair the previous year. He also noted his hogs were much in demand by Bubba Don's BBQ restaurant chain.

To Taylor, it appeared the jury pool system had produced a reasonable cross-section of Laurel County folks, or at least what he assumed they might be.

"A coroner's inquest is not like trials you may have seen on TV or read about in books," Clyde began. "It's a process to help our community try to understand why someone died. In most cases the good Lord takes one of his loyal subjects when they are ill, have lived a long and good life, or have faced a tragic accident. In those cases we know what happened and come together only to grieve a loss. But, sometimes, folks die for unknown reasons or when a close examination is necessary to find what might have caused their deaths."

Clyde closely looked at each juror and made direct eye contact with each one before moving on to the next. He gave a slight nod to each juror.

"Ezra Blair died after he encountered several Spirit Lake police officers. Ezra, you'll hear, was a troubled man suffering from mental illness. The officers were called to his home by his wife, Sadie." Clyde turned and looked back at Ezra's widow.

"The nurse who had been treating Ezra for several years encouraged the call. The two women couldn't control him on that tragic day. Ezra had chased Sadie out of their home the night before. The police officers called used force against Ezra to bring him under control in an attempt to get him the professional help he desperately needed. Ezra lasted nearly six months until the good Lord took him at the young age of sixty-eight."

Clyde stopped and looked at each juror. He turned and looked at the courtroom audience, stopping to glance at a group of uniformed officers on one side of the room and then at a small group of reporters busily writing in their notebooks. He walked back to his table and took a deliberate drink of water before turning back to the jurors. The button on his suit coat strained to keep his bulging belly from escaping.

"Your task as jurors is to evaluate the testimony and the evidence that will be put before you and make a decision. Was Ezra Blair's death an accident, or was it a homicide? Homicide means a death was caused by the hands of someone else. It doesn't mean that the death was murder or wrongful, however. If you find Ezra Blair's death was the result of actions by others, you'll need to decide if those actions were justified, accidental, or criminal."

Clyde paused, punctuating the last word.

"These are difficult decisions that you should not take lightly or determine in haste. Your decision will assist me and the State to decide what the next step will be. You are here to assist me to perform my job as the Commonwealth's attorney and I am in your debt. Thank you."

Spirit Lake employed a part-time city attorney like most small towns do. Jacob Samuels enjoyed a comfortable retainer for this position, but his main source of income came from marital law, drafting estates and wills, and handling a few personal injury lawsuits primarily relating to traffic accidents. He had been an attorney for nearly fifteen years and had been retained by the city for the past five years. As city attorney his duties included approving contracts, settling small civil lawsuits, dispensing legal advice on a myriad of topics, and sitting in on city commission meetings once a month. Jacob Samuels was not a trial attorney and it showed in his fumbling and disjointed presentation and questioning.

Jacob quickly handed the ball to Captain Lewis Shakelford. Lewis started by playing the 911 call from Nurse Thelma to the police station. Following he used a document camera, called an Elmo, to project scribbled notes he said were the operational plan of the Spirit Lake SWAT unit that stormed the Blair house. He also showed the log maintained by an officer at the field command post. This new high tech device replaced the older bulky overhead projector.

Captain Shakelford turned next to the massive structure positioned on the left side of the courtroom. Lewis was allowed to present a demonstration using Sergeant Bruce Adams and the five SWAT officers involved in the operation.

Taylor considered this to be a bad tactical move since it created discovery evidence that might be used against the officers should they be charged criminally or find themselves in a civil lawsuit regarding the death of Ezra Blair.

The officers went through a choreographed demonstration of what had occurred in the basement on the night of Ezra's "capture." For authenticity, the five officers wore their complete tactical uniforms, including gas masks. Every officer was forced to stoop while entering the cellar so their heads wouldn't bang against the low ceiling.

With five crammed in the small space, they were almost standing shoulder-to-shoulder. Josh was holding the exact same Sage weapon he carried that night and Zeke held his shotgun with the bright yellow stock.

Lewis found someone about Ezra's size to sit under the stairs as Ezra had been doing. The actual knife used that night was taped to the stand-in's forearm with duct tape as indicated in the reports of the incident. Overall, it was a very effective demonstration. The jurors were captivated as they watched every move the officers made. The older female juror appeared exceptionally startled when Ezra's stand-in suddenly lashed out with the knife from between the stair steps.

"I'm so sorry Mr. Blair died," Josh blurted as he walked out of the plastic mock-up, allowing the Sage to drop down his leg. "We just wanted to help him. God, we didn't want him to die. We just wanted to get him out so he could get some help." Josh choked up and used his uniform sleeve to blot moisture gathering in his eyes.

"Now, these are what the fine officers had to use to try to subdue Mr. Blair," Jacob explained as he handed the jurors the projectiles fired from the Sage and shotgun.

Jacob waited until the jurors could touch and examine each projectile. Some lifted them as if to test the weight. The Amerigas guy slammed the wooden dowel into his hand as if demonstrating what the impact might have been.

The hog farmer held the beanbag in his palm and pulled at the tiny wings that stabilized the projectile when it was fired. The retired Land Conservatory secretary quickly passed each projectile to the next juror as if it was on fire.

"The officers had to keep their gas masks on during the entire incident," Jacob continued. "If any of you want to try this mask on, feel free. You'll find the mask is very uncomfortable and will limit your vision substantially."

UK sweatshirt asked for the mask, but gave it back quickly when he realized strapping it on would mess up his hair.

The next witnesses called to testify were the four paramedics who responded to the scene. They were the ones who administered first aid to Ezra and carried him out of the basement to the waiting ambulance. They methodically explained the life support techniques used, which was really just a fancy name for basic first aid.

"The patient was moaning a lot," the first medic noted. "We couldn't see most of his injuries because of clothing. But, we saw a lot of hematomas and a few open lacerations. There wasn't much treatment we could administer in the cramped basement. It was a bitch… excuse me… a real problem getting him out of the basement.

"Mr. Blair was a big man and was dead weight. We ended up putting him on a backboard and enlisted a couple officers to help us get him up the stairs. We transported him to the new St. Joseph's Hospital along Interstate 75. They were waiting for us when we arrived at the emergency entrance. I guess that's about it. Oh, the patient didn't say anything in the ambulance." The medic shook his head and lowered it.

A doctor was called to review the hospital in-take records and read out loud what they said. Surprisingly he was dressed in green surgical pants, clog shoes, and a pale blue polo shirt with the St. Joseph's Hospital logo on the front. He reviewed the vital references and summarized the treatment Ezra received during his month in the hospital. The young doctor did a good job dumbing down medical terms and interpreting Ezra's medical records into common English.

An attractive, slightly plump young lady dressed in a pink patterned nurse's smock was next on the witness stand. She was the representative from the rehab facility where Ezra had been transferred after thirty days hospitalization. She gave a summary of treatment received and detailed the slow decline in Ezra's health until his death five months later.

The medical examiner read the autopsy results into the record and gave his final conclusion that Ezra Blair had died from respiratory failure resulting from pneumonia caused by extensive blunt force trauma.

Sadie Blair was called to the witness chair next. She was a small woman sporting the obligatory blue helmet hairstyle women of her generation love. She was dressed in a black tailored suit with a single string of seed pearls ringing her neck. A purse was clutched in her gloved hands. Sadie grasped the railing as she mounted the two steps leading to the witness chair.

Sadie recounted her life with Ezra. They had been sweethearts since the seventh grade and had been married just shy of fifty years. She allowed a tear to trickle down her cheek when she shared the couple had been planning a large family anniversary party the month after the police encounter occurred.

"I was never frightened of Ezra. He was a big man, but a gentle giant. He would often sound gruff and I could see how someone who didn't know him might be afraid. He never hurt me. I knew when he was falling into one of his spells. I knew how to keep away from him. Yes, sometimes I retreated to my sister's house.

"I called the police that day because I wanted to pick up a few sets of clothes and Ezra wouldn't allow me in the house. I knew it would take a couple days for my husband to come to his senses and I planned to stay at my sister's until he was back to normal. In the past, he always calmed down."

Nurse Thelma took the seat on the witness stand next. Blue scrubs and Dansk shoes gave her an air of authority. Her jaw was clenched and Taylor noted her fist was tight creating pale knobs where her knuckles should be. She didn't look directly at Clyde when he initially addressed her, but her pointed stare pierced the assembled group of uniformed officers in the audience. Her blatant hostility was evident.

"I had been treating Ezra for the past four years, that is before the cops snuffed out his life," Nurse Thelma recounted angrily. She delineated her treatment plan for Ezra and listed the various medications his doctors had prescribed. She told how difficult it was to determine the proper blend of medications and how hostile and irritated Ezra became when they didn't work or when adverse side effects frustrated him.

"We called because we wanted assistance from the cops. We called them to help Ezra, not kill him! And that buffoon...the officer with the stars on his collar...degraded and dismissed me without even asking if I might give the officers helpful information. He was just a pompous ass! I get mad every time I think about that day. It was horrible! Just hideous!"

To her credit, Nurse Thelma kept her composure throughout her testimony although she continued to glare at Chief Summers. She left the witness stand and walked down the center aisle of the room. As she passed the group of officers she turned and accused, "You killed a good man! Shame on you!" After the outburst, she walked out of the courtroom.

Taylor was surprised when Clyde Smith asked the jurors if they had questions. That was not the usual procedure in this type hearing, including grand jury hearings. Questions were typically presented in writing and the prosecutor would decide if and how he would present the question. But, as the judge initially announced, this was the prosecutor's show.

"Why didn't the gas affect Mr. Blair?" UK sweatshirt asked.

Clyde turned to Captain Shakelford who then turned to Sergeant Bruce Adams for an answer.

"OC, or pepper gas, isn't always effective. It will debilitate probably nine out of ten people, but some people have a higher tolerance for it than others. Police studies have shown that highly intoxicated people, and some mentally ill folks, don't react as immediately to gas as others do." UK sweatshirt nodded with understanding.

"How many times was Ezra hit with them things the cops shot at him?" the hog farmer asked with a frown.

Clyde walked to the table where his materials were spread out and bent to whisper something into Lewis' ear. Clyde straightened up and admitted in a bland, muffled voice, "One hundred and twenty-four."

The hog farmer gave a low whistle and shook his head.

"Why didn't the officers listen to the nurse or Mrs. Blair?" the young girl in black demanded.

"Chief Summers might be able to answer that best," Clyde said as he reviewed the audience.

"Captain Shakelford can answer that, Clyde," Art Summers nervously responded.

Lewis got up, rounded the table, and stood in front of the jurors. "I'm not the person who normally handles such police operations. But in my training with barricaded subjects, which Mr. Blair would have been under the circumstances, police don't normally bring in non-police people. Sometimes that creates more problems than it solves. Non-police personnel won't know our tactics or the equipment we use." Lewis paused as he grasped for words to clarify what he just said.

"But, the women only wanted to give you information that you could have used to help the situation," leather girl blurted.

"I'm sorry; maybe we should have asked questions. But at the time we did the best we could. We believed we would be able to bring Mr. Blair out and get him the help he needed." After that admission, Lewis walked around the table and sat down.

"Any other questions?" Clyde asked. None of the jurors raised their hands or spoke up.

"Now it's time for you good people to enter the jury room and deliberate." The jurors were escorted out of the courtroom in a single file.

Prosecutors frequently convene grand juries and coroner's inquests. These hearings help prosecutors make the difficult decision about prosecuting a case. It allows the prosecutor to expose evidence for public consumption. Such hearings can take public heat and pressure off a prosecutor, although most of the time hearings are not made public. When they are, it's a good indication that the prosecutor wants the public to come over to his side, either for building his case for prosecution or supporting his decision not to prosecute. The prosecutor in these hearings acts like the conductor of a symphony. The prosecutor plans what the jury will hear and what evidence will be presented. Some refer to the process as a "kangaroo court." That's probably a poor indictment of the process. It can be helpful for a prosecutor to ensure his office doesn't forge ahead with a case that has little merit.

Taylor had no indication how much time deliberations would take so he settled in for the long haul. Just as he was getting comfortable, a small man wearing an off-the-rack grey suit approached.

"Mr. Sterling?" the man asked extending his hand. "I'm Ben Franks from the KLC. We spoke on the phone. Let's go get a cup of coffee. I've got a member of my staff in the courtroom to alert us should the jury come back."

The men sat down on a bench outside a small snack shop in the lobby of the courthouse. An organization assisting the blind ran the shop, as is common in courthouses throughout the country.

"What did you think, Taylor?"

"Pretty usual approach by a prosecutor who doesn't want to charge the cops. And, it seems his approach was very effective. I was watching the jurors. Most seemed on board with a decision not to charge the officers."

"What do you think he left out?"

Taylor was acutely aware of what had not been presented to the jurors. "Ben, some major issues were omitted. First was the entire lack of negotiation, as the young juror pointed out in her question to the prosecutor. With incidents like this, you contain the subject, negotiate, and wait it out. It was almost like they didn't want to pay the cops overtime." Ben nodded.

"The other big thing was the use of force. SWAT tools, particularly wooden dowels, are called 'less than lethal,' but they still can be fatal. I'd have to do research on these particular projectiles, but I think that they way the SWAT team used them in this case cranked it up to being deadly force. It looked like none of the cops were more than ten feet from Mr. Blair and they all acknowledge he wasn't a threat to them. On top of that, the officers said they weren't fearful and were only trying to get the subject out from under the staircase. It's a shame no one really took charge of what was going on. I've got some real concerns about the chief, too."

Taylor's dialogue was cut short when a young man interrupted them.

"Boss, the jury's back."

Ben and Taylor glanced at their watches. Just over thirty minutes.

"That's pretty quick, huh, Taylor?" Taylor nodded.

Inside the courtroom the audience was whispering. After the judge was seated, the bailiff ushered in the jury. Taylor noted the six jurors appeared to avoid eye contact with anyone sitting in the courtroom.

"Who have you selected to be the jury spokesperson?" the judge asked.

Surprisingly, the elderly retired secretary from the Land Conservatory rose. "I've been asked to represent my fellow jurors, Your Honor."

"And it was a unanimous decision?"

"Yes. We had very little conflict reaching our decision based on the definition and paperwork the Commonwealth's attorney gave us." The woman paused and looked at the prosecutor, then back at the judge. "We find the death of Mr. Blair was a homicide, but not of criminal intent."

The cops were shaking their fellow officers' hands and jabbing each other on the arms. Sadie Blair allowed her head to slump to her chest as she dabbed her eyes with a hanky.

The jury spokesperson continued. "But, we were all very concerned about the conduct of the police and feel the outcome would have been different if they had exercised more restraint. None of us feel the officers meant Mr. Blair harm, and certainly didn't anticipate their actions would result in his death. It's tragic. Someone needs to look closely at that police department."

With that statement, she turned to her fellow jurors who all were nodding their agreement. As if on cue, every juror fixed a stare at Chief Art Summers.

* * *

Taylor drove to the Spirit Lake Police Department office. It was nestled between City Hall and the three-bay fire station. Just beyond the chain link fence securing the cop shop parking lot, but still in clear view, was the large black van with white letters on the side—S.W.A.T.

Forty officers! Taylor thought to himself.

Taylor walked through the front glass doors into the lobby of the station. He noticed a trophy case on the left side of the lobby. Several small trophies and awards won at police shooting competitions filled the shelves. Three photographs indicated the town had three successive chiefs, including Art Summers. From the caption under his photo, it appeared Chief Summers had been in charge for the past five years. Numerous photographs showing SWAT officers in training also hung on the wall. One of the photographs featured a younger Art Summers with sergeant stripes on his BDU shirt. Several trophies had his name inscribed on the base.

"Halp you?" A voice broke Taylor's concentration. The voice belonged to a woman in her forties. Her hair was drawn back in a tight bun and she was wearing an ill-fitting dress, most likely from the racks of the local Wal-Mart.

"Taylor Sterling here for a meeting with Chief Summers."

"You the LA guy the pool brought in, huh?"

"Yes, and you are?"

"Carol Upton, Chief Summers' secretary."

"You been here as long as the chief, Ms. Upton?"

"It's Mrs. Upton, and yes, I have. Been secretary to all the Spirit Lake chiefs, I'm proud to say." The secretary noticeably lifted her upper torso with pride. "Know pretty much everything that's ever happened with the police here."

"Had this SWAT unit in the department the whole time, Mrs. Upton?"

She studied Taylor for a minute and then turned abruptly and said, "I'll tell the chief you're here." Mrs. Upton disappeared behind a heavy door.

A side door opened a few seconds later and Mrs. Upton announced, "Chief Summers will see you now, Mr. Sterling."

Taylor squeezed by her Wal-Mart sized frame and mouthed, "Thank you."

Chief Summers had already rounded his desk and moved to shake Taylor's hand. He circled his hand around Taylor's back and gave him a friendly but serious pat.

Taylor looked around the small office and found it messy, immediately noticing the carpet hadn't been swept or vacuumed in some time. Dust balls slowly circled as air from the oscillating fan nudged them along. More shooting trophies lined the chief's bookshelves.

One photograph caught Taylor's attention. Eight officers in black BDUs stared back at him, all carrying automatic weapons held at port arms. The officers were positioned in front of what appeared to be an old Army armored personnel carrier. Chief Summers was sitting on top of the hulk of metal holding some sort of rocket launcher.

"You got a tank, boss?" Taylor asked with surprise.

Art Summers was a short, squat man carrying probably forty pounds more than he should have. He had a ruddy complexion and thin red strands of hair were fighting for prominence on the top of his head. Four stars lined the collar of his uniform shirt and four rows of campaign ribbons filled the space just below his badge on the left side of his shirt. Taylor decided not to venture into asking what campaigns they might represent. It surprised Taylor to see the chief was carrying what appeared to be a six inch .44 caliber wheel gun in a shoulder holster. Taylor identified the cannon as a 629 stainless stain Smith and Wesson. Dirty Harry would have been mighty proud.

"Yep, one of the many things I got from the military. Hell, they were just begging us to take that carrier off their hands."

"Ever use it, boss?"

"Officially?" A smile spread across the chief's face. "Nope, not officially, not yet."

"Unofficially, boss?"

He started to chuckle and momentarily turned away from Taylor. "Couple of my guys on the graveyard shift went out to the Public Works yard where we keep it. Hell, they got into it and drove it around like they was something special. Looked like Governor Dukakis in that ad when he was running for president." He broke into a full laugh. "Then the dummies puts it out on YouTube. How stupid can you be?"

"Did you create the SWAT unit, boss?"

"Not really. We had an early version of one back when I was a sergeant. One of the first things I did when they appointed me chief was to formalize the team and add a bunch of equipment, like the SWAT van outside. Old chief thought it would cost too much money to field a full team so he kept us on a tight leash."

"Why did you think a SWAT squad was necessary?"

"Hell, you got to be ready for the unexpected. Got them type of units all over the country. Bad guys got more firepower than the cops do. I wanted to even the odds." Summers slumped back in his chair and smiled. "You had one of them units in LA, didn't you? Probably had more than one team, huh?"

"We did. But we could show the need. We ate the cost of equipment and the extra training. How about your unit?"

"Got most of my equipment donated. Had to buy the uniforms, but got a lot of the weapons from the military. That old van used to be an electric company truck they gave us. Current chemical agents cost a little, but I've got a slush fund from seizures my guys make from time to time," Summers continued. He straightened up and leaned forward toward Taylor. "KLC nervous, huh?"

"Got a right to be, wouldn't you say?"

"Guess so. But we were cleared on both the SWAT operations. Just had a little bad luck. That happens even with the big boys. Don't it, Taylor?"

"Now and then. But your men had two incidents and two fatals in less than a year. That's not so common, boss." Taylor knew most SWAT units own stellar records of resolving standoffs without firing a shot. In fact, most SWAT units prided themselves on that record. A shooting often meant the unit did something wrong.

Taylor asked Chief Summers if it would be okay to interview some of his cops, specifically Sergeant Bruce Adams and Captain Lewis Shakelford.

Summers squinted at each name, but said he would arrange it. Taylor could almost read what Summers was saying to himself, *What the fuck he want with Shakelford?*

* * *

Taylor wasn't certain when his meeting with Adams and Shakelford would happen. It was a little after noon and his stomach was starting to growl—a good sign it needed to be serviced. As Taylor left the Spirit Lake PD, he glanced right and left to see if any restaurants had signs hanging over the sidewalks in this little town in the middle of nowhere. About a block down he saw several people going in and out of a nondescript building carrying what appeared to be take-out food sacks. He wandered down the street to check it out.

The front of the restaurant was faced with wooden siding that needed coats of stain or paint to cover years of having the elements beat down on it. The sign painted on the front window stated, "Murray's Café—Best Dawgs in Eastern Kentucky." Inside, the ambience complimented the exterior. The walls were covered with mismatched cheap paneling in complicated patterns. Most were plastered with photographs and local memorabilia…dated photographs of beauty queens riding on springtime parade floats, basketball and football players, and cheerleaders. Young men who looked hardly old enough to vote were outfitted with military gear from WWII, and the Korean and Vietnam Conflicts. One large sign appeared to be a campaign poster announcing that S. McFadden was running for Sheriff of Laurel County in 1936. It pictured an unshaven huge man wearing a floppy hat and holding a sawed-off shotgun and proclaimed, "I'm an honest man. Vote for me, even if I am a Democrat." Looking down the Wall of Fame, Taylor spotted the same photograph he'd seen in Chief Summers' office, showing the chief and his officers around their tank, looking like proud fathers announcing the birth of a bouncing baby boy.

"Hey, kin ah halp ya?" a soft voice asked.

Taylor glanced at the business end of the cafe and saw a young girl behind the counter looking at him questionably. She pointed to the menu board above her on the wall.

"Oh sure, what do most folks get here?" he asked.

The girl smiled at Taylor, "You ain't from around here, right? Well, the chili is a family recipe, goes back fifty years. My daddy told me that in the old days this was a pool hall…men only… but we still had the good chili. Women would send in a man to pick up carryout orders. I guess we served women, but jist weren't allowed to come inside. They's a window right behind me, still here, where they passed through carryout dawgs. So now, folks come from all over to eat here. When there's a reunion, out of town folks come here first for the chili and then to see people they know.

"So what to eat? Mainly dawgs or chili, or chili dawgs. A chili dawg comes with no dawg, just chili. But a dawg with chili is just what it sounds like. You can get hot Velveeta cheese or onions if you want for no extra charge. We'll put it on for you. Chips is extra. You visiting kinfolk or jist passing through?"

"Nope, just doing a little work and then I'll be on my way."

"What kind of work? Don't look like no laborer. You with the government?"

"Nope, just looking at your police department."

"Dem shootings, huh? Sad. Old Ezra used to come in here all the time. He'd sit back there at the regulars' table."

"Cops come in here?"

"Of course. They want the best dawgs hereabouts. Most really like to eat. They mix with the customers, too. Even the chief comes in here quite a bit. He and the mayor sit back at the regulars' table. Nice, polite man, that chief."

Taylor realized he hadn't checked out the customers eating in the restaurant. It surprised him because that was usually the first thing he did when entering someplace new. Surveying the scene was a throwback to his days on the force. You always wanted to know who was filling a place and where you might find cover if shooting broke out. Not that this had ever happened in Taylor's twenty years with the LAPD, but he figured he was just lucky. A few guys he'd known had unknowingly walked in on robberies in progress.

Taylor noticed that folks were comin' and goin' and would call 'Hey' to each other. He guessed most of the town was on a first name basis.

Murray's interior was typical of most restaurants in small towns. A line of booths along one wall, a parade of tables running down the length of the place, and a large table in the back where regulars could gather and rule the place. This was the kind of place where folks knew each other's business. Taylor guessed this was also the kind of place where folks were willing to talk about that business if they felt something wasn't right…even to a guy who "ain't from around these parts."

"Ezra was a little strange, but he didn't bother nobody. He'd order two plain dawgs and a bowl of chili. I'd watch him dip the dawgs into the chili before each bite. Almost like some ritual thing. I knew the Philpots too, but not the one that got kilt. Some of their kinfolk. Kept to themselves, them Philpots. Kind of clannish, if you ask me. Figure what you want, mister?"

Taylor got two dawgs with chili and cheese and watched the young girl pump a large stainless steel container that laid a line of cheese down the center of each bun. He elected not to go with the onions. The chili was smooth with meat that was cooked to mush, but had a sweet tang to it. Taylor noticed the chili didn't have beans as an ingredient. The dogs were good, but he wasn't sure he would classify them as the best in Eastern Kentucky. However, he had never been to Eastern Kentucky before so he figured he wasn't much of a connoisseur of vittles in the Bluegrass State.

His cell phone interrupted his lunch. It was Sergeant Adams. When he heard Taylor was having lunch at Murray's, Adams said he would meet him there.

* * *

"Guess you're lookin' fer that out of town stranger over there, Sergeant Adams," the young counter girl said as the uniformed officer came through the front door. She pointed at Taylor with a garishly painted fingernail. "Want me to bring you a Coke?"

"That would be nice of you, Jean."

Bruce Adams was exactly what you'd expect a SWAT guy to look like. He was probably six feet and about 220, but carried his weight well. His uniform shirt strained to cover his large, well developed biceps. Taylor assumed his shirt had met a tailor since it clung to his flat stomach like white on rice. It was obvious this guy was a power lifter, but not to the extreme of adding excessive bulk. Of course he had the obligatory buzz hair cut.

"You Taylor Sterling?" the young man asked as he pulled out the opposite chair and settled his bulk comfortably. "Boss said you wanted to talk with me."

"I am and I do," Taylor confirmed as he watched Jean deliver a Coke and set it in front of the sergeant. She lingered next to him until he turned his head and smiled. She was satisfied, so she went back to her place behind the counter.

"Understand you're the guy in charge of Spirit Lake SWAT."

"Actually, we're a special ops unit. SWAT technically means you need to do certain things that we can't, but the chief likes to call us SWAT," Adams admitted with a crooked smile.

"Chief Summers seems to like his toys...big ones!"

"Apparently you saw the boss's tank."

"Picture of it. Ever use it in an operation, sergeant?"

He laughed. "Shit, I don't even know how to drive the damn beast. Chief has to drive it when the PD has a public relations event. Kids love to crawl all over it."

Taylor pushed to the next subject. "He really have a rocket launcher?"

"Yeah, but never got any rockets for it," Adams said as he continued to laugh. "But Chief Summers means well. He's a good guy and has his heart in the right place. He's proud of our little police department and works hard to keep it going during these tough budget times."

It was obvious Bruce Adams liked and respected his chief. Taylor realized those traits were becoming a rare commodity in most towns these days. To the majority of cops their chief was someone aloof, unaware of their needs, and spent more time politicking than policing. Maybe Taylor's early opinion of Summers was being tempered by this dedicated cop sitting with him in a cracker dive in Eastern Kentucky.

"Taylor, I know all the guidelines and standards the big SWAT guys advocate. I'm a member of the Kentucky Tactical Officers Association. I go to the annual meetings. I've been to, let's see, three SWAT schools. I do what I can here in Spirit Lake. We struggle with our budget and the allotment the boss gives us. I know seven guys and I aren't enough for a full SWAT operation, but it's good enough for Spirit Lake. My guys are dedicated and would give me 110 percent if I asked them. They're good people." Adams stopped and fixed his stare on Taylor, waiting to catch his reaction.

"You've had two operations that ended up with fatals in the last year or so," Taylor said slowly and quietly. "That's unusual for any unit like yours, especially in a small town like Spirit Lake. Let's go back to the station and you can walk me through what you've done with your guys. Okay?"

Returning to the police station, Bruce suggested they start with the SWAT van parked in the lot. He pulled out a ring of keys and searched until he found the right one, then opened the rear doors of the van.

"Chief got someone to donate this old van. Me and the guys did all the inside work. Boss got another business to paint the thing for nothing."

Inside, the van looked like most vans used by special operations units. Shelves and containers lined one side and the other side featured a long bench where officers could sit and wait for the shout to jump out and engage the unknown.

"In this locked box we have our four MP5s and ammo magazines. This box contains our shotguns. We have two with yellow painted stocks signifying they're used with bean bags." Bruce opened a hinged door and pointed to the various canisters containing different chemical agents.

"We make sure the oldest is at the front."

Bruce pulled out a small notebook next to the array of chemical agent canisters, opened it to the last page and pointed to the last line. "We check the canisters once a month and rotate out any gas that's beyond its expiration date."

"Are you aware of the ATF requirements regarding storage of the distraction devices you got in there, sergeant?"

Adams' quizzical stare told Taylor he wasn't.

"ATF classifies them as 'explosive devices' and mandates they be kept in a locked, metal insulated container. Been the requirement for several years now."

"No cain't say I knew that. Don't remember anyone bringing it up at our association meetings. But, you know, I'll check into it after we're done. Thanks for bringin' it to my attention, Taylor."

Inside the station, Bruce took Taylor into a room with a sign warning KEEP OUT—SWAT CERT ONLY. Taylor noticed the room was much cleaner than Chief Summers' office was. The lone small conference table had only two chairs pulled up to it. There was a four-drawer metal file cabinet in one corner. On one wall was a white board that had been wiped clean. On another wall two framed motivational posters featuring American eagles hung proudly. Taylor knew eagles were symbols favored by special ops teams indicating strength and solidarity. He noted there were no weapons or evidence files scattered in the office as Taylor had discovered during several agency audits he had recently conducted.

"I use this as my office, that's why there are only two chairs. Not much room for anything else. It keeps the guys on their feet during ops planning discussions," Bruce explained as he opened the top drawer of the cabinet and pulled out a file. "This here is our training file."

Taylor quickly leafed through the pages of reports. Each was dated and gave the number of training hours spent, usually four. A few lines indicated what the training had covered and who was present. There wasn't much consistency to the dates and sometimes a couple months passed between training sessions. Sometimes there were magazine articles from various police periodicals. There were no lesson plans included.

"You probably see that our training is kind of erratic," Bruce admitted. "We're a part time unit, remember. We can't take any more time away from regular shifts to do the training we should."

Taylor didn't respond. There was no need to chastise the man for what the unit commander knew was a problem.

"Tell me about the Ezra thing," Taylor began as he and Bruce sat down at the table.

"I saw you at the coroner's inquest so you heard and saw it all. Not much else to say. Feel sorry for the old guy."

"Your men used a lot of less lethal rounds in a pretty small space."

"I know what you're getting at, Taylor. It was so crowded in that damn cellar that I had to supervise the operation from the top of the stairs. Between gas billowing in the room and the cluster fuck going on, I know most of the rounds fired from the Sage were under the spec range of the tool. Specs said they were potentially lethal, and in the end they were. Every one of them rounds was fired less than ten feet from Ezra. We were wrong. You and I know it."

"At the inquest, no one mentioned any kind of negotiation had taken place," Taylor flatly stated.

Bruce leaned back and appeared to be pondering how to answer the pointed question.

"That's true. Probably should have started negotiations before we went down there. But Chief Summers is our hostage negotiator, even taught negotiating techniques at some school. He was on the scene at the field command post. He knew everything we were going to do. I guess I just figured if he had wanted to negotiate, he would have told us early on. He didn't, so I didn't ask."

Police negotiate with people in crisis in a wide range of incidents. Hollywood has sensationalized this police task in films like "Dog Day Afternoon" with Al Pacino and "The Negotiator" with Samuel L. Jackson. Most police negotiation training is multi-session and becomes more advanced with each session. Formalized negotiation training started in the late 1960s and since has become more consistent and exact.

Most hostage or barricaded subject incidents end successfully after negotiations between the police and the holed-up subject take place. It's never an exact process. Sometimes negotiations might take a couple hours, other times the process could last several days. It's a difficult call for a cop on the scene of a hostage or barricaded situation to determine when "enough is enough." There is no science or formula that can be used adequately or effectively.

"Tell me about the Philpot incident."

"What about it?"

"Talk to me about the officer who fired the shots."

"He thought the woman attacked me and fired to stop her assault," Bruce firmly stated.

"Could it have been an accidental or unintentional shooting?"

"Timmy shot to protect me. End and final!"

Bruce leaned back and folded his arms over his chest; a chest that Taylor saw was pumped out more than it had been a minute before. Taylor knew this wasn't the time to challenge the obvious defensive position Bruce Adams had assumed. Taylor would have to find another avenue to pursue this aspect of the Philpot incident.

* * *

Captain Lewis Shakelford was waiting for Taylor in his office next to Chief Summers' domain. Shakelford's office was orderly and clean. Two certificates hung square on his wall. One was earned from the Southern Police Institute and the other from the FBI National Academy. A photograph on his desk showed an attractive woman and two nice looking teenage kids.

"Taylor, good to see you. Hope you can help us out. Troubling times for our little department."

"I imagine so, Captain Shakelford."

The captain chuckled and said, "That's a mouthful. I didn't have any say in my name. I simply go by 'Shak' most of the time. Where do you want to start, Taylor?"

Shak was about forty, Taylor figured. He was trim and wore his uniform well. He, contrary to the armament Chief Summers carried, simply wore a standard issue equipment belt with what appeared to be a 40 or 9 Glock attached. He didn't display campaign ribbons on his shirt.

"Been here long, Shak?"

"Last fifteen years. Only police time for me."

"What's a captain do here in the Spirit Lake PD?"

"Pretty much try to keep the chief out of trouble."

"How you doing on that front?"

"Not so well lately. I'm kind of like the good little fella sitting on the boss' shoulder whispering in his ear why he should or shouldn't do something."

"He listen to that little fella?"

"Lately, the chief's been listening to that fella with the horns sitting tall on his other shoulder. The one that's red and got a trident, pitchfork, and dangling tail. You know, the fella who's up to no good." Shak chuckled at his analogy.

"Been there, done that myself, Shak."

"Well, which role did you play, Taylor?" Both men laughed.

"Were you out there at the Philpot raid?"

"No, I was involved in the Task Force planning operation, though."

"There were plans?" Taylor asked facilely.

"Actually there were a lot of plans. Good ones. Biggest problem was the powers that be seemed to pick the wrong ones, if you ask me. I pushed to affect the raids either where the suspects worked or at the upcoming shooting competition they were scheduled to attend." Shak put both hands in front of him like a school crossing guard might do. "Definitely got out-voted on that one."

"Who pushed for the early morning raids at the homes?"

He pointed to his left shoulder, "The little fella in red, Taylor."

"Why'd you think they shouldn't hit the houses?"

"Kids. Wives. Dogs. Shit, everything they didn't need to get in the way."

"How about the Ezra incident?"

Shak got up, walked around his desk and asked, "How about some coffee?" Taylor figured Shak wanted a timeout before bad-mouthing his boss, so he agreed to have a cup.

"Ezra Blair incident was simply a cluster fuck, excuse my language," Shak said as they returned to his office. "We got a good policy on how to handle barricaded subjects. We get these incidents a couple of times a year. Usually surround the house, make sure no one is in harm's way, and wait 'em out. We're supposed to talk...then talk some more...and then continue talking. In the past the subjects have all come out eventually and all was okay."

"What was different about Ezra? Were you out there?"

"Yep, I was. At the command post with the chief. I was setting up the perimeter to make sure nobody got in at the wrong time."

"Why didn't the chief use any negotiation efforts? I hear he's a certified hostage negotiator and even trained others. You avoided that issue at the coroner's inquest, Shak."

"I wasn't expecting to be called to give testimony at the inquest. The chief suddenly up and threw it at me. I was doing some pretty fancy tap dancing up there, if you hadn't noticed," Shak smiled. "I did ask the boss to try some talking out there at Erza's. He turned to me and said it wouldn't work. I guess he figured Ezra wasn't talking to the SWAT guys in his basement, so why expend the effort?"

Taylor didn't find Ezra's lack of response unusual. Five SWAT guys in gas masks who were dumping canisters of gas into his basement, and crowding around him with heavy armament wasn't going to lead to a Chatty Cathy moment. A bi-polar personality like Ezra owned wasn't going to feel reassured hearing the words, 'We're here to help you.'"

"What's with the chief's fixation on heavy guns, Shak?"

Shak began laughing, "Oh, you noticed that?"

"Well, duh!"

"Art always wanted to be in the military, ever since his folks sent him away to military school. Unfortunately, he was born at the wrong time. By the time he was eighteen, there wasn't a war to fight. I guess being a cop was the next best thing. So the chief is kind of playing war now. Nobody seems to want to pop his bubble. It's really not harmful, you know."

Taylor slowly shook his head. "Actually it can be harmful, and is. You've got this tank that no one uses, officially that is. You've got a SWAT unit without need or the necessary support to make it effective. You've got guns that most of your people aren't trained to use. You got a nice little armed city here, but without any war! Some might say the chief starts his own wars!"

"But, Art's a good man. He lives for the Spirit Lake department and our troops. He loves our town and I think most folks here know that and like him in return."

Changing subjects, Taylor asked, "What about this kid, Timmy?"

"Timmy Gould? Nice young fella. The Philpot incident really tore him up...what happened to that woman. Hurt even more that she was shot right in front of her daughter and those other young girls. The guy was never the same after that. All his life he wanted to be a cop and then that happened."

"What's he doing now?"

"Fixing tires down at the Firestone store. Nice young fella, Timmy."

"Can you call him and convince him to talk with me?"

"I'll give it a try. Say tomorrow morning? I'll text you the okay on your cell phone, Taylor."

* * *

Taylor asked the hotel desk clerk if he had a recommendation for a dinner place.

"Not much here in Spirit Lake. You can go down the road about thirty miles to Corbin and eat at the original Colonel Sanders' place. You do know Kentucky Fried Chicken started right there?"

"Nope, can't really say I did." The thought of commercially fried chicken didn't rev Taylor's appetite. "Anywhere else?"

"We got a damn good BBQ shack outskirts of town." Taylor shook his head. "How 'bout Lone Star, Cracker Barrel, and a bunch of fast food places?" Taylor shook his head again.

"Say, what kind of food you exactly lookin' fer?"

Taylor decided asking for Thai or another ethic food was probably out of the question. "I always like someplace interesting with different kinds of food."

The desk clerk scratched his head and then his eyes widened. "Say, you might get a kick out of the Boone Tavern in Berea. About a half hour north of here. It's in the hotel in the center of town run by Berea College. Ever heard of it?" Taylor shook his head. "Most students attend the college for free, but they got to work. Some work in the hotel where the tavern is on the ground floor. It's an arts and crafts school. Got good Kentucky food. Kinda served with flair like them big city restaurants. 'Course it's not the caliber of the Brown Hotel up in Louisville."

Taylor headed north and approached the center of Berea, running almost directly into the Boone Tavern Hotel. Most of the town appeared closed, but then it was nearly seven o'clock. The dining room of the tavern was typical of older Southern hotels. It was a large room with highly polished wooden chairs marching around square tables topped with white linen. The crowd filling the tavern was sparse. But then, it was the middle of the week and smack between the numerous festivals Berea College hosted during the summer months.

Before grabbing a table, Taylor paused to read descriptions of the college lining the wall of the hotel foyer. He was intrigued to find that Berea College was founded in 1855 and was the only Southern college that was integrated and coeducational for the next forty years.

A young waiter guided Taylor to an open table. The menu was unexpectedly large and diverse. Taylor settled on a smoked trout salad to start. He asked if the tavern featured local microbrews and was pleased when served a draw of Kentucky Bourbon Barrel Ale out of Lexington.

The young man serving Taylor offered a basket of spoon bread and convinced him he would be remiss and disappointed if he didn't take the obligatory helping. The server was right. The cornmeal was ground so fine that the bread had a pudding-like consistency.

Taylor's entrée, pan-seared scallops, were the large ocean variety and presented perfectly seared with slight browning on the edges and firm, yet tender inside. The scallops were nestled into a serious helping of cheese grits and topped with a tomato/orange salsa.

Years before, Taylor had become a grits fan before they were made famous by Joe Pesci in *My Cousin Vinny.* Taylor always searched menus for stone ground grits topped with generous sprinklings of sharp cheddar cheese. Of course, he usually added a good sampling of Southwestern green chilies to the pot when he made grits at home.

The Boone Tavern dessert cart was formidable and the heavy chocolate creams had appeal, but following his custom, Taylor was drawn to the fresh mixed berry cobbler topped with vanilla bean ice cream.

* * *

Taylor received a message from Captain Shakelford that Timmy Gould would be available to meet at the Firestone Store located near the on-ramp to I-75 outside Spirit Lake.

"You must be Mr. Sterling," a tall lanky young man said as he stuck out his hand. "Captain Shakelford said I should talk with you and it'd be okay to be frank."

Timmy looked like he was still in high school. His complexion was pale, the only color being a band of freckles cascading across his nose. His hair was shaved close, but a noticeable cowlick shot out on the top of his head. His carriage was stooped and he allowed his arms to hang at his sides without tension.

"Boss says we can use his office," Timmy suggested as the two left the garage bay with its continuous clanking of pneumatic wrenches working lug nuts off wheels of cars and pick-ups.

"You from the insurance people, huh?"

"Yeah. Brought me in to look at a couple of your Spirit Lake shootings, Timmy."

"Figured that. I really loved that job. All I ever wanted to be was a cop. Chief Summers was real good to me. He's a fine man and I feel I let him down," Timmy admitted as he slumped into the chair in front of the manager's desk.

"How's that, Timmy?" Taylor asked. He figured Timmy wanted to tell his side of the story and was relieved he was getting another chance to do that.

"Mrs. Philpot. God, I've relived that moment almost every day since the shooting. I kin still see the side of her head open up like a smashed gourd and gush all over those little girls. I remember the Hello Kitty sleeping bag all bunched up and wet with blood."

Timmy began to shake and grabbed the sides of the chair. He took several deep breaths, then straightened up and looked directly at Taylor.

"Mr. Sterling, I tried to do my best. But Sergeant Adams gave me this automatic weapon I had never held before, let alone fired. Least don't remember ever firing the darn thing. I didn't want to let him down so I didn't tell him I didn't know how to use it. I tried to be careful. But the woman suddenly rushed down the hallway screaming louder than I've ever heard anyone scream before. The little girls were all screeching too and my ears were buffeted by the blast of the flash-bang. The whole scene startled me, absolutely. Then the damn gun went off. It wasn't supposed to. It just went off and snuffed out that woman's life. Somehow my finger slipped into the guard and onto the trigger. Got no recall of that…none at all." Timmy stopped and slumped in the chair, dropping his head and eyes down.

Taylor knew Timmy had been suppressing his genuine version of the event for over a year. The terror of it must have been eating away at his insides. Timmy had parroted what the other guys told him to say. He knew the truth and wanted to get it out to ease his conscience. Taylor was simply the vehicle that allowed him to start the healing process.

* * *

Ben Franks, Taylor's contact in the Kentucky League of Cities, answered at the other end of Taylor's cell phone.

"I'm going to set up a meeting with Chief Summers for tomorrow, Ben. Can you come down?"

"What you got planned?"

"Well, I've pretty much got the info I'm going to need for my report to the insurance pool. I wanted to give the chief an opportunity to respond to my observations."

"Can you make it around lunchtime? I'll finish what I'm doing here in the morning and make it down there in the very early afternoon. Will that work for you?"

It would be fine for Taylor as it allowed him the morning to start a preliminary draft of his report. Using the KSP investigative report detailing the Philpot raid, the coroner's inquest on Ezra Blair's death, and Taylor's on-site interviews and observations, it would be easy to draft out the liability and agency issues.

There was really no way Spirit Lake could reasonably sidestep liability issues. It would definitely cost the city a chunk of money. But, more importantly, it would put to rest some of the negative community capital that was lost by these two unfortunate police operations. Taylor wasn't sure how Art Summers would react to his analysis.

Chief Summers suggested they meet at Murray's and said he would be honored to buy lunch for Taylor and Ben. "Now I'm not trying to bribe you or compromise your report, you understand," the chief joked laughing into the phone.

"Fer a stranger in town you're gettin' to be a mighty common face here at Murray's," Jean remarked to Taylor as the three men walked into the restaurant.

"Hey, Chief, this fella a friend of yours?"

"Don't rightfully know, Jean." Chief Summers looked at Taylor and added, "Maybe. We'll see, huh, Taylor? I guess you can almost sit at the regulars' table now, Taylor?"

"I think it best we find a table out of the mainstream travel route, boss," Taylor answered.

They settled in a far booth with their loaded baskets of dawgs and spent the first several minutes barking them down and washing the residue with sodas.

"Before you start, Taylor, let me say a few things," Art Summers started as he jockeyed for the lead. "I've been talking to my people who you interviewed. Got some interesting feedback I hadn't heard before. Made me stop and ponder a bit."

Art sunk his body into the worn booth, cracking the vinyl with explosive reports. He pulled his holster around so it wasn't in contact with the booth back. Taylor realized Summers wasn't wearing the shoulder holster carrying the Dirty Harry cannon.

"Art, your people seem to think a lot of you. They almost love you, which is unusual in any police department. You must be doing something right," Taylor remarked.

"I do appreciate them. I do love this little community. I guess I've let both down lately," Art said with a shrug.

"When I was sitting in the coroner's inquest and saw that demonstration, the problems with what we did jumped out at me. I didn't realize how crowded that small basement was when my guys staged the take-down. Hell, my men were put in a position that was untenable. I realized I had done that to them. I've been kicking myself in the ass for not pulling back and trying to negotiate. Damn, I should have taken charge. I let my men down and I let ol' Ezra down."

Taylor was about to say something when Art held up his hands and wagged a finger at him.

"Let me finish, Taylor. You know, Lew, ah Captain Shakelford, was telling me the right things to do for both these incidents. He works hard to cover my ass. I need to listen to his wise advice. I get impatient sometimes, I know it."

"Timmy told me yesterday that his shots fired in the Philpot house were unintentional," Taylor said.

Art looked at both men and replied, "I pretty much expected that's what happened. I just didn't press my men about it. They would have been honest with me if I had. I was just trying to protect them. It was a tough spot we were in. See, Lew was telling me to hold off and run the raid away from the assholes' houses. The Philpot event was the first really big operation Spirit Lake was involved in. We were the lead for once. I was in charge of a really big operation." He slumped back in his chair as he remembered that day. "I guess I let Timmy down. All he ever wanted to be was a cop."

"Chief, can I give you a little advice as one good cop to another?" Taylor asked. Art nodded. "You got a great department here. Got good people. Got lots of community capital because the people seem to love you. It's time to retrench and give them what they want and need—solid community policing. Get rid of the military shit. Tell Adams he's doing a good job and you need his expertise to develop a team to perform warrant services, but not SWAT. Enter into intergovernmental agreements with KSP and Lexington to handle any incidents that really call for a full-blown SWAT operation. Paint that bread delivery van from a SWAT unit and make it a Spirit Lake PD Mobile Command Post."

Art Summers sat quietly for some time. He took a deliberate sip from his Coke and studied Taylor and Ben. "You know anybody who might want to buy a tank?"

All three laughed.

"Ben, I think it's time for you and Chief Summers to talk with the mayor. I know you can reach reasonable settlements," Taylor noted rising from the table. "You don't need me at that meeting. Art knows what needs to be done with his agency. I've started my report to the KLC and it'll be ready in about a week."

Taylor knew he wasn't really a necessary part during the actual discussions of settlement terms. That really wasn't his area of expertise anyway. He felt confident that the Spirit Lake Police Department was in good hands. Every now and then Taylor got a gut feeling that things would work out for an agency in trouble. He felt particularly good about this one.

As Taylor drove back to the airport, he smiled knowing he didn't have to resort to using an axe on this case.

* * *

Taylor arranged to meet with Ginger, his new part-time secretary, in the Hotel St. Francis garden dining room. The hotel was kitty-corner to Pasqual's off the Old Town Square. It was much quieter than Pasqual's and there always seemed to be an open table available, even at lunchtime.

Taylor walked through the dark, cozy lobby before being welcomed by bright sunshine filling the garden. The center small fountain tinkled with a slow cascade of water dropping from one basin to the next. Ivy growing on the old mottled stone was beginning to turn brilliant red as it crawled up the outside walls of the hotel. The jungle of ivy was neatly trimmed around the windows and doors to expose their painted accents of bright azure blue.

Taylor had just pulled out the table chair and was about to drop into his seat when

Ginger's booming voice announced her presence.

"Chief T, here I am! Got a room booked upstairs yet?" Ginger teasingly asked as she approached the linen covered table.

Ginger was in typical form...typical for her, yes, but a sight for everyone else.

Today Taylor's Girl Friday was wearing baggy full bib overalls in a light grey hue with navy pinstripes running vertically. A dark blue button down silk blouse peeked from beneath the bibs, sleeves buttoned around the elbow. Her Doc Martin glossy red patent leather boots planted her firmly in place.

Taylor offered Ginger the chair he had just pulled out.

"You forget your conductor's hat and punch, miss?"

Ginger flipped him the finger and unceremoniously plopped herself into the chair.

"You getting ready to fire me, Chief T?"

"Why would you think that?"

"Last time you asked me out for lunch was when you hired me. So, I figured this might be something really important, like giving me the boot."

"No, no, not at all. I just wanted to thank you for your help and see what's been going on in the pursuit of your new life." Taylor smiled as he watched his secretary bring both hands to the sides of her face as if she was shockingly surprised. Taylor saw Ginger was wearing silver rings securing each of her ten fingers. She was making an all-out fashion statement this day.

"Thanks. Same old, same old. Paralegal school's good. Sergeant A thinks I should apply for my PI employee card. Start the path to becoming a real PI like he is. But I'd rather be a consultant like you, Chief T. Shit, you charge a bundle! I could stop being the Zumba Queen and the always intoxicating Allure with money like you get."

"Someday you just might, especially with your many talents, Ginger. Never know."

"I wasn't spying, Chief T. Just happened to see your charges in your report on that mess down in Kentucky. That was tragic with that Philpot woman getting her head blown off right in front of her kid and the other little princesses. Now, she was married to a real shithead. Of course, so was I, once upon a time. I could see that Kentucky stuff happening big as life. Then the same cops really messed up that old man, what was his name again?"

"Ezra, Ezra Blair," Taylor filled in.

"Say, Chief T, how come those cops didn't get prosecuted?"

Taylor let Ginger's question rest while he took a few bites of his Southwestern Cobb salad.

"Well, they were wrong. What they did was really negligent. But that adds up to a lot different sum than criminal conduct does. Those cops were trying to do the right thing, but didn't know how.

"In both of those cases they made tragic mistakes. But mistakes rarely end up being criminally prosecuted against cops for on-duty actions. I guess most prosecutors figure any civil lawsuit will bring the proper amends. And, in most cases that's true.

"Sometimes, however, cops never learn, even when it costs the city or county a pile of money. I think the cops in Spirit Lake did learn. I felt good about that case."

"Well, you should. Shit, you made more money on that one case than I make in a year. Of course, that's not figuring in my fuck voice job as the charming Allure." On cue,

Ginger reverted to her misty, sultry voice.

This woman could go far, Taylor thought and fantasized what his secretary's future might hold in store.

The Big Chief

Allegation: Corruption, theft, abuse of authority
Client: Morgan City, OH, City Manager
Agency: Morgan City Police Department
Employee: Chief of Police Nathan Turner

Raa Farah was a frail, petite woman in her early thirties. A heavy, dark traditional scarf was always worn over her head to show respect for her Muslim beliefs. Raa and her husband Albert were first generation Americans born to parents who had emigrated from Iran. Extended family members who had left Tehran before the fall of the Shah in 1979 sponsored Raa and Albert's parents. Albert had adopted a more American name from his traditional Muslim name of Albara. The young couple met while attending Vanderbilt University and was allowed to marry as the two families were well acquainted. It wasn't exactly an arranged marriage, but close to it.

When Albert's parents retired, it was natural for them to try to convince Albert to take over the family business, a small neighborhood convenience market. It was a well-kept shop, but unfortunately was located in the crime infested south side of Memphis. Albert did as his parents wanted and over the next ten years

Albert and Raa acquired two more small markets. If the markets had been located on the east coast, most people would refer to them as bodegas but as it was, they were known by the locals as simply "the grocery."

The three markets provided quick and easy access for the neighborhood folks to get necessary sundries, but cigarette and beer sales created the primary income stream. Of course, lottery ticket sales provided a steady, but small income flow, but none of the markets had hit the big payout bonanzas that would have given the couple's bank account a genuine shot in the arm. Raa and Albert knew most of their customers, but didn't socialize with them. None were of the Muslim faith. They socialized exclusively at the local Muslim facility that housed a community center adjacent to the large mosque.

It was a constant struggle for the Farahs to justify the sale of liquor, cigarettes, and other items prohibited by their Muslim faith. This was not a singular conflict, as many Muslim-owned businesses fought the same conflict. National groups such as IMAN, Inner-City Muslim Action Network, explored alternative ways to keep this type business alive and yet remain within the teachings of the Muslim faith. The black Farah customers sought out Colt 45, round tins of Copenhagen snuff, and large bags of pork skins.

Raa, her real name was Raaz, was filling in for a sick employee at the newest market she and Albert had acquired. It was two blocks off Beal Street, the legendary line of rockin' city blocks that touted BB King's joint, the original Sun Records Studio, and a dozen or more barbeque places. Sounds spilled out of the restaurants on the shoulders of smells wafting from brisket, ribs, pork butts, and chickens roasting over burning embers mounded in aged stoked pits.

This particular market closed early at nine o'clock. Albert and Raa didn't want to deal with the hordes of drunken Beal Street patrons that blanketed the area as the night wore on. It was nearly closing time as Raa busied herself stuffing money, checks, and credit card receipts into a worn zippered First Fifth Bank canvas bag. She could hear her daughter Asha reading aloud in the small office behind the counter. Asha, whose given name was A'shadieeyah, was the couple's youngest child at eight years old. It was common to bring one or more of the Farah children to the markets when both mom and dad were working.

Raa allowed her eyes to flick to the front door when she heard the chime ring, signaling the door was being opened. A man filled the doorway, a man that inspired fear. A pervasive sense of alarm pierced Raa's senses as adrenalin rushed through her body.

Jake Jebson was hurting and his body was screaming for the drugs he fed it to sustain him. Crystal meth was his latest craving, but his body was tearing itself apart searching for the ingestion of *any* drug. Jake was small, pushing five feet and weighing just over one hundred pounds. His color was turning mottled grey as his punished body begged for relief. Jake's stringy blonde hair was streaked with oily grease indicative of forgotten showers. His arms protruded from a dirty T-shirt that cried lyrics from an ancient blues festival; his forearms revealed track marks from ulcerated injections.

Jake walked directly to the counter, lifted his T-shirt to his nipples, and pulled out a gun, nearly losing his grip on it as it cleared his waistband. It was a huge gun for his slight frame and it looked like the gun owned him.

"Money," was the only word Jake growled as forcefully as he could muster. A noticeable quiver unbalanced his voice.

The gun looked like a cannon to Raa as the barrel rose shakily and was pointed directly at her breast.

"Ma, I have a question!" Asha called as she came out of the office and approached her mother. She wasn't able to finish her request as her deep brown eyes focused on the wavering gun. She stopped and instinctively cupped her hands over her delicate ears.

What Jake didn't know, and Raa had apparently forgotten, was the customer lingering in the rear of the market.

Sam Wilson's day shift had been uneventful, until the last hour. He caught the emergency call from one of the many cut-rate dives located down the street from the motel turned museum where Martin Luther King had been assassinated in 1968. The call brought him to investigate a vacationing family's motel room that had been criminally invaded and was now empty of anything worthy of a pawnshop's attention.

Each of the three kids visiting from Chicago had two or three Gameboys, video players, or tablets. Both computers owned by the parents were gone. For Sam, his investigation included fielding minutia to locate serial numbers or other distinctive markings to identify the items, if they were ever found. He knew the family would never see their possessions again, but also knew it was important for him to appear concerned and conscientious.

Two hours of overtime were under his belt before Sam could get back to the police station, get his burglary report approved, and stow his equipment belt and gear in his locker. After leaving the crime scene, Sam had thrown a windbreaker over his uniform shirt and stuffed his duty Glock .40 into his off-duty holster before heading to the station and finally home.

Sam stopped at Farah's Market to grab a pack of cigarettes, but was sidetracked by a sudden thirst and wandered back to the refrigerated drinks. While he was debating between Coke and Pepsi, he heard Jake's loud command. Sam silently drew his Glock and did a quick peek around shelves loaded with bags of chips. His hidden position allowed him a tunnel view of the aisle capturing the counter action as he focused on Raa, the gun, and Jake. Asha was small and her body was hidden behind the counter.

Sam wasn't a gun nut, but he knew the guy's gun was a six-inch revolver in a heavy frame. He saw the hammer cocked back and knew the weapon was now in single action mode. It would take only a low poundage trigger pull to discharge and could easily be shot accidentally.

Jake saw Raa's eyes dart to her right. Following, he turned to his left allowing the gun to move with his body. The robber caught a glimpse of the dark figure darting behind the rack of chips and flinched. The flinch caused him to squeeze ever so lightly on the hair trigger.

The discharge of the .357 magnum Ruger was deafening in the small confines of the market. A thick blue flash erupted from the muzzle as bags of potato chips, pork skins, popcorn, and pretzels exploded sending white, yellow, and orange fragments blasting into the air.

Sam dove to the floor and slid into the row. He figured this would give him an advantage since the gun guy would probably not be looking down. Sam inched far enough into the row to target the robber without jeopardizing Raa who was now cowering behind the counter. He rapidly squeezed off five rounds as the Glock barked at each squeeze.

The first round found Jake's right hand and tore through his wrist, sending the Ruger tumbling to the floor. The next three rounds tracked Jake's body, marching from his stomach to his chest. The fifth round entered Jake's neck, severing his spine and the carotid artery. Jake crumpled to the floor in pools of blood. His battered body no longer craved to be fed.

* * *

"You ready to talk, Sam?" the detective asked.

Mel Tucker was the lead investigator on the Memphis Major Crime Squad assigned to the shooting at the Farah Market. Mel was a chain-smoking detective straight from the old school. His suit hung on him like a burlap bag and probably hadn't been pressed in weeks. It was the middle of July and humidity bore down like the innards of a Finnish sauna. Mel's tie hung loose and he had unbuttoned the top button of his shirt for blessed relief. Sweat stains darkened the top edge of the shirt collar.

"Union rep not here yet, Mel."

"Shit, Sam, you got nothing to worry about on this one. You probably gonna get a medal. Yeah, probably the big one—the one for Valor!"

"Don't know, Mel. Union says always to wait. But, I do know I'm righteous on this one."

"Hell, yes. Mrs. Farah says you're her hero because you saved her baby girl. Dirtbag had that damn cannon and the fucker shot at you! Let's get it over with, Sam."

The interview lasted only twelve minutes. Sam answered all the leading questions with the right answers. Of course he did. Wasn't much to remember and Mel led him to the answers that would satisfy any prosecutor and grand jury.

"Guy's name was Jake Jebson. At least from his ID in his pocket. Lookin' at him, he was a junkie."

"That was some gun he had, Mel. Big ass one!"

"Haven't seen one of those in a long time. Was shooting actual

.357 magnum rounds. Would have ripped you apart, Sam. One of them big ass magnums on a .44 frame. Got special handles for it. Figure Jake must have stolen that piece. Gun like that was someone's pet. Real beauty. We'll run it through the ATF database to check."

* * *

"Morgan City Property, Sally here," the full figured woman announced as she answered the page from the front desk.

"Mel Tucker with Memphis PD, Sally. Had us a robbery down here last week and the suspect got hisself kilt by one of our off-duty cops."

"Lord watching over him, your officer, that is. Blessed be," Sally whispered as she clutched the top of her dress stretched to cover her large breasts.

"Yes, ma'am. Yes, the good Lord was sure lookin' out for Sam that night. But the dead robber had a gun the computer says you're supposed to have in evidence."

Mel gave Sally the serial number, description of the Ruger, and the case report number of the investigation completed by the Morgan City Police. Sally's finger deftly ran over the keys of her computer.

"Must be some mistake, Detective Mel, that was your name, wasn't it?"

"Yes, ma'am. What's the problem?"

"We show picking that gun up from a domestic a couple years ago. Shows here that Officers Stockbridge and Worth booked it for safekeeping. We do that when we have a domestic, and then wait to see what the court says to do with it. If the prep is convicted he, usually it's a guy, loses the right to own guns."

"Same down here in Memphis. What happened to the gun, though?"

"We show it was destroyed. We melt guns down when we do that. Got the date of destruction right here in my computer, detective."

"Must be some mistake, Sally. I've got that monster gun right in front of me down here in the Land of Blues. Tell you what, I'll take a few pictures of it. Maybe you can use those to find out what happened. Ain't no big deal for us. We got this case all wrapped up. Just me crossin' all them T's and dotting all them I's. Pisses my wife off how anal I kin be. Thanks for doing your part, Sally. You should let a cop in your shop know what happened. Don't want it to happen again when it might be important. These kinds of things kin bite you in the rear, knows what I mean?"

"I do, that I do. Thank you, Detective Mel."

Sally tried to forget the incident. She sat on it over the weekend but the discrepancy kept nagging at her. She prided herself on keeping her property and evidence room in order. She had attended several training programs on how to run her operation. She had tried to get a modern bar-coded system, but couldn't shake the money out of the city. Instead she had paper files and a couple 5x7 card files that kept her stuff in order.

"Commander, got a minute?" Sally asked as she crowded the doorway to the Support Commander's office.

Neil Crowder served the Morgan City Police Department his entire eighteen years in law enforcement. He had competed for the chief's job four years before, but the city selected Nathan Turner to be top cop. Neil was upset about the choice and never let councilpersons, the mayor, or the city manager forget how he felt he'd been shafted. To Neil, the appointment of Turner was a slap in the face for the entire police department and old Chief

Topson. When Topson suddenly dropped dead from a heart attack, Neil assumed either he or the other commander, Sid Small, would be picked for the vacated position. Instead, the mayor and city manager chose a young, pretty boy Turk from a small police agency in southern Ohio. They made a big deal about Turner having a Ph.D. in Justice Studies. What they never mentioned was the degree was earned from a mail order mill somewhere in the bayous of Louisiana.

"What's up, Sally?"

She ran down her conversation with the Memphis detective and expressed her concern about the gun supposedly being destroyed, but then showing up at a crime scene in Tennessee. Neil took her information and the printouts she carried in a folder.

Annually the Morgan City Police Department held a burn. Guns were smelt down in an old iron works factory on the outskirts of town. Narcotics collected were also burned, but in a high intensity incinerator. The entire process was done under the watchful eye of the department's Office of Professional Standards, or OPS. There was a special name for this unit since the new chief had come on board, Turner's Rat Squad.

"Chief Turner," Neil Crowder began as he was waved into the office. Neil noticed Burt Munson had taken a corner seat. Burt was the head of OPS brought in from another agency after Turner had been chief for about a year.

"What's up?" Turner asked. "Okay for Burt to be here?"

Neil considered the question. Burt could be part of the problem, but Neil knew when to steer clear of trouble. And, Burt was trouble.

"No, no problem, boss." Neil went on to describe what Sally had discovered and detailed the Memphis incident.

Chief Turner sat back in his chair and glared at Neil. "So, what's the problem?"

"Our gun is the problem. One we should have destroyed now turns up in Memphis at an officer involved shooting. That could be very embarrassing, boss."

"Don't see the problem, Commander Crowder." Turner used rank title when he was upset. "Seems like it was a screw-up, probably another one that Sally had a hand in. We've had a few things disappear in her shop. Maybe we should audit *her*. Maybe she's taking things she likes. Let's see, her shop is part of your command, isn't it?"

"Chief, Sally's been here longer than I have. She's proven herself capable and dedicated. I'm not happy when you diss her. It's not warranted."

"And your point, Commander Crowder? Let the damn gun issue drop. Sounds like a good shoot. Not going to be a problem. If there was a problem, it was in *your* shop, *your* problem. Got that? Anything else today, Commander Crowder?"

* * *

The area around Cleveland, Ohio was essentially a cluster of small communities trying to avoid being lumped under the problems and general ineptitude that permeates the actual city of Cleveland. Most of the smaller suburbs were well run, had well-meaning elected officials, and aimed to hire competent employees.

Morgan City was one such community. Positioned on the outskirts of Cleveland, the city was far enough away to avoid the corruption and mudslinging occupying the bigger city. Two private religious-backed colleges were within the city limits. One had a Lutheran affiliation and the other obtained most funding from the Evangelist Christian mega churches dotting the city.

The Morgan City Police Department hovered around one hundred employees, three quarters of them being sworn officers. Inside the station a line of photographs was hung on the entry wall depicting the department's past chiefs going back to 1892. Some of the top cops looked like they had been kidnapped from Appalachian hovels or were members of a motley group of horse thieves. To its merit, the city paid its cops a good, comparable wage and there was never much job movement, unless a cop was fired or retired.

The state of Ohio has been known as a solid bastion for police unions since cops were given the right to collectively bargain in the early 1970s. The Fraternal Order of Police and the Police Benevolent Association are the two principal police unions fighting each other to represent cop shops. Cops in Ohio like to challenge their bosses. This has led to hundreds of arbitration and court decisions being published, thus announcing to the world the internal bickering, ineptitude, and stupidity that often goes on when cops try to bargain for positions.

Morgan City was able to stay out of the fracas involving constant lawsuits under its past chiefs and city administration. That was, until the last three years.

* * *

"And what the fuck are you going to do about it, Luther?" Adam Lester roared as he wagged a finger at the uniformed cop standing beside Lester's squad car.

Luther's fist appeared out of nowhere and shot through the open window. Lester's nose cracked and two rampaging rivers of blood gushed from his nostrils, creating a map of red on his light blue uniform shirt.

Lester's partner, Byron Jones, quickly positioned himself outside the squad car and menacingly rushed toward Luther, bouncing over the trunk of the car. Luther's partner, Shaun Avery, rushed to step between the two and tried to grab Luther by the shoulders. The three officers continued their struggle as they tumbled in a heap of thrashing bodies on the ground.

"911…What's your problem?" the operator said into her headset.

"I'm at the Pantry Pride on State Street. You ain't gonna believe this, but there are cops outside fighting."

"How you know they're police officers?"

"They're wearing uniforms and their cars say Morgan City Police. That 'nuff for you, lady?"

"Who are they fighting with, sir?"

"Themselves! Ain't no civies involved."

Sergeant Thames flicked on his unit's flashing blues and siren as he raced to the Pantry Pride. His saw Luther, Byron Jones, and Shaun Avery rolling on the parking lot pavement between the two police cars. Lester was still seated in the driver's seat of his patrol car, his head pillowed on the headrest. A fixed stare filled his glassy eyes.

"Stop it! Stop it now, assholes! What the fuck is going on?" Sergeant Thames yelled at the tangled mess gyrating on the ground.

Nothing! Zero response. There was no indication the brawlers had even heard him. The three were zoned out and focused only on whatever they thought they were doing. Sergeant Thames pulled a small black canister from his equipment belt and shook it three times.

"Stop now, or I'll spray you with OC!"

Still nothing! Not one change in the altercation.

Thames squeezed the canister and a steady stream of liquid hell penetrated the mass on the ground. Once liquid propellant chemical spray dissipates, particles of pepper spray invade the skin, nose, and eyes of the subject who'd been blasted. People react differently to OC, but most immediately sense severe burning on the skin and eyes as a choking sensation builds in the throat. Cops aren't any different.

The uniforms untangled and rolled away from each other. Shaun tried to stand and move away from the offending spray, but he careened blindly into the side of Lester's patrol car. He fell on all fours as mucus ran freely from his nose.

Luther rolled a few feet away and simply lay on his back, desperately resisting the urge to grab at his burning eyes. Byron Jones turned to face Sergeant Thames as if nothing had happened.

"What the fuck, sarge?"

The sergeant and the three officers on the ground turned to the front of the Pantry Pride and saw a crowd of eight kids laughing and pointing at the cops. Half had cell phones raised in a photo salute; Thames knew they were going to have starring roles in a YouTube viral hit. The scene was sure to make the local news channels. Maybe the national news would pick up this sure hit. The Keystone Cops never looked so good.

Back at the station, Sergeant Thames called an EMT from the adjacent firehouse to tend to Adam Lester's damaged nose. Thames ordered each officer to pose for shots taken with the digital camera kept in the watch commander's office.

The sergeant dreaded making the call, but knew he had to pick up the phone before the rest of Morgan City called the chief. Thames disliked Chief Turner and thought he was a pompous asshole. He knew the big boss would go ballistic at this exceptional fiasco.

"They did what?" Turner barked when Thames briefly described what had occurred at the Pantry Pride.

"Seems the fight was over a police groupie both Lester and Luther have been pounding. Most of the department knows her. She's a skag, but more than a few of our guys have had a piece of her. Seems neither cop knew the other was getting it at the same time."

"And you're telling me you had to spray the shit out of those assholes to get them to stop fighting? Tell me you're shitting me, Sergeant Thames. These are your boys, on your watch. What the fuck you been doing out there, sergeant?"

Thames knew this would be Chief Turner's response. He would be looking for someone to take the blame. Thames thought about letting the chief know that every cop on the job knew the boss was screwing the new little girl in records and the rich bitch volunteer who ran the neighborhood watch. Thames thought long and hard about making the disclosure, but kept his mouth shut.

"Put them assholes on admin leave! Tell them to expect a good suspension coming down."

"Chief, that'll leave my shift pretty bare."

"Do I give a shit, sergeant? That's your problem. You live with it. I better inform the mayor and council before the news snipes get them," Chief Turner growled and promptly slammed his phone shut.

* * *

The lone Morgan City paramedic unit skidded to a stop under the expansive portico of Valley Eternal Care. While the place was being built, most in the town thought it was destined to be a funeral parlor, but Valley Eternal Care turned out to be a rehabilitation and assisted care facility. Most patients, or clients, as the staff liked to refer to them, were there under Medicaid or Medicare. It was a struggling operation filled with folks who were waiting out their lives in humble surroundings.

Two medics ambled out of the unit. Morgan City used part-time attendants or volunteers for Basic Life Support service. The county fire department with a fulltime Advanced Life Support unit handled serious calls for help. This call had been designated as an "Assist the Staff" run. Neither Joe Samples nor Nick Carlson knew anything more. They just showed up when called.

"Goodness, thank you for coming!" a middle-aged woman wearing a pale yellow nurse's uniform exclaimed as Joe and Nick entered the front doors carrying a black bag with the familiar Rod of Asclepius symbol on the top. Large white EMT letters were blocked on the side. Joe nodded his head in acknowledgment.

"It's Samuel Whitestone...again!"

The name meant nothing to Joe or Nick. "And exactly what's Sam's problem, ma'am?" Joe inquired.

"Oh Lord, don't call him Sam! The man goes berserk when people don't call him by Samuel. He's in one of his weird moods right now."

"I'm guessing something more than a mood swing is happening for you to call us, ma'am."

She gave Joe a perturbed glance. "Of course! Don't you go giving me an attitude, young man!"

Joe looked at Nick and shrugged.

"We found blood in his commode. Samuel gets urinary infections pretty regularly. Our head nurse, she's not on duty right now, says we need to get a blood sample and then put a catheter in place."

"We don't do either of those procedures, ma'am."

"No, we will do it. We just need you to stand by in case we need help."

"That's what you got cops for. We're here for medical needs only. If the old guy is a problem, why not just wait 'til he calms down a bit?" Joe asked.

"Listen jerk, we pay your salaries! We got a schedule to keep around here. Samuel isn't cooperating at all and we need help now," Yellow Dress screamed.

"Call the cops! Better still, we'll call them!" Joe barked as he and Nick spun around and walked through the front doors that automatically parted. The two medics turned back to see Yellow Dress with one hand cradling a broad hip and the other flipping them the finger.

Two Morgan City marked police cars arrived at Valley Eternal Care from different directions and pulled behind the paramedic unit with synchronized precision. Both cops left their cars and sauntered over to Joe and Nick.

"What ya got, guys?" Shaun Avery asked casually.

Joe started to tell the story, but stopped abruptly as he gave Shaun the once over. "Say, aren't you one of the Morgan City cops I saw on YouTube fighting in a brawl?" Joe started to laugh and nudged Nick with his elbow.

"No, asshole, it was my partner that clopped the cop for fucking his whore without his permission. He's on suspension. I'm the good guy. I separated the jerks and saved their asses. What have you guys done lately that hit YouTube? We got over fifty thousand hits on that video!"

The four uniforms walked into the lobby of Eternal Care and were met by a now fiery Yellow Dress.

"'Bout fuckin' time you showed up!"

"What? Been less than five minutes since we got the call. Don't get your panties in a wad," Shaun blurted angrily.

"They got some old fart pissin' blood here," Joe inserted into the dialogue.

"That right, lady?" Shaun asked.

"Yes, and Samuel has already fucked up my schedule. I got a cart full of pills to deliver to the old people. They'll revolt if I don't get around to them soon."

"So why not leave the old guy alone 'til he calms down?"

"I got a schedule and the head nurse told me to handle it. Besides, Samuel's got his roommate so scared that he's hiding in the room behind the chair. Cartoons are blaring on the TV now. Samuel's roommate never misses his cartoons. He can almost recite them word for word. Does a great imitation of Daffy Duck, he does."

The four uniforms followed Yellow Dress down the hallway like chicks following a Canadian goose mother hen. Yellow Dress stopped abruptly without the customary STOP NOW beep that would toot from a Caterpillar tractor. The four almost buckled into her broad backside and all had a hard time keeping a straight face. The nasty nurse pointed to the open door on the left and mouthed, "He's in there."

Shaun took the lead and stepped in front of the open door while the second cop, Byron Jones, stood a foot behind him. The paramedics backed into the wall opposite the open doorway so they could view what was happening.

Samuel Whitestone was a small man, not much over 120 pounds. He appeared to be somewhere over seventy. Mismatched pajamas ragged over his bare feet. The knuckles on both hands were white from firmly griping the handles of a banged-up walker with tennis ball shoes on the front legs. He was hunched over like Quasimodo with his hairless dome jiggling like a bobble head on his narrow shoulders. His pajama crotch was stained with a dark substance. Hanging on one arm of the walker, a metal cane looped precariously.

From behind a large recliner chair huddled an even smaller man. All the officers could see were beady eyes peering around the chair.

"Wha' the fuck you cops want? I'll give you a lickin' if you come in here," Samuel yelled at the assembled uniforms.

"Sam, we're here to help you," Shaun murmured in a hushed, reassuring voice.

"Sam? Goddamn it—it's Mr. Samuel Whitestone, you whipper-snapper piece of turd!" Samuel screamed at Shaun.

Samuel grabbed his cane and waved it menacingly over his head and then jabbed it into the air in front of him. "I'm a vet! You know what that means, pussy face?"

Shaun wasn't baited by Samuel's outburst and even smiled in return. "Me too, Mr. Whitestone. Me too. Desert Storm, the old man's war; not W's war. Got a Purple Heart and a chest full of campaign ribbons. Proud to be in the company of another vet, Mr. Whitestone."

"You're not pulling some shit on me, are you son?"

"No, sir!" Shaun issued in a command voice worthy of a military drill sergeant.

Shaun could hear his partner trying to relay to dispatch what was going on. Unfortunately the dispatcher didn't get the complete picture.

"All units, cars 53 and 54 are at Valley Eternal Center with a patient threatening with a cane."

Shaun heard the approaching sirens and hoped Byron would intercede and stop the cops from rushing into the confrontation he was trying to control. Shaun was trapped in the situation and couldn't back away. Any interference would break the delicate relationship and communication he had developed with Samuel. Shaun heard yells echoing down the hallway as the new batch in blue rushed to help.

By this time the foyer and halls of Valley Eternal Care were packed with curious residents, staff, and the tidal wave of uniformed officers. Joe and Nick, the original paramedics at the scene, were slowly slinking down the hallway in the opposite direction. Byron Jones was nowhere to be found.

"What ya got, Shaun?" the first officer asked as he waded through the mass gathered in the hallway.

Shaun turned and saw Rodney Cains cradling a shotgun. The shotgun was one with the stock painted yellow, almost matching the yellow dress broad in the hallway.

Police have an arsenal of tools called "less than lethal" weapons. They are designed to give street cops and special operations officers an alternative to using regular firearms. They are intended to prevent killing someone who may be emotionally disturbed, suicidal, intoxicated or carrying a knife or other bludgeoning weapon.

Some of these tools are shotguns that fire beanbag projectiles. Others are weapons specifically designed to fire projectiles that deliver wooden bullets, foam bullets, or have a chemical irritant agent secured in them. But even less than lethal weapons can kill a subject. The projectile might hit the person in a vulnerable location like the sternum, throat, kidney, or anywhere on the face. There are minimum ranges that designate how far away an officer should be positioned to ensure the projectile actually remains "less lethal."

"No, Rodney!" Shaun shouted as Rodney raised the shotgun to his shoulder in response to Samuel again swinging his cane threateningly over his head.

The shotgun belched and discharged a beanbag round at Samuel. The sound wasn't as loud as a regular double-ought buck magnum round would make, but was deafening in the confines of the small room shared by Samuel and the frightened little man still crouched behind the lounge chair in the corner of the room.

The beanbag hit Samuel square in the center of his chest. Samuel's eyes grew as large as saucers as he took the impact. His cane careened to the right and shattered the glass mirror hanging on the wall. The force of the blow lifted the small, frail man off his feet and propelled him directly into the lounge chair. The chair slid backward from Samuel's weight and pinned the little man hiding behind it into the corner, forcing a series of gasps from his lungs. Samuel's crotch darkened wider with a growing stain. He had urinated in his pajamas.

The little man now pinned behind the chair came alive, "I thought I taw—I did! I did! Holey puddy-tat...jest like Sylvester!"

Shaun grabbed Rodney by his shoulders, forced him out the door and ran him down the hallway. As Shaun passed the two paramedics he yelled, "Get the fuck in there now. It's a medical emergency, *finally!*"

"Rodney King! Yes, that officer gave old Samuel a real Rodney King beating," an elderly woman screamed from the room opposite Samuel's.

Yellow Dress was making her way through the gawkers, elbows flailing as she ran. Bodies were pushed into the walls as Yellow Dress descended on Joe and Nick when they entered Samuel's room. Her high-pitched screams resonated down the hallway.

Shaun dragged Rodney and the errant shotgun through a side door and made their way back to the front portico of Valley Eternal Care. By now the driveway and parking lot were teeming with police cars and emergency vehicles, all with flaring blue emergency lights and unattended sirens squealing as if auditioning for a bizarre symphony.

"Shaun!" The sharp command from Sergeant Thames pierced through the chaos.

Shaun lowered his head as he approached Thames with Rodney in tow. "Sarge, let me explain," Shaun stammered. Shaun noticed Byron coming at them from between the stopped cop cars.

"Not here, not now, Shaun. Just tell me what I need to know to dismantle this circus."

Thames did what good field supervisors do when the shit hits the fan and is trying to plaster anybody passing by. Thames calmly put things in order. Samuel Whitestone was taken out of Valley Eternal Care on a stretcher and Joe and Nick accompanied him to the local hospital.

A somewhat surprised new officer had just arrived and was ordered to secure Samuel's room and wait for detectives to arrive. Thames told dispatch to make the critical incident notifications. He specifically told the dispatcher to make sure Chief Turner was alerted. Thames grabbed another uniformed officer and ordered him to take the names of everyone in the vicinity of the incident.

Three hours later, Morgan City and the Valley Eternal Care facility were back to some semblance of normalcy, but the shit was beginning to pile up inside the police station.

Chief Turner pulled Shaun Avery into his office along with Commander Burt Munson. He didn't bother to shut his office door, knowing full well the hallway was still crowded with officers, detectives, and clerical personnel.

"Tell me again what the fuck your name is!" Turner yelled at Shaun. He was close enough to Shaun's face that punctuating spit propelled into Shaun's face.

"Shaun Avery!"

"You mean…Shaun Avery, SIR!"

"Yes, sir," Shaun answered as he stood erect in front of the chief.

"What the fuck did you cause to happen there, officer?" Turner demanded, elongating the last word.

"Chief, I was actively calming the incident. Mr. Whitestone was hyped and I was able to start bringing him down. Rodney, that would be Officer Cains, mistook Samuel's cane swinging as a threat to me, he didn't know…" Shaun wasn't able to complete his response.

"Who the fuck is this Whitestone guy?"

"He…" again Shaun was cut off.

"Oh shit, I don't give a rat's ass about him. You're the one I'm pissed with. You caused this fuckin' thing to get totally out of control. You fucked me, officer. You did it again! You know what happens to someone who fucks with me?" Turner swung around and pointed at Munson with an order. "Put this deficient asshole on administrative leave and get him out of my station. Do it now!"

Shaun was about to lose his cool when Sergeant Thames entered the chief's office and grabbed his arm, pulling him away from Turner and hustling him out the door.

"I'll deal with Officer Avery, sir," Thames announced as he left without waiting for a response.

"Sarge," Shaun pleaded.

"Not now, Shaun. It'll all be righted in the Critical Incident Investigation. Now's the time for you to get the hell out of here. Go home early, son."

A detective approached Thames as he watched Shaun sulk out the station's rear door emptying into the employee parking lot.

"Sarge, we got a problem," the detective whispered to Thames. "The gal from the old persons' place just called me. I thought it was regarding a follow-up to questioning her earlier. She says there's a bunch of prescription pills missing from the nurse's cart. Says one of the old farts told her she saw a cop lift them during the scuffle with the guy who got bean bagged."

All Thames could think was, shit, shit, shit! Will it never end? He knew what he now had to do, and didn't like it. Not that it wasn't the right, proper thing to do, but he knew what the chief's response would be when he delivered this news.

"Chief Turner and Commander Munson, got some more bad news."

Both men glared at Thames.

"A facility nurse is accusing a cop of taking some medications from the nursing cart during the incident."

Munson yelled, "Who? How they know it was a cop? Who's the complainant?"

Thames knew which cops had been at the Valley Eternal Care during the incident. All were accounted for during the time of the actual incident, except Byron Jones. He remembered Shaun telling him that Byron had suddenly disappeared and then reappeared outside after things settled down.

"Boss, I think the guy was most likely Officer Jones," Thames offered. "He's still out on patrol, however. I needed someone to cover the field during the time we were cleaning up at the scene."

"Get his ass in here…now!" Chief Turner thundered.

Sergeant Thames met Byron just outside the back door of the station. Byron was a young officer who looked like he wasn't old enough to shave, but had collected more than enough red craters on his cheeks to be declared a hazard zone. The young cop allowed his hair to grow to a point where it hid the collar of his uniform shirt. Thames liked the young officer, but remembered he avoided any continued contact with other officers. He was dependable, but a loner.

"What's up, sarge?"

"Chief got himself worked into one of his stress stages. Got a bad report from the Valley Eternal Care place."

"You mean 'cuz the old man got blasted with the bean bag?"

"No, something more. Got anything you want to tell me, Byron?"

"Like?" Byron stammered and looked away from his superior. His feet were bouncing like oil on a skillet as he stuffed his hands deep into his pockets.

"I may be able to help if I know what's going on, Byron."

"Nothing, sarge. I'm good."

"Well, let's go see the chief and his henchman Munson." Thames offered Byron an opening, but the young cop didn't grab for the carousel ring. He was going to have to take this ride on his own.

"If there's one thing I can't stand in my department, it's a thief! You understand?" Chief Turner started yelling at Byron the moment he entered the office. Turner's face was morphing red like a thermometer left in the hot sun. His voice quavered as the harsh pitch ascended.

"You hand over the pills from the old farts' home, NOW! Don't make it harder for you or for me. I'm not going to stand for some asshole tarnishing the reputation of my department. One way or the other, you'll not be part of this place. You hear?"

Byron simply stood glaring at the chief with an off glance directed at Munson.

Turner continued his rant. "Hand over that gun, young man. You ain't going anywhere and sure as hell won't need a firearm anymore."

"Am I under arrest?" Byron quietly asked.

Thames was surprised at Byron's calm demeanor. He was a young officer just off probation and had no experience in police disciplinary matters, at least as far as Thames knew.

"Well, you're sure as hell not free to go. You figure what that means…shit bird?"

"Sounds like it's an arrest, Chief Turner. I'm asking for a union rep and an attorney. That's my right, *SIR!*" Byron heavily punctuated the last word.

Thames thought this young officer sure had balls the size of a prized breeder bull.

"You got no rights in my shop! Munson, search this asshole!"

Munson looked surprised as he glanced at the chief and then at Thames.

"Chief, we should read the officer his rights first."

"Fuck that! Munson, do it!"

Fortunately Byron didn't resist and simply stood at attention, rigid as a Buckingham Palace guard.

Munson did a cursory pat down and then examined each uniform pocket. He backed away and shrugged his shoulders. "Nothing, chief."

"Thames, you go search his unit. Munson, search this asshole's private vehicle. Officer, give Commander Munson the keys to your car now. What you driving out there?"

"Chief, we just can't search his personal car without probable cause. Are we going at this as a criminal matter or just internal?" Munson asked, backing up to avoid the barrage he knew would be coming from Turner.

"Munson, you challenging my authority? You really want to go there?"

Thames knew the entire episode was going down the toilet. He knew from his training and experience that there was a lot of leeway available from an employment standpoint, but it was looking more and more like the chief was making this situation into a criminal offense. Cops don't give up their Constitutional rights when they pin on the badge. Thames saw a smirk building on Byron's face and wondered if he knew his rights were being trampled, both as a member of the police union and a citizen with the same rights as anyone under arrest. As ordered, Byron handed over the keys and identified his car.

"I'm giving you these keys under duress. I'm not consenting to any search of my private car, Chief," Byron calmly stated.

Thames had just finished examining the cop car trunk when he saw Munson hurrying from the employee parking lot carrying several white canisters in his hands. Munson flashed by Thames without saying a word. Thames followed him into the station, directly to the chief's office. Munson dropped the canisters on the chief's desk. They obviously were prescription drug containers.

"Fuck! This guy's a pill head on top of being a thief!" Turner exploded as he examined the canisters. "Oxycodone, Percocet, Ambien, what are these things in this packet?"

"Morphine patches," Thames replied without hesitation.

"Munson, arrest the thieving bastard and get his ass out of here! There's no place in my department for a thief. On top of everything else, he's stealing drugs from old people. He's tarnished the badge for every one of our officers."

* * *

It was a four-hour drive from Morgan City to Chatham-Kent. Nat Turner was used to the monotonous drive to Detroit and finally through the tunnel to Windsor. The drive didn't bother Nat Turner much; he'd made the trek once a month for the past year. Reaching Canada, Nat was able to wind down and relax. Sometimes he'd dip south on a rural highway and leisurely drive along the banks of Lake Erie, but this particular day he took the faster 401.

Nat glanced at Emily who was busy playing a stupid game on her iPad. Brightly colored figures dropped from random squares as she tried to figure out their magical sequence. It was blind luck if she achieved success with any game she tried. Not that Nat thought she was stupid; technology simply wasn't her forte.

Emily was a woman just passing fifty. Most people would consider her attractive, but it could be a difficult call. She rarely wore obvious make-up, other than a hint of lipstick. She dressed like Mother Earth personified and favored casual baggy outfits when she wasn't attending political meetings. Then she was a fashion plate in tailored slacks and silk blouses. Emily was a tall woman and kept her body taunt by playing tennis and participating in daily yoga and stretching exercises. Nat liked his isolated escapes with this interesting woman. The sex was great, but he gained even more from the relationship.

Emily Stanton was one of Morgan City's elected councilpersons. Her husband was a well-respected attorney in the area and his firm acted as the contracted city attorney. He was a Republican mover and shaker in this part of Ohio. Emily and Nat's relationship slowly developed from flirtatious glances at council meetings to secretive touches, playful bumps, and longing stares at a budget retreat over a year ago.

Nat was on his third wife who refused to move when he accepted the Morgan City Chief of Police position. She reluctantly visited when Nat felt it was important to show her off to the community and remind them of the sacrifice he was making to be their head cop. Any intimacy the couple shared disappeared after she found Nat in bed with a probationary officer in his last job.

"Nat," Emily began as she laid down her iPad. "I think Ernie knows about us."

"How so?"

"Just some comments he made yesterday when I said I had to go to Detroit. Like, 'How come all your meetings seem to be out of town? The first couple years you never went to anything that involved traveling.' Just odd comments like that."

"What did you tell him?"

"I told him I'm now more involved in the League of Cities and the Ohio Elected City Officers matters. But, I don't think he believes me."

"You worried he might find out about us and our relationship?"

"Find out what, Nat? Is there something more than you and me fucking like rabbits in heat?"

Nat knew to keep his mouth shut when Emily acted this way. He didn't want his time and money wasted once they reached the B&B he had selected for their rendezvous.

* * *

Artesia, New Mexico was over two hundred miles from Santa Fe. Plenty of drives in New Mexico were beautiful, showcasing mountains and sheer cliffs shaded in red and purple hues thrusting upward to the sky. Occasionally the scenery was punctuated by meandering streams with clumps of cottonwoods crowding the banks, begging for moisture.

This trip wasn't pretty. Barreling down Highway 285 with an expanse of flat, high desert on either side was downright boring. Dodging tumbleweeds circling on the highway was the only excitement offered on this trip Taylor was making.

Taylor had briefly considered flying to Artesia. If he opted to fly, he would have to drive to Albuquerque and then catch a puddle jumper to Roswell, followed by renting a car and motoring down the short distance to Artesia. The same, if not more, time would be consumed.

Taylor was glad he had finally laid his Jeep Wrangler to rest, most likely in a scrap metal heap somewhere, destined to raise from the dead in a far off country where sweaty, underpaid workers would turn it into a Kia or Nissan. Down deep he hoped the Boys and Girls Club was able to find it a home with some kind soul with a knack for tinkering. His new heavy Dodge Ram pickup devoured the road and almost lulled him to another dimension with sounds from its uninterrupted satellite radio connection. No static. No more flapping window inserts. No more fighting every gust of wind attempting to upend the top heavy Jeep.

This trip to New Mexico's southern wasteland started with a passing question posed by Amos, the landlord for Taylor's new pigeonhole office. "Taylor, can you help out a friend of mine?"

Amos' friend was a fellow recent retiree from the New Mexico State Police. Sal Dominguez was now an instructor at the Bureau of Indian Affairs' Indian Police Academy in Artesia. It was one of several training elements in the Department of Homeland Security's Federal Law Enforcement Training Center. This one was affectionately called "Flectsy West."

"Taylor, my man Amos says you're the man for the job. I need somebody to teach a short class. He says you're retired from LAPD, that right?"

"True, Sal. But, why me? What's the topic?"

"Ethics. You got some, huh?" Sal replied, offering a rumbled laugh.

"You got an outline you want me to follow?"

"Fat chance you would use it if I did have one! No, I want you to use your years of experience, and maybe spice it up with interesting cases you've worked on. Amos told me about some of them. Seems you just can't think of enough ways some cops will fuck up, huh? Know anything about tribal policing?"

"A little. Probably enough to get me into a heap of trouble."

Taylor was just entering Roswell after three hours on the road. The Dairy Queen sign was like a beacon drawing Taylor into its sheltered red and white building. Treats found at DQ were Taylor's reward for enduring a road trip. The ice cream joint was the equivalent of a Waffle House, but with a younger clientele. A cross section of a community's teens, all chewing gum, stealing secretive glances at the opposite sex, and gawking at new cars in the parking lot usually filled the seats.

Taylor always ordered the same when he reached the counter—a Snicker's Blizzard. Lately he'd dropped from ordering a regular to being satisfied with the smaller mini. He was sure the company had included minis on the menu board to placate the senior crowd.

Following DQ's protocol, the young girl behind the counter turned the filled cup upside down to demonstrate that its sweet innards wouldn't plop onto the counter. This fanciful ceremony made every DQ in every state the same. Taylor had no idea what this ritual was supposed to signify, but, just like the rigmarole surrounding post time at a horse race, turning DQ cups upside down was an American tradition. Taylor took the offered cup and scooped up a mouthful.

It was a short drive further south before Taylor entered Artesia. It appeared to be a small, uneventful town with not much more to offer than a lazy Main Street. He knew only eleven thousand folks called the town their home. Lately the population was growing with the rapid influx of energy workers drawn to the newfound developments that appeared as a result of fracking.

Sal Dominguez offered Taylor the option of staying the night at the residential dormitory at the training facility, but Taylor remembered the cautionary advice Amos had issued to steer clear of that suggestion unless he had an aching to relive military boot camp.

His three-hour class could be scheduled for either the morning or afternoon periods. Either way he would have to spend a night in Artesia.

That almost sounded like a tune from the 40s. What was it? A Night in Tunisia?

Burgundy awnings tried to make the façade of the Heritage Inn inviting. That was hard to do since the inn was a dull, squat square brick building. Sal recommended the Inn over the traditional chain hotels outside the heart of downtown Artesia. Taylor was glad he had a reservation when he noticed the glowing red neon sign jutting from the second story flashing the warning, No Vacancy.

"Halp you?" the young man behind the small counter asked as Taylor opened the door to the hotel's lobby.

"Got a reservation. Taylor Sterling."

"Yes sir, Mr. Sterling. You teaching over at the Indian school, huh?"

"Got that written on my forehead somewhere?"

"No, your forehead's clean, but I just had a call from a lady at the school who told us to expect you. She didn't know you'd already made a reservation online. First time with us, sir?"

"Yep."

"Well, breakfast starts bright and early at 6:30. Continental style it is, meaning you halp yourself. If you wants to use a gym, this key will open the door at Pop's around on First Street. Pop closes about five each afternoon, but members have keys to get in anytime. Instructors seem to take advantage of that."

"No, not today. Gonna drive around and check out Artesia. Never been here."

"Not much to see, Mr. Sterling. When you come back, you needs to park in back. Cops will ticket you if you're on the street overnight."

"How about dinner?"

"Couple of places are good. I'd recommend the Wellhead. Okay food and good selection of micro brews. Some say it's over-priced, but nowadays most places are with the energy boom and all."

The Wellhead was a good recommendation. Taylor ordered an Indian Basin Wheat to start, along with an order of chili poppers. The poppers were battered nicely and fortunately were tame. His green chiliburger and onion rings were served with a Wild Cat IPA. Taylor finished off the night with a heavy Crude Oil Stout. He was glad he still wore his jeans, T-shirt, and boots. The crowd was made up of locals, some probably just off the fields. Some were definitely roughnecks judging by their gritty appearance. Taylor didn't earn glances or comments as he sat at the bar and enjoyed his meal in relative peace.

It was a little after seven the next morning when Taylor pulled into the sprawling training center. He wanted to get a feel for the place before the training started.

Three large 727 aircraft parked at one side of the campus intrigued him and warranted a look. The bleating sound of a bugle assaulted Taylor's ears as he jumped from the truck. He glanced around and noticed several uniformed groups standing at attention in a semi-circle around a tall flagpole. They were saluting as the Stars and Stripes slowly left the hands of four officers. Taylor stood at attention and was taken back to his police academy days for a brief moment.

Taylor got lost as he tried to navigate his way to Sal Dominguez's office. He found himself standing near a brown planter surrounded by three towering granite walls reaching to the sky. A sign proudly pronounced, "Indian Country Law Enforcement Officers' Memorial." Too many names were etched on the walls. Taylor noticed the first on the list was identified as "1852 Chin-Chi-Kee of the Chickasaw Nation." He caught the names and agencies of others and realized some must have been Native Americans working for police agencies other than tribal forces, like the Border Patrol or the Sandoval County Sheriff's Office.

He thanked the gardener who eventually directed him to Sal's office.

After the usual introductions, Taylor asked Sal, "What's with the planes?"

"Air Marshals. We train a lot of different law enforcement elements at the Center. Border Patrol. Counter-terrorism units. FBI. Lots of local police agencies train here, particularly from New Mexico. And, of course, we train tribal officers," Sal replied.

"What do you know about tribal policing, Taylor?"

"A little, Sal. I know it's a tough job. Mostly understaffed offices. Real political arena with tribal councils wanting to control everything. Lots of problems with sex crimes, drinking, and domestic abuse. Most councils want to keep their problems hidden. FBI has some jurisdiction over felonies and a few other crimes. Police chiefs are usually short term and are often driven out by politics or scandals."

"Well, you sure got that in a nutshell, Taylor. Then too, some tribes are filthy rich from gaming money and others are forgotten and steeped in deep poverty." Sal slowly shook his head. "But, we try to give new officers the best entry training we can in the sixteen weeks they're with us."

Sal opened the classroom door precisely at nine o'clock. A commandingly loud *"Atten...hut!"* filled the room as it came alive with the cadence of forty chairs moving back followed by forty cadets jumping to their feet to face the front of the room. All the rigidly standing cadets were dressed in khaki T-shirts and dark green fatigue pants that ballooned over the top of shiny dark brown combat boots.

"Take your seats!" Sal barked at the group. "I know you've read the section in the instruction book titled "Ethics." We're trying something a little different for this class...your class. We've invited a guest speaker to review the scope of Ethics as it relates to your job.

"Taylor Sterling is a retired Deputy Chief of the LAPD. You know, that department famous in TV and movies—Jack Webb, T.J. Hooker, Hunter, Columbo, and all four, all four, Lethal Weapons. We've all seen them: the good, the bad, and the ugly. Taylor lives in Santa Fe now where he's hung his shingle as a consultant. But, I know most of what he deals with involves cops who get jammed up and police departments that need help. He'll be with you for the next three hours. Listen up and learn something that might help you in the real world after you graduate."

Taylor decided to dress down for his presentation. He wore jeans, boots, and a blue button down shirt clasped with a double eagle bolo tie to make his statement. Forty fresh faces were staring at him without giving any indication what was going on behind their fixed eyes. Only four females filled seats. He doubted a physical agility exam was required to gain admittance to the class. Some male students were crammed into their chairs with ample amounts of flab cascading over the seats. A palette of complexions from dark mahogany to Nordic pallor greeted him. Taylor guessed the ages of the assembled group ranged from early twenties to mid-forties.

"Today I'm going to talk about temptation. All of you will be faced with temptations on the job. Will you give in? What will your limits be? Will you snitch on a partner who's caught by the lure? Will you stand up when your boss cuts corners and shaves the truth? You are going to be tested, no doubt about it. The question is, will you pass?

"I never got the chance to work for Chief William H. Parker of the LAPD. He died on the job about fifteen years before I joined the California force. He was a god. Parker was the one who dragged the department out of a sea of muddy corruption and adverse political control and elevated the department to a well-deserved and recognized reputation. It took years of hard work and discipline to rid it of compartmentalized evil.

"I heard every class graduating from that early academy, as you will be doing in several weeks, got an earful from Chief Parker. He'd start out by saying, 'Men,' but keep in mind only male officers were in the LAPD back then."

Taylor noticed smiles spread on the female officers' faces after that admission.

"There were three things that would get you fired from the

LAPD; they were known as the three Bs: Booze, Broads and Bills."

Taylor paused and knew he'd gotten their attention. "That's equally true today, but you'd have to add a fourth B for Brutality, as well as a P for Perjury, otherwise known as lying.

"Booze is still big, but today prescription pills and steroids should be added to the mix. As an officer, you'll be encouraged to pump up, to add bulk to your torso, instead of adding it around your middle.

"Women can cause you trouble with a capital T. You'll have unbelievable control over women who will be caught in a very vulnerable state.

"You'll see money, sometimes enormous amounts of money and valuables that will be so impressive your eyes will pop out. And, often you'll be the only one around the stash, so who's to know? Suspects may beg you, 'That stash is not mine and I urge you to take it.'

"To add to your misery, some bad guys you encounter will run from you, assault you, or spit in your face. They'll piss you off, oh yes, they will. No one is around, so why not teach the punks a lesson or take a little flesh back? You'll be tempted to write reports or swear testimony to something you know isn't true, but you'll feel justified because the bad guy is just scum or a known criminal."

Taylor had downloaded a series of video clips detailing police corruption and misconduct onto a thumb drive. As part of the class he'd play a clip and then discuss the implications, ending with identifying various ethical decision points. Every cop portrayed in the videos was offered more than one decision point where he or she could have reversed the course of action, but didn't.

The first hour of class was grueling and tedious. The students sat motionless, with blank faces. They were attentive, but no one raised a hand or asked a question. During the first break Taylor wandered by the groups clustered in the hallway, but not one student approached him or gave him an interested glance. Were they purposefully avoiding contact? The ten-minute break ended and the forty were back in their seats, once again focusing their gazes on Taylor.

"Mr. Sterling?" an older man in the group suddenly asked. "You mean to say you've never taken a free cup of coffee?" A few snickers exploded and several younger trainees glanced nervously at the questioning member of their group.

"Of course, I did. That was not the limit I set for myself."

"What was your limit?" the same trainee questioned.

"When I was a young cop, it was common for restaurants to give discounts or free meals to cops on the beat. When I was driving, we didn't stop at those places. When my partner was driving, he did stop. I would always leave a tip big enough to cover the meal and a tip. This was my little personal protest. That still goes on. Is it corruption? Will a free meal tempt me not to enforce the law equally when it involves that restaurant? That's the key question you have to ask yourself."

"You never 'tuned up' some asshole you arrested, Mr. Sterling?" another senior trainee asked.

"No. Never!" Taylor responded. "That was one of my limit lines."

"But what about your partner?"

"Never had to worry about that. My partners knew what my limits were and respected them. Some cops didn't want to work with me. That was okay; I had more than enough good cops to claim as partners. My limits never wavered when the color of someone's skin was a factor.

"You're going to run into a nasty, belligerent, foul-mouthed drunk one day. He may even spit on you. Your natural reaction will be to lash back and smack the sucker in the face. But you know, that same drunk would have probably spit on me, too. See, he's not spitting on Taylor, he's spitting on the uniform. When situations like that become personal with you, you'll get into trouble."

"That video you showed about cops stealing from drug dealers was pretty bad," a small-framed trainee noted. "Most of us are going to be working in poor tribal villages and won't be making much money. Where can you draw the line on that type behavior, Mr. Sterling?"

The question was framed in an unusual way, Taylor thought.

"Good question, sir. What you're really asking is, when and where is the line crossed on theft. The old chief, Bill Parker, simplified that situation when he said, 'Theft is theft.' When you put a dollar amount on it or when you rationalize a situation because you don't make much money, you begin to trivialize the action. It's not just a question the cop on the beat faces. Lately chiefs and sheriffs have been getting caught with their hands in the proverbial cookie jar. Officers have been found stealing from fellow officers when managing downed officer funds and union dues.

"I know some law enforcement officers have rationalized their actions by insisting they'll pay the money back. Of course, they never do. Rationalizations for theft could include gambling, addiction, family problems, surefire investments gone south, or too many lady friends."

At that comment, nervous laughs erupted from sections of the room.

"But, theft is theft, no matter who's doing the stealing. You can try to rationalize that siphoning a few gallons of gas from the motor pool for your own car is okay because the tribal council is cheap, or they're stealing from the tribe, or you'll pay it back. But, know this, you won't! You've allowed temptation to alter your limit line."

"But you can't be a snitch, Mr. Sterling! You'll never be able to work with other cops if you snitch," exclaimed a young man owning the darkest complexion in the class.

"Officer, that's the hardest choice you'll ever have to make. It's easy to jump into a fight to save your partner, confront a robber armed with a gun, or run into a burning house to save a kid. But, standing up and coming forward when you see misconduct or corruption is the most difficult choice you'll ever have to make. There will be consequences for whistle blowing; I'll guarantee that. On the other hand, I've arrested several cops and caused others to be arrested. Each of those dirty cops then had to face the consequences, which often included personal shame and humiliation, loss of family, and the possibility of unbearable days in jail. Choices all rest on what limits you set and what you will or will not accept on the job."

Another hand shot up in the back of the room. Taylor acknowledged the dark complexioned, small, round man who stood at rigid attention. "Most of us will be working for small tribal departments. The chief is beholden to the tribal council and everybody knows somebody. How can we be true law enforcement officers when everybody gets special treatment?"

Taylor noticed most class members were nodding their heads in agreement.

"That's true. But you'll be in no different position than eighty percent of the country's police agencies. See, those agencies all have less than fifty employees. Most of them are manned with fifteen or twenty cops, max. They all have elected town councils.

Everybody knows everything that happens in these small towns, just like happens in your villages. Does it make it harder? Sure, it does! But it also can help. You can get tips when cops in big cities can't. You'll be an integral part of your villages. You'll be like the old Irish cops known as the 'Garda.' That means 'guardians of the peace.'

"In big cities, cops rarely live in the jurisdiction they police. Many will tell you they purposefully avoid that so when they're off duty they don't run into the people they police. Unfortunately, these cops end up being like an occupation army. They think of themselves as 'warriors' or 'law enforcement officers.' There's a big difference in the two underlying philosophies.

"There are good and bad things about each and every jurisdiction. You have to feel proud inside here," Taylor said tapping his chest. "If you don't, you'll have to make a big decision. Another choice will be called for. Do you want the job? Our job is always about choices. Do you make good ones and resist temptation? Or, do you tarnish the badge you'll be carrying on your chest?"

The three hours came to a close much sooner that Taylor expected. Somehow he'd stimulated enough discussion to make ethical behavior something personal to the class. At least that's what Taylor hoped had occurred. He didn't know if he'd really changed any personal views, but he felt good about his presentation.

The four-hour trip back home to Santa Fe was anticlimactic, until strange marimba sounds invaded Sirius' Franco Country rendition of Jerry Lewis. It took Taylor a moment to realize his phone's Bluetooth was signaling him that a phone call was coming through. He fumbled to find the right button to push to answer the call.

"Taylor, here…" he uttered with hesitation.

"Mr. Sterling. Hope I didn't catch you at a bad time," the strange voice replied.

"Nope, just motoring back to Santa Fe. Actually the scenery is rather boring, so this is a welcomed interruption."

"We'd like to hire you to help us unravel what's becoming a tangled web. Our insurance carrier told us you might be able to help."

"Where are you and what's your problem?" Taylor asked, trying to avoid bantering back and forth.

"Oh, sorry. I'm Karl Unger from Morgan City in Ohio. I'm the city manager here. Our chief of police was killed in a car accident a few days ago while coming back from somewhere out of state. Unfortunately he was traveling with one of our council members whose husband happens to be our city attorney. She was killed, too."

"You're not looking for an accident reconstruction, are you?"

"No, that's not our problem. We have three female police department employees coming forth with allegations of sexual harassment now. Seems our chief couldn't keep his privates in his pants. Also, we have reason to suspect that there might have been irregularities with city funds and property. It's looking like a big mess. We need someone without ties to Morgan City to get involved. You interested?"

This was the usual pattern for developing situations that drew Taylor away from Santa Fe these days. Strange, unexpected calls from people he didn't know that were facing a problem that needed to be brought to light and ultimately resolved.

* * *

"Taylor, good to meet you in person," Karl Unger welcomed as

Taylor was ushered into a spacious office in the sprawling City Hall complex. Karl seemed young for his position, considering the staid, upscale feeling Morgan City oozed. Karl was lean and fit, his dark green polo shirt showing taut abs. On the left of the shirt, an umbrella tree spread over a modern font showcased Morgan City's logo. Surprisingly, Karl was wearing light grey slacks rather than Dockers.

"Done much consulting in Ohio?"

"A couple jobs. I'm familiar with Ohio policing from reviews of what seems to be a continuous stream of litigation between the police unions and local cities and counties."

"Morgan City has been spared a lot of that, until recently."

"What happened to change that?" Taylor inquired.

"I've been here just under five years, but the old timers tell me the relative peace the city enjoyed was the work of the former chief, Stanley Topson. He basically carried the title of Chief for Life. Came up through the ranks and was chief for nearly twenty years. Knew everybody inside and outside the police department. Everybody liked Stanley, but more importantly, respected him. He was fair and treated everyone with dignity. Had that 'Andy of Mayberry' personality and he knew how to use that nuance effectively. Unfortunately he keeled over with a fatal heart attack while giving a talk to the local Kiwanis Club. That tragically happened during my first year in Morgan City."

"And the chief who was killed in the traffic accident?"

Karl leaned back so far in his overstuffed chair that Taylor thought it was going to flip over. He crossed his arms across his chest. Taylor interpreted that body language as an attempt to protect himself.

"Nat Turner was different."

"You picked him, I gather?"

Karl sat upright. "I did. Obviously I made a mistake. Problems began within a couple months of his arrival. Nat didn't win friends in the department. He bullied his people. But, to the public and city council he was charming and was actually quite endearing. Sounds weird, I know."

"Karl, you mentioned on the phone that Turner had a problem keeping his dick in his pants."

Karl smiled and let a snicker escape. "Apparently so. First I got wind of it was early last year. Apparently he went to a chiefs' meeting in San Diego and took a local volunteer with him. She was recently separated and ran the police community watch program. A real looker. Well, one of our dispatchers was also being bedded regularly by our man Nat and was furious when she heard about the San Diego trip. She posted a ranting on her Facebook site detailing Nat's sexual proclivities in some pretty racy verbiage. Even had a picture of Nat in her bed lying bare-chested. Somehow the link started making the rounds at the chiefs' conference. Added some real spice to what was probably a boring event."

"And what did you do?"

"I told Commander Munson to open an investigation," Karl sighed.

"Where's that gone?"

"Still in the works, or so I've been informed by Munson. I have concerns about Munson. Turner brought him in from the outside his first year on the job. Said he needed someone in the department without skeletons and long friendships."

"How'd you select Turner?"

"I went to a national group, the Association of Police Executives Council. I was familiar with their services since they did a search for the last city where I worked. The selection was good for us then, but it cost plenty. Paid for the search and then the new chief gave that search outfit a no-bid consulting contract. Same with Turner. It's a racket, if you ask me," Karl sighed and leaned back in his chair.

"What do you want from me, Karl?"

Karl left his seat and walked around the chair, stopping to look out the window behind his desk. He put his hands into his pockets that Taylor recognized was an excuse to delay answering.

"I need to know what's really been happening in the police department. We've got three EEOC harassment complaints in the works, litigation started over the termination of another officer, an arbitration matter going on with a current field officer, cliques in the police department forming and biting each another, and I've got concerns about money and other projects being mismanaged by members of the police department. There's a shit storm whirling in the department, Taylor, a real shit storm."

* * *

Taylor checked into a Residence Inn. It was one of the older versions often found nestled along winding paths and looked more like an apartment complex than an inn. He wasn't sure if the inn was located in Morgan City or the neighboring community as they seemed to merge without markers.

He noticed a restaurant that could have been a Pizza Hut in its past life, but now wore a subdued carved sign announcing it was the Beverly Hills Supper Club. Something about the place caused Taylor's salivary glands to dance; he knew that was a good sign indicating exceptional food…usually.

"How's that Supper Club place?" he threw out to the desk clerk.

"Local place. I hear it's got great food. Nice people; both customers and staff."

Inside his room, Taylor unpacked his suitcase. About a year into his consulting gig, he realized he would need something more substantial to carry than a Wal-Mart suitcase. The clerk at the Fashion Outlet Samsonite store south of Santa Fe promised this model was indestructible and was the lightest weight available. She'd been telling the truth as evidenced from the marks and scars crisscrossing the body of the suitcase. Most of Taylor's clothes were still on the clothes hangers under the cleaner's plastic protection and he methodically placed them away from the row of provided hangers in the closet. Next he unpacked each plastic zipper case. One contained underwear, another workout clothing, and the last one often held extra shirts and belts. Taylor took his Dopp kit and opened it on the counter in the lavatory. He found if he used the same kit at home, he was more likely to be well supplied. But more than once he had visited a local drugstore late at night when something went missing.

Before setting out to fill his belly, Taylor decided to make a call.

"Al, Taylor Sterling here," he said into his cell phone. Al was an attorney Taylor often worked with on litigation cases in Ohio. Al was one of those tenacious, but cautious, civil rights attorneys who was like a bulldog once on a case.

"I'm here in Morgan City. City manager called me in."

"Tragic thing, that car crash. Is it true the chief was having an affair with the council woman?"

"Seems that way. Why did you ask that question, Al?"

"Friend of mine up in Canton had a sexual harassment case brought against the chief at his previous job. Small department of maybe thirty officers. My friend deposed him after he left and was already working in Morgan City. She found him charming, but sensed underneath he was a vicious snake." Al laughed with bluster and then continued. "Seems the case involved consensual sex with a young probationary officer. Anyway, the chief's wife saw his unmarked car at a local motel the middle of the day. Guess the sucker left his police radio on the front seat.

"Wife took the radio and drove off. For the next forty-five minutes she tooled all around town bad-mouthing her husband over the open mic, telling all sorts of sex stories about him. She wouldn't shut up. Now, the open mic ranting was broadcast to every small town cop shop in the county over the regional dispatch system. Her stories proved to be pretty popular listening until she was finally stopped by GPS tracking. Really surprised me when I heard Morgan City picked him up to be their chief."

"What's new, huh, Al? What happened on the case?"

"Settled. Heard about seventy-five thou passed hands. Probationary officer wasn't fired since the sex was consensual and all."

Taylor walked the few hundred yards to the Beverly Hills Supper Club. The owners had done a good job obscuring the obvious Pizza Hut identity, but the roofline gave it away. The inside was bright with plenty of natural wood trim, paintings of Western scenes, and an expanse of plants to make diners feel they were entering a private garden.

"You eating or just drinking?" a soft voice purred at his right. He turned to see a trim young woman wearing tight jeans and a peasant blouse hanging loose above her waist.

"Eating, but I don't mind sitting at the bar."

"So you're alone?"

"Yes, I am."

"Shame," she commented as her eyes gave Taylor the once over.

Taylor noted the bright tattoo spidering up her bare back until the blouse covered it.

The bar was empty with the exception of an older man somewhere in his seventies. Taylor mounted the exceptionally high stool that was necessary to reach the towering and ornate heavy wooden bar that was reminiscent of those found in Old West saloons. He sat two stools down from the old-timer who seemed out of place. The guy wore a black cowboy hat that Taylor knew was a Stetson "Boss of the Plains" model. The large hat hid most of his hair. It had a stiff, flat broad brim and a high crown with rounded, straight sides. The hatband was a triple strand comprised of bone and beads and looked authentic Native American Indian. The old timer's black cowboy shirt was fastened at the collar by a bolo with a large hand tooled silver oval.

"Fine hat, mister. Don't see too many wearing that style," Taylor offered.

The old man turned from the drink he was nursing and stared at Taylor. His was a longer than normal examination from Taylor's point of view.

"You're right, it is. Bet you don't know what kind it is."

"Boss of the Plains, mister."

A broad smile lit the lined face as the old man nodded.

"That's right. How'd you know?"

"Live in Santa Fe. Get to know things there. That hatband looks original. Get it from some Indian?"

"You a cowboy?"

"No, just a cowboy wannabe."

"Me too, fellow. Did you know Roy Rogers was from Ohio?"

"Didn't know that," Taylor lied.

"Yep. Born down in Cincinnati. Name was Leonard Franklin Slye. Can you imagine that?"

"And what do you do, Mister Cowboy?"

The old-timer smiled again. "I own this place. 'Course my boy, Ivan, runs it now. I just hang out since my little flower passed a year ago. Why you here?"

"Doing some work in the area."

"What kind of work? Don't look like you're into construction or anything like that."

"Looking into the police department business."

"Morgan City?"

"Yep."

"Sure needs some looking at. That new chief was no good."

"How so?"

"Women and arrogance. He'd come in here regularly with women. Some young. Some old. Didn't seem to matter to him. Always paid with an organization credit card. Never liked him. He'd hit on my hostess even when he was with another woman. Didn't like him at all. Tragic him with Emily. She and her husband used to come here all the time. Nice people, but I don't know what got into her."

"Unfortunately, that's the stuff I get involved in all the time. Tragedy. People getting hurt. But you know most cops are good people. Say, what's good to eat in your fine establishment? By the way, what's your name?"

"Petrus Gorigan." The supper club owner extended his hand across the empty bar stools. "If you're from out of state, order the Walleye."

Taylor upgraded his house salad to the Belgium endive with bacon infused vinaigrette dressing. He thought the bacon might overpower the delicate endive leaves, but was delightfully surprised when it didn't. As Petrus had predicted, the Walleye was superb. It came as a large filet dredged in egg wash, then rolled in pecan meal before being sautéed to a golden brown edged with a dark lace. Taylor wondered if his fish was caught that afternoon in a pond behind the restaurant since it was so fresh.

Taylor was almost finished with his meal when the hostess placed a simple white bowl in front of him. "Compliments of Mr. Gorigan. He was sorry he had to leave before you finished your meal. This is our house specialty dessert."

It was easy to see the bowl was filled with bread pudding, but the aroma hinted at surprises. Taylor quickly picked up on the pungent bourbon swirling through the butterscotch that circled the top of the pudding. Whole toasted pecans crowned the succulent dessert.

* * *

Karl Unger had completed the assignment Taylor had given him the day before. He had asked Karl to pull together a meeting with the police department's command staff. Three police commanders were waiting for Taylor at nine o'clock sharp. Taylor was directed to a room adjacent to the one that held the placard Chief of Police on its door. The large space was well equipped as a conference room with a long rectangular table commandeering the center of the room. Seven mesh backed armchairs and a larger padded desk chair circled the table. Four matching chairs flanked the wall. A large flat-screened TV filled one corner of the room while the opposite corner presented a white smart board fastened to the wall.

The three men seated at the table rose and shook Taylor's hand as introductions were made. Sid Small and Neil Crowder were wearing standard field uniforms for command officers—white long-sleeve shirts and black pants boasting a narrow gold stripe running down the sides.

Burt Munson was in a dark blue blazer, white button-down dress shirt knotted with a subdued striped tie, dark grey slacks and shiny black wing-tip shoes. The three men took back their seats and Taylor noticed the two uniforms sat opposite Burt Munson. Taylor pulled out one of the mesh chairs and sat next to Munson. The padded throne at the end of the table stayed vacant.

"Who's acting chief?" Taylor asked abruptly.

Neil raised his hand, but didn't add anything.

"Tragic about the accident. Any drugs or alcohol on board?"

Neil shook his head.

"You guys do talk, don't you?"

All three laughed in unison.

"I'm not here to bust your balls. Naturally there's a lot of concern expressed by folks inside the city and in your community. I understand many people thought very highly of Mrs. Stanton," Taylor continued as he purposefully and strategically omitted any reference to Chief Turner.

"Yes, she and her husband were very good to the department," Neil finally offered.

"I noticed you didn't mention Chief Turner, Mr. Sterling," Burt interjected.

Taylor noticed the quick glances between Neil and Sid.

"Burt, of course you're right. I didn't mean to diss your chief or anything like that. But, it seems strange that with the chief's death only ten days ago, officers aren't wearing black armbands or black ribbons over their badges. Why is that?"

Neil and Sid leaned back in their chairs and threw the ball to Burt. *Would he catch it?*

"I know those guys over there don't think much of me," Burt

said pointing across the table at Neil and Sid who both allowed a smirk to show. "I've been holding the shit end of the stick since I was the boss's hatchet man. I know that and everybody else knows it too. That's why Turner brought me in from the outside. Sure, I did his dirty work, but that was my job. I'm IA…the headhunter."

Taylor began his spiel. "Guys, I look at IA differently. If you do your job right, you protect everybody. If someone screws up, we can deal with that. Everybody gets treated with dignity, respect, and in a professional manner. If you've been doing it some other way," Taylor turned to face Burt squarely, "then somebody gets fucked."

Sid suddenly piped up, "Yep, and I think we've had too much…"

Taylor cut Sid off by raising his hand and interrupting the direction of the conversation. "Now's not the time to start pointing fingers, guys. We've got to get things in order. We have to find out what might have gone wrong. I can't stay here forever."

The three looked at each other as tension in the room subsided.

"What happened to Turner's personal effects, on his person and in the car? By the way, was it his personal car involved or a city issued vehicle?"

"Personal," Sid said. "The bodies were brought back to one of our local mortuaries. Emily's items were handed over to her husband. Her funeral was two days ago. We all went to the service at the Stanton's church. Nice service. Lots of relatives. Emily and her husband didn't have kids.

"Turner's body and his stuff are still at the mortuary. I'm not sure what his wife wants to do. Probably nothing. You know they weren't still married in the literal sense."

"We've been questioning whether the department should take over that end of this awkward situation, Taylor," Neil added.

Taylor was glad to see his first name had now been ushered into the discussion without prompting. It signaled the Morgan City boys were making him part of their team.

"You got any ideas, Taylor?" Sid asked.

"Not really. I'm most concerned about retrieving evidence that might have been collected by the Highway Patrol."

"Evidence?" Burt asked with surprise. "What kind of evidence do you think there might be?"

"Don't rightfully know, guys. Don't know what we're getting into with this matter. Unger is concerned there might be financial issues involved. I got a feeling he felt Turner was living a little large for his salary. Takes a heap of money to have as many affairs as he apparently was having."

"You sound like you're thinking something criminal was going on," Sid commented.

"Don't know; could be. I think we should consider it might be a criminal case until we discover we're wrong. We should go the warrant route."

"Normally we would get someone outside our police agency if we're doing a criminal investigation on one of our own, Taylor," Sid said.

"I would agree normally, but this time the targeted employee is dead. Besides, we can do it in a way to preserve the proper chain of evidence, just in case."

"Then, why worry?" Burt asked.

"Burt, we don't know where these cases might lead. I've been surprised in the past, haven't you?"

They all nodded.

"And, let's get that warrant to include Turner's office, where he's been living, the car he was driving, bank accounts, and any credit cards he had access to. Also include storage lockers he may have rented. You should throw in his phone records if we can't get information from the actual phones without going to the phone company for access."

"Shit, Taylor, I'm not certain I like where this is going," Sid sighed.

"It goes where it goes, guys. It goes where it goes."

* * *

"Ms. Blanchard, thanks for making time for me," Taylor said as he sat down at a desk piled high with folders and scattered papers. He noticed another dozen or so boxes stacked along one wall of the small office. "I'm sure you're buried," Taylor added as he shot a glance at the paper chaos.

"It's Sylvia, Taylor," the middle-aged woman said from behind her desk. She was wearing a plain, pleated silk blouse and he noticed dark blue linen slacks when she stood to acknowledge him.

"I'm not really prepared to conduct sexual harassment investigations, let alone three at one time. I'm the Human Resources person in Morgan City, not an EEOC expert."

"I gather the common denominator in all three cases is the deceased, Nat Turner?"

She nodded and continued, "I really can't discuss the specifics of the investigations, and you know that."

"Who are making the complaints? I've been told complaints might be coming from one of your dispatchers and a civilian clerical lady stationed in records. You have another one in addition to those two?"

"Apparently so. A young probationary officer."

"I gather Chief Turner was the type who never tried to hide the fact that he was still married."

"That's true. All the women knew that, but two thought they would be the woman who could win him over as an exclusive," she smiled. "Between you and me, there was a fat chance of that happening. His marriage, sham though it was, gave him an out when the ladies started pushing."

"Sylvia, did you have a relationship with Turner?"

She stammered and grasped her throat. "You *are* kidding, aren't you? The man was a pig, a loathsome pig. All sweet and condescending to your face, but that was a caricature he portrayed when he thought a good imitation of Cary Grant or George Clooney was required. He never tried anything with me!" She stiffened and gripped the arms of her chair.

"Have any of the women actually filed a lawsuit?"

"Not yet. Seems remote that they will. It was consensual sex with all of them and none seems to have suffered a loss or job alteration."

"How about the volunteer woman?"

"I doubt she'll do anything. She's battling to put her marriage back together."

"Sylvia, thank you for making time for me. Guys like me come on the scene and sometimes try to pack too much into a few days on site. You've helped me understand one aspect of this incident. It's like so many other cases when multiple issues and innuendos come into play."

Taylor left the Human Relations office feeling somewhat relieved. It seems sexual harassment was an issue of concern for people serving in the police department, but had minimal impact in the total picture.

* * *

"Mr. Sterling, got a second?" a voice called from the open door of the office Taylor was using in City Hall. He had selected a place to work far away from the police department to avoid wandering eyes and ears.

Mike Able was the detective Neil Crowder had assigned to help Taylor with legwork. Taylor had asked for a detective with the most years in the department, but who still had a passion for the job. Mike was nearing fifty, overweight, and should have shaved the few remaining wisps of hair remaining on top of his head.

"Didn't get much from the car, boss," Mike admitted. Taylor enjoyed watching the way Mike slipped into his role. He particularly liked that he called him "boss." It made Taylor feel he had become part of the police department.

"But, a couple of items piqued my curiosity."

He tossed three sealed evidence envelopes and a photograph on the small conference table Taylor was using as a desk. The photograph showed two boxes of condoms lying in the car's trunk. Taylor picked up one of the sealed evidence envelopes and flattened it on the tabletop to better see the document housed inside the clear plastic. It appeared to be a lodging receipt. The second envelope was a handwritten list on a three by five index card.

"Mike, what do you make of this index card?"

"To me it looks like a series of passwords. I have a bitch of a time remembering passwords myself. Keep forgetting the sequence or I use the same words over and over, which I know, is stupid. I've got no idea what Turner might have used them for."

"We'll have to wait and see what files we get into, Mike. Tell me about this other envelope."

"It's from a B&B in Canada. A place called Chatham-Kent. Small town on the banks of Erie. Got to go through the tunnel in Detroit to get there. Well, I guess you could take a ferry, but that would take a lot of time.

"I called the B&B, boss. Nice lady answered. She got choked up when I told her about the traffic accident and the deaths. Accident happened the day the chief and Emily checked out it seems. The lady said they were a nice, quiet couple and thought they were another happily married couple from the States spending quality time with each other. Enjoyed eating out at different restaurants and they loved telling her all about each meal they had. She laughed when she said if had she been twenty years younger, she'd go after the man. She referred to him as 'luscious.' The lady who ran the place was surprised that he paid with a strange credit card."

"Was it their first time at the B&B?"

"No, she said they had been there twice before."

"Mike, I need you to find out Turner's schedule for the past year. Identify the days he took off as well as the ones he was out of the office on business. Make sure you note what he was supposed to be doing. You may have to get access to his calendar. We were able to obtain his smart phones, weren't we?"

"Yes, we found three, boss. One agency issued, one personal, and another one I haven't been able to place yet."

* * *

"Shamus O'Brien," a rusty Irish brogue bellowed over the phone.

"Shamus, still hard for me to get through to you. Don't know much French and I don't think your people understand my California accent," Taylor laughed after maneuvering through censuring by various clerical personnel at the Surete au Quebec, the provincial police of Quebec.

"Taylor Sterling! You in Montreal?"

Taylor met Shamus at a police training conference nearly fifteen years before. The training concerned managing special operations units. Taylor maintained his relationship with the Irishman over the years with telephone calls a few times a year and occasional visits to Montreal. The city was one of Taylor's favorites, particularly the old section. The food was varied and excellent with a definite French flavor. Asian cuisine of all kinds was readily available, and there were, surprisingly, quite a few vegetarian restaurants.

The first time Taylor traveled to Montreal was in a cold January. It was horrifically frigid in the city, but the catacombs of walkways under the downtown proper made strolling easy, even with snow swirling and the harsh wind biting noses with a vengeance outside. Taylor remembered the next time he visited when he coordinated his trip so he could attend the Montreal Francofolies, a plethora of French music from jazz to reggae to blues to zydeco, and all genres between.

Shamus was a third generation Canadian. His family migrated directly from Ireland before the turn of the 19th century. When Shamus used French, his Irish brogue dropped to just a whisper. Canada had become a mecca for the displaced from many foreign and non-French speaking countries. Of course, Shamus had an uphill battle getting selected to serve in the Surete, but now he was a staff inspector and a respected member of the elite police unit.

"No, unfortunately I'm not in your wonderful city. Say, how are your kids? Six of them, isn't that right?"

"Right you are, Taylor. My oldest boy is with the RCMP stationed in God forsaken Newfoundland. He hates the assignment, but loves the job. Still single, so that uniform is like a magnet for the girls. Oldest daughter is third year at McGill. Eighteen-year-old just moved in with her boyfriend, a minor league hockey player. You can guess how excited I am about that. Still got three at home; all in Catholic school so that's driving me further away from any thought of retirement. What brings you calling, my friend?"

"I'm down in Ohio doing some consulting work for a small city with big police problems."

"And how can your French ami help?"

"I've got a police chief who was having an extra-marital affair," Taylor started.

Before he could finish his comment Shamus interjected, "And what's the problem? Love takes many strange turns. Why does a love affair bring you all the way from Santa Fe, Taylor?"

"The chief and his paramour died in a car crash coming home from their latest tryst in Canada. I'm hoping you can help with your contacts, specifically your border people. Need to know the number of times and dates the chief may have made entry, probably through the Windsor tunnel."

"That's a long way from Quebec, Taylor."

"I figure you've got a computer system that can compress the distance."

"I do, and I can do. When do you need it?"

"Day or two?"

Shamus whistled as if this was an enormously complicated request, then laughed and said, "But, no problem for you my good Yankee friend."

Taylor gave him Turner's full name, vehicle plate number, driver's license information, and passport number.

* * *

Taylor made arrangements with Neil Crowder to get a night ride-along with a beat officer. It was nearly six and he had an hour to spend before they were expecting him at the station. Taylor wasn't really hungry, but he knew he needed something in his belly, knowing full well you could never anticipate what might happen once he got in the cop car.

The Morgan City Diner was crammed between a furniture store and second hand clothing store. The furniture store was one where $999 could buy a complete living room or bedroom set. The furniture might last through the last payment if luck was with you. The clothing store looked a little more upscale. "Delicately pre-worn designer clothing" the sign in the window proudly purred.

The diner was an original Worcester Lunch Car, at least that's what the back page of the menu touted. The diner craze began in the nineteenth century in Worcester, Massachusetts. The inside of the car was honed in rich, deep-hued wooden shades from years of service and clouds of cooking. The ceiling was made of curved wooden panels anchored by a ring of hidden lights beaming upward. Eight wooden booths along one side were armed with brass hooks on posts to collect coats, hats, and umbrellas. A long counter separated diners from the cooks. Taylor picked the counter for his dining spot, swung a stool outward, and slipped in. The counter was Formica, crisscrossed with more than one deep gouge where a knife had slipped.

Two women appeared to be running the whole operation efficiently. A stocky woman with a severely masculine haircut ending in a long rat-tail tasseled down her back was busily working a double griddle, four burners, and two deep fryers.

Her movements appeared to be a choreographed dance as she added and subtracted the makings of meals on her cook tops and loaded plates lined on the wooden ledge atop the cooking area.

Her waitressing partner was tall and slender. She wore a black T-shirt and jeans under a heavy black apron. Her arms were well toned from either flinging hash at the diner or pointed free weight exercises.

"See something good, mister?"

"Maybe…Edna," Taylor replied, noticing the name embroidered on her apron. "I'm not from around these parts. What's this Cincinnati-style chili?"

Her smile was broad and exposed almost too perfect lines of teeth. "Well, we got our own take on chili in most parts of Ohio. No beans, not one. We load it on spaghetti and top it with grated Cheddar cheese. You can get onions on the top, if you want. We got something most places don't offer though. We can give you a blend of Asiago, Gouda, and Cheddar cheeses. It's our little twist on the Cincinnati specialty. We also add a couple pieces of toasted sourdough bread on the side, instead of the basic boring Midwest white."

"You convinced me to give your Morgan City Diner version a shot, Edna," Taylor said smiling back. Taylor figured Edna and her cook were partners. Certainly didn't bother him.

The chili was good, almost excellent, and the cheese blend was interesting. He thought about asking for a bottle of hot sauce, but reconsidered. It might not be proper after hearing the pride Edna exuded in her vivid description of the dish.

"So?" Edna asked as Taylor soaked up the last bits of chili with a final sliver of bread.

"Very good! Got a new convert, Edna."

Smiling again, she inquired, "What's a guy like you doing in Morgan City eating chili at dinner time?"

"Working."

"What kind of work, fella?"

"I'm a police consultant."

"Hmm. Imagine you're looking into that terrible accident. Emily Stanton was a fine lady. Helped me and Sadie out on licensing problems with the city now and then. Don't know what she saw in that Turner guy. He was just downright nasty. Came in here once and that was the last time."

Sadie spun around with spatula in hand and added fiercely, "He said something ugly about me being gay. Edna took the plate right out from under his fork and told him to haul his skinny ass out. I remember him saying something like, 'You bitches ought to be careful. I can put the hurt on you.' But the bastard never did."

* * *

Sergeant Thames was in the watch commander's office when Taylor threaded his way past the security systems. Thames was in his fifties, a little overweight and fairly grey on the head. He was busy looking over police reports on his expansive computer monitor. Reading glasses were perched on the bridge of his nose ready to pounce on unsuspecting words. He turned when he sensed someone standing nearby. Good cops have a knack for that.

"So you're the guy the city hired to do some snooping, huh?" Taylor shook his head and stuck out his hand.

"Still can't get used to reading police reports on a screen. Guess I'm one of those old farts who remember the good old days when paper ruled. Do old-timers ever get used to reading on this contraption?"

"Eventually you'll master it, sarge. I had trouble at first but got over it and now I really like not having all that clutter and weight spilling over my desk."

"It's Jim. You go by Taylor?" Taylor nodded his head affirmatively. "What you interested in seeing on your ride along?

"Let's talk some first, Jim."

The sergeant leaned back in his swivel desk chair. Questioning eyes suddenly pierced through Taylor. Thames was definitely on the defensive.

"Maybe, Taylor. But I'm no snitch. I'm going to be here long after you fly back to wherever you make your home these days. Morgan City will still be standing and so will I. How do I know you're some kind of righteous guy?"

"You don't, but check me out if you have questions. Give me a chance. I have no stake in Morgan City. I always call 'em as I see 'em, and never sway because somebody is footing my bill. All I've got is my professional reputation, just like you. You willing to sell your reputation, Jim? How much would you take? I'm guessing there's no price on you and you're not for sale." Taylor stopped his spiel, grabbed a chair from against the wall, and plopped himself down.

"We'll see," Thames uttered as a slight smile twisted the corners of his mouth.

"What kind of boss was Turner?"

"He sure wasn't a Stanley Topson," Thames said

"How so?"

"Topson was like your father, brother, or best friend. He knew everybody on the job and knew their families, too. Every cop knew exactly what Topson demanded on the job. He was fair, but didn't flinch when he had to fire someone. Turner wasn't, and that's about all I'm going to say about the recently departed."

Thames folded his arms tightly across his chest, emphasizing his final statement.

"What about that Byron Jones kid?"

"You always so pointed, Taylor?" Thames asked grinning broadly. "Jones fucked up. Maybe we could have salvaged him, who knows? Maybe we coulda put him in some kind of rehab. The guy apparently got hooked on painkillers. But, having said that, we fucked up the investigation. I doubt the DA can get his case past motions to exclude the pills we collected from Byron's car. We really botched the whole investigation."

"You mean Chief Turner did?"

"I was there, too. We all botched it up. I thought about interceding, but you didn't do that with Turner. 'His way or the highway' crap. All the while this is happening, the chief's into shit up to his eyeballs. Two faced bastard, but you didn't hear that from me, Taylor!"

"What about this guy Avery?"

"Shaun, you mean? Solid officer. Solid person."

"Seems he was in the middle of everything, right?"

"That's Shaun. He never turns away from a problem. Say, he's working tonight. You should ride with him if you're interested in getting a real look at the shit we sometimes have to wade through."

Taylor walked out the back door of the police station to find a waiting black Chevy Tahoe. The Tahoe's front doors were painted glossy white and awkward, uneven block lettering proclaimed, MORGAN CITY POLICE. Under that was printed the motto, *Policing with Pride.* The driver's door opened and a uniformed cop jumped out. Shaun Avery was small, stretching to reach five eight. He had the taunt, compact build of a runner or gymnast. Bright red hair and a face full of freckles gave him a boyish look.

"Sarge says you want to ride with me, huh?"

"Yep. Hear you're always in the middle of anything and everything that happens in Morgan City," Taylor said as he offered his hand. Shaun's grip was firm but unassuming, showing the man had nothing to prove.

The Tahoe was a welcome ride over Chargers or Malibus usually used as cop cars. Those beasts were packed with electronic gear, computers, and videos that made the ride uncomfortable. Extreme agility was needed to wiggle into the smaller cars. The Tahoe was filled with the usual gear, but the passenger seat was broad and empty waiting for a human to fill it. Taylor climbed in and swung the seat belt across his chest.

Unit 26...fight at Smalley's...27 will provide back up.

"We're 27, Mr. Sterling. Smalley's is a blue-collar bar across the tracks in Coon Bottom. Not my name; been that for years."

Shaun's unit arrived about the same time as Morgan City 26 pulled up. The driver got out, hitched up her equipment belt, slid a PR24 baton into the ring dangling on the belt, and threw an acknowledgment signal at Shaun.

"Betty Baker. Good solid cop. A talker like me," Shaun told Taylor.

Both officers were slow to approach the front of the bar. It was a small building in need of serious painting. Narrow windows under the eaves were filled with neon beer signs, giving the building a weirdly festive look.

The front door suddenly swung open as loud, heavy sounds from James Brown assaulted ears like gusts of wind. Raucous yelling created back-up for the wailing Mr. Brown.

"Best not rush in," an elderly black warned from his station chair by the door. "Dey be fighting over some whore."

"Guns? Knives? What they got in hand, mister?" Betty demanded as she stepped back and to one side of the door.

"No guns that'n I sees, officer. One's holding a carpet knife. Other fella gots a straight edge. Ain't seen one of dem in years. Cuts ya before you knows it and ya won't even feel it 'til you bleed out. Nasty!" The old black stood, turned, and shuffled into the crowd.

Smalley's was more like a social club than a bar. It was simply a large room with tables scattered around and folding chairs wherever they could be placed. Wall lamps gave the room a muted glow. At the back of the room was a simple wooden barrier surfaced with a narrow top. The wall behind the barrier was festooned with more neon beer signs that seemed to pulsate to the musical beat. Above the barrier an industrial fluorescent fixture illuminated the two people standing behind it.

Like so many social club bars in black communities, beer and wine were kept in large Coleman-style coolers against the wall behind the divider. Racks of chips, pork skins, and nuts stood like colorful columns anchoring the bar. Two large glass containers filled with opaque pink liquid cradled dozens of white hardboiled eggs that seemed to bounce to the rhythm of the bass blaring from an enormous pair of speakers.

The place still carried the Smalley name although Reginald Smalley had been in his grave for nearly ten years. He was shot accidently while trying to break up a fight between patrons. Vera and Edgar Black took over the bar and had been trying to make a go of the place ever since. Most who entered Smalley's knew a stash of liquor, usually bourbon and scotch, was hidden someplace. The bar's license covered only beer and wine. The place might have been a throwback to prohibition days.

At least twice a year state liquor enforcement officers would descend on Smalley's and find more than enough violations to cost Vera and Edgar several hundred dollars in fines. After each inspection, the front door would be slapped with a yellow sign announcing 'Suspended Premise' and padlocked for a week. For the most part, Smalley's didn't add many pins to the Morgan City police crime map.

Betty and Shaun entered the front door and sidestepped to opposite sides of the doorway. Taylor remained outside, but leaned forward so he could take a look into the bar. Six people were huddled on the left side of the room using upended tables as shields. A female and male were standing behind the barrier, backlit with the reds and blues of the beer signs flashing behind them.

In the center of the room, two middle-aged black men circled each other menacingly. One man was wearing dress slacks and a dark grey luminous shirt. Silver chains around his neck flickered as they twisted with his moves. He held a curved carpet knife in one hand and kept brandishing it to the right and left. A dark, heavy stain was spreading across his shirt.

The other male was much shorter and had a stocky build. He was also in dress slacks but wore a white starched short-sleeved shirt. A heavy piece of clothing wrapped around his left arm that crossed his torso. His right hand was held close to his waist and an extended straight edge razor protruded between his thumb and forefinger. The blade danced under the neon hues. He was obviously the more skilled knife fighter.

"Cut him, Jacob, cut him hard!" a voice screeched from the crowd.

"Stay back, Ditto...Jacob got that razor of his," another voice bellowed.

"Jacob, that bitch ain't worth going back to jail fer," a booming voice called.

"Poleece here, boys, five-oh here *now!*" the male behind the barrier yelled.

The two circling men were oblivious to the chants of the crowd or the sudden presence of two cops. Knife Man incessantly jabbed the curved tip of his carpet knife at his opponent between swipes across his body. Razor Man shuffled in position, never dropping his wrapped arm or moving the razor from its protected side perch.

Betty took another step into the bar, slid her PR24 baton from the holder and grasped the protruding short handle. She slammed it repeatedly on one of the upended tables. Her snappy movements produced a staccato of sounds reminiscent of a snare drum that was not stretched taunt.

"POLICE! Drop your knives," commanded Shaun from the right side of the room. "POLICE! Do it now!"

Both men stopped dancing, backed up a pace, and turned to stare at the two officers they suddenly realized were taking charge of Smalley's. Taylor noticed Shaun had his handgun out and held it along the back of his thigh. Betty had slipped her baton back into its ring and traded it for a yellow Taser now in her right hand. Its laser sight cast a stream of scarlet as it bounced across the front of Razor Man's starched white shirt.

The carpet knife clattered to the floor and lay between both men. Razor Man's fingers moved slightly and the straight edge suddenly disappeared. He spun the blade into the handle and simply dropped it into his pocket and held his hands shoulder height as if nothing had happened.

From his secreted vantage point in the open doorway, Taylor saw the straight edge disappear. He wasn't sure the officers had witnessed the sleight of hand since it had happened so fast. Taylor opted to hold back with the announcement until the two fighters were controlled and handcuffed, but kept a watchful eye on the knife positioned on the floor and the guy wearing the white shirt.

"Both of you, down on the floor!" Shaun commanded.

"Man, the floor's dirty. Ah gots my best pants on!" Razor Man complained.

"On the floor, assholes!"

Both men slowly dropped to their knees, then to their hands, finally lowering themselves onto the floor. Without being told, they interlaced their hands behind their heads. They had been through this drill before, Taylor thought. Shaun holstered his gun and moved closer to the guy in the white shirt while Betty kept her Taser targeted on both men as Shaun handcuffed each with hands behind their backs.

During the handcuffing process, a male from the group huddled behind the tables slowly began moving toward the action on the floor. Taylor took a few steps into the bar and moved to intercept the man as he dipped in an attempt to collect the carpet knife on the floor. Taylor slipped his hand inside his waist-length windbreaker as if he was reaching for a gun. Of course he didn't have one, but the guy didn't know that.

"Back off, fella, and leave that knife be," Taylor ordered. Betty jerked her head in the direction of the unfamiliar voice but Shaun held up his hand to signal Betty that things were okay.

"No need to go for your gun, officer," the male said as he straightened up and shuffle-footed back into the crowd.

Shaun finished ratcheting the cuffs on Razor Man.

"Shaun, better turn that other dude over quickly," Betty shouted.

Betty had noticed the widening pool of dark liquid spreading from under the suspect. When Shaun turned Knife Man over, the front of his silk shirt was soaked with blood. The shirt had been neatly severed across its lower half from both sides. The suspect's dark skin could be glimpsed through the sharp gap. Pink shades of the fallen guy's stomach pockmarked the darkness of his skin while an opaque tubular mass of intestine was beginning to protrude from the deep gash across his midsection. The straight edged razor had done what it did best—slice.

"Vera! Vera, get me a load of towels!" Betty yelled. Shaun was on his radio ordering an ambulance.

"What's wrong?" Knife Man asked. He had no idea his innards were exposed.

"Motherfuck," one in the crowd cried out. "He belly been splayed open by the other nigger's razor. Looks like a gutted catfish. Shit! Dat bad."

"Jacob, you be in a shitload of trouble now," another voice from the crowd added.

"Shaun, the guy dropped his straight edge into his right front pants' pocket," Taylor whispered into Shaun's ear as he turned to help Betty.

Shaun grabbed a napkin from the floor that had fallen when the tables were upended. He reached for Razor Man's pocket and yanked it violently. The seams gave way, exposing the mother of pearl handle razor. Shaun used the napkin to grab it and then wrapped the weapon in an unused towel Vera had piled on the floor.

"Hang onto this," Shaun ordered as he gave the wrapped evidence to Taylor.

Shit, now I'm in the chain of custody, Taylor thought.

Taylor made the coffee run to Dunkin' Donuts and returned with brews for Betty and Shaun. Both officers were busy completing the crime report, probable cause affidavit for arrests, arrest report, and evidence sheet. It would take them awhile.

"Got that I'm the one taking custody of the razor, Mr. Sterling. City can't afford to bring you back. Anyway, we got more than enough wits that saw him, and put the damn straight edge in Jacob's hand. Agg assault since Reggie Stanford, aka Ditto, isn't gonna die. Betty or me get a scratch during a fight and we'd probably croak."

"Sarge said you'd get me in the thick of whatever might be going on, and that you did," Taylor threw out jokingly.

"No lie. That's my life. Try to do the right thing and I always seem to step right into the shit. Like that fight between a couple cops a few weeks ago. Wasn't my problem, but I still got three days suspension. Hell, I tried to stop it from getting out of hand," Shaun complained.

"I heard it did get out of hand though."

Shaun broke into uncontrolled laughter at Taylor's comment. "Damn right it did! Had three cops crying their eyes out, snot pouring out of their noses, faces burning like a son of a bitch, and there stands Cool Hand Thames shaking his OC spray can in case they needed another burst.

"I looked over and saw a crowd laughing, hooting, and hollering while three or four aimed their cell phones at us letting that video crank away. We were instant stars on YouTube. Guess I had some time coming after that. Sure embarrassed the job. Really didn't give a shit about Chief Turner. He's nothing but a two-faced ass, if you ask me."

Taylor liked what he saw in Shaun Avery. He was a cop who enjoyed the *work* of being a cop, not like so many others who simply enjoyed the *position* of being a cop. Those guys like the uniform, badge, authority, and power. Shaun truly seemed to enjoy doing the job. He seemed to be a guy who didn't pussy foot around or run away from problems, instead he faced them head on. Shaun was a cop without pretense.

"What about the rest home incident, Shaun?"

A scowl shadowed his face as his laughter evaporated. "Yes, sir. Now, I got a real raw deal on that one. Chief Turner gave me a seven-day suspension. Union and me won't stand for that or any discipline like it. Our grievance took the normal route and it's now scheduled for arbitration. I did the right thing on that one. I got the old man calmed down. We were talking. No threat. Then the damn hotshot rushes in and takes the old man down with a beanbag. No need for that, and I told him so."

Shaun dropped his head and shook it slowly. "No, I done the right thing, Mr. Sterling." Now he was back looking Taylor square.

"I won't lie to you, I didn't like the chief. Pompous guy. Understand he had his dick into every willing hole around here. Not my problem, though. I'm not sorry he's gone, but I wouldn't wish how it happened on anyone. The asshole took down a right nice lady; that council lady, with him. But, he did me wrong! If Commander Neil or Sid is made the new chief, or even acting the position, bet they'll rescind my disciplinary action. It just wasn't right."

Taylor left Betty and Shaun an hour later after he made a final coffee run for the cops who now were working overtime. He felt good about these two cops. However, that old uncomfortable feeling Taylor often sensed when things were running amuck told him he would find out a lot more about Chief Turner than he initially assumed. He hoped his search to uncover the extent of the man's misconduct wouldn't take others down. But, it usually did.

* * *

"Mr. Sterling, got a second?" Burt Munson approached Taylor as he pulled into a parking stall on the far side of City Hall.

Burt was a tall, lanky man with sandy hair that flew all over his head. He always wore the same ensemble—a dark blue blazer, white button-down dress shirt knotted with a subdued striped tie, dark grey slacks and shiny black wing-tip shoes.

"Sure, Burt. Come into the room I'm using while I'm poking around."

"Rather not, Mr. Sterling," Burt whispered as he glanced furtively around the parking lot. "Can you meet me at the Dunkin' Donuts on Main?"

Taylor agreed, but then realized he didn't have a clue if he should turn right or left when he got to Main Street. Right was the easier turn, so it was his pick. Two blocks down he spotted the familiar orange and brown awning announcing Dunkin' Donuts. Burt was already seated at a booth at the back of the store. He got up as Taylor approached.

"Didn't know how you take your coffee."

"Black, no sugar," Taylor said as he slid on the bench opposite where Burt had parked himself. Taylor chuckled as he remembered his first visit to a Dunkin' Donuts shop when he ordered a regular coffee. He was served a mug loaded with cream and double sugar, the "standard regular" since the chain's birth in New England.

Burt popped the lid off his coffee, shook the corners of the three sugar packets in his right hand and tore the tops off all three with one motion, allowing the white granules to escape into the steaming dark liquid. Burt stirred the cup in a ritualistic manner, a sure sign he had a serious touch of OCD or was stalling for some reason.

Burt launched into a game of twenty questions touching on

everything from Taylor's time with the LAPD to the artsy life-style of Santa Fe. When he segued into the world of hobbies, Taylor raised his hand.

"Burt, knock off the bullshit banter. What do you really want to talk about?"

Burt took two sips of his coffee, set the cup down, and launched into a monologue. "Don't know how much you know about me. Chief Turner approached me about four months after he was hired by Morgan City. I was a sergeant serving a couple towns over. Don't know how or why he zeroed in on me, but I was impressed with the man. I was stuck in my job with little room for upward movement. The chief offered me the rank of commander and a raise. Of course, I jumped at the offer."

"What did the chief want from you, Burt?"

"Loyalty. I remember he made a point of using that word over and over. Said he didn't think he could trust the other two department commanders. Felt like they might try to sabotage him since they had been passed over for his job."

"And?"

"Found myself stuck again, but in a more tenuous way."

Taylor didn't respond. He wanted to hear what was coming next without breaking Burt's train of thought.

"Mr. Sterling, I despised the man, Turner, that is. Womanizer, arrogant, and something else."

Taylor waited. He was really getting good at this role.

"I don't think Turner was an honest man. I found out pretty quick he was using me as his bad guy, his hatchet man. So there I was, stuck between a man I was learning to hate and the rest of the guys who thought I was a brown-noser asshole."

Burt stopped his story to tend to his cooling coffee.

"Give me a few examples, Burt."

"Well, the chief had three phones. One was the official city phone, one was his personal phone, and then there was an iPhone that I'm not sure what it was used for. He had at least two checkbooks for police operations. One was connected to a community action grant and the other was for a charity the department created. Never knew exactly what they were for and never saw the statements or accountings. Shortly after I signed on, the chief pulled the department out of the area-wide HIDTA task force to create our own small street narcotics group. He picked the four guys to be in narco without input from the rest of the department."

"And what did you think was going on?"

"I think he may have been using money for his own little slush fund, Mr. Sterling. But that's just my opinion. Got no evidence to back it up."

Taylor sensed Burt was trying to distance himself from Chief Turner and whatever was happening under the table. Taylor suspected Burt probably knew a lot more than he was telling. It would all come out in the end most likely.

"Tell me about Officer Jones, Burt. The cop who's being prosecuted for drug use and was fired by Chief Turner."

Burt looked like a deer caught in the headlights; he obviously hadn't expected this question. His mouth opened, but he avoided a quick response. He picked up his cup and raised it to his mouth, but didn't take a sip. Taylor thought he could hear the gears in the guy's head beginning to crank.

"I thought the chief acted precipitously on that one. Not that Jones deserved any special treatment. Hell, he was a frigging thief! Most likely a pill head on top of that. I tried to slow the chief down when his ranting got the best of him, but he was geared up for blood. Jumped on that officer and probably fucked up the case when he did, if you ask me."

"How do you think Turner compromised the case, Burt?"

"Jumped the gun. Mixed the administrative case with the potential criminal offense. Young cop probably didn't know what to do. Sergeant Thames tried to get Chief Turner to slow down and think before he took action, but with Turner you could go only so far before he'd jump on your ass. Vindictive bastard. Had a long memory, too. I was his IA guy and I know he screwed up. But, what could I do, huh?"

"What should have happened?" Taylor asked. He wanted to see if Burt was familiar with the proper course of action when dealing with an administrative and criminal matter affecting the same case.

"I think it was okay to have Thames search the police car in the parking lot, but not Jones' personal vehicle. There's a reasonable expectation that we aren't going to do something like that to the guy's personal car, especially when an officer might be facing a possible criminal charge. Turner was wrong telling me to get Jones' keys and do that search. Me being the IA guy and all. Jones wasn't going anywhere. Should have gotten a warrant, if you ask me."

"Why didn't you say that, Burt?"

"What could I do, Mr. Sterling?"

"As the IA guy you got to protect everybody, Burt. The boss, the cop, the department, and the city. You got a pair of balls or do you need to grow them, Burt?"

Burt started to answer, but stopped short as his words morphed into glares. He didn't like what Taylor was insinuating.

"Yeah, what would you have done?"

"Stepped in and done the right thing, Burt." Taylor knew Burt was feeling pressed by the questions and his stress level was elevating rapidly.

"Why do you think Turner wanted out of the HIDTA operation?" Taylor asked, attempting to redirect Burt's focus.

It took a few seconds for Burt to calm himself and realize he was being asked about something else.

"Control, Mr. Sterling, it's all about control. Turner couldn't control what the task force was doing, who they were targeting, and what they were doing with the two guys we assigned to them."

"Didn't Morgan City get its fair share of seizures?"

"I guess, but Turner wanted it all. That's why he appointed special reserve officers."

"What special reserve officers, Burt?"

"He had a couple retired officers who lived in Florida and a PI living in Seaside, California. He gave them a badge and a pocketful of flash money and assigned them to work narcotic deals there. If the local cops made a bust, we got our share of the money. Actually, I think we got a couple big pops outta their work."

"Where did the money go, Burt?"

"Beats me, Mr. Sterling. I sure didn't see any of it. Guess the chief kept it. Must have funneled it into a fund, but I doubt he gave it to the Morgan City general fund." Burt laughed at the thought.

"Glad you reached out to me, Burt. You gave me valuable information. I can see why Turner liked to have you around." Taylor fawned at Burt, trying to sound honest and impressed. Taylor considered Burt to be a pussy and would do whatever Turner told him to do, and probably a little more. Taylor had suspicions about Burt, but tucked his thoughts in the back of his mind for the time being.

* * *

Taylor checked e-mail on his Apple laptop and saw one had arrived from Shamus O'Brien.

Well, friend, you owe me. Guess that means we'll see each other again soon, huh? Your chief came through the border checkpoint at Windsor eight times in the past year. Same car and registered to him. Same lady friend riding shotgun. I've attached the exact dates of the entries and exits. You can open an Excel spreadsheet, right? Of course you can, you're a big time consultant now! Stay well, friend! Shamus

Taylor printed out the spreadsheet and set out to find Mike Able's office in the police building. Taylor dropped the spreadsheet on Mike's desk after exchanging hellos.

"These are the Canadian comings and goings of Turner and the councilwoman. Check them against the timekeeping records Turner submitted. Did you find anything about those phones?" Taylor asked, noticing three cell phones lined in a row on the desk.

"Learned something, boss. Gave them to one of our in-house geek experts, a sixteen-year-old Police Explorer Scout." Mike smiled at the thought that teen-agers seemed innately attuned to this new world of gadgets.

"He pretty much confirmed that the Blackberry was the city-issued data device with mostly job-related shit on it, including a detailed contact file.

"His old flip version, hardly see those babies these days, appeared to be his personal phone listing his wife's number and not much else.

"But, this fancy Verizon package is different. Got a bunch of contacts I don't know, with the exception of Emily Stanton and, based on the EEOC complaint I hear is in the hopper, the three other women the chief was fucking are on it. Several other females were on file, some with local numbers. Other contacts showed numbers in the area code where Turner last worked. Bunch of other contacts I know nothing about. I thought we should send the Verizon phone out for a forensic examination. We can get his text messages with a warrant. Know anyone who works on these devices?"

"Actually I do, Mike. A company down in Indianapolis," Taylor admitted as he pulled out his iPhone and fingered a number. "I'll tell them I needed it yesterday and maybe they'll put my request on the front burner."

"Rubbers came from Wal-Mart according to the receipt in the bag. Didn't figure I'd pursue that with the volume of skins that comes and goes from that store. None of the phones had risqué photos or macho selfies on them. That surprised me. Usually these horny types keep trophies. By the way, found out the chief had a small storage locker at a place near the Interstate. I was fixin' to go out there this afternoon. Want to tag along?"

"No, Mike. You can handle that. Look for stuff that might help our case. Videotape your search from opening to closing… but you know that. Make sure you fill out the warrant service return with a copy of the evidence report. Leave anything else, but you better put an evidence seal on the door. Tell them the city will be good for any additional charges."

* * *

Edna smiled when Taylor entered the Morgan City Diner with Sid and Neil in uniform close behind. "Not here to arrest me are you, Taylor?" Sadie turned from her griddle to check out the threesome.

"Do I need to give you the police discount now?" Sadie asked with a broad smile.

"Nope, I don't believe in that old school stuff, Sadie. Just having coffee with a couple of my new friends like you and Edna," Taylor answered, sliding into the booth at the rear of the diner. He wanted Sid and Neil to meet him away from the station where ears were everywhere.

"You know these ladies, Taylor?" Sid asked.

"Nope, just met them the other day."

"Seems they like you."

"Hey, most people like me, Sid. What's not to like?"

"My experience with consultants tells me you guys can be brutal."

"True, and I can be. One thing you'll find, I don't have time to pussy foot around."

"And what's on your mind today?" Neil asked.

"What financial accounts does the department have that Turner would have had access to?"

Neil and Sid exchanged glances.

Sid offered, "Shortly after the chief arrived, he ended the department's involvement with the area HIDTA drug unit. We'd been providing two guys and think they put two or three thousand dollars in the unit's operational kitty. We got a lot more back from seizures. They weren't the most active unit, but it was an okay return for us. Turner insisted we could do better on our own so he set us up with a departmental unit. Not sure how well we did since the chief never shared results with me or Neil."

"Ever do an audit of the confidential monies fund?"

"Nope, not that I know. You ever hear of one, Neil?" His partner shook his head.

"Who's in charge of that unit?"

"Burt heads it up. Strange thing I heard, they had a couple alleged reserve officers working cases in strange locations. Once

Burt let slip that at least one officer lived in Florida. Don't know what they could do out of state. What do you think was going on, Taylor?"

"Could be giving leads to local drug units. If they developed them, they would be in line for some of the seizures. Big money in drug units these days. Lots of unexplained cash floating around. Property like cars, planes, boats, houses, and buildings are another matter. A paper trail is needed for those seizures. But actual folding money can be a little slippery," Taylor explained. "Any others?"

Neil piped up. "We've got a PAL program. One of those youth athletic things. Get some funding from community groups and I think maybe the United Way."

"How's that maintained?"

"Oh, there's a board of community bigwigs that run it. One member was that nice looking rich broad Turner was poking. Took her to the IACP convention this past year and caused quite a stir when the other broad he was screwing found out about it. She was pissed and wrote some pretty caustic things on Facebook." Neil and Sid laughed.

"Then there's that grant we got from COPS, a community action grant from the Feds. You know, trying to enlist the business community to help with crime prevention. There was a governing board on that one, too."

"Headed up by Emily Stanton, poor woman," Sid interjected.

"Either of you guys have anything to do with those programs?" Both shook their heads.

"Turner and Burt kept those pretty much to themselves," Neil offered.

Taylor thanked them for their time and slid out. He dropped two dollars on the table and moved to the cash register, peeling off a five.

"Let me get it, Taylor," Sid said.

"No, got to keep up my good rapport with these fine two ladies."

Outside Sid whispered, "You know they're a couple? Lesbians, that is."

"And your point is, Sid?"

Sid elected not to answer and he and Neil got into their police car and drove off.

More complications as the tentacles of misconduct creep further into the police department. Budgets and bottom lines were not his forte and the new funding revelations would take someone with a head for numbers to figure out.

* * *

Taylor was in the City Hall parking lot heading back to his office when he noticed Mike Able. Mike was having difficulty opening the rear door to the police station while carrying a box balanced on his shoulder. Mike had just inserted his key in the lock when Taylor gave a pull to open the door. It was a case of too many hands in the mix. The box on Mike's shoulder toppled over and crashed onto the pavement splitting open at one end. Two handguns slipped free and spun like wobbling tops on the asphalt until the manic circling stopped.

"Shit, Taylor! You scared the crap out of me!" Mike exclaimed.

Taylor smiled. He liked that Mike was considering him as just another cop in the shop. Mike was a seasoned, older cop himself so he got it. Taylor bent to secure the opened box at the same time Mike did, resulting in Mike tumbling over the box, finally ending on his butt. He roared with laughter.

"So sorry, Mike."

"Like hell, Taylor. You'll probably start telling everybody how you knocked me on my ass. Insinuate we were in some kind of brawl. I know your type; guys like you always try to one up the locals. All you West Coast pricks are the same. But, I know under the fancy façade you're just an aging surfer dude." Mike smiled as he grasped Taylor's extended hand to help him get back on his feet.

"Got the shit from Turner's storage locker. Eight handguns. Most are fine pieces, too. One is some kind of old wheel gun, looks like a Western piece. Probably like the one you used to use when you were out on the street," he laughed loudly at his own joke. "One's a sweet Sig Sauer 250. Got one of those Commander style Berettas from storage, too. Turner kept a couple boxes of fuck DVDs. Left them there. Not homemade stuff, just store bought flicks. Figure you didn't want shit like that, huh?"

"Figured right, Mike. Got any idea about the guns?"

"Yep. Few months ago we got an inquiry from a detective in Memphis. One of our guns that was supposed to have been destroyed ended up on a punk dude pulling a robbery. You'll have to check with Sally over in Property and Evidence for verification. I think Commander Crowder may know something about that incident."

"How the hell did that kind of screw up happen?"

"Don't ask me! I heard Chief Turner jumped all over Sally and insisted it was her fault. After the initial yelling and screaming, the gun incident just kind of disappeared. Beats me, boss."

"Mike, let's you and me go over and talk with Sally. Bring those guns of yours along," Taylor said with a smirk.

Sally sat behind a small desk just inside the room labeled Property/Evidence. The room was adjacent to the sallyport common in many police stations. That particular room placement allows officers to move property from their cars into the storage room easily. Several rows of tall shelving loomed behind Sally, all filled with bagged or tagged items. Taylor remembered seeing a large screened section at the side of the sallyport that held a collection of bicycles, lawn mowers, garden equipment, engine hoists, and other rusted metal hulks.

"You must be that consultant I've been hearing about," Sally welcomed as she rose when the two men entered her office. "By the way, my friend Petrus, at the Beverly Hills Supper Club, said you seemed like a pretty right fella. He figured any dude who knew what kind of cowboy hat he wears must be okay."

"Word does get around. They saying good things or grumbling?"

"Neither, just saying you're asking a lot of questions. Most think the questions are right on. What do you need from me today?"

Mike placed the box of handguns on Sally's desk. Her eyes blinked as she looked at the assortment of metal spread before her.

"Those ours?"

"Don't know. Could be."

"Tell me how you dispose of guns, Sally," Taylor asked.

"Well, Mr. Sterling, we don't have a bar code system here in Morgan City. I've tried to get one, even from the old chief. Seemed there was always something more important standing in the way," she sighed and sat down. "Lord knows, I've tried. I know how we should be handling and storing property. Most officers don't seem to care until their case is called on the carpet. Then the storage issue becomes important and usually jumps into emergency status.

"Under the old chief's direction, we'd smelt down guns no

longer needed for prosecution or when they hadn't been retrieved by the rightful owner. I'd pull the guns with a copy of the property report. We'd take a picture of each gun and then an officer would take them to the old ironworks plant outside of town. The guns were lined up on the ground and photographed again. A plant worker would throw them into the fire. We'd get the guy to sign a document indicating he appropriately disposed of whatever number guns there were."

"Seems like an adequate system, Sally," Taylor acknowledged. "What happened when Chief Turner came on board?"

Sally crunched her face in a sign of disgust. "Chief Turner was different."

"How so?"

"He'd have me pull the guns. Then he and Commander Munson would simply throw them in a cardboard box and take off. He said he was taking them to the ironworks factory, but I never saw anything saying he did."

"Sally, I'd sure appreciate it if you'd run these guns Mike collected against your system. I suspect they're yours, but I want to make sure. Mike, you make copies of the original property reports, but let Sally rebook the guns into her system," Taylor ordered and smiled.

Taylor wanted to let Sally know she was the person in charge. He was also being cautious about the chain of custody. He suspected this investigation would end up becoming a criminal case and he didn't want to be obligated to return to Morgan City should a trial be set. Taylor was pretty sure Turner was selling the confiscated guns on Craig's List or eBay and pocketing the cash.

* * *

Taylor found Burt Munson in his office at the far end of the police building near the exit to the rear parking lot. Burt's office was small and cluttered with file boxes and stacks of reports. The office walls were bare without the usual training certificates or accolades from one professional group or another. When Taylor knocked, Burt was focused on a small stack of police reports occupying the top of his desk.

"Burt," Taylor called as he filled the doorway. "Got some time?"

"Sure," Burt answered sliding the reports into one pile and placing it on one side of his desk.

"Hear you've got the narcotics operation."

"I do."

"Tell me about the reserve officers you've got working for you. Where are they now?"

"One is down in Florida around Boca. Another one in the Bradenton area. The other one is down in Southern California around San Diego, I think."

"What are they doing?"

"They're retired cops who Chief Turner knew from one of his other assignments. Made them reserve officers for Morgan City. They communicated directly with the chief and made a couple of cases now and then from shit leaving their sunny states bound for Morgan City. Eventually we got a taste of the seizure. Not sure how much. Chief put it into a slush fund for informant payments and flash money for buys. Chief kept the slush fund in his office. It's in the keyed lower right drawer of his desk, but I don't have the key, Taylor."

"Let's you and me go take a look."

"Won't help. Got no key."

"I've got a warrant to search it, Burt. Ought to be able to open it with a screwdriver, huh?"

Taylor called Mike Able and asked him to come to the chief's office.

The drawer didn't even splinter when Mike pried the lock down. There was a metal box inside that filled the expanse of the drawer. It was unlocked. Taylor flipped out his iPhone and keyed open the camera function. He took a close-up of the open drawer and metal box. Documenting finished, Taylor placed the box on top of the desk and opened it.

"Shit!" Burt exclaimed. "Looks like a pot full of cash there, Taylor."

Taylor took another photo of the contents of the box. Between Mike and Burt they counted and confirmed each other's count. Forty-two thousand, four hundred and seventy dollars, mostly in hundreds and fifties with a small stack of twenties. Normally a ledger would be with the cash to document the flow of money, in and out. None was found.

"Mike, I want you to find an evidence bag and get this sealed up while we're all here. You complete the evidence report. Take this cash stash to Unger and have him put it in the city safe. After that's done, Burt, I'd like to meet you and go over to wherever the narcotics unit hangs out. Understand you have them holed up in an out of the way storefront. Give me a call when you're ready to go."

Taylor wasn't worried about the possibility Burt might notify the unit. Most they would have time to do was straighten up the place. What Taylor wanted to find was either there or it wasn't.

* * *

Karl Unger was coming down the hallway as Taylor approached the small room he was using as an office.

"What are you finding, Taylor? I was quite surprised when a detective came over with a bundle of money and asked me to put it in the safe."

"Unfortunately I'm discovering quite a bit. I've got a few things still to look at, but I think you've got some heavy criminal misconduct going on here."

"With Chief Turner?"

"Yes, and maybe others, but I need another day or so to put all the pieces together. I've been careful not to leave my fingerprints on any evidence so it'll be an easy transition if you decide to go the criminal route."

"You think the department can do it if it comes to that? You know, handle it in-house?"

"I'd recommend against it. It's always best to bifurcate a criminal case like this to another agency. In Ohio, that probably would be the Attorney General's office"

"Should we bring them in now?"

"No, I think that would be a bit premature. We still need to determine the extent of vulnerability. Once you bring in an outside agency to file a criminal case against your own people, the flow of information seems to stop."

"What do you think of Sid and Neil?"

"Nice people, why do you ask?"

"Need to have someone in charge. Which one of the two do you think might be a good choice for chief?"

"Karl, I really don't know either one well enough to make a determination, but, either one would do for an interim choice. Neil seems to be doing a good job."

Taylor's cell phone chirped. "Taylor here."

It was Burt Munson announcing it was time to visit the narcotics unit.

"Karl, who's your financial person? The person who would be on top of grants requested and received, and maybe credit card use?"

* * *

Burt drove Taylor to a part of town he hadn't seen before. At one time this section of Morgan City might have been bustling and clanking with small industrial works and machine shops. Now most of the buildings were vacant. Windows were covered with ravaged plywood or left open to reveal the guts and lost souls of now deceased small businesses. The expanse of walls was a canvas for aspiring graffiti artists. Some street hieroglyphics were good; others weren't.

Burt pulled up to what appeared once was a car repair shop. The doors to the four bays had long disappeared. A rusting Chevy four-door filled one of the bays.

Taylor followed Burt up a flight of stairs at the rear of the building. Taylor noted a collection of surveillance cameras focused on the stairway and the door at the top of the stairs.

"Curt, it's me, Commander Munson," Burt called as he opened the door.

Taylor was surprised Burt would use his rank. Narcotic operations usually were very informal. Using a title either meant Burt was uncomfortable with the unit or needed to throw his rank around for protection. A voice from the back signaled the way the entering duo should go.

The main room held three tables, a few chairs, two upright

file cabinets, a row of old school lockers, and a wall littered with photographs of apparent targeted suspects and locations, and yellowed newspaper clippings. Taylor didn't notice any weapons left unattended or evidence bags lying on tables. So often he had seen narc units like this one—far out of sight of police management, leaving them basically uncontrolled. This unit, from his first impression, was messy, but not uncontrolled. Of course, Taylor recognized the unit had probably been forewarned of his visit.

"Curt Vinson," the large man said as Burt and Taylor entered the rear office. The guy was bald with the exception of a small rat-tail dangling from the base of his scalp. He had to wiggle to dislodge his flabby bulk from the wooden armchair before sticking out his pudgy hand for Taylor to grab.

"What you need, Mr. Sterling?"

"I'm interested in informants and confidential monies, Curt," Taylor began. He noticed the heavy man looked down before shooting a glance at Burt.

"You do have an informant file and a way of knowing how much money is paid for the info informants give up, don't you?"

"That's big time stuff. We're small time here in Morgan City. Each narc got his own snitches and pays them what he figures the info is worth. I know that's not how it's supposed to work, but it's the way we been doing it ever since we split from the area-wide HIDTA task force. Those guys did it by the book, we don't. Even Chief Turner had snitches, or at least he must have because he used the narc slush fund just like the rest of us. Say, where you get off confiscating that slush fund anyway? How are we supposed to do our job without that money?"

Taylor saw Curt was visibly upset as he slowly rounded his desk and approached them. Taylor purposefully didn't respond. He figured silence would tweak Curt into saying something he might not want to. Curt faced Burt and jabbed his index finger into Burt's chest.

"You knew what was going on, Commander Munson!" Curt emphasized the name with shades of disgust. "You knew. You and I both knew Turner was using that slush fund as his own piggy bank. We brought the cash in, and he took it out. Shit, it ain't my responsibility to tell him what he can and can't do with confiscated money. I used the cash for my guys and narc work. We might not have done everything proper and up to code, but we done it for good. None of my guys took any money they didn't have cause to use."

Shades of red were quickly covering his face as Curt continued his rant.

"And those alleged reserves living in who knows where? Sure, we all liked the money they brought in, but no one asked what they were doing to get it. Just loved the money flow. Commander, you knew!" Curt again punctuated the rank title. He looked at Taylor. "You done things for some asshole boss of yours, haven't you?"

Taylor nodded and said, "Sure, but there is a line that we all have to draw for what's acceptable and what's not. I always knew exactly where that line was, Curt."

There wasn't any reason to stay and watch Curt's anger mount. He knew what he had allowed to happen in his unit. Taylor's suspicions were confirmed.

"What are your concerns, Taylor?" Burt asked as they were driving back to the station.

Taylor thought about how to answer what seemed like a straightforward question. He could spend time outlining his concerns and the problems he had uncovered, but decided not to.

"Burt, I think you better get yourself an attorney, and a good one. I suspect that a lot of the money Chief Turner messed with had federal strings attached to it. That would make it a federal felony. There's going to be a shit storm coming down and you might be a star player."

Burt didn't respond, but Taylor saw his knuckles whiten as he gripped the steering wheel.

* * *

"Taylor," Mike Able said on the phone as Taylor was pulling into the Beverly Hills Supper Club parking lot. "Got some things wrapped up for you. The guns were all originally booked into Morgan City's property section and were supposed to have been destroyed. I booked them back into Property/Evidence. I've got copies of the original evidence reports and attached them with the photos from the storage locker.

"Got a return call from the phone company about the texts on Turner's third phone, too. You remember, the secret phone. A lot of racy banter back and forth with several of the women he was seeing or dating. He also got a lot of text messages from a guy named Stan Best. They were cryptic enough to pique my interest. Ran the name and it came back belonging to a known fence in the Toledo area. He might be our connection to what was happening with the guns."

"Can you check with the Toledo PD and see what they can give you?"

"Can do. Also, I compared the dates of Turner's rendezvous in Canada with his timesheets held at Accounting. Seems all but one showed him attending various conferences or training sessions, but there was no record of him showing up for them. On one occasion he took comp time. Obviously Turner was abusing his time records."

"And that's theft anyway you figure it, Mike."

Taylor told Mike how he'd like him to report and detail his findings and then walked into the restaurant to enjoy a meal.

"Nice to see you again," the same young woman greeted as Taylor entered the foyer and glanced around the half filled restaurant. "You want a booth or table?"

"Neither. I'll sit at the bar by Mr. Gorigan," Taylor said as he spotted the familiar Boss of the Plains hat. This time the band featured rattlesnake skin with menacing rattles cascading down Gorigan's back.

"Mister Cowboy, how you doing?"

Petrus Gorigan spun around on his bar stool and squinted at Taylor, then beamed as he jumped off the stool and gave Taylor a bear hug.

"Well, Mr. Santa Fe Cowpuncher, glad to see you again. Thought you had already left town. You consultants seem to do that. In and out and raise a ruckus."

"Nope, still here snooping into things. Had to come back for one more outstanding meal."

"You find anything interesting in Morgan City?"

"Unfortunately, I have. But you must know I can't tell you anything. It'll probably be front-page stuff when it does get out, though. How come you never ventured out West, being the cowboy you are?"

Petrus dropped his head and slowly shook it side to side, "I did. Yes sir, I sure did many years ago. Went to one of those dude ranches with my little flower. The ones where you saddle up and ride the hills, eat chuck wagon slop, and help move over-aged cows. My ass was sore for weeks. Cow shit stink was everywhere.

Guess I liked my delusional visions of the West from movies and TV. But once back home, my cowboy outfits set me apart from everybody else in this Midwest town. They think I'm an eccentric old goat and I like that. Say, you eating tonight?"

Taylor nodded.

"You eat on old Petrus tonight, or Mr. Cowboy as you like to call me. Tonight you get the crab bisque with a splash of sherry in it. Then you get the braised oxtails along with my son Ivan's signature side of vegetable lasagna. His cheese blend is to die for. Hell, he don't even tell me what cheeses he uses!

"But first join me in a toast to poor old Emily. We'll toast with Willett single barrel bourbon from Kentucky, a bottle I break only with friends. No water, no ice. It's my version of "Red Eye" like the dusty, trail-tried cowboys ordered at the local saloon." Petrus laughed heartily and almost lost his hat as the effects of his joke resonated up and down his body.

* * *

The next morning Taylor found the dangling sign "Accounting" two doors down from Karl Unger's office. A nameplate announced one Florence Mays was in charge. Florence, a middle-aged black woman, was settled behind a desk piled with stacks of spreadsheets serving as a barrier against anyone entering her lair. Her short hair was grey stubble and framed a round face accented with large eyes. The expanse of white sclera in her eyes was highlighted by the tangled dangle of ivory earrings she wore. Florence's face belied her trim figure. She was wearing a starched black blouse and burgundy skirt accented with a faux leopard belt.

"You must be Taylor Sterling," the accountant said rising from her swivel chair and circling to the small conference table that was holding court in one corner of the office. "Let's sit here."

As Taylor took his chair, he watched the woman continue to stand behind a chair as she focused her eyes piercingly on him. Hands on both hips, she cocked her head to one side. Taylor thought about interrupting whatever process she was going through, but decided to wait and see what she would say. Florence pursed her lips and then drew in a deep breath.

"I sense you have some pointed questions for me, Mr. Sterling. I'm not one to beat around the bush and waste time. Are you?"

"No, I'm not, Mrs. Mays."

"Florence is fine, Taylor." She smiled as she sat down opposite him.

"Well, Florence, you know why I'm here. I won't waste your time with chitchat. I'm interested in what you know about police accounts, credit cards, the accounting of funds held for the Police Youth Athletic program, and whatever grants the police department was given by the U.S. Department of Justice COPS program."

"All goes against my better judgment, but I don't know much, Taylor. I always feared one day someone would come asking questions just like you are. I told Mr. Unger about my concerns," she said as a sinking sadness softened her face. "He wasn't much concerned since each group had a board of directors made up of good people from the community."

"Good people sometimes don't know much about finances. Sometimes they can be led down the path of impropriety and won't know it."

"Lordy, Lordy, isn't that the truth! The devil never seems to sleep, Taylor. You and I know that, for sure. We've had the Police Community Enhancement Grant from the feds for a little over a year. Councilwoman Emily Stanton was the chair of the advisory board handling it. I heard that board rubber stamped whatever the chief wanted," her voice lingered on the word "chief."

"You didn't like Chief Turner?"

"You picked that up, huh? Good listening. He was all sweet-talking and gracious around folks. My momma always told me to hold onto my pocketbook and panties around men like that. I always figured he was one of those men, a real shyster. I stayed clear of him. Yes, Lordy, I kept my distance from that man! That poor Mrs. Stanton. She seemed like a fine woman. A shame what happened to her. Like I said, the devil never sleeps and works in strange ways."

"Where would I find documents detailing the finances for that program?"

"They had a checking account at the Buckeye Savings and Loan on Main Street. I'm pretty sure there were credit cards linked to the account as well. Chief Turner once came into my office and said he had misplaced his card and wanted me to get another one from the bank. Told him he had to do it himself or get one of the directors who had signing privileges do it. I didn't have those privileges, you know."

Taylor recalled looking at the receipt from the B&B in Canada and remembered the stay was paid for with a credit card. He made a mental note to check with Mike Able to determine which card was used.

"What about the youth program?"

"Same thing. Most of that money came from the Chamber of Commerce and fund raising the kids did. I'm sure the Chamber's liaison has documentation for that one. It's pretty well run. They did buy a lot of sport equipment for the youngsters. Took them on several trips each year that had to cost a bunch. They usually rented vans for transportation."

"When the chief went to conferences, did he get an advance from the city?"

Florence paused and put her finger against her cheek. "I think he did. He never took his police car, though. Used his personal car and submitted for mileage. I think I can get that documentation, Taylor."

"Would you, and give whatever you find to Detective Able?"

Taylor was pretty sure Chief Turner had been misusing funds from both sources, and maybe even from Morgan City. This was fast becoming a complicated investigative process. Financial crimes had never been Taylor's forte and were usually done by someone who specialized in that task. The warrant Mike Able secured would cover getting access to the data at the bank. This task would become one for a forensic accountant and would be pursued during the eventual criminal investigation.

* * *

Karl Unger was not looking well as Taylor entered his office for his exit meeting.

"Got this report from Sylvia Blanchard; I think you met her. Sylvia is my human resources person," Karl added. Taylor nodded.

"That Nat Turner had his head in his crotch. What pisses me off is I should have known what was going on. The outfit that vetted him had to know about his escapades in the last city Turner owned. Hell, Sylvia found out details with just one lousy phone call. I think that cop buddy club that calls itself a professional group bamboozled me. I should have known, or at least suspected. I keep telling myself I need to get out of the office more and walk and talk with the employees."

"At least there's not a lot of liability on the sexual harassment allegations, Karl."

"True. Sylvia says we should reemphasize our written policy and conduct another round of cultural diversity training. I guess that's as nice a name as any for keeping your dick and pussy in check," Karl said, snickering at his feeble joke.

Taylor laid out what his investigation had discovered. The Canadian connection and obvious abuse of city time led the list, followed by the apparent misuse of grant and charity funded program monies and credit cards. The gun issue and the poorly run narcotics unit also were identified.

"Karl, I strongly urge you to bring in the Attorney General and do a criminal investigation. Detective Mike Able could be detailed to work with them. He's been a prince on this case and I've managed to keep myself out of evidence collection. You've got a few people in the department who might be caught up in the criminal aspect. Commander Burt Munson and Curt Vinson in narcotics may not have had their fingers in the pie chockfull of misconduct, but they both knew about what was happening. A lot of the money had federal strings attached and that makes the theft even more significant."

"What do you think I should do with those two?"

"I think you should put them on administrative leave with pay. When and if they're indicted, you can reverse that decision to leave without pay. You probably should talk with Neil and Sid and ask them to consider rejoining the HIDTA task force," Taylor advised. "Also, do you know if the directors on the youth and community action boards have policies that might give them indemnification protection?"

"What do you mean?"

"Many organizations buy insurance to cover their boards of directors, particularly volunteer members. Doesn't cost that much and gives protection via a "hold harmless" clause. In this case, some directors may have unknowingly signed checks or credit card issuance documents that allowed Turner to misappropriate funds. Most are good people who think they're doing good work, but sometimes they get sucked in. Emily Stanton, however, may have had more than a passing role in some of that, but with her death it really won't be a factor for her or her husband."

"Other than a pile of embarrassment for the husband and Morgan City!" Karl exclaimed.

"I'll send you my report a couple days after getting back to Santa Fe."

* * *

The lunch crowd had vacated the Morgan City Diner when Taylor entered. He had asked Sid, Neil, and Mike to join him for a debriefing session.

"You alone, Taylor?" Edna asked as Taylor headed for the back booth.

"Nope, got my cop friends coming. Where's Sadie?"

"In the back. Lunch crowd beats her up. That grill is smokin' and everybody wants to get in and out in thirty minutes. That Sadie is an organizational genius, but her knees are getting worse and worse. Too stubborn to get them fixed. Says what would happen to the diner if she took time off, like I'm chopped liver! Shoot, I could handle everything if I had an hourly worker."

As she placed a fresh cup of coffee in front of Taylor, Mike

Able entered and found the booth. After Mike settled in, Taylor pulled an envelope from his pocket and slid it across the table to Mike. He opened it and pulled out a card.

"What's this, boss?"

"It's a gift certificate to the Beverly Hills Supper Club. For you and your wife. You been there?"

"We have. It's one of our favorite places, but this is too much!"

"It's my favorite too, and you earned a dinner there. Tell the guy with the cowboy hat sitting at the bar, he owns the place, tell Petrus the Santa Fe cowpuncher sent you."

"Thanks. Say, Taylor, remember the name I found in Turner's phone who turned out to be a fence in Toledo? My contact said he specializes in guns. Gets a couple hundred apiece. What I don't understand is why would the chief throw away his career for a couple hundred bucks?"

"Mike, that's small potatoes. Turner's theft is going to add up to the tens of thousands. He was just a credentialed slime ball."

Sid and Neil slipped into the booth.

"Got Unger pretty concerned, Taylor," Sid said. "Bringing in the AG is the right thing, but Unger looks at it as a sign of defeat. Hell, it'll actually take the heat off all of us. Some of us, including Unger, will probably be embarrassed and get a slap here and there. We should have known what was going on and should have done something about it. Turner was such a dictatorial asshole, though."

"True, but you have to draw that line. Each person has a different line. It's all about choices." Taylor had a sudden flashback to his recent lecture in Artesia.

"Listen, I want to thank you for pulling out Mike to help me. Fine detective. Keep him happy, guys. Neil, you might revisit Shaun Avery's discipline. Hear it's waiting for arbitration and you might want to take a fresh look at it. Do the right thing. You're chief, even if it's just a temporary position.

"That Jones kid, though, you can't do much for him. With the evidentiary mess, he might not have been convicted criminally, but he had to go. Too bad someone didn't see his addiction problem earlier. That can usually be handled and most employees can be saved and rehabbed. Too bad a young career ended."

Like so many other meetings with fellow cops, the conversation gravitated to Taylor's experiences with the LAPD, but to outsiders it would seem like four cops bullshitting over a cup of coffee, minus the donuts.

Most police departments have highs and lows during their history. Some have more peaks and valleys than others. With the exception of a few very small departments, most stay in business. Reforms come in and bring the department up to some degree of acceptability. Most seem comfortable to remain in a calm sea of mediocrity. People come and go without much reflection. New programs are tried, but most are just recycled from past eras with new organizational buzzwords attached.

Maybe the police become the ballast in the ship of government, trying to keep it steady as conflicting trends in the community attempt to change its course. Of course the cops have to resist becoming an anchor.

ABOUT THE AUTHOR

Lou Reiter has been active in law enforcement for over 50 years. He served with the Los Angeles Police Department for 20 years and retired in 1981 as a Deputy Chief of Police. Since that time Lou has been a private police consultant.

Every year Lou conducts multi-day training seminars for over 1,000 police, sheriff, state police, and other criminal justice personnel teaching how to perform Internal Affairs investigations. He has conducted audits of troubled police and sheriff agencies for insurance and risk management pools throughout the country. The smallest agency was a three-man police department and the largest agency he audited was the N.Y.P.D. Lou has served as a consultant for the U.S. Department of Justice investigating police departments accused of Constitutional enforcement problems, including those in New Orleans, Buffalo, Pittsburgh, and Cincinnati.

Lou has testified as a police practices expert in over 1,100 civil lawsuits. He has worked for police and sheriff agencies as well as for citizens bringing suit against police departments. He has testified in over 250 trials in Federal and State courts.

When Lou is not on the road consulting, he lives in the North Georgia Mountains near Atlanta with his wife Marilyn, an attorney, and their dog, Shakti.

Book Club Questions

1. If Taylor Sterling had been a female, would that change the story line?

2. When they make a movie from this book, whom would you like to play Taylor? And whom do you see as his girlfriend, Sandy Banks? How about Ginger, Taylor's new part-time secretary?

3. What did you learn about police misconduct investigations?

4. Do you think police officers really engage in misconduct like that represented in this book?

5. The author makes a point of saying that police misconduct can be a product of a bad chief or sheriff. Do you agree and did the book give you any new insight into this?

6. Taylor Sterling obviously is a "foodie." Did this add or detract from your reading of the book?

7. Did the language offend you?

8. This book was a series of independent cases or short stories.

Did you enjoy this format or would you have rather had one storyline?

9. What did you like or dislike about the author's writing style?

10. What surprised you about police Internal Affairs procedures?

11. Do you think that this book will convey the wrong message to readers?

12. Were you transported to a geographic location you believed was realistically portrayed?

13. What was the most surprising revelation for you?

14. Do you think that police corruption is worse in some regions or states than others?

15. Do you think police corruption occurs more at the top ranks than among regular street cops?

16. Several of the stories concern police involved in highway interdiction. Do you think this should be outlawed?

17. Does officer suicide occur often when an officer is caught engaged in misconduct?

CPSIA information can be obtained
at www.ICGtesting.com
Printed in the USA
FFOW04n1153250615
14634FF